# *I Got Next*

# Godfather

DC Bookdiva Publications
Washington, DC

DC Bookdiva Publications
#245 4401-A Connecticut Avenue, NW
Washington, DC 20008
www.dcbookdiva.com

Publisher's Note: This is a work of fiction. Names, characters, places, and incidents are a product of the author's imagination. Locales and public names are sometimes used for atmospheric purposes. Any resemblance to actual people, living or dead, or to businesses, companies, events, institutions, or locales is completely coincidental.

Ordering Information:
Quantity sales. Special discounts are available on quantity purchases by corporations, associations, and others. For details, contact the "Special Sales Department" at the address above.

I Got Next/ Godfather -- 1st ed.
ISBN 978-0-9907854-1-5

# *Dedication*

For Mama.
I've never handed you anything: Not a trophy, diploma, wedding picture, or a grandchild. Not one moment for you to stand up in a crowd, point at me, and celebrate, "There Goes My Baby..."

I've given you nothing but tears of regret and misery, but it is my hope to one day stand up and receive the NAACP Image Award: something I can hand you with great pride. But, until then, it is my hope that this book should suffice.

My gift of Ghetto Gumbo. Enjoy.

*"The truth is often avoided because
It is ugly and unpleasant."* - Robert Greene

# Chapter 1

**Saturday, December 18**
**Approx.: 1:00 A.M.**

Sometimes you face challenges in life: you see things and experience things; become confronted by things long before you should, and more than you wish you ever would. Thrust into conflict, the damage peeling you apart, leaving you exposed and raw, 'til, finally, you feel literally and totally fucked. Like a used condom tossed in the wind, important to no one, and destined to who knew where. It's a grown ups' pain but even at 13-years old Jaquanna understood the weight of its burden. Even at 13, Jaquanna knew that shit had to change and she wasn't beyond shaking some shit up. In a major way. To do it.

"Bitch! Didn't I tell yo' stupid ass to lay the fuck down and leave me the fuck alone?" *Blam!* At the sound of the meaty crack, Ricky jumped and Jaquanna cringed. The door was closed to their bedroom but not to the cries beyond.

"Benny!" their mother yelped, "No, Benny, please no!" Her cowering cries were filled with tears. The tears of a woman bullied beyond despair.

"Huh? Dumb ass bitch, didn't I?"

"Why! Why?" Lay-Lay wailed. "Why you treat me like this?"

"Shut-up!" he insisted. "Shut the fuck up!"

Emerging from their bedroom, Jaquanna stood in the open doorway. 9-year old Ricky was right behind her. He had on his red pajamas with the little footies. Green Christmas trees all over. He was holding the back of Jaquanna's thick cotton gown, wide-eyes frozen by fright. Jaquanna looked and took it all in. It was almost one a.m. Saturday morning. Benny hadn't been home from work.

"You don't be asking me where the fuck I been." Benny was a big ole brute and he stalked the tiny woman as she tried to slide behind the tree. "I come in this house anytime I get good and god damn ready!"

"Okay. Okay." Lay-Lay dabbed her lip with the collar of her flimsy pink gown. "Okay. Oh-ohhh!" She sounded suddenly more distraught after having seen all the blood. Her hair was everywhere. The small tree could barely conceal her.

Benny shrugged off his big rain soaked jacket. Breathing hard, with an alcohol inspired flame in his eyes, he turned, chest stuck out and lips all twisted. "What the fuck you lookin' at?" he asked as he finally took note of Jaquanna.

"Jaquanna," Lay-Lay warned. "Don't say nothin', Jaquanna. You...go," her mother pointed. "Go in the room now." But she was still behind the damn tree.

Benny sneered a mocking smile.

Jaquanna stared him in his eyes and slowly shook her head.

It was a week before Christmas, and all through the house, a couple of creatures were staring and maybe even a mouse. This was the shit she had to put up with.

"What?" he challenged with a toss of his chin. "Huh, what?" He reached in his back pocket, pulled his bottle, and took a swig.

"Come on, Quanna," Little Ricky tugged.

"You better get yo' little stupid-ass kid," he said over his shoulder with a smile. He was still facing the girl, and looking at her in a way that he shouldn't. Another swig. Even over the stench of pine, the room reeked of the cheap sweet wine.

Jaquanna hadn't budged. She was too disgusted to be afraid.

"Go away little girl," he took a swig. A long long good one. "Go play." His foot crept forward slowly.

"Quanna!" Ricky cried. "Let's go-ooo!" He was bouncing up and down behind her like he would pee on himself if she didn't. "Come on-n-n."

"Go Jaquanna! Go!"

"Or do you need me to make you?" He was slowly taking his second step, his foot was about to fall.

"Ain't nobody scared of you," Jaquanna said with a calmness beyond her years. She was breathing hard, short and deep: Too afraid to be afraid.

"What? You little bitch? Huh? What?"

"You heard me. And I ain't no little bitch eith…"

He struck like a cobra and grabbed her by the collar.

"No!" Lay-Lay screeched and ran to aid her child.

"Ahhh-hh-h!" Little Ricky was jumping up and down crying.

"Let go of her you bastard!"

"Bitch, who the fuck you thank—"

With a sideways fist, Lay-Lay hammered into his back.

"Ho!" he threw the bottle.

Lay-Lay ducked but still it struck her in the eye. Blood spurted from her battered face. "Ah! You son of a bitch!"

He picked her up and slammed her to the floor like a dead-weight dummy, then kicked her square in the ass. "Don't..." *kick* "you..." *stomp* "ever..." *kick*. Lay-Lay was balled up at his feet trying her best to shield her face with her arms, shoulders and the floor. "Put-yo-stupid-ass-hands-on-me!" He picked her up and slammed her against the wall. "Bitch!" He felt enraged. Empowered. Like a demon possessed king. Unbeatable, unchallenged. Raaahh! He was the beast of this jungle. *Kick. Stomp.* The feel of his foot bouncing off her quivering flesh, the sound of her pleading cries, and the splatter of blood, all added to his raging insanity. In this moment, she was not human. Like a dog, she needed to be trained. How dare she challenge him? How dare she break a rule? Did she not know who he was? What he was capable of? Damn what the world might've thought of him, in this home; in this land, he was to be feared; he was to be respected. Served. Honored. Obeyed, catered to. For, here unlike anywhere else, he was an invincible tyrant. King. Raaaahhh! And he kicked her again, for good measure.

"Oh-hhh! Please stop!"

The smell of Christmas; the lights flashing on the tree. The 10 or 15 gifts...it should've been a happy time filled with good cheer and sweets. They even had the white tree this year and a stream of lights around the outside of the house with frosted snow to rim the windows and even a wreath on the door. It was Christmas time. A time of joy, but, instead, they had to put up with this shit.

"What you doing, Quanna?"

Ignoring Ricky, Jaquanna reached in the drawer and pulled out a butcher knife; the biggest butcher knife she could find.

Lay-Lay had crawled under the tree. She was face down and holding the tree at its base.

"Let go of the tree, you stupid-ass bitch!" Benny kicked her in the hip. Then stomped her on her butt. "Let go!"

"Stop Benny!" Lay-Lay cried. "My God will you stop? That's enough, baby. That's enough. I'm sorry, 'kay?"

"Bitch, you don't tell me when it's enough. You don't run shit up in here. I don't give a fuck who house this is!" He reached down and grabbed her by the ankles. "Now let go!"

"Noooo, baby!" She held on tight. "Stop!" The tree rattled, shook and banged. Gifts were ripped, torn and scattered. There was blood every bit of here and there. The lights on the tree tinkled and blinked. The candy canes had fallen from the limbs.

"Let go of the tree, now," he smiled. "Come on, stupid, let it go."

"No, you gon' hit me."

"I'ma hit yo' dumb-ass anyway." He tugged. The tree toppled. He drug her to the center of the room. "Stupid bitch!" And he socked her with such force that it sounded like her head would go straight through the fucking floor. *BLOOMP!* It was a thunderous blow. And as if it were some sick synchronized harmony, there was a flash of lighting then a burst of thunder outside.

"Ahhh!" Little Ricky was out of his mind.

"Stop!" Jaquanna had the knife in her right hand, hidden just behind her thigh. The winds rushed and the windows rattled. The rain slammed against the window and came down in a pour.

He was stooped over with his fist drawn back. The calm sternness had caught his attention.

Jaquanna looked right at him, "Don't hit her no more."

"What?" He chuckled with a scoff, "What you say?" He stared back with total disbelief.

A tear ran down Jaquanna's face. Little Ricky looked worried to death.

Benny stood and turned. "Didn't I just tell you to stay up outta grown folks business?" He bit his lip. "Huh?"

Behind him, Lay-Lay was a whimpering mess. She'd confronted him and now, like a deadly snake he'd turned and bitten. He was used to whipping Lay-Lay's ass and Lay-Lay was used to accepting it.

If only she knew telekinesis, she'd make his ass do a back flip and bang his head off the fucking wall! Urgh! Man! Jaquanna couldn't stand him.

She stared at Benny. She stared at Benny long and hard with an intensity bordering on insanity. "Don't kay?" It was slow. It was calm and barely above a whisper. "Just don't." She flexed her fingers around the knife. Her palm sweated as she clenched it in her pulsing fist.

"Or what, you little bitch?"

"I told you I whan't no bitch."

Again, he came and stalked his prey. One step. Two steps. The floor creaked under his weight. "Retarted ass kid," he mumbled. "You gon' learn to stay up outta grown folks business, little girl. I bet you that." He'd been meaning to teach her a few things about being grown anyway. With her little wide-butt self. He took another step. "I'ma learn ya," he promised. "I'ma learn you something real decent. Keep it up." *Little wide ass booty. These kids growing up way too quick, and thank they grown.* "Yeah, you just keep it up. Keep that shit up that's what you do. You hear me Quan? I'ma grow yo' ass up."

Oh she hated when he called her Quan. And he knew it, because she'd told him not to do that shit. It wasn't her fuckin' name. She had an uncle who called her Quan. Man, she missed her uncle. He was the only one who could call her Quan. Not this bitch. He did that punk shit on purpose.

"That's not my name," she said.

"Yo' name whatever the fuck I say it is."

Something warned him. He stayed his distance.

She waited in the doorway and flexed her fist over the hard weapon again. "No it's not."

"Stop, Quanna," Little Ricky tugged from behind. "Stop."

Benny scoffed and shook his head in disbelief. He was five feet from her with a quivering lip, red eyes, and a simmering stare.

"Leave her alone." Lay-Lay had crawled to her feet. With a busted lip and one eye swollen, she tried to smile and even look cute. "Please baby, please."

He turned to look at the forlorn creature. "You better learn to raise yo' little stupid ass kids," he told her. As he tossed a thumb over his shoulder towards Jaquanna. "Or I'ma learn the little bitch somethin' real decent."

"I ain't no bitch."

"Don't call her that."

"What?" *POW*! He snapped forward with an open palm and smacked the dog shit out of Lay-Lay. Dropping her where she stood. "Don't you ever speak outta turn."

"Stoooop!" Ricky wailed. "Stoo-op," the halpless tyke was beyond himself. He was helpless and he was afraid.

"And you is a little bitch," he pointed at Jaquanna, "You little tramp." Lightening flashed and thunder clapped. The window shook as if it would break. "Now get yo' little stupid ass outta here," he pointed.

"I ain't going nowhere." She stood stern and stubborn. "You ain't my daddy." She dug his eyes out. Her spirit urging her on. "And I ain't stupid either."

A white Christmas with snow on the ground. Gifts piled high with love in the air. Hugs, cheers, and smiles. A roasted something, a baked something else. Mistletoe, tinsel and carols, Not a care in the world; not a cause for concern. Just where does that happen and how?

"Come on, Quanna." Little Ricky was jumping up and down and tugging with insistence. "Quanna, come on."

"Go in the room, Jah!" her mother insisted," Go in the room!"

Jaquanna's eyes shifted from Benny and over to her battered mother.

Lay-Lay was on hands and knees; spit, snot, and slobber all mingled and spilled from her face. Her voice was a husky rasp, from all of the hollering, "Please, Jah. Please, baby girl, just go. Oh, just go!" she cried. "Go for Mama, kay? It's gon' be alright, baby. Mama alright. Benny love Mama. Mama love Benny, kay? Mama got this. Just go."

"This shit is crazy." He had his hands folded over his chest turned sideways, looking back and forth between the women, as if watching a tennis match. His smile was more of a scowl.

"Come on, Jaquanna. Come ooo-on!"

Slowly Jaquanna took a step back.

Benny bent over to pick up his bottle. Turning it up, he was about to sip when he saw it. "What the fuck is you doing with that knife?"

He'd caught the glimpse as she'd turned away, about to put it away. She'd been discovered.

Jaquanna froze and turned to face him. Exposed. The shining sword was out in the open now.

Another flash. Another roar. There was a rage inside the storm.

"You don't hear me talkin' to you?" he asked the silent child.

"She didn't mean nothing, baby." Lay-Lay grabbed his arm and stroked his chest.

"Booooy, I'm telling you," he scoffed again. Shook his head. Paused and took a good little guzzle.

"Put it away, Quanna. Just put it away." Little Ricky took the knife.

"Girl, get yo' ass back in there," her mama pointed towards the room. "And don't you come out no more tonight."

Jaquanna shook her head but felt like the victim. As the tension died, her eyes poured. "This shit is stupid, man."

"Don't be cussin' in here either!" Lay-Lay yelled after the retreating girl, "You ain't grown." As if, some moral was to be taught by the measure. "These kids is something else," she heard her mother say.

"I'm tryna tell you."

At the sound of the bottle being turned up, Jaquanna slammed her door.

"And don't be slamming that fucking door either!" her mother warned. "Little heifer."

"I don't like it here, Quanna." Little Ricky was on the top bunk. He'd climbed up there and had his pajama covered feet dangling off the side. He was wiping his nose on his sleeve and sniffing, "I wanna go."

The lights were still off and the door was closed. The darkness gave her comfort.

"You mad, Quanna?"

"Not at you, Big Boy." That's what she always called him. That was her own little name.

"You mad at Mama?"

"I don't know who I'm mad at," she answered honestly, "I'm just tired, man."

"You sleepy?"

"No. Not that kinda tired, Big Boy."

"Oh."

It was the thought of her mother standing there comforting him and talking about her. It hadn't always been like that. Lay-Lay was a cute little thing and barely 28 years old. Benny was a bugga-monkey and damn near 40 himself. They'd been together for just over a year. And while Mama was happy that they could afford a little car and pay a few bills and had even managed to move into a house, Jaquanna wasn't feeling it and neither was little Ricky.

"Things was better the way they was, Quanna."

"I know."

"I miss that old house. I miss my friends."

"Me too."

"I don't like it here, Quanna. You?"

"Nah-uh. Big Boy, me either."

"Wanna just go?"

The house was struck by another sheet of storming rain. The cracked window whistled. The drops dripped in the pot in the corner where the roof always leaked.

"We ain't got nowhere to go."

"Yeah-huhn!" insisted Ricky, "We can go stay with Jeremy."

This made Jaquanna smile and chuckle a bit. Jeremy was Ricky's best friend who lived in an apartment next door in the building where they use to stay. Jeremy was only eight. Had a brother and two sisters, mother and father, all living in a one bedroom.

"We gon' be alright, Big Boy. She reached up and squeezed his little foot. "Quanna ain't gon' let nothin' happen to you, kay?"

"I love you, Quanna," he said as she smiled. "I do."

"I love you too, Big Boy, more than anything in this world."

"More than anything?"

"Yep."

"More than Mama?"

Damn. What kinda question was that? Where did it come from? What did it mean?

"What kinda question was that, boy?" He could hear her smile as she shoved his foot.

"Well, I just asked, dog!" He chuckled.

"Now take yo little butt to sleep." She stood up and helped him to lie back down then tickled him, loving the way he giggled. He even pooted as she did it. "Ugh!" She fanned her face as she fell away.

"That was you," he said, "that whatn't me."

"Yeah right."

The air was contaminated but it could just as well have been laughing gas the way the two of them chuckled and giggled.

"Ugh, Quanna!" He ducked under his blankets. "Oops!" The second one hadn't cleared the sheets yet and he'd damn near choked himself to death.

He fanned the blanket to air out the funk.

"Stop, boy!" Jaquanna pulled her gown over her nose and giggled as she tried to catch a clear breath, "with yo' nasty butt."

"That's you!"

"Yeah, right." She smacked him on his ass. "That's why you couldn't go under your blankets, huh?"

As the giggling settled, she tucked him in.

"You the best sister I could ever have, Quanna."

"You're not so bad yourself." She smiled and kissed him on his little cheek.

"Ugh!" He wiped it off. "Don't be kissing on me."

"Alright well gimme my kiss back then."

He giggled.

"Uh-huh. That's what I thought."

At least all men weren't bad. Big Boy was proof of that. The bathroom was between the two bedrooms. Jaquanna had heard the water and seen the light on. Her mother must've been cleaning herself up but the light was off now. The water had long since stopped.

"Go on go to bed. I'ma use the bathroom, kay?"

"Kay."

The rain fell in heavy drops. The house creaked and shifted, but even still, there was no denying the squeak, thrusts and thunder of merging bodies. Just on the other side of the thin bedroom door.

"Oh that's good," she heard her mother purr, "Oh damn, that's good."

"You like...Oh!" Benny gasped. "Ummgh."

"Oh that's nii...oh, yeah! Oh Benny! Oh! Ooh! Right there."

You could hear the wet smack. The rattled bed and shuddered cries.

Jaquanna reached to pull down her panties then sat on the toilet.

Wind banged at the windows with irregular bursts and slams, as thrashing sheets of rain crashed with rapid gusts.

Squeal, squeak. Rattle. Bang. Oh! Ow! Umm! There was a symphony of grunts and a drive towards completion.

As Jaquanna relieved her bladder, she had the toilet paper at the ready. She hated this bathroom. It never felt private and she never felt safe here. She always felt that either someone could hear, whatever it was she was in there doing, or that someone would pop in there on her. As Benny had not so accidently done twice, once when she was taking a bath and the other when she was sitting on the toilet. She had told her mother to get locks, but her mother swore there was no need. "Girl, don't' nobody wanna see you" Was actually what she said, "So ain't no need in wasting no money on no locks."

Squeak. Squeak. Smack. Smack. "Oh Benny! Ooh, boy! Yes!" The bed rattled with a quickened rhythm. The headboard banged *bloom*! A jolting clap of thunder shook the skies.

Jaquanna pulled up her panties and made with haste. In a hurry to get away from the giggles and cries of passion which selfishly assaulted her young ears. But, more so than that, for the life of her, she couldn't understand just how her mother could comfort and pleasure a man who had just disrespected her child and beat her ass.

*How could she?*

Lying there broken and bruised, just barely this side of bleeding yet her legs wrapped around the man. Her body used for his comfort. *Was it really that good?*

*How? How? How?* Jaquanna was disgusted. It happened every time, as if sex was just part of the whole pattern, but still. Jaquanna never made peace with that. She lay there with tears in her eyes and tried to go to sleep. Wide-eyed, she couldn't.

Thunder cracked. Lightening flashed. The light in the bathroom came on. Benny barked with a loud burp. The stream of his piss was loud and continuous. Another burp and then he flushed.

And so it went on, as if it was just another night but tonight was not just another night because tonight Jaquanna had had enough and tonight she'd made up her mind. If you can't beat 'em, join 'em. There were two ways to skin a cat.

Yeah, no matter what. You only get one mama, no matter who she is or what kinda troubles she's got, but, you also only get one childhood and once that was fucked up, everything was different; your whole outlook was twisted.

"You sleep, Quanna?"

"I'm 'bout to be."

"Me too."

"Good night, Big Boy."

"Good night, Queen."

"Awww," she purred.

"Shut up."

# Chapter 2

In every hood, every hamlet, every project, quarter, quad, borough, region, yard or turf, there is always a "royal family" the "entitled" bunch: the do-no-wrong-boys: those whom you either liked, feared, admired or respected, "just because." It was like learning to chew bubble gum: It seemed natural; expected even.

The royal family were your local celebrities. Your first taste or experience with status. The gravitational pull of it all. The will to wanna be like that. Like them. Like they. Like those. This was the ready-made in-crowd. The crew to be close to…to be a part of…to be seen or in bed with. They were usually a part of a huge family, with hangers on and claimers of, you know: "I use to go with one of they cousins," or "My brother's baby mama got a brother who run with them and we use to be over there allllll the time, so I know everybody." Until pretty soon, half the hood was somehow attached to or thought themselves a part of The Royal Family.

People claimed these folks and acknowledged their status from as far back as they could remember. Even in elementary school, you knew who was who and what was what with them: your mama told you, your sister told you, your big brother told you what he knew, and pretty soon, it was just like a game of hide-and-go-get-it: you knew the ins and outs: the twists and turns; the rules. "Aw, that's Drippy and them little cousin, his mama go wit' Big Coota," instant status. Something that the rest would have to spend years and years and take many risks in search of and probably still would not achieve. It's a trip when you stop to remember.

The way they walked, dressed, talked, stood, smiled, or even stared became the talk of the town and the newest trend. These were people you knew and paid attention to, even when they didn't know or acknowledge you. "Oh, I went to his party before." "Oh, I met him once." "Aw yeah, my uncle and them use to kick it over there, they know all them dudes." Sorta like the Queen of England, Princess Di, Prince Charles and William and that whole clan, or how about the Kardashians, Oprah, the rappers, actors: The TMZ Stars. You get the picture. We studied them: learned what we could, copied what we needed or thought that we should, and eventually claimed it all as our own. The way we laughed; our idea of cool. Our earliest ideas of life within our most vulnerable and impressionable years, in a large way came from, by and through: The Royal Family. *Our* Royal Family. In the hood. And, if the Blackmans were the royal family on Wall Street then young Kirk was its reigning prince. Oh, and that was another thing: The royal family very seldom, if ever, had way out nicknames. They were never clowned with a name that stuck, like Nose, Pig head, Dumb-Dumb or Dunce and they didn't have to create names to stand out and draw attention. In fact, they'd be the first to tell you that they were too smart to label themselves and they tried *not* to stand out. Because standing out was for fools. Besides, there was no sense trying out or advertising for a role that already bore your name. It was yours; and all you had to do was claim it. The ghetto's version of the Silver Spoon.

The Blackmans had been on top for a long time. Jackers, dope dealers, street hustlers: owned a few things, made a few twists; had they hands in all types of shit. It was a beautiful thing when your mere name transcended you beyond any need to commit murder. You were royalty; no one would dare offend. But, that is not to say, it didn't have to start somewhere.

They had originally come from the south somewhere. Nine brothers, four sisters. Attitudes, beauty, muscles, cunning, connects. FAME. Same story; different family. Facts vary little. We all knew them. How could we not?

But Little Kirk Blackman was a true insider. A direct descendant of the throne. He wasn't a "married-in" or a "tag-along-could-be."

His daddy Big Kirk was a baby of the original nine. But it was Richard who everyone said Little Kirk looked like and took after. And that was all fine and good because Richard was the eldest brother and defacto king a.k.a. Head of the Family. Kirk looked up to him and admired him; studied and copied his moves. Some even said Kirk was Richard's little twin. Richard had a nickname: They called him Big Dick. But, there was no way in hell Kirk would even think to call himself Little Dick. That just whan't finna happen. Fuck all that. No way, José. Not even. K.J., Little Kirk, or Kirk Jr. was his name and those who knew him praised him. Just as they should.

It was a California winter, Saturday, 11 a.m. and the sun began to pound: beating down on the rain-drenched city that now soaked up the sun. The weather reports had said it would probably hit close to 70° with a lingering slight chance of rain for later in the evening. The Wall Street Boys had set up shop and K.J. was posted at the new house on the corner. He was 16 now and already well on his way with things: if crack was "Black man's oil," then he was a full-blown pump and the Wall Street Boys were his well.

"What's up, Little Kirk?"

"Hey, what's hap'nin?" He was sitting on the concrete steps at the side of the small vacant white house on the corner of 105th and Wall. The sidewalk bordered the steps.

"What's up with you, homie?" The man smiled 'til his face glowed. He had a small bag in his hand and was coming from the store. An around-the-way cat. More than just a passerby.

"Just kickin' it." Smiling, Kirk hugged his elbows, rocked back and forth, kicking his feet. His patience came with a calm endurance. He never really seemed quite rushed with things. This added to his gravity and made him more endearing. Like Barack: For you he had the time.

"That's right," the eager guy nodded, happy to have simply been acknowledged. "That's right, my nigga. Just straight kickin' it, huh?"

Kirk Jr. smiled and nodded.

"Alright then, Young Kirk." The young thug patted himself over the left breast. Head eagerly bobbing as he nodded. "Holla atcha boy."

"Fa sho'."

"Alright." He felt he'd made a connection. "Alright, bet." The way he walked off, you'd think he'd just kicked it with Dr. Dre or some shit.

"Who's that?" Leon twisted his head in the direction of the fading teen.

"Shit, if I know," K.J. shook his head and shrugged.

Leon smiled. *Another fan.* "That shit's crazy" He shook his head. As an active member of the Wall St. Boys and longtime friend of Kirk Jr., Leon was more than used to the extra attention that his boy got but he still took humor in it all. "These niggas be needing a hug."

The door to the house was open. It was clean and neat inside. A mattress on the floor in one bedroom and an old couch in the front room. An old boom box did the entertaining. It appeared to be a trap house. A dope spot. A place to catch some fades but in truth, it was more of just a clubhouse where the young Wall St. Boys had started to come and hang. When the family who lived there had moved out a month ago, Kirk Jr. had kept a copy of the key. And, if history was any indication, the house would probably be vacant for a while. Just like the three others on the block, real estate had gone sour; evictions had swept the hood, the state, and the nation. Kirk lived a couple of doors down and they normally hung out over there. But now, they had their own little fort to kick it in and it was right on Wall Street. How perfectly fitting was that? Big Dick was even thinking of buying the place. And, knowing him, he probably would. He liked having the younger crowd pushed off down the street. And, he'd already been considering buying the other vacant homes on the block anyway There were a couple of good deals on the market and he loved a good investment. So this was right up Big D's alley.

"What y'all up to?" Preach had just hit the corner, cheesing.

"Shit," K.J. kicked his feet. Nodded his head and smiled, "What's good with it?"

Leon also smiled. "What you got cookin' in that noodle of yours?"

Preach shook his head and smirked as if the weight of the world was on his shoulders. Something was on his mind.

"Aw, shit," K.J. teasingly pointed "There he go. There he go y'all."

"Go on give it to us, Preach," Coo-Coo urged him on.

He was an outsider in the inside circle. They called him Preacher because he loved to teach with words. The nickname worked. The nickname stuck, but the street life wasn't his thang.

However, K.J. made him feel important and welcomed, so he often came around. Using knowledge as his entertainment until it soon identified him.

"What you got for us, today, man?" Kirk loved this shit. "Go on give us what you got."

"Okay." He rubbed his bony chin in thought. "Okay. Okay. Peep it," he pointed and said, "Here go something for y'all. I was on the Internet last night, right?"

A couple of the fellas nodded.

"And I was thankin' 'bout how y'all be calling y'all selves Black Wall Street Boys and that kinda thang, right?"

They nodded some more. Not sure where he was going, but willing to take the ride.

"Yeah, so I thought back on something I'd heard once about a place called Black Wall Street and decided to look that up."

"Yeah?" K.J.'s face was twisted with interest, "And what you get?"

"That shit prolly just say something 'bout that nigga Game from Compton" offered Coo-Coo.

"Yeah," said Leon, "What it say, something about dudes label and shit?" Black Wall Street is the rap record label pushed by the rapper called The Game.

"Naw, but there was a place named Black Wall Street," said Preacher.

"OH, serious?" asked Kirk, Jr. "What that was about?"

"It was a spot down in Tulsa, Oklahoma," Preacher explained, "Which went on to become the site of the largest massacre of non-military Americans."

"Massacre?" Coo-Coo asked, "What kinda massacre? What like some shoot 'em up type shit?"

"The Ku Klux Klan and some other folks got together and bombed it then set the town on fire. It destroyed something like over 600 businesses, fifteen hundred homes and killed like two or three hundred folks. Ten thousand were left homeless and people were buried in mass graves or thrown into a coal mine, or rivers or wherever."

"The Klan?" K.J. asked. "So Black Wall Street was Blacks?" He loved to learn and was always impressed whenever the 22-year old Preach came around to share new wisdoms.

"Blacks and Indians. It was also known as Little Africa. We'd come over with the Indians during "the Trail of Tears" in the 1830's, that's when they were being forced out of their land and ushered to different spots. At the time, Oklahoma was set aside to be a Black and Indian state and there were close to thirty townships there. They'd even chosen a Black governor to represent their proposed state. But the Ku Klux Klan whatn't feeling it and said they'd kill him within 48 hours if he tried to take office."

Traffic was light to non-existent. Across the way, K.J. watched as one of his boys caught a fade and slid the money to one of his other workers. He had a kid on a bike who roved the streets keeping an eye out for cops. Chirp at the ready.

The gentle breeze was cool but not that crisp. It was light-sweater/T-Shirt weather. Even in the middle of December.

"But I don't understand," said K.J. "I thought they wanted us to be there and outta they hair and shit. Why care what we do?"

"Okay, but we gotta think about the times though," Preach went on, "This all happened on June 1, 1921, and though slavery was over, there was still a whole lotta racial stuff going on in this country.

"We weren't yet able to do a lot of things or go a lot of places. We were looked at as only three-fifths of a human being. We couldn't vote, go to school, or basically do nothing. They considered us stupid and didn't think we could do nothing with it. Some of the Blacks who inter-married with the Indians even received their 40 acres and a mule…"

"I ain't never heard that before," Coo-Coo braced with full attention, offering a look that both questioned yet accepted.

"Yeah," Preacher admitted. "This whole thang was kinda new to me. I'm surprised our culture doesn't talk more about it because it's really some powerful history." Preach could speak on many levels and usually preferred to use the chosen dialect of the gathering.

"So, what, this came from like some book or something?" Coo-coo asked.

"Naw, I guess it was like an article which had been posted in the Bay View newspaper up in the Bay Area, up near San Francisco and Oakland."

"So, what else it say?" Kirk Jr. was still smiling. A handsome kid with puffy lips, an athletic body, charm, and charisma. And he even had money, status and a brain.

"It talked about how this was one of the most affluent all-black communities in America. Like a little Beverly Hills."

"Yeah?"

"Yeah. We had our own schools, bank, post office, library, hospitals, churches, lawyers, restaurants, grocery stores, movie theaters, everything. You name it and we had it. We even had a few airplanes and they had just came out," Preach nodded proudly.

A black on black 750Li BMW floated past on all black rims bumping an old classic by Tupac, *I Ain't Mad Atcha* and the warm sun acted as the background as Jaquanna pranced across Wall Street in some tight fitting jeans. The boys noticed. She looked over her shoulder just as she disappeared up the block headed homeward.

Leon looked at Kirk Junior. Kirk Junior smiled and nodded. He'd been looking to pick that cherry and he made sure the little sweet thing knew it, every chance he could. It was only a matter of time, he told himself. Time and opportunity. He nodded and watched the dance then shook his head at her youth.

"Black Wall Street was an example of us getting it right and working to empower our own selves without waiting for a job or a gift from someone who despised us," Preacher said. "They say, that it whatn't even uncommon that if someone's home burned down accidently, they'd have it rebuilt within a few weeks."

"Damn!"

"They worked together and they spent their money within their own community which helped other blacks to help themselves. As a matter of fact, it said that in their community, a dollar bill circulated from hand-to-hand, paying bills and buying stuff, some thirty to a hundred times! And that it stayed within the community for as long as a year, changing hands sometimes. Whereas now a dollar lasts in the black community an average of no more than fifteen minutes, before we done took it somewhere and spent it."

"Damn, that's crazy." Leon shook his head. "We cain't wait to go buy shit."

"We don't spend with our own and then we don't even encourage it or understand the importance of it. Our attitude is simple, if I buy what I want, who cares! Black empowerment or helping each other to grow is no longer of any concern; Until you the one with the business then you sitting in there wondering why nobody comes by, then you happy as hell when one do. Like a dope spot with no customers."

Kirk Jr. nodded his support for its truth. "So where'd they get all this money, though? I don't know if I got that."

"Well, some of the land had oil on it so once they tapped into that, that helped a great deal. Remember we're talking the early 1900's, the car was just being invented; the plane had just proven real. All that makes a difference. Plus, they understood the principle of spending within their own communities. 'Cause if we spend with you, it made your business strong. You made a profit and you were happy. So, now, then whenever you were ready to spend you came over and you spent with me and some of our other folks, that helped us to make a profit which gave us more to come spend with you and on and on."

"Yeah," said K.J. "That's some cool shit right there," he chuckled.

The others chuckled to join his symphony

"But it's kinda hard to spend with our own folks when our folks be charging an arm and a leg. It's like we be having the highest damn prices in town," argued Leon. "That be the damn problem."

"Yeah, I hear you, Leon, but there is a bigger picture," Preacher explained. "You see, the more you and the rest of the community spends with me, then the more I can go down on my prices. Because then I can buy in larger bulk and get a better deal, and I ain't gotta charge so much, but if I'm only getting a few sales then I gotta charge the max I can. Just so I can pay the bills to keep the doors open."

"Yeah, shit." Leon shook his head, "Yeah." He wasn't feeling it.

"Okay, peep, in the dope game if you buy one ounce of cocaine you pay like what? Let's say six-hundred dollars. But if you pay six-hundred dollars then you really have no room and you have to make every dime: You can't really afford to give any deals because your profit margin isn't that big. Let's say you only make back a thousand on each ounce. So your profit is only four hundred. Right?"

They nodded that they followed his logic.

"But what if you were able to buy four ounces and got them for say eighteen hundred dollars?" Preach went on, "Well, that means you can now serve bigger pieces and give better deals because now you only have to make eight hundred and fifty back, on each ounce, in order to see the same four hundred dollar profit. because you're, basically, unpain four-fifty each."

"Yeah, that's how it be too," K.J. chuckled. "Then by giving bigger shit that just be having even more muthafuckas coming. So you making more money and getting even a better deal." He looked across the way and noticed another customer had come up. The guy on the bike cruised by. Things were nice and quiet.

"And that's what they understood on Black Wall Street," Preach said, "Because, at the end of the day, it was about loyalty and self-empowerment. I understood that by helping you I was also helping me, because it kept money circulating right in our own little 35-block radius, and the more people had, the more people would spend. It whatn't just that the rob-you-blind-store-on-the-corner, Perse had the same shit for a little less. That woulda just been selfish, and kept the people of the community all running to the rob-you-blind-store-on-the-corner and leaving nothing to do business with in the hood."

"And if you ain't making no money then you might as well close your doors."

"Yeah, and they whole little community woulda like crumbled," offered K.J.

"It woulda been just as if some group called the Enemy Boys popped up and put a dope spot in the hood next door. Of-fering bigger pieces at cheaper prices…"

Coo-Coo laughed, "Like on some Wal-Mart shit."

"No, you laugh, but that's real," said Preacher. "Because now here you are, all out on the corner, begging for your local customers to still deal with you, but now, they going to 'the Enemy Boys'."

"Boy, I'd be hot!" confessed K.J.

"Like Wal-Mart, the Enemy Boys come in with their awesome, amazing, wonderful deals. They buy in huge bulk and serve at discounted prices, under cutting every local guy in the area. The local guy can't compete. The local customers may want to be loyal and still deal with you, but money is money and so now, to save a buck, the customers start doing their business with the 'Enemy Boys!'"

"That shit'll prolly start a war in these streets, if some crew tried to come in like that and just shut niggas down." Leon was agitated even by the very notion, "Got niggas families starving, and making it hard for nigga's to eat."

"Yeah, huh?" Coo-Coo agreed as K.J. nodded. "Nigga bet not get too close with that bullshit."

"That's how shit be getting started," offered Leon. "Cain't just shit on niggas like that."

"'Shit," Coo-Coo's voice grew a pitch with emotion. "And Wal-Mart is in niggas hoods! We all love Wall-Mart!"

"But see, let me show you something," Preacher thought as he explained. He loved to reach the guys with words and examples of things they understood and lived with every day. It was one thing for them to sit and read some newspaper or watch it on some television, but those things spoke in a different language than these young men understood. It's like the average citizen, when faced with some contract or warranty and it's filled with all of those legal heretofore's and ipsofacto's and all of that other mumbo jumbo. No matter how well you knew and understood the English language, these things could still be a bit confusing as they snatched you out of the comfort of your realm. Like a housewife in a mechanic's garage, or a grown man helping his wife give birth: you'd do what you could, as best you could, but you couldn't help but feel challenged and discomforted by the unknown. Some you taught with examples of pinches and measures and what it took to make a gumbo; others you taught with examples of fast pitches, long strokes, par courses, and touchdowns! In the hood, as a general rule, it was probably best to stick to examples of the hip-hop world, rap music and the dope game.

These men knew and breathed these streets, its rules, its measures, and all of its subtle silent bylaws. They knew it the way a mechanic's ear knew a sound and could diagnose it. The way a doctor knew the feel of a pulse and a mother knew the sound of her child. It was their language and their world. And so he used it as he spoke to them, and taught them with their words.

"Now, let me show you," Preach continued. "That would be like you had yo little operation tryna make a $1,000.00 off each ounce. Just barely tryna pay your workers and make a profit. You know, just tryna get ahead."

The guys nodded.

"But, then here come 'the Enemy Boys' and they just move right in on your turf, with 10 kilos of product. But instead of them selling you and the other dealers in the area a bit of wholesale and letting you guys make a few dollars, they decide to keep it all for themselves. They chop it all down and bully the market, selling it all rock-for-rock. Huge rocks at great prices, because basically they're only paying like $350.00 an ounce, or close to that, and so they can afford to give crazy deals and still make the same $400.00 profit off of each. They only gotta make $750.00 back off theirs; you still gotta make a $1,000.00. So you look like the greedy bad guy and he's just sitting there smiling. Guess who's going outta business?"

"Damn," K.J. said. "That's crazy."

"They'll take all yo' customers and take that money out of the hood to go do something else with and leave you, and your homies, starving. Or who knows, maybe they'll offer you a job shaking hands and smiling for them at their front door, so you can help them to lure in more of your folks to buy their product. There's a new boss in the hood and your homies ain't got nothin' and ain't runnin' nothin'. "Hey, how you doing? Welcome to Wal-Mart."

Coo-Coo laughed out loud.

"That's crazy how we keep going for the same ole shit, from Ronald McDonald with his painted on smile, Bill Clinton with his sax and a smile, the pimp with his chalice and a smile, or Magic Johnson and his theater and a smile. Smile at us and it feels good and sure enough we go for it every time and will defend it to our death. It's the same banana in the tail pipe. Just a different clown putting it down."

Coo-Coo and Leon were caught in thought, mostly agreeing but not totally buying. It was a broad net and not all of it actually made the same sense. But for the most part, they got it.

"Okay," Kirk Jr. said, "So what's the answer? I mean, what do we do about it? I mean you cain't think Black folks is finna just like stop going to McDonalds..."

"Hell, naw!" Coo-Coo grinned, "Shit, I need my Big Mac's."

Leon smiled and nodded his agreement.

"And you know our folks love some Wal-Mart and with the cheaper prices, man, shit, they done just already did that shit, homie. Ain't much we can really do."

"No," Preach agreed. "You right, ain't much we can do about what they've already established," he explained. "But the key is to at least be aware."

They all nodded.

"You see, now that we've had this conversation, you guys will never be blind to those facts again. And, from now on... from now on," he repeated, "You will look at things just a little bit different. Awareness is everything, because the mind cain't forget what the mind has been exposed to and what the mind has learned."

"So, basically," Coo-Coo nodded, "You just waking us up."

"Not only that, Coo-Coo, man, but going forward, hopefully you'll also try and spend more money with our own folks. Just like the folks in Korea-town or China-town, and all them other places. They spend a lot of money with each other and don't feel no need to so quickly run out and buy the latest foreign car, foreign clothes, and all that other nonsense. And they don't feel a need to have to explain that or be all angry about it."

"Yeah, but you know people still gon' do they thing," said K.J.

"And ain't like niggas is making our own cars," offered Leon.

"Shit, at least we are buying our own hip-hop gear and clothes and shit," Coo-Coo nodded.

"True to all of that," Preacher agreed, "and I'm not trying to change the world. It's just..."

"Plus, we ain't got no like Africa-town or no shit," Coo-Coo chuckled.

"No, but we do have black owned businesses, and up on Crenshaw, they actually do have a little area where a group of blacks have been trying to build something meaningful."

"Oh, is that right?"

"Yeah," said K.J. "I think I heard about that."

"All I'm saying," Preacher went on, "Is we've gotta be conscious of the power of our dollar. And maybe, instead of just running off to Zale's we might stop to check out what a local black owned jewelry store has to offer. Or for times like this, when everybody is Christmas shopping, or whatever, maybe we could go out and buy a few trinkets from our own, and show our support. Just like, we do with the hamburger stand in the hood. Let's go to the one that's black owned. If there's two markets, or stores nearby and it really doesn't matter to you which one you buy your milk or cigarettes at, then go to the one that's black owned. We know better, we do better. Pure and simple. If we keep taking our money out of the hood, then there won't be any money, in the hood to be made."

"And if you ain't making no money then you might as well close your doors."

"Or go borrow something from the rob-you-blind-store-on-the-corner," Preacher said, "you understand: the situation was bigger than just a simple deal, and our folks understood that. And, if somebody was gonna have a nest egg, and extra money to spend, then, they'd rather for it to be one of their own, as opposed to the rob-you-blind-store-on-the-corner, with its shiny bait of a cheaper price and fake sugar-coated smile," he said. "I mean I love Big Macs too, but I don't wanna see the little mom and pop shop, down on the corner, get closed. I simply don't want Aint Meme's spot to disappear."

The guys chuckled and nodded, acknowledging the power of unity.

"It's no different," Preach expounded, "than if you had been buying kilo's from your boy at fifteen thousand, but then, some new joker comes along and entices you, by telling you he'll serve them to you at fourteen thousand. And so you ask yourself, then, I mean, do you up and just abandon ship?"

"Well, shit, that depends," K.J. shook his head. No matter what the emotion, money always made you do your math.

Coo-Coo nodded and looked at K.J. to let him know he was in agreement.

"Let's say he put you in the game and helped you get started and you been messing with him from the jump."

"Oh, well, naw," said K.J. "I'm not gon' just bounce on my boy like that then."

"You'd pay the little extra to help him through."

"But at the same time I'ma let his ass know though," offered Leon.

"Okay, so you give him a chance to match the price?"

"Yeah, I mean…"

"But, either way you understand that by spending with him you're showing loyalty and in exchange as he grows and you spend more and more you want better prices As he gets better prices from people he's buying from?"

"Hell yeah."

"That's what they understood." Preacher pointed at Leon, "That part right there and they were loyal to it."

"Okay, so let me ask you this," K.J. began, "They just bombed us and burnt our shit up and ain't no body say nothin'? Ain't nobody do nothing?"

"No restitution or insurance was ever paid," Preach said simply. "But, I tell you something else I didn't know though."

"What's that?" Kirk, Jr. asked.

"There used to be this old R & B group from like the early 80's called the GAP Band and they were named after the town…"

"How's that?"

"The main street in Little Africa—as Black Wall Street was also called—was a street called Greenwood Ave and it was intersected or crossed over by Archer and Pine streets. Gap was the acronym of the first letter from each of those streets. Because it turns out, that they were from Tulsa Oklahoma. It was their way of playing tribute."

"The Gap Band," Coo-Coo nodded.

"Black Wall Street," said Kirk Jr. "that's some cool shit."

~ ~ ~

Jaquanna suddenly appeared at the corner.

"Aww, shit." Leon bent over and slapped Kirk, Jr. on the shoulder. "There go yo' girl."

K.J. smiled. "Yeah. Look at her little chocolate ass."

In Los Angeles, Wall Street is a narrow little side street. It's a residential street nestled between two bigger streets: Main Street to the west and San Pedro to the east. At the corners where 105$^{th}$ and Wall Streets met, there were houses on three corners, but on the southwest corner was the back of 107$^{th}$ Street Elementary School. Jaquanna lived on 105$^{th}$, between Wall and Main, right behind the school.

K.J. and them had the house catty-corner to the school, so as Jaquanna turned to head toward the schoolyard, they admired the swaying swell of her budding curves.

"Ooohh!" Leon breathed into the side of his clenched fist.

Kirk Jr. smiled.

"She twisting that little shit for you, dawg."

Kirk, Jr. kicked his feet, stared and nodded. *13 years old* but he knew she'd be 14 soon.

Jaquanna was walking with two other girls but then she stopped, suddenly turned, and beckoned. "Kirk? You got a minute?"

As he jogged over, she crossed her arms and struck a pose, smiling in that way that girls often do, when they know, they're being watched by someone who thinks they're cute.

"What's up, hot stuff?"

"Hot stuff, aw, uhn-uhn."

"Girl, you know you sexy."

"Yeah," she waved him off, "Whatever."

"So, what's good with it, ma?" He smiled and licked his lips as he stared her up and down. "How can little Kirk service you?"

She grabbed his biceps and pushed him back separating themselves from the others. "Come here."

"Heeey Kirk," the one named Suzy waved, with her little hot tail self. At 14 she was a little bit older and a whole lot more active. Jaquanna knew her friend was gaining a rep, and she also knew that that reputation was more than good and well earned.

"What's up, Suze? What's up, Meesha?"

"Nuuuthin'," Suzy purred. "What's up with you?" She bit her lip with her smile.

"I'm good."

"I know that's right." She turned her head and cut her eye. "Um."

"Come on," Jaquanna pulled his hand. "Come here."

"What's good?" He stumbled along. "What's up?"

"I need a gun."

"You what?" he reared back and looked at the girl; head twisted he wondered what he was seeing.

"You heard me." There was a sudden sadness but her eyes were firm.

"For what?" he asked her. "What you need a gun for?"

She dropped her head but just a bit. "It's personal."

"Whoa. Whoa. Whoa. You serious?"

"I am so serious, little Kirk."

"So, what, like some small shit?"

"Yeah, something I can handle."

"Damn," he smiled and nodded. Looking her up and down with a renewed interest. "A muthafucka gotta be careful fucking with you, huh?"

"I wouldn't advise nobody to just fuck over me." She looked up and stared him in the eyes.

"Aw, wow." He enjoyed the mystery of her fire.

"So, you got me?" She pulled out a pack of Bubblicious, offered him a piece.

He leaned his head forward and opened his mouth, offering himself to be fed.

"Boy." She held it out to him. "Here."

He wiggled his tongue with his mouth still open.

"Uh-oh!" Suzy offered from the distance. "I want some."

Kirk Jr. was facing her. There was no doubt what or who she was talking about. 'Cause she was already chewing some gum.

"Oh, Lord." Jaquanna hastily ripped the wrapper then poked the gum between his teeth.

In a sudden move, he reached out and bit her finger.

"Uh! What the…"

He licked the tip and stared into her eyes then slowly grew closer to her.

She left her finger.

He sucked it.

"Oh!" She gasped as the others cheered in the distance.

"What's in it for me?"

"Shit," she twisted her frown and lifted a brow, "Nothing."

"Nothing?"

"Well, what you want? I mean…what?"

"I want it all."

"All what?"

"I want everything." He bit his lip and walked up on her pulling her warm body close. "I'm tryna be yo' first."

She loved the feel of his hands on her hips; the bubble-gummy breath that they shared as they stared into each other's eyes only inches apart.

"How you know I ain't had my first?" She pushed up off him. "Move."

"Make me," he slammed into her, hugging her tight. His hands cupping that wide softness he'd so admired.

"Aw, shit!" the boys yelled.

"Uh-oh. Go Quanna. Go Quanna." Suzy ass knew she was jealous but she made that shit sound good.

"Boy, you is too old for me!" Jaquanna shoved at his wrists to break his embrace. "Let go."

"Oh, that's how you getting' it?" He loved the challenge and smiled. "That's how you gon' do yo' boy?"

"Man, ain't you damn near grown?"

"You ain't no little girl."

"Yes I am, shit."

"You almost 14."

Her brows shot up, "How you know?"

"My nigga Little Ricky told me."

"Oh, yo' nigga huh?"

"Yeah, that's my boy."

"Man, my brother ain't nothin' but 9 years old."

"Yeah," Kirk Jr. nodded. "He say he gon' hook me up with you."

"Hook you up with who?"

"With your fine ass."

She crossed her arms over her chest, smirking, smiling, and blushing, "Boy, please."

"Please what?"

"I be seeing you with all them girls."

"But they ain't you though."

"Oh, but they ain't me, huh?"

"You know you top of the game."

"Yeah, well, I don't do a whole lotta playing."

"Oh like that?"

"You gon' be my baby mama," he declared.

"I'ma be yo' whata-whoda?"

"You heard me."

"I'm afraid not." She rolled her eyes and stretched her neck. "I ain't finna do the B.M. thang."

"What you mean?"

"I mean I'm tryna be somebody's wife. I'm cool on just raising a group of bastard kids. Four kids and three different daddy's, uh-uh. Not the Quah. Jah ain't havin' that."

"So, what, you asking me to marry you?" And he had the nerve to look all serious.

"Boy, if you don't go the hell on."

"That ain't the way to get me to say yes."

"Okay," She looked all sexy, face melting into a softer glow. "So how I get you to say yes then?" she whispered.

"Well, first of all," he pushed back up on her with a whispery tone of his own, "You gotta learn how to be nice to me."

"Aw. Uh-huh."

"And then…" He tried to kiss her.

Jaquanna dipped away and leaned back. "Boy!" she pushed him. "Get yo' old ass up off of me."

"You gon' gimme some?" He held her by the waist. "Huh? You gon' hook yo' boy up?"

"Nope."

"Oh, well, then I ain't got nothing for you either then." He let her go with a gentle nudge.

"Aww. Like that?"

"Fair exchange."

"How's that?"

He smiled all flirty. "I need you to help me shoot my gun."

"You what?" She beamed.

"You heard me."

"I'ma help you shoot yo' damn gun alright."

"Yeah?" he glowed.

"Yeah, I'ma kick you right in that muthafucka and we gon' watch it explode!"

"Aww!" Kirk Jr. shook his head with a broad smile. "You cold. You cold for that one."

"Well, shit."

"So, I cain't be yo baby daddy?"

"Man, I oughta kick you for even asking me that stupid shit!"

"You mean."

"I ain't no damn mean."

"Yeah you is," he said. "Hell, you even wanna shoot people."

"Some people deserve to be shot." Her mood suddenly grew sadder and quiet, as she thought about the late night drama.

"Like who?"

"I cain't really talk about it."

"If I get it for you," he told her, "you cain't tell nobody where that shit come from."

"I ain't."

"No, I'm serious, Jah, 'cause they could stretch my ass out."

"I got this."

"You sho'?"

Jaquanna nodded with a solemn expression.

"Let me see what I can do alright?"

She nodded. "I appreciate it," she told him. "Thanks."

"Nah, nah, not thanks. Remember, this some serious shit."

"I know."

"I'ma see what I can do and I'ma think this shit through and I'ma try to do it 'cause I really do dig you, but I don't know what you got planned and I don't want my name caught up in this shit."

"I know."

"This is real serious shit right here, ma."

She nodded.

"So, you sure?"

"Yeah," she said. "Yeah. I need it."

He nodded. "Okay, alright. So, just one question," he told her.

"Huh?"

"What color are they?"

"What color is who?"

"Them panties you got on!"

"Boy," She slapped his arm. "Wouldn't you like to know?"

"Damn, a nigga cain't even get the color? Ain't like I asked to sniff them muthafuckas!"

"Aw, you crazy."

"Come on, girl, just gimme the color," he said like a fiend in need.

"Why?"

"So I can add color to my dream."

"You mean yo' jack off image?"

"Come on, just gimme the color."

"They the same color as the ones yo' mama got on."

Aw, kill joy. "What?"

"Yeah," she laughed at his visible reaction, "That's what I thought."

There was something about this girl. Jaquanna may not have been the most beautiful girl in the world but she sho had his

number. She was sexy and chocolate and curvy and unpredictable. Like fire: Magic. Sweet. Meaningful. Dangerous. Irresisti-
ble. Every time he looked at her, he felt he was missing
something but she was kinda young though, he had to admit that.
Still, he couldn't change what he desired. And as she stepped
away, he shook his head.

"They like a peach color," she turned and said. There
was a wicked twitch to her eye and a subtle tease in her tone. "A
reeeeal, real soft like peach color and they smooth." She rubbed
her hips. "They fit me real real smooth and like really, really
tight. Um."

"Oh my God!" He touched his chest like Fred Sanford
right before the big one.

She grinned with a tinkly giggle. "You stupid."

She walked away and he stood there watching. *Soft.
Tight peach.* "Um."

# Chapter 3

In life, we are taught that things are generally fair. You join a team, play by the rules, and, win or lose, it's fair. The main thing is to keep playing, for, in the end, you will win. Never give up. Keep fighting…But, now, let's be real about it: Life isn't always fair. We don't all have an equal chance and some of us have head starts and advantages while others do not.

Of course, there're the obvious examples of "privilege" such as Lil Romeo, Willow Smith, Janet Jackson and that whole bunch, but those are the glaringly easy examples. More less-known examples include the light-skinned-pretty-girls, the big-butt-beauties, and the big-baller-families, and then, at the very very end, right at the tipsy-twirly-tip, on the bottom, are the lone wolves; no money, no family, no inside connects and no assumed status. Just the lone wolf. The wolf all by his lonesome.

"I got next," Mark said, as he walked up beside the court.

"Uh-unh." Jaquanna approached from the rear. "I got next," she said, "I already called it."

Mark nodded his head as he stole a glance, instantly enchanted by the young woman who popped her gum with an attitude and posted up on the small bench, hands reversed to cup the front of the bench as she leaned forward. Mark was standing just to her left. Her head wobbled as she ducked back and forth. She didn't look at him. She watched the game.

"Could you move?" she said with a bit of attitude. "You like kinda like in my way."

"Oh, shit!" Mark was startled and hadn't even realized that it was him who she was ducking and bobbing around in order to see. "My bad." He took up a seat on the bench beside her.

"You good." Her eyes were still locked on the game.

Though the court was in front and he had to look leftward to follow the down court progress, Mark couldn't help but steal another glance to his right. As he looked at her, Jaquanna stretched up to look up and over him. She smirked, like *Pa-lease*.

It was about 5 pm and there were a few kids scattered about the asphalt slab of a playground although the schools are actually closed on weekends. There is no nearby park in the area;

no place else for the kids to go to just run and play, so a lot of the locals simply slid through the cracks or jumped over the fences and brought their own balls, Jax, and jump-ropes, and came over to the schoolyard to play. There was no tetherball or caroms but they could still run and have a bit of fun as long as the rain held back. The winds were already becoming a little brisk. As the cusp of the evening lost its shadow and became filled with the haze of a dying sun.

There was a chill.

"Why you keep looking at me?" Her focus appeared to be on the game but obviously, she'd noticed him too.

Mark shrugged and turned to face the court. "Naw."

"Naw what?" Her face was twisted, left brow doing a dance. "What, you whatn't looking at me?"

"My bad." He watched the game. Three on three, one girl on each team. They ran, they laughed, and they played. Future leaders. Future losers. The workhorse of America. Some would make it out. Some would stay and cry. Some would end up for long stretches in somebody's prison; maybe even for life. While others would undoubtedly die, destined to wear their Easter clothes one last time before being returned to the dirt well before the age of 18.

"Nanna-nanna-bo-tanna-fee-fi-ro-danna-nan-na!" Pitty-pat patty-cake, whatever the hell they called it, the girls in the distance were doing their thang.

Watts was just to the east of here. Though some actually called this Watts. 107th Street School is nestled in a lower-income working class area. Lots of houses. Lots of apartments. More houses than apartments. The houses were the saving grace. More apartments were usually a pretty good indication of more poverty. More poverty, of course, equaled more desperation and more desperation, in turn, equaled more crime. This was still a high-crime, bloodthirsty area. Just above-or right at-the defined poverty line.

"Go Shamika! Go Shamika! It's yo birthday! Have a party!" The Double-Dutch girls were in full swing but the wind was just starting to give them a bit of trouble. Shamika was spinning and jumping and smiling her little ass off. She felt like she was on top of the world.

"Go Shamika! Go Shamika! You can do it! You got it!"

Like Double-Dutch, someone is always behind you watching and anxiously waiting. They may be smiling and saying how happy they are for your glowing success but deep inside, do believe, they're hating. For hating simply equals waiting. And they got next.

It ain't their turn until you fall. So, of course, they can't truly wish you well. Well, not unless they just some sideline chick destined to just spin ropes and cheer all they damn life.

"Go Shamika! Go Shamika! It's yo birthday! Have a party! You can do it! You got it."

You see, in the streets, every move is like a game and in a game timing is everything. Like Jump Rope, you get in when it's your turn; misstep and step the hell off. Get yo rabbit-ass back in line and don't be tryna look all pretty and shit.

"Aww!" The jump rope crowd moaned in the distance.

And just like Shamika, yo sweaty ass ain't that bitch no more. It's the next Ho's time to shine. So, who's cheering now?

"Whoa!" Some girl on the court had took a three point shot. There's no net but *whoosh!* She nailed it.

"That's my muthafucking girl right there!" Jaquanna was on her feet. "That's what the fuck I'm talking 'bout." She yelled to a cute slim Mexican Girl. Rosa was only 12 years old but she was practically the tallest girl at her school. Star center; WNBA hopeful. They were already saying such things. The lanky girl waved over to Jaquanna as she ran backwards. Hands up. Defending against the other team.

"Fifteen to ten!" Rosa's teammate yelled.

"She's good," Mark said.

"Yeah, that's my girl," she accepted as she sat.

He was looking at her.

Her eyes were still focused on the court. She saw him look down at her breasts. Blew a bubble with her Bubblicious. Checked her phone as if waiting for a call.

Scared of getting caught, he turned away.

"You just move around here?" asked Jaquanna.

"Naw," he answered. Happy as hell she was talking. "I'm coming to visit Moms."

"Visit Moms?" This made her look at him. Even her gum chewing stopped.

"'Yeah, I stay with my granny and them."

"Oh." She turned away and tucked her phone back in her rear pocket.

"Yeah." He watched the game.

"And where they stay at?"

"Who?"

"Your granny and them." She gave him that look like *Duh.*

Mark was nervous. He was sweating under the arms. He read her lips as she spoke each word. She had him all discombobulated and he had no idea why. He was 15 and pretty out spoken; this wasn't a feeling he was used to. Especially not with her. Huh. She wasn't even all that cute. Well, okay, she was cute but she wasn't all that. I mean, not even hardly all that. I mean, okay, she was fine but not like that ruby red diamond, which is the hardest to find, rarest to touch and worth more simply by its miracle type of fine. Close maybe. But not exactly. But still he was nervous though. So, whatever.

"Oh," he answered calmly. "Yeah," he said, "we live in Mississippi."

"That's a long way."

"Yeah." He scanned the court. "It's far."

"You like it?"

"Huh?"

"Mississippi."

"Yeah," Mark said, "but only sometimes. Not really like all the time though like."

"I don't understand."

"It's country. It's cool. Still got some little racism stuff though."

"Now?" She looked at him like 'what the fuck.' "I thought that stuff was over."

"Most of it," said Mark, "not all of it."

"Uh." She rolled her eyes. "That's crazy!" Through the fence and across the street, Jaquanna could see Kirk Jr. He had left for a while but now she could see that he was back. She wondered if he had gotten the gun.

"What about you?"

"Huh?"

"You new around here?" Mark asked. "I've never seen you before. I'da remembered," he blushed, hoping he'd sounded smooth.

"Yeah. Few months."

"Uh."

She turned away as if captured by the game.

"You always suck yo thumb?" he asked her.

"Huh?"

"You always suck it?" he pointed at her flattened thumb.

"Damn." Jaquanna chuckled. "Sometimes." She tucked her thumb, self-consciously. "Not always."

"You know that'll buck yo teeth," he smiled.

This made her giggle. "I know."

"You have pretty teeth," he told her.

"Thanks."

"Pretty smile."

"Aww. Thank you."

"You shouldn't buck it."

She laughed. "I won't."

"Promise?"

"I don't owe you nothing."

"Well," he'd found his cool, "not yet anyway."

"What you mean not yet? What's that s'pose to mean?"

"It means if I give you my heart I'ma want something back."

"Your heart?" She looked at him like he'd lost his absolute last God given sense. "Boy, you gotta be kidding me."

He smiled. Pleased with both her shock and joy. "Never know."

The nanna-nanna-bo-danna girls were wrapping it up in the back and as the wind picked up the meager crowd grew even thinner. It was December, after all, and the slight chance of rain still lingered. A charcoal colored sky was beginning to claim its stake.

"How old is you?" she asked.

"Fifteen."

"Um."

"You?"

"Thirteen and a half." Of course, at that age, the 'half' was very extremely important. "Or thirteen and three-quarters actually." She flexed her math. "My birthday's in March."

"Pisces."

"Yep. You?"

"Birthday's in July," he said. "I'm a Cancer."

"Um. Scared of you."

"Should be."

"Why?"

"Cause I bite."

She rolled her eyes.

He smiled.

"Oh, is that right?"

"Lord knows I hate when I'm wrong."

A sharp wind blew. "Ooh!" She hugged herself and rubbed her arms. "That was a good one."

"Want my coat?" He shrugged it off and extended it to her.

"Naw. I'm good."

"What's wrong?"

"I don't need no favors."

"Huh?"

"Favors cost too much."

"Girl, if you don't take this coat and quit playing."

"Naw, I'm good." She waved it off nicely. "Fa real though. I am. But thanks."

He laid it on the bench between them to make sure she knew it was available, in case she changed her mind.

"Oh!" Rosa was out there at it again. She'd stolen the ball and rushed down court. then took it in for a quick lay up.

"Point! That's point! Point game muthafuckas!" Her teammate taunted the competition. "Make some room on that bench over there, 'cause these fools 'bout to have a seat!"

"So what about you?" she brought him back.

"Huh?"

"You always bite yo nails?" she pointed.

He looked down at the stubby digits. Bitten, ripped, and torn till they bled. The thought made him bite his thumbnail now. "Sometimes."

"Ugh!" She slapped his hand from his mouth. "Stop that."

He shook his head and smiled then rubbed where he had bitten, checking to see if the curvature of the barely-there-nail was smooth.

"That's bad." She laughed at his discomforted smile. "I guess we both got hang ups, huh?"

"Alright. You got me."

"Ahh!" It was Rosa all the way. She'd scored the winning basket.

"Move over," her teammate yelled. "Move over. Make some room for the losers." He was smiling broadly. "Who got next?"

Mark looked at Jaquanna.

Jaquanna looked at Mark. "I got next," she said.

Just then, a heavy drop of rain hit the court.

"Ah, shit!" someone yelled, "It's 'bout to straight rain."

A gust of wind swept through the playground. The sky grew suddenly dim. Another drop. Thick. Heavy. Hard.

"What the hell?" They all stared up at the moving clouds. One shifted, the others stayed. The last light was upon them. As the ominous skies took on an even darker grey.

"Y'all better look out for Freddy Krueger."

*Bloom!* There was a thunderous roar and a squeal of tires. The sky erupted as the shooter pulled away.

"What the heck was—"

"Oh my God!"

The car zoomed by just outside of the school's fence. There were two of them. One drove. The other was in the passenger seat looking around as he brought the big gun down. The shotgun blast had rocked the senses and shattered nearby nerves.

"Ooh! Look!" a girl pointed as the car retreated. "That was them. That was them."

Across the way, Jaquanna could see the men all scrambling into action.

The big gun had made a lot of noise but it didn't look like it had hit shit. But, even still, the Wall Street boys had been fired on and it wasn't gonna rest at that.

"I'm gone."

"Shit. Me too."

"Iknowhuh?" Rosa always made it sound like just one word. I know huh? One word, three syllables, almost like aloha. Iknowhuh?

Everyone quickly gathered their things and tried to beat the rain.

"I gotta go." Jaquanna was side-stepping as she ran away visually searching for Kirk Jr. as cars pulled up then disappeared, racing to catch the offenders. "See you, kay?" she waved.

"Aw. Uh." Mark was caught off guard and kind of confused. He waved. "Yeah." He'd never even gotten her name. "Damn!" he muttered as he watched her fade away. Like a magnet, his eyes followed. Drawn by love and lust. "Damn." He could only hope he'd see her again.

# Chapter 4

"Where's Kirk?" Jaquanna asked as she ran up to the 'new house'.

Leon's eyes were scoping the block back and forth, left and right as he barked out instructions and looked for the cops. "Not now," he told her.

Inside the house, she heard a boy's voice yell in agony.

"Not now." A small Kia sedan pulled up. To the men in the house he yelled, "Come on!"

"But I need to see him."

The skies had opened and the rain was falling. *Bloom!* The sound of the thunder made everyone jump. Nerves were still on edge.

"Where he at, Leon?"

Two men rushed out carrying a third. He was walking, his arms hung over their shoulders. The side of his face and his upper body had been sprayed with a bunch of buckshot and there was blood everywhere.In the distance, sirens could be heard.

"Fuck!" With the police station basically around the corner on 108th and Main, Leon knew they didn't have much time. "Let's go. Let's go" He waved the three men forward as he held the rear door of the small car open. "You know what to do," he told Poo-Poo Patty.

Poo-Poo nodded. "I got this."

"Police 'bout to hit the corner in a minute so bounce." Leon slammed the door and she raced way. The three men in the car ducked down.

Sirens were less than a block away.

The clouds were thick and dark. Night had fallen early and without much warning. Soon Christmas lights would be on because it was Christmas time, even right here in the ghetto.

Jaquanna stood there watching it all, not sure what to do but not yet ready to leave.

"You gon' catch a cold." Leon shut the door then jumped from the steps of the side porch. "Come on." He grabbed her hand and pulled her off. Walking calmly like two lovers.

The first car hit the corner fully activated. Lights strobing, siren screaming. It paused for a second, then *Whoollp*, the hungry engine purred with the sound that only cop cars make. Moments later, three more units hit the corner. The first one pulled up in the driveway of a nearby house effectively cutting Jaquanna and Leon off at the pass.

"You." The driver had thrown his unit in park then stood from the car with his door wide open. One foot out, the other in, side arm pulled and resting near his thigh. He pointed to Jaquanna and Leon. "Keep your hands where I can see them." He was in full 'felony stop' mode.

The other cars had pulled up, and double parked, and had sirens wailing. The kids had suddenly become the focus.

Rain fell and neighbors stepped out. Curtains opened, necks craned to see.

"Turn around slowly and put your hands behind your head."

"For What?" Jaquanna demanded, "What we do?"

"Just do it!" The demanding cop barked. "Now!" His face was a vibrant red.

"I ain't do nothing."

"Just do it!" Leon was already in compliance and now he urged her to follow his lead.

Other officers were fanning out behind the kids; side arms unclasped or pulled, batons at the ready. Contain and apprehend. Ready to chase if needed. They weren't sure of the call but they'd support their own without question. Like a football team: nothing mattered more than the uniform. Period. At least, not in this moment. Not now.

"Aw, uh-unh." Jaquanna wasn't having it. She faced the cops as she angrily threw her hands on her hips. "This shit—"

The officers jumped and some moved forward. "Don't do that!" Red Face pointed and shook his head. "Don't."

"But what I do?" Her hands were out at her sides. Palms open.

The tension built as the rain poured down. Neighbors looked and everyone wondered. There might've been some Christmas music playing somewhere but you couldn't hear it beyond the sirens.

Mark was across the street frozen with concern, looking, but not knowing what to do. Preacher and Kirk Jr. stepped out. Big

Dick drove up at the corner, looked around to assess the situation, and then slowly pulled off.

"I'm finna call my mama," Jaquanna reached as if to go in her back pocket.

"Nooo!" Red Face yelled.

There was a female officer right in front of her. She whipped out her Taser and aimed it. Resting the red beam on Jaquanna's chest, she shook her head.

"Man, y'all cain't tell me what to do." Jaquanna reached for her phone. "Y'all got me—"

The trigger was pulled, the dart fired. Jaquanna's body locked up and froze till she fell over like a timbering tree, then shook on the ground in full convolutions flopping like a dying fish.

The dart of the Taser was hooked in her, as the contraption crackled and popped. Surges of electricity flowing through it and into the body of the defenseless girl. On some new age, Frankenstein shit. 'It's alive' my ass.

"Hey, man, what y'all do that for?" Mark had danced in as close as he dared. "She ain't even do nothing."

"Hey, man. Hey!" Preacher walked in until he was stopped by an angry face with a badge. "All that there is uncalled for." He shook his head and pointed angrily. "Y'all need to stop that."

"What's all that for?" Kirk Jr. was right beside him.

The neighbors were now coming out in the rain. Umbrellas and raincoats to cover them. Yet driven by the desire to know.

The officer approached and stood over Jaquanna still attached by the tether on the dart.

"Let her go!" Mark insisted.

"What y'all doing?" Lay-Lay demanded angrily, breathing hard from her dash up the block. "That's my daughter," she told the cop who stopped her. She'd donned dark shades to cover her eye but from the side you could still see the darkness and puffy swelling.

The sirens wailed. The lights flashed and now there was a helicopter.

"That's my damn daughter!" she repeated. "What the hell are y'all doing?"

The popping stopped; the body rested.

"Stand back, miss. Stand back."

"Ohh! Ohh!" Jaquanna moaned as she journeyed back into consciousness. "What the—oh." She was trying to remember where she was and regroup her scattered bearings.

An officer rushed over and grabbed Jaquanna. "Just stay still," he told her as he cuffed her. "Stay still. Relax. You've been tased. Medical team is on the way." Once she was cuffed, he rolled her on her side then let her back rest against his leg.

"Uuhh. Ahh! Oh." She shook her head from left to right still tryna get it together. Her body just felt weak. Her thoughts were groggy. She could almost barely speak. "Mamaaa!" she cried out. "Oohhhh."

"What y'all doing to my baby?" Panic and worry was all over the woman's face. "That's my baby!" Lay-Lay cried. With the realization that there was nothing, she could do to comfort or protect the life, which she'd created.

They'd already managed to get Leon searched and cuffed then shoved into a rear seat of one of the cruisers. The plan now was to secure the area as quickly as they could and then try to figure things out. By now, there were 12 units on the block with sirens and lights flashing. The sky had dimmed and the ghetto-bird hung low with its search light on, beaming down to try and help the cops and generally just adding an extra sense of chaos to the whole disturbing melody.

The crowd of neighbors was growing, already they were at 30 plus. Containment was priority. Safety of the officers held weight over anything else. So what if it resembled a war zone.

"Excuse me, sir." Jaquanna could hear Preacher yell. "Excuse me, but is all that really necessary?"

"Stand back, sir," Red Face warned. "This doesn't concern you."

"The hell it don't. These are my people. And what you doing is harassment."

"Stand back," he warned more sternly. "I'm not gon' tell you again." He had his hand on his weapon and his finger in the young man's face. Two other officers approached; one had a Taser at the ready.

"That's my baby! That's my baby! What're y'all doing?" Lay-Lay cried. "That's my baby!"

"Stand back, ma'am! I'm not gonna keep warning you."

"Oh-hhh what did I do?" Jaquanna cried. "Oh-oh-ohh!" Her face was a mess and the rain only added to her discomfort as the winds blew. She shivered while soaking wet. The EMT had just pulled up.

"I need everybody to stand back!" an officer yelled with more force. "Now!" He thrust his arms in the get-back motion and shot fire from his eyes with meaning.

*Bloom!* The clouds opened and the rain poured down. *Bloom! Bloom! Bloom!* The thunder rocked the ground and shook the trees.

Christmas lights flashed on the frames of a few scattered houses. In the windows, there were a few colorful trees.

"Just be cool, Jaquanna," Preacher yelled to her. "Just be cool."

The EMT's rushed over to tend to Jaquanna, first slowly removing then tugging the dart free. They then patched the wound in her stomach with gauze. As soon as this was done, the officer tugged her to her feet then walked Jaquanna over to the rear of one of the cruisers where he handed her off to a female officer to be frisked, rubbed, checked, and searched.

Tears poured down the little girl's face. "Uuhhh. I didn't even do nothing," the child inside emerged. "Where my mama? Mamaaa?"

"Yeah, baby, I'm here."

Christmas time in the ghetto. It was Christmas time. It was Christmas.

"What I do?" she cried. "What I do? Mamaaa?"

"I'm right here, Jaquanna."

"Hey, quit yelling!" The officer shook her. "And settle down. I'm not gon' tell you again."

"But I didn't even do nothing though."

"Well, we'll work it out when we get to the station." She opened the rear door to the cruiser then placed her left hand on top of Jaquanna's head. Her right hand gripped the girl under her arm as she helped her in. "Watch your head."

Once inside she slammed the door, then quickly they all raced off before the locals lost their senses and thought to do something stupid. Whatever had taken place, they'd sort it all out down at the station.

## Chapter 5

"This makes absolutely no sense." Preacher's angry face was shown on the nightly news. "You take a little girl; a thirteen year old little girl and you abuse her, then you kidnap her. You abuse her and kidnap her in front of her family and in front of her friends. And then you detain her?" He asked of the mystical nobody. "First you tase the child. Then you leave her on the ground, in the rain. And then you whisk her off to the station to be asked a question." He was angry and sounding every bit like a budding Malcolm X. "And all the while, mind you, her mother is standing there being ignored, while the community stands there, in the pouring rain, and watches as this goes on. You cain't tell me this would've happened in a middle-class community. In the suburbs little Laura woulda never've been treated like this. Yet, you come into our community and you kidnap our children and then dare us to say anything about it! This is not war and you don't treat us like POW's where you apprehend and then ask questions later."

He went on, "If you have questions, then you ask them. You're entitled to that. But why is it fitting to place one of our children in a cage, just so you can talk to them? Can they not make sense of the English language without being shackled with fetters and shot with Tasers? Show me just one time, just one time, where anything even remotely similar has ever occurred in suburban America. Police in the suburbs have probably never even used their Tasers, let alone approached with a weapon drawn. And God forbid should any 13 year old child, in suburban America, be tased and tossed in a cage without having committed any crime whatsoever." He continued, "That girl today was mistreated and abused, not because of the foolish and senseless crime, which took place in this community, but because she didn't do what the officer said do as soon as he said do it. And that is not acceptable!" Preacher was pointing and jabbing with fierce intent, to add emphasis to his every point. "That officer's order became more important than the crime which had actually been committed. Now how does that justify force? And what does that say to our people? What? Are you to tell me that

*obeying an officer is more important than finding a shooter?
What is the message here? What are we to learn from this?
What're you tryna tell us? Are you tryna tell us that it's more
important for Blacks to stay in line, than is it to uncover those
who threaten a Black life? Is a black life that meaningless? Is a
shooting that unimportant?*

"*That officer should be disciplined. Those officers need
to answer for this! And I mean now!*" *He took a breath and
shook his head.* "*They should not be permitted to harass the lives
they were sent to protect, not if this is an America where we truly
believe that all people are to be treated equal.*" *He took another
breath and smirked disbelief, as he got ready to step away. Lean-
ing back, he paused.* "*And Merry Christmas, America,*" *he said.*
"*Merry Christmas from the ghetto.*"

*Someone had taken video footage of the young girl being
tased and flopping on the ground. And the image had caught
syndication. Those images, along with the angry retort of
Preacher's rant, were being streamed into every home in America. And people were paying attention.*

"Why you so into that?" Mark's mother asked as they
ate. There was a TV right there in the kitchen, something Nana
Mama never would have allowed.

He barely turned away as he chewed his food; even the
commercials were a comforting distraction from the awkward
company of his mother and her boyfriend. "I met her today."

"Um." She nodded. "The girl?"

He nodded. "Yeah." Forks hit plates. The TV filled the
silence.

"Were you over there?" His mother's tone was tinged
with accusation.

"Yeah. I went to the school."

"The school?"

"A Hundred and Seventh."

"That's over there?"

"She had just left the school," he explained. "It happened
on a Hundred and Fifth."

"A Hundred and Fifth?"

"Yeah." He elaborated, "The back of the school ends on
a Hundred and Fifth."

"Um."

"And that's where it happened," he added.

Food moved. Forks scraped. The TV filled the void.

"They messed her up, huh?" Randy asked.

Mark nodded as he chewed. "They went too far."

Randy nodded. "How did you feel about it?"

Mark shrugged. "I don't know." He shook his head with a helpless smirk. "It was messed up

"Yeah?"

"Yeah." He nodded as he peeled at the thought that bloomed at the front of his brain. "I mean, it just wasn't right, you know?" He set down his fork and took a sip from his glass. "It made me feel maybe even a little scared even." The thought was forming.

Randy nodded.

His mother chewed at a slower pace, watched him, and waited to hear what he'd say.

"Well, scared but not really scared, just like..." He searched for the word.

"Vulnerable," offered Randy.

"Vulnerable. Yeah, vulnerable." He nodded his thanks. "Like they could do whatever they wanted and nobody could say anything, not even her own mother."

Randy nodded and smiled.

"They came in. Created the situation and then, just like that, they could do whatever they want to her and nobody can stop them or say nothing."

"You sound just like your grand-daddy." His mother smiled. "I see he got you thinking, don't he?"

Mark smiled at the thought of his Civil Rights beacon. Big Daddy loved to preach and share the light. "Yeah. You know Big Daddy," he said.

"But that's good though." Randy smiled. "That's how a boy becomes a man."

"Big Daddy say, the true essence of a man is one who accepts responsibility, even when that responsibility may not otherwise be his own."

"That's good," Randy pointed. "I like that."

"Yeah, Big Daddy's something else," said Mark. "He says a lot of stuff like that."

"His personal proverbs," Wilma offered. "That's what Daddy always called 'em."

Mark smiled broadly, as he nodded harder. "He also says: The true measure of a man is not what he has, but for what will he stand."

Randy smiled and nodded some more. "So that guy there," he pointed to the TV, "you feel he stood up?"

"I don't know." Mark's mood again grew somber. "I mean…" He shook his head, "I saw him out there, and he was yelling. I mean, a bunch of people was yelling, but really, what could we do?"

"That's what made you uncomfortable?"

"Yeah, I mean, that coulda been any one of us and who's gonna say anything? Who's gonna do nothing?"

"Well, why'd they mess with her in the first place?" Wilma asked. "She had to do something."

"Well, there was a shooting—"

"Oh okay," Wilma said. "I ain't catch that part."

"They mentioned it," Randy informed her.

"But it wasn't her. She had nothing to do with it."

"So why they mess with her?"

"I think the cop was just looking for somebody, anybody that he could talk to and, then, when he saw her and the guy she was walking with, he figured they might know something."

"But why?" she asked.

Mark shrugged. "Everybody else had basically already left and then the guy she was with, I guess he kinda looked like a street guy or whatever."

"Hm-hmm," Wilma nodded. "A street thug."

"Well," He hiked his shoulders and twisted his neck like he really wasn't sure that was his answer, but, "Okay."

"But they still didn't have to tase that girl," Randy said to Wilma. "She was just a kid."

"Yeah, well, I don't know." Wilma stood up and began to clear the table. Mark knew the subject was starting to take her to a place that was a bit uncomfortable.

Wilma was only 31 years old but she'd been out in those streets for years. By 14 she hung with the in crowd; by 15 she was smoking her chronic and playing with the primos. A little bit of ecstasy here and there and even some crank sometimes. Just a kid being a kid; adventure and good times. Invincible and full of the world's knowledge. By 19, she was a full-fledged user and by 20, they'd taken her kid.

That was how Mark ended up back home in Mississippi. Big Daddy had come and got the boy himself. She knew the streets, the games, and the characters and you'd think she'd be a bit sympathetic, but she'd had a long journey towards recovery and an even longer journey in the gutter. She'd seen more than she cared to recall.

"So did you have fun?" Wilma was at the sink starting on the dishes.

"Huh?"

"Your visit. Was it fun?" He'd been there for a week already. "Seeing your ole mama and how she living."

"Yeah," he uttered slowly, "It was cool."

"But you ready to get back?"

He paused a minute. "Yeah."

"Wish you woulda saw yo daddy, huh?" They'd both come down from Mississippi. Young, bright eyed, with the world by the tail. He was 20 and she was 15. You couldn't tell them that they had wasn't love. But once she started with the drugs ole Billy pulled away. And the further she went, the further he'd get. By the time that baby came, he was gone and he wasn't right ready to claim it. He swore it belonged to some dealer; the one he'd walked in and caught her with. Now, here the boy was at 15 and there still hadn't been any tests. Mark didn't know the full story, but he didn't really know or feel close to his "dead-beat Dad." All he knew was that Billy was a hard working truck driver who did damn well for himself, his wife, and their two daughters. But it seemed Mark always had to beg. He couldn't count all of the fishing trips and other dates Billy had promised to attend but to which he never came. For Christmas, he was sure he'd get his usual card and fifty dollars.

"Yeah," he said, "but I called him."

"What he say?"

"Said he had to make a quick run up to Oregon and he whatn't gon' be back till the day before Christmas Eve."

"Um." She smirked and rolled her eyes. "Boy, I tell you..." She shook her head. "That Billy is something else."

"Said he thinks he'll be running through Mississippi sometime in a couple months though and that he'd try to visit me then."

"That man don't live but an hour from here. He coulda come saw you."

"I know."

"That shit don't make no sense." Dishes clanked and the dishrag sloshed. Soap was all over her arms.

Lightning flashed outside the window. Randy excused himself to the restroom. *Bloom!* The thunder roared as Mark wondered if he'd ever see her again. Jaquanna was like a mystery for him; he couldn't understand what it was about her, or even if there was anything.

He'd gotten her name when everyone was hollering at her but he still didn't know exactly where she stayed or... Man! He wished he'd gotten her number.

"...that last time, huh?" His mother's voice rushed back into his conscious space.

"Huh?"

"What you doing?" She glanced back over her shoulder. "Watching TV?"

"Aw, naw, I was just thinking about something."

"Hm-hmmm." Mama nodded knowingly in that way mama's always somehow do. "Thanking 'bout that girl ain't you?"

"Naw." He smiled. "Why you say that?"

"Boy, I made you, you don't thank I know you?" She turned and propped a wet hand on her hip with that don't-play-me-for-no-fool look.

"Yeah, okay." He smiled broadly. "A little bit."

"Hm-hmm." Wilma returned to busting her suds. "Take that trash out, lover boy."

"Aww, man."

"Boy, you bet' not gimme that." Her hands stopped moving in the sink.

Mark got up with a smile on his face. He had no problem with chores. He really just didn't want to go out in all of that storming wind and rain.

"And how's that scholarship thing looking?" Randy came back from the restroom.

"Pretty good." Mark smiled proudly. "I'm sure I'll make it to college."

"That's music to my ears, boy." Wilma reached for him with wet hands. "Come here and give your mama a kiss."

"Hey!" He jumped back.

Randy laughed.

She shook her head and smirked. "If you don't brang yo ass here…" she beckoned.

Obediently he complied.

"I want you to know, Mama real proud of her baby."

"Big Daddy say you get two chances in life," Mark offered as he tied the trash bag at the door.

"Oh, yeah?" said Randy. "What's that?"

"Those of your own and those of your child's."

Randy nodded.

"And I'm gonna be a big success so I can take care of you, Mama."

"Aww," she beamed. "You hear that?" She looked at Randy. "That's my little man."

"You're every mother's blessing, son." Randy patted him on the shoulder. "And our hope for a brighter future."

He chuckled and nodded. "Thanks." Randy was a good man and Mark knew it. He and Wilma had been together for going on three years now and he'd really helped to rebuild his mom into a strong and beautiful woman. Helped her through her recovery, helped her get a job, helped her to buy the house they shared, and helped her to hold her head up proudly. Randy was a hardworking man who bared the burdens of life with sureness, fortitude and strength. What they felt for each other probably wasn't love but they each held a strong and mutual respect.

"I appreciate that." Mark slid on his coat and headed out the door.

"Oh," Wilma called, "and you know your train is leaving real early in the morning, so you might wanna get your stuff packed, before it gets too late."

"Okay." He nodded. Opened the door. Then *Bloom!* He stepped out into the rain, wondering if he'd ever see Jaquanna again and why did it seem to even matter.

# Chapter 6

The flash and bang of the storm raged on. Rain fell in droves and the winds whipped fiercely. It was almost 9 pm and the land was shrouded in a cold, cold darkness, when in from the drips they drained.

As they walked in the house Benny was already posted and they hadn't even closed the door good before he was all up in their faces acting like a bear with a bull up his butt.

"That girl's a headache," Benny said. "That girl's always into something."

"But it wasn't her fault now, come on now." She still had her keys in her hand. Jaquanna dipped her head and slid on by them. After two hours of sitting in a police station answering dumb questions about something she couldn't know, she really wasn't in the mood for this King of the World bullshit.

"What?" He turned to Lay-Lay with a vicious expression, Hell bent on intimidation. "You don't know who fault it was. You whatn't there."

"I was too there."

"Not from the damn beginning, you whatn't."

"So?"

"So my muthafuckin' ass!" He grew louder and got right in her face, pointing while biting his lip. Finger hovering, it could turn into a slap or a fist. It was already cocked and loaded. "Bitch."

"Oh, what you gon' do, hit me now?" Lay-Lay stood with her arms folded over her there-nothing breasts, defiance turned up full steam. "Huh? That what you finna do? You finna beat my ass? Beat me like I stole something?"

"You betta get the fuck up out my face," he warned, looking just this side of the edge. Like a cock-eyed ape on crack.

"Come on, Mama." Jaquanna tugged at her mother's coat the same way little Ricky had tugged on her. "Just come on."

Benny's angry eyes fixed on Jaquanna. "Boy you just love getting in grown folk business, don't you?" He nodded and sneered. "Cain't wait to grow yo ass up, huh?"

She just rolled her eyes and pinched her lips together. He whatn't the only fool in this house.

"Keep it up." He pointed and bit his bottom lip, eyes shifting in ways that they shouldn't. "You just keep it up, miss thirteen and some change."

"What that s'pose to mean?" She fired the darts of her eyes right at him. "That s'pose to mean something?"

"Don't worry about it." A smile played at the corner of his lips. "Don't even trip."

She sucked her teeth. "Yeah, whatever," she said, "I sho wish my uncle was here."

"And then what?" He pushed up on her. Facial expression hardened. Personal space violated. Lay-Lay rushed in and placed her hand on his meaty bicep, hoping to deflect his attention. "Huh?" He was right up on her. Breathing down on her with his hot ass breath. As usual, he'd been drinking. She could smell the funk of the stale liquor now. Not that it was ever any mystery. "And then what, bitch?"

"Oooh!" she roared from deep within a hollow chest. "I cain't' stand you."

"Oh, but you can stand to eat my food though, cain't you?"

She looked over at the lop-sided Christmas tree with its broken limbs and its gangster lean. The lights still worked but it wasn't pretty and it stood more as a reminder, now, than a decoration. The gifts had actually been re-wrapped, though the shapes of them couldn't hide the damage beneath, to the packaging at least. Bah, humbug! "Maaan!"

"Yeah, that's what I thought."

"Whatever."

"Yeah," he said, "whatever." He nodded. "Just remember, I pay for the clothes that's on your ass too, and I'll make you take them muthafuckas off."

"Man, I don't owe you nothing," she said, "and what that s'pose to mean?"

"Look," Lay-Lay said, "this is getting too crazy. Y'all need to stop."

"He needs to stop, Shoot, not me."

"Both of you!" Lay-Lay insisted. "Now stop."

"I don't know why you even mess with this man," Jaquanna said.

"Cause I want to," Lay-Lay barked, "and I'm grown." Now she was looking all cock-eyed and crazy. "Dammit!"

"Yeah, whatever." She waved them off then posted like a crosswalk guard. "Well, just leave me alone then , shoot."

"Girl, you ain't grown," Benny insisted, "and you don't tell no grown folks what to do."

"Well, why don't y'all just do y'all and leave me alone."

A gusty wind rattled a window. Winds whistled, no one noticed.

"Cause you's a kid," Lay-Lay said.

"And we pay the bills in this house."

"Oh, so now it's we, huh?" She whipped off her coat and stormed away.

"Little girl," her mother called.

Jaquanna was just about to exit.

"You don't hear me calling you?"

She had tears in her eyes. "What?" she cried. Her mother was standing by the tree.

"What?" Benny corrected, as if to teach her manners. "Girl, that ain't how you answer no grown up."

"Well, yes Mama?" It dripped with sarcasm. "Shoot."

"I think you need to apologize." Lay-Lay pointed to Benny.

With a barely hidden smile, Benny held his royal, expectant chin up high.

"For whaaat?"

"For being rude," Lay-Lay told her, "that's for damn what."

"Maaan."

"Man what?" Lay-Lay demanded. Oh, she was gon' teach this child about minding her damn manners.

"Seem like that's the only time y'all get along, when y'all jumping all down my throat."

"You ain't hear what yo mama said?"

"Man, I ain't finna apologize, man, fa'get that," Jaquanna turned to leave.

"Don't you leave this room, little girl," Lay-Lay told her. "I ain't through with you."

"Well, whaaat?" Jaquanna turned.

"What the hell Benny just tell you 'bout some damn what?"

"Dog, man." She shook her head. "This is crazy. Shoot!"

"What's crazy about it?" her mama demanded. "Huh? What's crazy?"

"It's like you just turn on me because you scared of him and whatever he say about me you just agree with."

"Girl, that ain't the damn truth."

"It is the truth, Mama," Jaquanna pleaded. "And you don't even see it."

"Girl, go on with all that," Benny waved her off. "You think you just so sharp. You little stupid ass kid—"

"Aw, come on now," Lay-Lay told him. "Don't call her stupid."

"Man fa'get that little conniving ass bitch."

"You the bitch."

"What?" Benny headed towards her. Lay-Lay threw her arms around him. Hugging the big man, but too light in the ass to truly anchor him.

Jaquanna dropped her coat and threw up her dukes. "I ain't scared of you...shoot."

"Keep it up, little girl." Benny shot a sinister smile. "Just keep it on up, and I promise I'ma learn your ass something real decent."

"Quanna?" little Ricky called from behind her. He was nervous, timid, and scared. Kinda hard to be the man of the house, when you're the littlest one in it. "Quanna?"

"What, Ricky?"

"You okay, Quanna?"

Her heart melted as she turned to her little brother. He was peeking around the doorway mostly, in his little long-john Christmas pajamas. He had his favorite little Doo-Doo Bear in his hand.

"Yeah, Big Boy." She smiled as she hugged him. "I'm okay."

"Oh," he said, "cause I was scared."

She giggled and nudged him.

"You whatn't scared, Quanna?"

"Boy." She looked over her shoulder at the two confused adults: the needy and the needer, the beaten and the beater. "Come on." She led her heart's joy. "I got you."

As they were in bed, over an hour later, Jaquanna just lay there in quiet silent tears wishing someone somewhere understood her. She felt so alone, so empty and so meaningless in a world that mattered to no one, and seemed filled with nothing but anger, revenge and pain. It was kinda hard to feel beautiful when things were so ugly inside. Maybe it was the weather.

"Do you ever get scared, Quanna?"

"I'm always scared, Big Boy."

"Me too."

Water dripped in the pot in the corner.

Earlier, while Jaquanna had been in the tub, she heard her mother and Benny in the next room having a damn hate fest: Jaquanna this, Jaquanna that. Jaquanna, Jaquanna. Jaquanna. She couldn't understand why she was even born if nobody wanted her. Her father had been killed right after little Ricky was born and it seemed like it'd been a constant stream of step-aside play daddy's ever since. Whoever paid the bills. A 'good man,' She'd actually heard her mother tonight tell Benny he was a good man, and "Jaquanna just needs to grow up a bit so she can see and appreciate how good you are." Ricky was on his back, stretched out in his bunk. Doo-Doo Bear was under his arm. The wind pushed the tree, the tree scratched the house.

"Quanna?"

"Huh?"

"You think we always gon' be close, Quanna?"

"I hope so, Big Boy." Her mind wondered; for no one could know what the future held and it seemed most people eventually just drifted apart. "I really hope so."

"We are close, right?"

"Well..."

"Aw, like that?" He reached over and threw Doo-Doo Bear and struck her in the stomach.

"Hey!" She threw it back up at him. "Punk!"

He shrieked and then giggled as Jaquanna jumped up to tickle him.

"Stop!" he cried in laughter. "Stop. You gon' make me pee on myself. Stop. Stop. Stop!"

They were giggling and laughing and having fun. Kids being kids for the moment.

There was a knock on the adjacent bathroom door. "Hey?" Benny yelled through the door. The laughter stopped. "Y'all need to settle down in there."

She rolled her eyes and stared at the door. "Urgh-uh," she said. "I cain't stand him."

Soon things settled and the house grew quiet. The plink-plink of rain dripped in the bucket, windows whistled with the gusts of wind. And Jaquanna laid thinking about Christmas.

"I wanna take care of you, Quanna."

"Huh?"

"When I grow up, I wanna take care of you, the way you always take care of me."

"I don't know what I'd do without you, Big Boy."

"You know what, Quanna?"

"What, Big Boy?"

"When I grow up, I'ma be really really rich, watch!" He promised, "And I'ma buy you everything."

Jaquanna smiled and her young heart melted. In that moment, she wished she could marry her brother, for he was truly the only love of her life. "You gon' get rich and you gon' forget all about me."

"Nah-uhn," he said seriously. "Watch," he declared, "and I'm never gon' leave you, Quanna, no matter whatever or what."

"And I'll never leave you either, Big Boy."

"Promise?"

"Pinky swear."

He rolled over and they did the little yet all so powerful pinky-shake.

Satisfied now, Ricky rolled on his side and snuggled up with Doo-Doo-Bear. He also liked to suck his thumb. Always tryna be like his big sis.

"You think it's always gon' be like this, Quanna?"

"No, Big Boy." She didn't know why she said it. "It'll get better."

"Good." He worked his little head down into his pillow. "I hope so."

"Oh and hey?" Jaquanna called as she stopped herself from rolling to her side and sucking her thumb.

"Huh?"

"You shouldn't suck your thumb no more."

"Why?"

"Cause you got pretty teeth."

"I do?" He smiled.

"Yeah, and you don't wanna buck 'em."

"Oh," he said. "So you gon' stop sucking yours too?"

"Yeah, we can stop together."

"Kay."

Jaquanna smiled as she thought of the boy who'd said the cute words to her. She wondered what his name was. And kinda looked forward to seeing him tomorrow. Well, if the rain let up. But, who knew, maybe she'd see him anyway. Maybe he'd still come around.

"Good night, Big Boy."

"Good night, Quanna."

"Oh, I ain't your queen no more?"

"You know you'll always be my queen."

It had been a real long day. And she was still hurting where she had been hit with that dart. She was amazed at all of the noise that was being made over the incident and she'd even caught Preacher on the news. It felt good to know that at least someone cared. She wondered what happened to Kirk Jr. She hoped that he was alright, but she also needed that thang.

"Hey?" She hit his bunk.

"Huh?"

"Try not to worry, kay?"

"Kay."

"Whenever, wherever, however, I'ma always be there for you."

"Whenever, wherever, however, Quanna, me too."

## *Chapter 7*

Money. Power. Respect. Even Lil Kim said it, when she did that piece with the LOX. It wasn't like it was nothing new, or a re-invention of the handbag. Money, Power and Respect, that was the recipe and all you had to do was get it. But trust me; getting it wasn't half as easy as it sounded. You had to have ass to give it and bring ass to get it. And though it wasn't always the biggest ass that you wanted, you got that ass if it flaunted. And then you claimed that ass as yours and the booty was yours too.

*Boom-ba-boom-boom.*

*Boom-ba-boom-boom.*

The deep bass knocked as he cruised up the block.

*Boom-ba-boom-boom.*

The music was on low, but it still sounded like a bass drum on wheels as the streets were empty and the rain fell slowly.

*Boom-ba-boom-boom.*

Like war drums in an African village, announcing the arrival of its king.

*Boom-ba-boom-boom.*

Today's activity signaled both the rise of a giant and the end of a war.

*Boom-ba-boom-boom.*

Victory.

*Boom-ba-boom-boom.*

Revenge.

*Boom-ba-boom-boom.*

And the Hail of a new King.

*Boom-ba-boom-boom.*

A woman's voice boasted over the bass line.

*I'm gonna sit on top/I'm gonna get it, get it*

*Every thang you got/You gonna give it to me.*

*Boom-ba-boom-boom.*

They were at the west side hideaway. It was a low-key spot, in the cut just off Western. It was a spot Big Dick had given to him a while back and he often came here to rest his head.

As Kirk Jr. pulled to the curb, his two car escort took up position; the men climbing out in long dark coats, eyes peering in all directions. Not in the least bit deterred by the storming rains.

The Get Money Crew had tried their hands, but now those GMC boys were has-beens. Kill or be killed. Conquer and be king. Never before had Kirk Jr. felt such a surge of awesome, raw, ruthless power. Things would be different from this day forward, and already he liked the chill, which ran through his veins.

*Boom-ba-boom-boom.*
Money
*Boom-ba-boom-boom.*
Power
*Boom-ba-boom-boom.*

The men fanned out, as he stood from the low-slung, steel-gray, Chevy Camaro. The mag wheels were basic, windows tinted. He had on a big, thick, puffy, black leather trench coat and he was carrying a backpack. Full of cash. Leon had the two big black duffels; Coo-Coo had a red Santa's bag slung over his shoulder. It was huge. He held and lugged it with both hands. This whatn't no romper room Merry Christmas shit, and whatn't hardly for entertaining.

Having arrived in a separate car, the two men were already heading inside. Two other men had gone in and cleared the house: like the Secret Service for a president. And as soon as clearance came, the men rushed in. Others posted and took up security outside. They were armed and deadly and there were no games they weren't prepared to play. With anybody. Be it the men in black or the boys in blue, it really didn't matter, because, tonight, there'd be no losing and compromise was not even possible.

*Jingle bells, Jingle bells, Jingles all the way*
*Oh what fun it is to rise and become a ghetto King. Hey!*

"They even gift-wrapped this shit!" Leon dumped the first of the duffels out in the center of the living room with a huge ass grin. "Look."

Huge blocks that looked like gifts tumbled and fell to the floor.

"It's Christmas time 'round this muthafucka." Coo-Coo's fat ass dumped his bag, looking like a Black ghetto Santa. Christmas gifts tumbled and plopped.

"Damn!" one of the men standing guard exclaimed.

Everybody in the house was cheesing.

One man's fall was another man's rise. And the Get Money Crew had fallen.

"Get some drank and roll this shit." Leon tossed one of the guys an ounce of purp and four big ass cigars.

Coats came off and the men relaxed. There was a huge pile of gift-wrapped product, and Coo-Coo and one of the other men were calmly unwrapping it while a third guy counted and stacked it.

Kirk Jr. cracked the backpack and nodded his head with a smile. Chunks of 20's and stacks of hundreds; there were no one's, five's, or ten's. He'd need to count this on the machine, but the damn thing was stuffed. Literally. Figuratively. However, this wasn't a knot it was a woo-wop, a woo-wop-wham. The shit that ghetto dreams were made of. It was snowing in Southern Cali.

They had blocks of Christmas trees and the powder. Now, tell me that whatn't a gift.

*I'm dreaming of a white Christmas*
*Filled with big o'huge blocks of snow,*
*A big bag o' cash*
*And pounds and pounds of pot.*
*Merry Christmas*
*Merry Christmas to you.*

Yeah, GMC had stepped to the stage and really wasn't ready to play. The Wall Street Boys and the Get Money Crew had had a long-standing beef, which had been going on way before any of the young men here were ever a part of it or knew anything about it. It wasn't their beef per se, but they had inherited it, and truly didn't even know why. Something Big Dick and them did way back. But, either way, the war had been going strong. They'd rob each other and take pot shots, or send some young kids like today, and it all just kept shit going. But today, shit had ended different because today Big Fleetwood and his boy Denali had gotten flat-lined and several of their main gunners had gotten busted. It was over, and because Kirk Jr. had done his homework and knew where their main stash house was, he didn't hesitate to go and get it. Though he knew he didn't get it all, they were sitting on a cool ass chunk. Tax free and pure profit.

"Fifty-five burgs and seventeen chronic," Coo-Coo smiled as he announced it. The cocaine wholesaled at $15,000 a kilo and the chronic was going at $4,000 a pound. The total was astronomical! "Nigga, we ain't never s'pose to look back."

Kirk Jr. sipped his drink and smiled broadly. He had a cigar. He didn't fuck with the pot. A simple drink on special occasions but other than that, he left the drugs alone.

"You hear this shit?" Leon slapped his boy on the shoulder. "You hear this shit?" He was smoking a huge ass blunt. "Nigga, you's a Boss!"

Niggas all laughed and cheered at that and K.J. smiled and nodded. It felt good to be surrounded by a team that wanted to see each other make it. It felt like some East Coast and Mid-West shit where niggas worked as teams, and put in as they rose to the top. But this was the Left Coast. Full of backbiting and every man for himself-ism. And only a fool would get it too confused. Yet tonight, tonight was a night to celebrate, and split up the booty. And boy did it feel good.

"Alright. Alright. Alright!" Kirk Jr. said. Everybody was laughing still, congratulating, celebrating, having the time of their lives. "Alright, I need to holla, let me holla."

The guys settled down and gathered close, forming a circle around the pile. Someone had called the other men inside and so there were nine of them now. Leon and Coo-Coo had been his boys from the start; some of the others were still kinda new, but you went with what you had and you built from there. That's what a leader does. And he was confident in his men.

"First of all y'all," Kirk Jr. raised his glass to his rag tag group of modern day pirates. "To the Raiders," he said, "Backs to the wall…"

"…we shall not fall…" they said together.

"…Balls in the street…" he led.

"…cause we bang…"

"WALL STREET," they all said together, as they threw up the W, then toasted and sipped from their glasses.

"Now," Kirk Jr. went on, "y'all should all know that the homie Chance is cool. That shit was all superficial. It just looked good, but the homie straight."

They were all nodding. Leon already knew.

"From here on out, we gon' need to put together a cool little structure," K.J. continued. "A lot of it we learned by what we seen Big Dick and them put down. But we on our own shit now. We bosses."

Leon smiled and took a huge pull from the blunt then filled the air with a cloud. He felt like a fuckin' boss. He looked like a boss.

"All of us, each one of us here, is gon' eat from this shit and from here on out, we the inner circle of this shit."

"Wall straight!" Coo-Coo whooped and twisted his W. staring down at the floor and nodding his head. He felt good as he bit his lip.

"But there's got to be a structure," K.J. said, "without structure we're just scrambling fools. Even corporations and businesses have chains of command, supervisors, and leadership. Someone has to be the eyes, someone has to be the ears, and someone has to be the voice. The arms, the hand, and the brain." He looked around. "And we, right here," he pointed to the floor, "are that. We are the leadership and together we gon' build this shit."

"That's what's up," said Leon. "That's what's up."

"Do yo' shit, my nigga," Coo-Coo offered, "whatever it is nigga. You know we got you."

"Okay, so let's do this. First off," K.J. pointed. "Coo, you made this day happen, my boy." He toasted the man's glass. "Today, your life forever changes," Coo-Coo beamed as his big block-head nodded. Only he, Leon and Kirk Jr. knew that he'd been the one to actually fire the pistol, which took Fleetwood and Denali down. He'd earned his bones and deserved his place. "Grab five of them white thangs and three of them green ones," K.J. told him. "Merry Christmas, my nigga."

Coo-Coo's eyes were big as fuck. "You serious? No bullshit? On errythang?"

"That's you, my nigga. You did that."

Leon stood by smiling proud. He had butterflies in his stomach. Like damn, so this is what it feels like to make it. Leon realized that Kirk Jr. had just given Coo-Coo roughly $90,000 worth of product. Enough to change the man's life forever. Hell, change his life, his people's lives and alter the course of his offspring's lives and every generation of his family tree, that came after. All depending on what he did with it and how he handled it.

Money. Power. Respect.

"Hey, K.J., man," Coo-Coo had real tears running down as he squatted and buried his face in his open palms. "Man." He cried openly as he shook his head. "Man." A couple of the men reached down and touched his shoulder. Leon hit the blunt forcing himself to hold his water. "I cain't believe this shit, K. J...man," Coo-Coo cried. "This what it's about right here," he said, "This is like a thugs fuckin dream."

Kirk Jr. nodded. "We're dream makers, my boy." He sipped his glass, "and you're a dream weaver."

"I ain't never gon' forget this." Coo-Coo stood. "Never, my nigga, never!" He looked Kirk Jr. right in the eye. "You changed my whole fuckin life, little Kirk. Nigga, I love you for that." He promised, "I'll die for you, boy." He reached out and hugged the man then started crying. "And that's real."

Coo-Coo was the one who fired the gun to do away with Fleetwood and Denali, but it was all just a natural chain of events. Kirk Jr. hadn't sent him to do it; he'd done it simply because he'd stumbled upon the cats and their crew had just bust on Chance. It was a retaliatory strike for Wall Street and Chance. Coo-Coo had no idea there'd be any sort of payday in it. Knowing about the stash house and the idea to go and hit it was all Kirk Jr.'s doing. This shit was Kirk's. Coo-Coo had no idea he'd be served such a full plate.

"And that ain't it," Kirk Jr. reached in the backpack and grabbed a rubber band wrapped bundle of hundreds. It was stretched out the long way; flat; like a brick, with three thick rubber bands stretched out around it. It was at least six inches high. "Do some Christmas shit, my boy." He tossed it to Coo-Coo and Coo-Coo caught it.

"Hey, man, I ain't never seen this much money." Coo-Coo cried some more. "And that's real." His voice broke. The tears ran. "Never in my whole fuckin life." He came over and hugged Kirk Jr. again. "I love you, dog. I love every breath you breathe, my nigga."

Kirk Jr. nodded and smiled. "Now let's get this shit over with." He pointed as he waved the men back around. "Alright, it's seven of y'all left, so this how we gon' do this. Every one of y'all get two white and one green, and on that, y'all just brang a nigga ten racks each."

"Aw, Hell yeah!" Hector punched his palm. "That's what's up right there!"

"Merry Christmas to you niggas." Kirk Jr. smiled.

All of the men gathered around hugging and exchanging pounds and promising an undying dedicated love. The drinks passed, the blunts blew. Dreams and plans were shared. 'Cause it was Christmas time. Christmas time in the ghetto; the ghetto. Where one man's fall equaled another man's rise and those wanting a turn, simply waited in line until they found a way to skip ahead, win, or lose. In jail or dead. There was always a line and always another man waiting.

"Kirk..." Coo-Coo was feeling his sauce. "I love you, man." It was obvious he was using the liquor to celebrate but also to escape the pain. "Let me know if you ever need me for anything. Anythang, my nigga. Any the fuck thang, and that's real."

"Thanks, boy."

"Don't even trip, I got you." Coo-Coo fell away.

"Lee?" Kirk Jr. called.

"Yo, what it do?" Leon came over.

"That two and one?"

"Yeah, what about it?"

"That ain't yours," Kirk Jr. said.

Leon frowned.

"I got something else for you."

Leon nodded.

"Give that two and one to the homie Chance and tell him to shoot back the dime on that," Kirk Jr. explained. "I'ma give you three burgs of that white and then you take the other seven pounds of green and then just shoot me back fifteen."

"Damn, nigga!" Leon shook his head slowly, the emotion showing through. "You's a real one." A single tear fell. With the back of his hand, he chased it. They shared a thug's embrace.

"We on top now, dog," said Kirk, "and we always said: when we get it we split. I wanna surround myself with successful niggas. And when I shine, I want it to be because my team is the shit. Besides," he said, "You're my number two and I know I'ma need you."

"Always."

"And forever."

Another thug embrace and they were gone.

# Chapter 8

***Thursday, December 23ʳ***
***Two days before Christmas***

"You know, as I stand here…" Preacher began, "I just want it to be said that I have a very great deal of respect and admiration for Senator John McCain, the former Republican, and current Independent out of Arizona. And the reason for my need to acknowledge this is that he is, in fact, one of my heroes. His story is a story of manhood realized. The story of a man who stood up in the face of danger and chose courage over cowardice. Senator John McCain is a man in the truest sense of the definition.

"He was a P.O.W. in Vietnam and he's never forgotten, not then or now, as he still takes concern for prison issues long after his personal return from a cage. Fact. It's a fact," he told his audience of wounded men, women, and children. "He's stood up for P.O.W.'s. He's stood up against the Republican Party. He's a man who's not afraid to take a stand for what he believes and that just makes him a stand-up guy. Yeah. Ole John is okay in my book. That's a real American hero."

They were at the hospital and people of all ages were ushered in. It was an impromptu spiel, without much of a point or meaning and based mostly on a matter, which he had read about, where John McCain, after having received a letter from a prisoner, had taken a brief moment to contact the warden of the prison where the man was being kept. He inquired about the treatment of the prisoner. He'd taken a moment. He'd cared. The Senator had not forgotten. And, just as he had in Vietnam, he showed faith, compassion, and solidarity with the less fortunate. He hadn't forgotten and he'd taken a moment, so Preacher took a moment to acknowledge and remember him.

Kirk Jr. and his whole crew were in attendance. It was his boy Preacher's idea but Kirk Jr. fully supported it and he'd had all of his boys buy up a bunch of toys and trinkets. And then they took a U-Haul truck jam-packed full of stuff down to the local hospital to hand out to the wounded and less fortunate.

They were now assembled in a staff meeting room, which was filled with chairs and had a podium up front. At K.J.'s encouragement, as always, Preacher was now up and ready to share. Kirk Jr. only hoped the man didn't come off too radical. He'd already heard the comparisons to Malcolm X, and knew that could invite a harsh and unjust criticism.

"Now, y'all probably remember John McCain's name from when he ran for President in 2008, the year that Barack Obama won. But he'd been around much, much longer than that, and his history is one of honor, commitment, and dedication. And now, I won't go all off into that. We'll leave that as home-work for you, because what I wanna talk to you about today is my number one true hero."

Preacher paused for a minute and looked around the room. White faces, brown faces, yellow faces, black ones. Young, old and undecided. All eyes were on him as he said it.

"Barack Obama is my hero." He paused again to gauge the reactions. A few nodded—mostly the Black ones— some looked perplexed; some filled with worry and concern. "President Obama. President Barack Obama is my hero. Because President Obama brought us to the meal. In the same house that was built by slaves, at the very table where we were only allowed to serve; where we bowed our heads in shame," he said and looked around. "Now we sit."

There was a pause and, in the quiet, they watched him.

"He not only got us a seat at the table," Preacher went on, "he got us a seat at the *head* of the table." Another pause. "So what's the big deal? Some ask as they wonder. Well, for starters I offer you this. There was a time, in not too distant America when a Black man had to go to the back doors of cer-tain homes and businesses. A dark skinned American citizen was not worthy to walk in the front door of a white man's house, and now, some 50 years later, he holds the key to the ultimate house. He holds the key to the White House, the most powerful house in the land. How is that for shattering a glass ceiling?"

He looked around and many nodded. Kirk Jr. was full of smiles.

"Barack Obama is my hero, not because he became some Black president hell bent on curing all of this country's racial ills. That's foolishness and too much for any one man to be expected to bear. As if he was to just go in there and just give us the land and rob and pillage the country." Preach shook his head in disappointment, for he knew that many expected such nonsense. "Too much for any one man."

There were only two more days before Christmas and many of those in attendance would be stuck here at the hospital over the holidays. This was a bit of escape and also an inspirational education though many seemed unsure and maybe even concerned. I mean it was one thing to be proud or even unhappy with a president, but it was a whole other something when "the racial card" became involved.

"Barack Obama is my hero, not only because his wife Michelle is so fine and classy—"

There were a few scattered chuckles at this.

"But because he is a Black man who became president and in so doing he has erased all other doubt or excuse," Preach said, "We're not serving the table, we're at the table. And though he can't just go and change everything, we now have an ear where it's needed; an eye where it wasn't; an insider within the fabric of America's woven workings. There's no more ready-made excuse."

Several heads nodded, most of them smiled. Preacher loved the feel of testing his thoughts and ideas on the masses. He felt that this was what he was born to do. And even now, he thought about how Kirk Jr. had inspired the fire within him and in many ways made all of this possible.

Preacher nodded. K. J. smiled.

"I cried the night this man was inaugurated, for 'I have a Dream' never rang so true. It was like Martin Luther King Jr. — *Doctor* Martin Luther King Junior" he corrected himself, "had been a visionary. As if he stood on that very spot and stared into the unseen, knowing that day would come, seeing the very shadow of the man who was to be Barack Obama. The personification of the dream, the fulfillment of a destiny."

Kirk Jr. gave him two thumbs up. The other guys smiled and nodded. It felt good to see and hear one of their own speak their truths. Many thought Tupac was the last chance at inspiring and leading a youth identifying social-politically conscious movement. Kirk Jr. wasn't so sure. He saw great potential in Preacher's future.

"Today, we see the likes of Dr. King's Dream everywhere. From Oprah Winfrey to Jay Z, from Puffy to that Black neurosurgeon dude, Dr. Ben Carson." The nurses and doctors all chuckled, as they too were familiar with the name of one of the greatest surgeons to ever touch a brain. And the book about him called 'Gifted Hands.' "It's everywhere," Preacher went on. "The dream has found life; the dream lives, so we gotta get off our knees," Preach told them, "There's work to be done. We can no longer cry. It's time now." He nodded with an emotional heartfelt expression. "The war is over. It's time to get up, shake it off, get that dirt off our shoulders, and lean. We have a nation to rebuild now. A war torn nation of deep scars and scattered roots. But it's our nation! The war is over. It's time to rebuild now."

As he spoke, Preacher thought of the Civil War and what it meant to truly fight for freedom. Slavery had ended, but not segregation, as the Confederacy in the Deep South would not and could not accept a Black man as an equal. It was that segregationist mentality that had kept the Blacks suppressed for so long. It was racial segregation that Malcolm and Martin and Rosa Parks and the Freedom Fighters and Brown vs the Board of Education, and many countless and unnamed others stood up against and risked or gave their lives to defend or defeat. And therein laid the dream. But.

"The war is over," Preacher whispered his declaration, "For today's youth are not of yesterday's thoughts. Today's youth have come to us with clean hands and an open embrace. For today's youth, the youth of *this* day, have elected Barack Obama. And I ain't mad at that." He shook his head and smiled. "I ain't mad one bit."

As Preacher stepped from the podium, Kirk Jr. began to clap. Pretty soon everybody was standing.

Leon looked at Preacher and beamed then slapped Kirk Jr. on the shoulder. "That's yo boy right there."

K.J. nodded.

"Man that dude can speak on some shit," Coo-Coo said to Kirk Jr. "You oughta see if Big Dick or somebody can plug that boy with some of them folks." Coo-Coo was shitty sharp and gleaming in his new jewels. But he'd played it smart; he'd went and got some of that hollow fake shit. He knew better than to fuck his off. He hadn't even gotten a car yet. He was still pushing in his same old beat-back regal. Coo-Coo was taking his time and tryna make that shit last forever.

"Yeah, I'ma have to see what's up," said K. J.

"Encore!" someone yelled.

"Speak on something else," a young brother in a wheel chair requested. "Spit that shit."

Preacher looked over to Kirk Jr. who turned his hands up and shrugged. He nodded as Preacher headed back to the podium.

"I tell you something that just struck me." Preacher looked down to the young brother who'd asked for more. "You sitting there in that wheelchair..." he pointed, "is it gang related?"

The young brother was only about 13 years old. His joy faded as he nodded. The occasion was no longer an escape for him. The moment had just been made real.

"You gon' walk again?"

There were six of them there, all huddled together. Young Blacks in wheelchairs like a club. The wounded thug gang. Another three or four were off to the side patched or braced or missing a limb.

The young brother shrugged and shook his head, unsure.

"Why is it so commonly said that 'most of the people I grew up with are dead or in prison'? We wear it like a badge of honor and say it as if it's nothing to dwell on; as if it's the norm." He continued, "But I guess it is the norm," and rushed on, "the problem is our normal is too messed up."

A bunch of heads bobbed at this. He knew he had their attention.

"How do we not see the future of our present reality, when we live the life that we do?" He looked around and saw the frowned brows and was kind of taken with the line himself. "Again, I ask, how do we not see the future of our present reality, when it is we live the life that we do?"

This whatn't no Sunday service and he whatn't tryna preach. They say Sunday is the most divided and segregated day of the week, as each racial group runs off to its private and sanctimonious little boxes, domes, rooms, closets and cathedrals to go worship their own individual gods in their own fanciful ways. And each one of these people would swear that they weren't hateful, bitter, judgmental, or divisive, because, to them in their world, it made sense. Preacher believed in unity and speaking to the streets, of the streets, from the streets, for the streets, by the streets and through them. He wasn't speaking from any particular angle or religion. He spoke what his spirit gave him as its truths. He would not be slanted, divided, or contained by the guidelines of one simple ideology. He spoke with Love. He spoke with Wisdom. He spoke with Fire and he spoke with Venom. Besides, the church had already had its turn. The fight was different now.

"When little Johnny goes overseas to Iraq or Afghanistan, or some other far reaching corner of our globe, he fights in that war and he comes home a hero. He puts his guns away and the war is over." Preacher was frowning with an angry scowl, the look of a man with things on his minds. "We," he said, "Us," he pointed at himself, the young brother, then twirled his finger, "we…we gotta fight every damn day, in a war that we can't win. We gotta fight every day," he said with added volume and strained emphasis, "just to survive." He paused. "We gotta fight every day because on every damn corner there's a Black man with a gun. The inner-city is a war zone." He shoved a finger to the floor as he declared it. "What the Hell's going on? What are we tryna accomplish? And what are we gonna do about this?" he asked. "Post-Traumatic Stress Disorder? War wounds? Hell, we need a damn V.A.! But first of all," Preach said, "we need to stop shooting at each other."

Preacher paused and saw that everyone was paying close attention. Kirk Jr. was in deep thought.

"It's not normal," he went on. "It's not normal for a human being to pick up a gun and shoot at another human being. Sure, people do it in an act of war. But you don't have to pick up a gun and go out and shoot your neighbor. What the Hell is going on?" Preach demanded in the famous words of Marvin Gaye:

"People don't shoot at each other in the suburbs. People don't ride around with guns like soldiers on a damn mission," he said. "I don't know if our reality is reflecting the damn TV or if the TV is reflecting our reality, and I really don't give a damn. But I tell you this: Little Johnny ain't running around the suburbs tryna be the terminator. And though they may rock our culture, buy the clothes, watch the videos, and come to the concerts, they don't go home and tryta re-create the Hood. How many of them you think be Ridin' Dirty?"

Several of the youngsters smiled as they noted the reference to the once popular song and ghetto slogan.

"It's crazy, you know how we say it. 'Aw, man, that's crazy.' Yeah, it's crazy," Preach declared. "You know what they say the definition of insanity is, don't you?" A couple of faces urged him on, as if they needed an answer. "The definition of insanity is repeating the same action, but expecting a different outcome." He paused. This was one he used often. It made people think.

They smiled.

"Now, ain't that crazy? But we gon' give this to our kids. Now, that's crazy. And every kid we stop to recruit, initiate, stomp out and put on, is just one more child to help us spread the cancer."

They all nodded.

"Naw, it sounds 'Hard' to say I'll die for my Hood and I'm in it till my death. That's some hard core shit to say." He wondered about the slip of his tongue. "But how many of y'all in them wheelchairs?" He pointed. "How many of y'all in that therapy with missing limbs; how many of y'all still feel like that? Who's got next, huh? Who's gon' take your turn? It's always somebody waiting; always somebody that thinks this is cool. You know why? 'Cause we ain't told them the truth, that's why. They see the videos, nod they heads to the songs; peep the homies in the hood, flossing, big money, big cars, top notch girls. They see the Bosses. And, Hell, yeah, that's part of it too. But that ain't no how, no way, no not even close to the major part, nor all of it." He was building steam and speaking with passion. "We need some videos that show y'all laid in y'alls' beds getting your diapers changed. We need videos of little damn kids shot in the head while they mama is sittin' there screaming. We need a song about the home girl who got shot, but ain't nobody but her mama and her kids coming to see her. Where the Hell her home-boys at?"

There was a chubby sister in the back by herself. She wasn't grouped up with the wheelchair clique, but she was stuck in that chair all the same. And she could relate. 'Cause she was bobbing her head something crazy.

"And instead of glamourizing the homies in the pen, like they just in there having a ball and posted all up like some super-solid gangsters so full of pride, commitment, and dedication. Let them write some damn songs and let's see how they really feel. Let's see what they tell you about sitting in the joint and ain't nobody coming to visit. Let's see what they tell you about how they ain't seen, and don't know they own damn kids. Let's hear about the tears in their hearts and the regrets in their souls and then let's ask them how many times they've ever heard from a homie, and if they got life they probably ain't gon' never hear from a homie again," he said angrily. "And somebody's got next for that, too, because that is a part of it. It's a large part of it. It's probably the largest part of it. But who's really talkin' about that, huh? Who's talkin' about that? Who's voicing those opinions or telling those truths? Who's warning the next kid in line? Every-body I know is dead or in prison. Humph!" He shook his head. "Now when do we tell them that? When do they get to hear that? Do we tell him before we put him on the set? Or do we wait until after? You might as well hand him a prison jumpsuit right along with his little gun and his gang colors and whatever else you gon' teach him as part of the Hood. When you teach him his gang sign, tell him his prison number too. And, I'm willing to bet you this," Preacher rushed on. "All them homies he out there hearing about, 'JoJo did this, Hank dog did that, the homie Kill-A-Fella was a god damn fool,' all of 'em as they sit in those cag-es wishing for a hug or a letter or a kiss from their child. All of 'em, no matter how many millions they done touched, or how much 'status' they thought they had, all of 'em as they push around in wheelchairs or wait for someone to come in and wash 'em or wipe their ass, all of 'em, each and every last one of 'em, would tell you it wasn't worth it and they wish they could take it back. They'd tell you gang banging ain't the bet, and they wouldn't want that for their kids. They'd tell you how the hood forgot about 'em. And those that's in the grave, man." He paused and shook his head. "You wouldn't hear nothing but they tears. 99.99 percent of 'em would tell you that the hood they died for or died representing, ain't even came to they funerals or chipped in to help they family plant 'em. And they'd beg you to leave them streets alone and stay the hell outta them gangs."

Kirk Jr. was nodding and deep in thought. He understood exactly where Preacher was coming from. He knew that some coulda took it as Preacher talking down on gangs and the whole street culture which consumed the youth and spit them out like the next rap song, but K.J. saw beyond that and knew that Preach was telling the truth. Hell, even his own father called from the pen and said such things. The only mystery was why didn't we hear more of this urban truth represented in rap songs, videos, and books. Yeah, some mentioned it as they gave a shout out but who really told the story? And who could tell the story without having lived it? Some of our greatest thinkers and leading authors have come out of the 'University of Prison'. The penitentiary is a hotbed of knowledge and untapped resource of some of the purest talent imaginable: look at how Harry-O helped put together Death Row Records and look at all the material Tupac put together during his brief stint in a cage. Could you imagine the lyrics in Rap music if we opened the door to accepting such material contributions from guys on the inside? The urban book game has somewhat cracked its doors, but in order to share the truth, we have to get to the truth, and we do that by peeling away the layers of bullshit and exposing the ugly sores. That was the way to make a difference and Kirk Jr. understood that, so he understood the position Preacher was in and he understood where he was coming from.

"It's hard sometimes to say some things, because you're not sure how others will take it, and, of course the last thing you want to do, is to offend the very people or person you are trying to reach." Preacher spoke calmly and softly. "But in order to get to the healing, we have to get to the sore. And it's no way we can fix a broken bone without first touching it."

They all smiled and nodded.

"We got some thangs that's broke y'all." He nodded and shook his head looking like a preacher in need of a Hallelujah. "We got some thangs that's broke, and I ain't afraid to brang the pain. And I ain't no Doctor Feel-good either." He shook his finger, in case anyone doubted. "I speak the truth as I hear the truth, as my spirit gives it to me. And right now, at this moment, right here and right now, I declare…" he was shoving his finger to the floor, "I said I declare we got some shit broke!"

Thursday, two days before Christmas. Cloudy skies and rain outside, but it felt like a sunny morning Sunday.

"It's broke y'all and, yeah, it hurts. It's broke!" he said, "But if we still got feeling in it then we can fix it."

He paused to let the thought absorb.

"And I don't know about y'all, but I'm feeling this shit." Preach continued, "I feel it when I look at a young mother tryna raise a young boy on her own, and she's scared to death she may lose him, because most of us end up dead or in prison. I feel it when she looks around her and she feels helpless, not knowing how to keep her son from following in the very footsteps of those of us who are dead or in prison. Yeah, I'm feeling it." He said, "I'm feeling her fear and her helplessness and I'm feeling the pain of her struggle. I'm feeling it. It's to the point where a woman has a boy and she says oh my God! She cain't even thank God no more, 'cause she scared and I'm feeling it."

It was feeling like a sermon and he knew he had to wrap it up. He'd spoken his piece and that was that.

"Now, because I don't like to present a problem without also offering a solution, I am forced to offer you this," he said, "For those from the Hood, let's quit rewarding foolishness. Instead of only chipping in and taking up a collection when a homie dies or comes home from prison—for those few who even get that." He added knowingly, for not all homies received even that. "Instead of only acknowledging a need once it's gone all bad, let's take up a collection, and pass the hat to send one of our own to school. Let's reward that single baby's mama, that home-girl who went back and completed school even after having a baby. Let's salute that like it means something to us. Let's reward the homie who gets his shit together and throw a party for him the day he gets off parole. Or how about a collection for him on his eighteenth birthday, but only if he's never gone to jail? Let's reward the men and women in our Hoods when they graduate; celebrate with them when they get a job. Pitch in for any of them who decide they wanna go back to school. Loan them the money to take job training or start a business. Let's go back and check on the kids of our incarcerated or fallen soldiers and tell the kids stories, give them pictures, make sure those kids are okay and be willing to take up a collection for them as well. There's pain but there's healing and we got the power."

There were several smiles and nodding heads. More and more people were packing in to catch the words of this man who spoke with such knowing passion.

"For those mothers caught with the pain or panic and not sure what to do; don't feel helpless. Don't give up, and don't be scared. You got this," he declared, "You got this. The key here is to spend time talking to him, spend time teaching him. Don't sit back and just wait till he's grown, thinking he's gon' figure out how to raise himself and all you gotta do is keep telling him to 'go to school'. That's nonsense. That's foolishness. That's giving up and you cain't do that. You can't do that. That's giving up and you cain't."

The big girl was feeling it.

"You have to get in there and take the gloves off, you have to get in there and man-up!" He told them, "The bone is broken but there's still pain, and if there's pain, we can fix it. We got this. You got it. Once he's dead or buried in a prison for years, you won't feel the pain no more. But for as long as he's alive and fighting it's gon' hurt 'cause it's broken, but we gotta reach in there and grab a hold. Yeah, he's gon' yell. Yeah, he's gon' cry. You gon' hurt him, 'cause you love him. You got this! You gotta reach in there and grab hold of that bone. We gon' break it and put it back in place!" He spoke with passion. "Now quit tryna pamper him and pat him and comfort him. It's a war out there and he's wounded. Get that bone fixed and get up and fight."

He loved what he felt inside but he had to give them more. "Teach your son to think. Teach him problem solving. You can do this by the gifts you buy from puzzles to chess games to whatever. Ask him questions, debate his opinions, help him to learn and grow. Read a book together, discuss what each of you thought, go to museums together, libraries, or simple day trips. Show him a world outside of the war zone and find out what interests him: what does he like to do? What are his hobbies? What is his natural talent? We've all got one and you gotta tap into it. God gave you that child, so that makes that your job. And no matter how deep it gets or how helpless and difficult it seems, remember on the other side of pain there is healing. There's healing on the other side, but first we gotta re-set that broken bone." He continued, "And once you've discovered that talent or interest in your child then get you some help to develop that talent or interest within him. Break out your yellow pages, pull out your phone, and then start dialing-for-a-future. You call any and every body you can with even a remote interest or attachment to the field he's interested in until you find somebody who's willing to mentor, teach, or in any way share the benefits of their field. 'Cause there's some good people out there and people do wanna help. We just gotta give them a chance. And I don't care if it takes you a month of calling 10 to 15 people a day in every airport, every shipyard, or every office building in America, you have your marching orders, and you find someone. You spend the time now or you'll spend it later when you're driving to some prison or you're sitting there making calls to arrange his funeral. You have a job. It's time for you to bring the pain or, if any way possible, simply get up and move out as far and as fast as you can. We're living in a war torn nation; these are desperate times. The Hood ain't safe. And if you don't pay attention, it'll be too late. Bring the pain; quit cooing in his ear and telling him he's cute. And I ain't talking about whipping him 'cause that ain't gon' mean a thang. Bring the pain." He pounded his fist like a hammer in his palm. "Bring the pain. Bring the pain. Bring the pain, 'cause we got some thangs that's broke and it's time for change."

# Chapter 9

**Friday, December 24th**
**Christmas Eve**

Memories. Memories are like private treasures: some you keep close and dear; some you bury and try to forget. Memories. Sometimes, people can even share the exact same experience and yet remember it altogether differently. Is one right? The other wrong? Or is it simply that memories differ? You know where your memory is yours and their memory is theirs, and it's simply the way that each of you remembers it. Kinda explains itself doesn't it? Memories, everything we do; everything we go through, it all adds up and sits there in the mind to be remembered. Good, bad or indifferent. We remember. And when we look back, it will always be exactly how we remembered it, even if it wasn't exactly how it was. Ah, memories. Some things we never forget.

"So what's up, baby. You gon' gimme some?"

"Boy." Jaquanna pushed Kirk Jr. up off her. "If you don't stop."

"Stop what?" They were at 'the new house' on 105th and Wall, inside, alone, at night. He was holding her waist and pressed all up on her. Her back was to the wall. He cupped her chin and kissed her.

As they kissed Jaquanna felt her body relax. Her nipples hardened, a shiver ran through her. He was tall, sexy. He smelled and felt good. She'd never been kissed like this before. Her body melted. Her body felt warm. As his hands cupped her ass, she didn't stop him. The kiss lingered. She hugged him. She wanted it.

"Ummgh," she purred.

The kiss went on for a cool little minute. Kirk Jr. took his right hand and cupped her nice meaty breast. Her body was young, tight, and full.

Jaquanna flowed with the oozing feeling inside of her. Her heart throbbed and pounded, as her hands clenched him, grabbing his waist. Wanting him. Feeling him. Holding him.

Taking him deeper into her essence as they shared a single space, a single breath, a single desire.

Kirk Jr. softly sucked at her lower lip as his hardness rested firmly against her soft warmth. His bulge was bursting with the need to be free. The need to be surrounded and stroked in her kindness. He pinched her nipple and groaned as he kissed her. Driving himself into her so that he knew she felt him.

As the fire sparked, and the burning flame lingered within, Kirk Jr. reached down and pinched the hem of her Levi jean skirt. "What color are they?" he whispered. He always asked her that and he always wanted to know.

"Um-mmm." She pushed him away. "Stop."

He kissed her again but she turned from his peck.

"Stop, boy." She pushed his hands away and took a deep breath to calm her.

"Come here." He pushed back up on her. "What color is they, girl?"

"Red. Now move."

"Ooh! Red," he said, as if he'd never seen such vibrant color before. "Lemme see."

"No." She slapped his hand away. "Stop."

"Why you playing all hard to get?"

"Boy, you ain't my man."

"Oh, so that's what I gotta be?" he asked. "Your man?"

"Yeah, if I wanted you to, prolly."

"Oh, like that?" He swooped in to kiss her neck

"Get off me." Jaquanna turned away. "Move."

"That's how you gon' do me?"

"That's how you did yo self."

"Look." Kirk Jr. gripped the angry swelling in his pants making sure the outline of his hardened penis showed clearly. "That's fucked up."

Jaquanna licked her lips then bit her tongue with an open mouth as she cut her eyes and stared. "You crazy," she chuckled.

He walked back up on her, still gripping the throbbing shaft of his misery. "You know you drive me crazy." He kissed her lips, just a peck.

"Move, boy." She pressed his chest while staring down at the angry trouble she'd created with pride.

"Come here." He grabbed her hand. "Just touch it." He guided her hand down into his crotch.

"No!" Jaquanna tugged her hand away. "Move." She pushed his chest. "I ain't with all that."

"You fucking tease."

"I ain't no tease."

"Yeah you is."

"No I'm not."

"Yeah you is," he told her. "What I say?"

"I don't care what you said; I told you, no I'm not."

"Prove it."

"Prove it how?"

"Gimme some."

"Yeah, right, boy."

"Just a little bit."

"A little bit how?"

"Let me just put the tip in."

"What?" She chuckled and pulled away.

"Come on, just the head. Let me just poke it in there a little bit."

"Boy, you got me confused." She twisted her smirk into a frown.

"Come on, I ain't gon' tell no body."

"Boy, I don't care who you tell."

"So you gon' gimme some?"

She pursed her lips in a cocky little twist and folded her arms over her meaty globes.

"You gon' gimme a little bit?" Kirk Jr. walked up and kissed her cheek. "Huh, baby? You got me?"

"Boy."

"Come on. Just a little bit." He pulled her into his arms and kissed her again. Deeply, slowly, lovingly. "Wanna be my girl?" He asked her.

"Aw, uh-uh, what?" She smirked as she reared her head back to look up into Kirk Jr.'s face. "Where that come from?"

"You know I been feeling you."

"Yeah, right, you just want you some, that's all." She shook her head. "I ain't hardly no damn stupid."

"Naw, seriously, Jah, I'm feeling you like that. I'm tryna real live do this shit."

"Hm-hmmm."

"So you with it?"

"Boy, leave me alone." She turned her face from his kiss.

"I'm tryna make you my Christmas gift."

"Yeah, well did you ask Santa Claus?" She smiled.

"Aw. You wrong."

"Shit, I ain't wrong, you is."

"Well, can I at least see 'em?"

She twisted her face then pushed him back. "Move." Jaquanna reached to her right hip and pulled down her skirt just enough so that she could pinch the top edge of her panties. She pulled them up. They were red.

"Aw, that's fucked up."

"You wanted to see 'em. I showed 'em."

"Aw. See, I'll show you some shit. You show me some shit."

"And what you gon' show me?" She rolled her eyes.

"You can see all this shit." He dropped his zipper and whipped out the hardened shank of his manhood through it.

"Ooh!" Jaquanna gasped and stared, frozen with an open mouth. "Oh my God!"

Kirk Jr. proudly stroked himself as he bit his lower lip while she stared.

"Aw, uh-uhnnn!" She waved her hand as if stricken by the heat of the Holy Ghost. And shaking her head, she declared, "I'm outta here. I am so outta here."

"Oh, like that?" He was still stroking and she was still looking. "You gon' be my girl?"

"That ain't finna get you none."

"Well, how can I get some then?"

"Shoot, I don't know." She shook her head. "This ain't that kinda party."

"Oh yeah?" He stepped back towards her.

"Uh-uhn!" She shoved him harder and slid out of his way. "Naw, uh-uhn."

"Oh, but you want my help though."

"You said you was gon' give me a gun." Her finger danced. Her finger pointed. "Not that little thang."

"Little?"

"You heard me."

"It's little?" He stroked it and smiled.

Jaquanna looked. "Well, whatever." She shook her head.

"Uh-huhn, I know my shit ain't little."

"Oh, them girls told you it was big?"

"What girls?"

"Unm-mm-uh, whatever girls you be messing with."

Kirk Jr. took a moment to tuck his shit. "Girl you know I been wanting yo ass."

"No I don't," she said, "I don't know that."

"Oh, so you don't see me when I be out there posted checking for yo ass?"

"I be seeing you out there doing something. But you don't be checking for me."

"Yeah I do."

"No you don't."

"You don't know, girl."

"Whatever."

"I don't even know if I should give you this gun."

"That's what I came in here for."

"And what you gon' give me?"

It seems men always wanted something. They gave; they wanted or they felt you were in debt. Anything to get what they wanted. That was her mama's sick-ass problem: always feeling like she owed some nigga something and always fucking with niggas who felt owed. Or entitled. Or owed and entitled.

"I ain't gon' give you nothing," she told him. "And I ain't gon' owe you nothing."

"Damn, that's how you getting it?"

She rolled her eyes.

"That's how you get at the boy?"

"Look," Jaquanna told him, "I need a favor alright—"

"Well, favor for a favor, ma."

"And what kinda favor you talkin' 'bout?" Head dipped she stared up over her brows. One brow higher than the other.

"I don't know…we'll work something out."

"Uh-uhn. No little Kirk, not even." She was waving and doing that I'm outta here dance. "I'm cool. I'm outta here. I am so outta here."

"Damn, you just went way big on a nigga, huh?"

"Naw. I'm just saying…"

"Girl, you know I got you, girl."

"Well, why you—"

"But you gon' have to give me another kiss." He walked up on her and looked down at her. Stared her in the eyes, waited.

Jaquanna stepped back up against his hard, warm body and allowed herself to be pulled flat into his youthful arms. Everything about him was strong and undeniably desirable. His soft kiss made her moisten again and she knew she was melting for him in ways that she shouldn't. But how could she stop what she felt?

Every fiber of her being wanted to fall to his rule. She wanted to be toppled and plundered and drug into passion. Taken and pounded, then cuddled and protected.

"I'm a virgin," she whispered into their kiss.

"Oh my God!" He smiled with excitement. "You serious?"

With a long face, she nodded. "I don't want my first time to be like this," she said. "I always wanted it to be special."

He nodded.

"And with the man that I love."

"Think you could ever love me?"

"Stop playing, boy."

"I'm serious."

"Yeah, right."

"Fa real."

"Hm-hmm."

"I'm tryna life some shit."

"And what that mean?"

"I'm tryna wife some shit."

"Boy, I cain't get no married."

"But you can get engaged."

"Engaged?" She frowned. "To who?"

"Be my girl, Jah."

"You serious?"

Kirk Jr. nodded.

"You really really serious?"

"I need a real queen, one I can build with and grow up with. Somebody that wants more than just, what I got. I need somebody that I love more than the streets or the money I make. Somebody I can trust when these streets turn against me—"

"Against you?'

"It happens, Jah, it always happens, 'cause there's always somebody waiting in the cut, waiting they turn and wanting what a nigga got." As he spoke, he reflected on the many lessons his father and uncles had shared. "Right now, it's my turn, but the streets ain't gon' always love me. Just like I ain't gon' always love the streets. And to be honest," he looked Jaquanna right in the eye. "I'm coming up so fast, and, so much, right now, I'm scared."

"Damn."

"I'm growing up too quick, Jah."

"You serious, huh?" Jaquanna realized that she was seeing a whole nother side of Kirk Jr., a vulnerable and emotional side. A side that needed her, that needed a woman. A side that she was sure he didn't trust to many if any. And, in that thought, she felt blessed. "You is so serious."

"I'm digging you, Jah."

"That's crazy."

"I'm crazy," He kissed her forehead, "about the little girl I see walk by me every day." He kissed her lips, "about her taste." He dropped to his knees and kissed her hip then pushed her skirt up and sniffed at the puffy red v. "About her scent." And then he kissed her little sandal-covered foot, "and the ground that she walks on."

"Damn." Jaquanna had her hands cupping both sides of her face. Her eyes were wide as the first tear fell. Then she cried, "Ain't nobody never said nothing like that..." She sniffled and caught it but cried, "Damn."

Still on his knees, Kirk Jr. pulled down her skirt and smoothed it back into place. "Don't trip." He stood. "Your first time will be exactly how you want it to be." He held her and kissed her salty tears. "And not until you want it to be."

Jaquanna was still cupping her crying face.

He kissed her again. "You tell me how and when," he told her, "Can you do that?"

Jaquanna sniffled, breathed, and nodded.

"Good." He kissed her salty lips again then turned from her and handed her a small brown bag.

Jaquanna wiped her eyes.

"You sho you want this?"

"Yeah." She nodded as she thought about the horror she faced so often. "Hm-hmm."

"Thirty-eight Smith and Wesson," he said as she peered inside. "Old school."

She nodded with a stern expression.

"Six shot. Bullets' in there. Be careful!"

Jaquanna wiped her eyes and nodded. "I better go." She turned to the door. "It's almost nine o'clock and I don't wanna be too late." Truth was she knew her little hot ass was supposed to've been home by 8:30 pm. She was already late. "I don't wanna get in trouble."

"No doubt." He opened his arms to her. She came. He pecked her forehead. "Think about things," he said.

"I will," she promised.

"I'm waiting."

"Kay."

## Chapter 10

As Jaquanna left 'the new house', her mind was in a million places. The weight of the gun was more than she'd imagined. As she hefted the bag, she wondered what to do with it. She wasn't some thug who would just plop it in her belt and bounce around like some beat-box bruiser. No, that wasn't gonna get it. And the light Levi jacket she wore didn't provide for many options. She was cute. The outfit was right. But she sure wasn't ready, not even.

The clouds were thick and the rains were just falling, a light sprinkle. And just the hint of a wind. Between the two big dark pillows of clouds, she caught the shining sliver of a full moon.

With her shoulders hunched, and her hands tucked under her pits, Jaquanna headed home with a sprightly step. She carried the bag in her hand. And still struggled with what to do. It was one thing to have a desire for a gun. But something else entirely to have a gun in your hand.

The day before Christmas. The eve of the celebration to honor the child. The day of happiness and joy, eagerly awaited year round. Lights flickered here and there and, as she passed, she heard laughter. In some houses, there truly was a home. *This Christmas* by the Whispers played. And Jaquanna's little heart melted.

Oh, why couldn't she just have the time that every other child had in the world? Why couldn't she have a mother and father who loved her more than life? A Christmas filled with gifts and goodies? A warm house of candles and light? Soft music playing, Christmas Carol singing, gifts piled at least knee high. Holiday pictures of smiles and cheer, a best friend to share it and understand. *This Christmas*, the Whispers sang, *will be a very special Christmas.*

Heavy drizzle was turning to rain.

As Jaquanna approached the darkened house, she slowed. There was a foreboding something that lingered in the air. A sixth sense, which told her to beware. But nothing seemed amiss.

The rain was building, but slowly though. Her little toes were wet. Her nose was cold. With the bag in her hand, her mind was racing. There was a stash in the back, under the house. But that would mean going through the gate. But then what good would a stash be if it couldn't be reached in time? No. This was not a plan, not a thought. She shook off the ill-formed thinking.

There was one thing though, which worked to her credit: Benny's car wasn't in the driveway. So this gave her time. She had no way to know when he would be home though. Fridays after work he took his time, sometimes not returning until the wee, wee hours. The thought made her smile but also worry, for whenever he was off, he came home drunk. And when he came, he came in a rage. No. The back of the house was certainly no good. She'd need it much closer than that.

As the rains fell in a consistent sheet, Jaquanna was beginning to get drenched. With the palm of her hand, she wiped her face, like a windshield swiping the rain.

She had the gun in her hand and was still unsure. There was the Christmas tree and its blinking lights. This she saw through the window. But the house seemed dimmer than usual. Something wasn't right. It was there. That spine tingling, knowing unknown, that fear without want, which breathes without cause: you know it before you knew it—but you could be wrong.

"I'm trippin'," she mumbled as she shook her head and smiled. After all, there was only one car, and this wasn't to be the first time she came home to an empty house, where the other three were out. And, besides, as she thought of it now, she remembered her mother was planning to do some last minute shopping. Benny got paid today, came home, picked up Rick and Mama and now they were all just simply off somewhere. "I am really, really trippin'."

Still cautious, Jaquanna reached inside and tucked the gun within the arm of her coat. She felt its heavy weight, down near her elbow. She kept her arms bent as she unlocked the door and as she opened it, she couldn't believe it.

Candles were burning and flickering inside, more decorations had been put up, and there were even stockings with their names on them now. Christmas songs sang on the turned down radio. And there was the Beach Cruiser she'd been so wanting.

Her eyes lit up as soon as she saw it. Her smile was one of amazement. Oh, how she'd wanted this bike for so long, she couldn't believe Mommy'd actually gotten it.

"You ain't all that, Quan." Benny was there. He was sitting on the couch and as she pushed the door wide, she saw him.

"I never said I was."

"Don't get smart."

"Man." Sucking her teeth, she closed the door. It squeaked. It groaned. It locked.

The rain was falling faster.

"Where you been, Quan?"

She put her left hand in her pocket. Felt the weight of the gun as it slid to her forearm. With her right hand, she wiped her face. The rain had washed away her tears. And the magical dream of just moments ago was now shoved aside by the nightmarish reality of her life.

"Huh?" He pestered. "Where you been?"

"I was out."

"Oh, you was out, huh?" He refilled his glass from the gallon of Jack. He leaned back on the black leather couch then stretched out with one leg up. Pajama bottoms, bare feet with no shirt. She hated when he wouldn't put a shirt on. Not only did he have a round little pig belly gut, he had nappy little salt and pepper bee-bees on his chest and had the nerve to think he looked sexy.

Jaquanna really wasn't in the mood for this. She tossed her key in the bowl by the door then turned to head to her room. "Where Mama and them?"

"Bitch, do I look like yo mama's keeper?"

Emboldened by the gun, she stopped and she stared. Locking her eyes upon his.

"What the fuck you looking at?" Benny rolled over and swung his ashy black feet to the floor. He didn't cover his bunions with socks nor care. He was big and foul and beastly. How her mother did it, she didn't know, but, to her young mind, there was nothing attractive.

Benny stood up and walked up on her, looked down into her face. "Oh, you don't hear nobody talking to you, huh?"

Jaquanna didn't break eye contact. She was nervous but she wasn't afraid.

"Where you been, Quan?"

There was no answer. Only silence spoke.

Like a cobra, he lunged and grabbed her. "Bitch." He had her by the throat. "You don't hear nobody talking to you?" He ran his hand up till he had her chin. Pushed it back till she was locked in place. Forced to face her master.

Her breaths came in shivering starts. Jaw clenched. Her heart was racing. She could smell the stench of the alcohol on his breath. His eyes were burning flames, topped off with little tiny black dots. The very picture of evil.

Benny looked in her eyes and saw her anger. "What, bitch?" He leaned closer. "What?"

His grim stare and his stern face were tinged with a certain pleasure.

"Oh, you cain't talk, bitch?" He stooped until they were eye to eye. He held her chin and looked ready to kiss her. "Huh?" he whispered harshly. His eyes dancing in the sockets of his head. "You cain't talk?"

"Yeeeh." Her jaw would barely move to form a word. Her breaths were starts and stutters.

"Then where the fuck you been?"

"Iwa owa my friend's whouse." She sounded like Elmer Fudd as she tried to form words. She'd pull away but he'd only pull closer.

*I wanna wish you a Merry Christmas*
*I wanna wish you a Merry Christmas*
*I wanna wish you a Merry Christmas,*
*From the bottom of my heart.*

The sounds of Christmas were in the air. Chestnuts roasted, maybe somewhere. But here there was only this.

"You smell like a damn boy." He leaned in close and whiffed her. He could smell the cologne on her too. "Been out there fucking, ain't you?" He nodded as he nudged her head back and let her go.

"Nope."

"Yeah you have, Bitch, I smell it."

She wondered if the gun was loaded at all, and how long it would take to get to it.

"I should tell your mama." He looked her up and down in a way that made her feel totally naked. "I bet it's good too, ain't it?"

Jaquanna sniffed her nose and wiped her face. Smoothed her wet hair back and hiked her shoulders. "I ain't having sex."

"Well, maybe that's what you need, miss high and mighty."

"I ain't high and mighty," she mumbled in a little girl's voice.

"Naw, but you thank you is though, Quan. You thank you the shit," he told her. "But I'ma show you, Quan. I'ma show you. 'Cause I ain't with no muthafucking games. This ain't no Nickelodeon and I ain't with no Funnies."

"Me neither."

"What?" He pushed in tight. "What you say?"

"Nothing," she muttered.

Nodding his head with satisfaction. "Yeah, I didn't fucking thank so."

"Can I go?"

"Did I muthafucking tell you you could leave?"

Jaquanna dropped her weight back on one leg and folded her arms over her chest. Looking down.

"With all that damn attitude."

"I ain't got no attitude," she mumbled. The gun was so close but it seemed so far. A million miles away. If only. If only, she thought. If only.

"I should make you gimme some of that shit." He smiled. "Since you out there giving it away."

"I ain't giving nothing away."

"Oh, you getting paid for it?"

"I ain't doing it."

"It might be what you need." He grabbed himself as he pulled back and looked up and down over her. "Tame yo' little hot ass."

"I ain't hot." She continued to look at the floor, not in the least bit turned on or tempted by the tight bulge he'd help himself to create.

"You is hot."

"I'm not."

"Bitch, what I say?"

"Humph!" She sucked her teeth. "Man." She shook her head.

"Man, what, Quan?" He smiled. "Man what?"

"Nothing."

"You know what?" He bit his lip and walked in closer and the cobra struck again. "Fuck you, Quan." He took her by the throat and shoved her.

Jaquanna stumbled and turned with a stare.

"Pull your skirt up, bitch."

"No." She twisted her neck and frowned like he was crazy. "I ain't finna do that."

"Bitch!" He reared back an open palm, advanced until he was up on her. "What I say?"

She winced and threw her forearm up intending to shield the blow she knew was coming.

Benny laughed at her frightened posture. "Yeah, that's what the fuck I thought." He backed away. "Bad ass."

"Why is you messing with me?" She was happy he hadn't seen the bulge when she'd raised her forearm up, or who knows what would've happened. "Why?"

"Pull it up."

"No. For what?"

"I wanna see if you got cum in your draws."

"If I got whaaat?" Mouth hung open; Jaquanna couldn't believe her ears. Benny was more than amazing; he was an absolute riot. An adventure all his own.

"You heard me. You ain't stupid," Benny insisted. "Pull it up."

"I'm not finna do that, Benny. No, I ain't finna do it."

"Alright," he conceded with a nod. "Well, take the muthafuckers off," he said, "and let me see 'em."

"No, Benny, come on now." She pleaded and noticed she sounded just like her mother. "That's crazy."

"Little girl," he told her, "I bought them panties and if anybody gon' play in 'em," he poked his chest, "it's gon' be me."

The gun felt heavy. The gun felt useless. Winds blew at a sharper pace. Jaquanna's head hung down.

"I should tell your mama." He reached for his glass and took a sip. "But I ain't gon' say nothing." He took a seat. "It's gon' just be our little secret." He took another sip. "You is good at secrets ain't you?"

"Yeah," she said, "whatever." She was tapping her foot. "Can I go?"

"Yeah, go wash your ass then come in here and keep me company. We can listen to music. It's Christmas."

She nodded her head as she walked away.

"And, hey!" he called. "You ain't even say nothing 'bout the bike I bought you."

Even now, she couldn't resist a smile. It was the big pink and black one with the bow on it. "Thank you." She blushed.

"Hmm-hmmph." He took a sip. "But you don't appreciate ole Benny though."

"Yes I do." Jaquanna went over to the couch and hugged him. "Thank you, kay?"

"Hmm-hmmn." He nodded. "Go in there and wash your ass. Your mama and them went and did some last minute shopping. Come on in here and keep me company."

She nodded and pulled away. Feeling the burn of his eyes upon her backside, she knew she was no longer safe. Sure, there'd been subtle threats before. A lingering stare here and there. But this was different. It was out there now; he'd made his move. The threat was real. She could taste it.

The winds whipped. The rains slammed. A flash of lightening flared. There was a rumble, a nice rolling rumble and a shiver danced along her spine.

> *Feliz Navidad*
> *Feliz Navidad*
> *Feliz Navidad*
> *Prospero Ano y Felicidad*
> *I wanna wish you a Merry Christmas*
> *I wanna wish you a Merry Christmas*
> *I wanna wish you a Merry Christmas*
> *from the bottom of my heart.*

Jaquanna walked in her room and she closed the door. Slipped the bag from her arm and gazed inside. The shiny nickel-plated .38 revolver was brand spanking new. It had the black rubber grip and the chubby little snub nose. She held it with her finger on the trigger. Power. Power. Power. Oh, she felt so powerful now. Inside the bag, there were six loose bullets. She took them and tried to fill it. Power. The power of life. The power of death. She held the great equalizer. Now she fiddled with the heavy armament and tried to get inside. It made no sense to her at first; she saw the empty chambers but couldn't get to them. She was wet and her clothes were moist.

"Quan?" She heard the foot falls on the creaking boards; the heavy man was upon her.

"Huh?" She dropped the gun and bullets in the bag, fell to her knee and rammed it beneath the box spring to her bunk.

"Quan?" He pushed the door as he always did. Feeling entitled he stepped inside. "What you doing?"

She had stood and whipped her jacket off and was working on her sandals. "'Bout to get in the water."

He took a step and stared down his nose. Swirling his glass he told her, "Well, hurry up, I got something I wanna show you."

"Kay." She wiped at her nose with the side of her hand.

His eyes burned slowly as he took in her form. He lingered and smiled as he leered. "You know you alright with me, right?"

Jaquanna refused to remove another item of clothing while he stood there salivating in a loud silence. The warnings were loud and clear. "Yeah."

"We could be real cool, Quan."

With her hands on her hips, she nodded.

"It ain't gotta be like this."

More nods and the bite of a twisted lip.

"Go on in there and get your shower."

"Kay."

The tiny bathroom had two doors, one opening to each bedroom. Neither had a lock and she didn't feel safe, but she'd

thought of it too late, so she rushed through, scrubbing her goodies and hell bent on getting out as quick as she could.

*Knock, knock, knock.* "Quan?"

*Oh, shit.* She froze. "Huh?" Her eyes were wide. Her
beating heart stopped. She peeked around the shower curtain.

The doorknob on her mother's side twisted both left and
right. "You already started in there?"

"Yeah. Huhn." She watched the knob. She clenched the
curtain. The shiver ran down her spine.

"Can I come in?"

"For whaaat? I'm almost out."

"I need to take a piss."

"Well, wait. I'll be through in a minute."

"Say what?" She could hear the agitation in his tone.

"Please, Benny, I'm almost through." *Damn, it ain't
even been five minutes.*

"Well, hurry up."

Jaquanna saw that the doorknob fell back in place and
she moved with a quicker pace. Determined to get done and get
out of there, but then there he was again.

"Quan?" He knocked and twisted the knob.

*Oh, shit!* His voice was inside. "Huh?"

"I'm just gon' use this right quick."

She heard the clink and clatter of the commode and she
stood with a frozen chill. The water rained down over her.

"Ahhh," he uttered, as the stream of his piss raced from
his penis and clashed in the bowl, creating its own little racket.
"Oh, man."

Jaquanna turned and faced him through the curtain,
afraid that he might peek in. Soapy bubbles covered her cunt.
The rag was at her breasts.

"You know what, Quan?"

"Huh?"

"I think it's time you became a woman," Benny said as
he flushed. "You all grown up. I can see it."

"But I'm still a kid though." The warm waters of the
shower seemed frigid. She clamped her thighs and stared.

"No you not." Benny calmly reached over and pulled
back the curtain.

"What you doing?" She squatted more and folded into herself, trying her best to conceal her treasures. The horror in her face was undeniable, as was her fear. "Wha—"

"Stand up." The stern face with the grim stare looked upon her as if disgusted. "Stand up."

"What you doing?"

"I said stand up."

Slowly she moved to comply. "But why?"

"Cause I said so."

A tear welled. Her face grew long.

"Don't you start no crying." He held his glass in his hand and he took a sip, as he openly, brazenly stared. "Wash that soap off."

Again, she moved to comply. "But why?" Jaquanna was confused. Jaquanna was scared. She didn't know what to do, and she seemed defenseless. If only she could get to her gun.

"You a fine little thang ain't you." Benny stroked her cheek with the back of his hand. "I'ma show you what it means to be a woman."

"But—"

"Get out. Get dried and meet me in my bedroom."

The tears flowed freely.

"Don't cry." He reached down and cupped her chin, then ran his musty Jack-covered lips gently across her wet cheek.

There was a loud bang. The house rumbled and shook. Jaquanna was under the weather.

"Just put on your towel, okay?"

Through her tears, Jaquanna nodded. *This is it*, she thought. Her time was now. There was no way. No way. She was going down. No way, she'd give up without a fight. No way! No way. No matter what plans he had in his head. No Way!

The storm rumbled. The house shook. The thunder raged. The wind swept. No way!

As he walked out, he snapped his fingers. *A very Merry Christmas.* He did a full spin as he sang. A two-step now, he jitterbugged out of the room.

As soon as he left, Jaquanna came to. This was it. Her time was now. With the water still running, she crept to her room, still wet and carrying her towel.

Quickly she dipped as she fell to her knee, reached under the box spring and searched. She couldn't hear if he was singing anymore, but she knew she had to rush.

Fumbling and fiddling, she found the bag. Dumped its contents upon the bed. The towel was on the floor. Her skin was wet. Like a sheen of beautiful brown gold, to be plundered. To be plundered if she did not protect it. Now.

"Oh my God," she fiddled and fumbled. "Come on, come on." Jaquanna couldn't get the dastardly thing open. "Come on." Without the bullets, it was only a weight, of no more use than a rock. "Oh my God," A bullet fell and bounced under the bed. "Oh Jesus," On all fours now she looked under the bunk. Booty tooted to the wide-open air. "Come on."

"Quan?" Benny yelled in the distance.

"Oh shit." She left that bullet and tried for the rest. She had to get it open in time.

"Quan?"

She heard the floor boards creaking as he slowly approached. Faster she fumbled and turned toward the bathroom. "Huh?" She hoped her voice threw in that way some bit. She raced with her fiddling now, until suddenly it made simple sense.

As she released the latch to drop the chamber, her heart banged in the cage of her chest. She was light headed, nervous and shaking.

"Quan?" He called with a bit more anger. He was closer to the door now.

It was taking too long to get the bullets in. One rolled. Another one fell. Two in, two gone and two more to go. Her hand shook as she reached again.

*Bloom!* The blast of thunder startled her beyond measure.

"Quan. You don't hear me talking to you?"

*Oh my God!* He was right— "Yeah."

The door came open and Benny stood there with a nappy chest, belly, and a bullshit smile. He was holding himself as he sipped.

Jaquanna was still on her knees by the bed. He was behind her. Her backside totally exposed.

'"Yes. Yes. Yes," he said. "Um. Um. Um."

The feeling in her stomach was one she'd never known. She was repulsed, but not afraid. Her nerves had her on edge. The gun was right there. But still she wasn't totally safe. Two in the gun. Two loose besides. Two others under the bed.

She'd shoved the open weapon and loose bullets under her pillow.

"What you doing down there, girl?"

"Nothing." She stood up now and grabbed the towel.

The *plink-plink* of the rain struck the bucket.

"Why that shower still on?"

"I was about to cut it off."

"Well, let's get that shit done. We ain't got a lotta time, and ole Benny wanna show you something."

"Kay."

"Come on." He pushed up behind her, herding her like an old cow.

As he ushered her into the bathroom, Jaquanna reached in and closed the water valve.

"Hm-hmmm." He gazed into her eyes and stroked her cheek. "Come on."

"Kay, let me just get something real quick." She tried to push past him.

"Uh-uhn." He spun in behind her and grabbed her little hips then pushed her on ahead of him. "You don't need nothing."

"Yeah I do," she protested, "I just gotta—"

"Uh-uhn."

As they entered the room, she looked at her mother's bed. Benny had prepared it with towels. "Ah, uh-uhn!"

"Lay down."

"No, Benny."

"Bitch." *POW!* He slapped her. "What the fuck did I just say?"

Jaquanna stood there holding her cheek. Diamond darts forming out of her eyes.

The thunder rumbled. The lightening flashed.

"Take this shit off." He yanked the towel she'd used for cover.

Jaquanna was an iron stone.

"Get your ass up on that bed. Don't make me tell you again."

*No way*, she thought to herself, *no way*.

"What the fuck is you looking at?" He grabbed her throat and squeezed it softly. "Lay down."

"Fuck that." She shoved him, and when he fell over the bed, she dashed and broke from the room.

"Bitch!" He was right behind, having bounced like a weeble-wobbling clown.

"Leave me alone!" she screamed. Clearing the second door, she slammed it then fell forward to the floor to grab her gun.

The door came open and there he stood.

"Leave me alone!" she grabbed it.

"What the fuck is wrong with you?" He snatched her and rolled her on her back.

The gun fell. She didn't know where. But it was no longer in her hand. "Stop!" She shifted to the side avoiding his tackling lunge. "Stop!"

"Come here, bitch." It was a sinister whisper.

She was on her feet.

He was on his back.

"What the fuck is wrong with you, Quan? Huh?" He sat up now and rolled to his knee.

She saw the gun there behind him.

"I don't wanna do nothing," she told him. Her naked body exposed, breathing hard. Heart pounding. Her mind raced to find a way. "Just stop, Benny. Come on stop, I'm serious. Stop!"

"Oh, you thank you really something, huh?" He lumbered to his feet with a smile. "I done told you, you ain't all that, Quan."

"Just leave me alone." Her arms covered her breasts. Her legs were clamped tight. There she stood. The hairy triangle on full display.

"Oh, naw, you finna gimme that pussy. That's what you is finna do."

"No! Why is you tripping, man? Why is you tripping, Benny?"

"I ain't tripping." He stroked her face. "I just want you to show ole Ben some appreciation for that bike."

"Keep the bike, Benny." She pulled her head away. "I don't even want it."

"Oh, what you gon' waste my money? Huh?" He pinched her chin to breathe down on her. "Is that what you thank?"

"Take it back and get the money, Benny. Come on, just leave me alone."

"I don't wanna leave you alone." He licked his lips as he stroked her upper arms. Then he let his hands fall to her young tight hips. "I been laying to make you a woman."

"Stop." She twisted away and looked past him to her gun. "Let me go." Sliding sideways, she tried to get past. Just five feet or so, out front, she could get it and hold him off.

Two shots. She knew she only had two shots. The gun was closed; a bullet was on the bed. Two shots. She didn't know where the other bullet was. But she knew that she had two, and two was more than enough.

"Come on." He herded the scared girl along. "Come on and play with Big Ben."

"Noooo!" she cried as she went. "Nooo. Why you doing this?"

"It's Christmas."

"You gon' just do me like this on Christmas, Ben?"

"Trust me, girl." He tapped her booty. "I'm giving you a hell of a gift."

In the front room again, where the candles flickered, soft carols played on the radio. Across the land children turned in their beds for the happiest day was upon them. Milk and cookies set out on the mantle. Gifts were wrapped and stacked. Turkeys and hams, cakes and pies. Every treat for a little kid's eyes. It was Christmas, a momentously happy time. A time of sharing and a time of warmth. A celebration of Christ and a fulfillment of wants. Even the ghetto had Christmas.

No fireplace, no chimneys or dreams, moms and pops simply bought a few things. So very few gifts laid under the trees. But, more meaningful, was the magic. Yet some kids didn't even have this. Instead, what they had was tragic.

*Bloooo-uh-oo-uh-rrmm! Bloooo-uh-rrmm!* It was a loud, raucous thundering roar. Reverberating almost endless. *Bla-bla-bla-bloooo-uh-uh-mmrrmmm.*

> *Jingle bells Jingle bells Jingles all the way*
> *Oh what fun is it to ride in a one horse open*
> *sleigh-Hey!*

"You see that?" Benny dropped his pajama bottoms and boxers. "That's a man." He pointed at his hardness as he kicked the material aside. "That's a big man." Though this she surely doubted.

Jaquanna was standing there with her head down crying.

"Now, come here." He uncrossed her stubborn arms.

"Nooo."

"Shhh," he shushed her. "Look." He took her hand and laid it upon him.

Like a fire had licked her, she snatched it back. "No!"

"Come on." He nudged her. "Lay down."

Jaquanna fell back a step as he guided her.

"We gon' do it right here next to the tree so you can look at that big pretty bike I bought you, kay?"

"Why you doing this, Benny? Why?"

"Trust me. You'll thank me later."

With a move deserving of Emmitt Smith's respect, Jaquanna cut to her right, ran around the low-slung table, and then quickly made her dash. "Aarrgh!"

But Benny, to his credit, was a lot faster than she'd thought, and he'd dived and snatched her by her ankle. "Bitch!" He said, as she crashed to the floor and fell flat on her face. "You thank this a muthafuckin' game?"

Her nose was busted and the blood poured. Her head had grown a bit dizzy as he stood over her and dragged her.

"Stop!" she sniffled and cried, but the drunken caveman drug her on. Her butt burned on the unforgiving carpet. She tucked her palms beneath. Captured but yet unbroken.

"I'm 'bout to teach yo little stupid-ass something." He fell down on her and pressed her with his weight. "Open your muthafuckin' legs." He shoved one and then the other. His hardness poked at her treasure.

"Uhn!" She wiggled and danced. "No!" She pushed and rocked, but the big man was too much for her. "Stop, Benny!" She couldn't close her legs. He had forced them apart and wiggled into her saddle. Raising her legs only seemed to excite him. She wiggled her ass but it caught her. "Noooo~" With a burning pain he pushed inside. "Ohhh!" It was a pain unlike any she'd ever known. "God!"

"It's gon' get real good in a minute." He pushed in harder, deeper, ripping her as he rifled her.

*Bloo-oo-rrmm-mm!*

More lightning, more rain. The pain was unbearable.

"Oh, yeah, girl." He pushed in deeper. She thought it would tear her apart. "Take Big Ben, come on." The lick of the flames flickered and flashed. A candle lit Christmas for two. Complete with tree. Bikes and goodies. And carols in the air.

*I'm dreaming of a white Christmas*
*Just like the ones I use to know*


With tears in her eyes, Jaquanna faded away, disappearing inside of herself as blood poured down her face. How could this happen? How could this be? In her own house? Raped under a tree? Her first time? Her virginity stolen. Stolen by some thief, invited home by her mother.


*Chestnuts roasting on an open fire*
*Jack Frost nipping at your nose.*


"Just relax and take it easy, Quan. Come on. You can do it." He began to work himself in and out. "Now wrap your legs around me." He tried to make her. "Hump me back like you want it, girl."

Tears welled and tears fell. Tears spilled from her very soul, very much like the rains outside.

*Bloom! Bloom!*

"Damn, this thang is tight. Uummm!" he groaned. "You like how I'm fucking you, Quan? Huh?" He grabbed her chin and pinched it hard, forcing her to look into his face. "Fuck you, Quan!" He pounded hard.

"Huu-ohhn!" She winced at the violence and pain of the assault.

"I told you, you ain't all that, Quan." He hunched his back and rammed her!

"Oh God!" she panted. "Oh my God!" she cried. "Please. Oh! Please. Huu-oh! Please!"

"Come on, fuck me, Quan. Come on; fuck me back. Come on." He humped her faster. "Where all that fire at now? Come on." He demanded her to challenge. "Let's see what the fuck you got, Bitch."

"Oh, stop. Oh, oh, uhn. Uhn. Sto—oh—oh!"

"Yeah, that's what I thought. Umgh!" It was hard and vicious. Selfish driving.

The thunder. The music. The rain didn't matter. The pine scent and the candle flick. Nothing mattered but her gun.

"I have to use the bathroom," she uttered.

Benny drove and hunched and rode, not giving a damn about her plea.

"Benny?"

He ignored her; his pace was building, hairy ass bouncing. Dick driving. Head sweating.

"I gotta use it."

"So what." He kissed her

She kissed him back. "Please?" she asked. "Please," she said, "then we can finish."

He kissed her.

She kissed him back. "Please."

He rolled over on his back. Reached up for some Jack. And as she walked away, he told her, "Yeah, I'ma hit that from the back."

Jaquanna looked over her shoulder and smiled. Then dashed.

With a bounding lumber, the big man was upon her. Storming into her room.

"Don't." She held her gun with both of her hands. Finger on the trigger. She pointed. "I ain't even playing. Don't."

Tears fell. Tears streamed. She saw the blood on his dick and quickly looked down. There was blood on her thighs trailing to her ankles. "Oh my God!" She looked at the big horrifying monster. "What did you do?" With her wrist, she wiped blood from her dripping nose.

"Hey, man." He had his hands in the air and a shriveling dick. "What's up with the gun?"

"What did you dooo-oo?"

"Look, man, put the gun down."

"No." She looked down again. "Damn, Benny, man, why?" she cried.

"Gimme the gun." Benny took a step closer and extended his hand. "Give it to me."

"Man." She shook her head with a new rush of tears. "This shit is crazy."

He was right there now. "Give it."

"Fuck you, man!" Jaquanna pulled the trigger. "Fuck you!"

"Ah!" He threw his hands up to block it.

*Clink!*

He looked at her.

She looked at it.

*Clink!*

"Oh shit!" She broke through to the bathroom. Ran to the front.

Benny gave chase and was right on her. "Bitch! Gimme that gun."

"I ain't playing, Benny." She pointed it again. He froze. "And I already dialed 911." She pointed down at the phone.

He looked with his searching eyes. "Oh, now, you done really fucked up."

"I got two bullets in here, Benny." She shook her head as she rounded the small table. Benny stepped around and towards her. "You got them white folks in my business, Bitch?"

"I'm telling you," she said. "Just leave me alone. Please."

There was a key in the door. They hadn't heard the car. But, suddenly, there was her mother. "What the hell is going on?" Lay-Lay looked around. "Jaquanna put that down!"

As Jaquanna turned, Benny struck and snatched the gun from her.

"What the—" She broke and ran out of fear and desperation. She didn't know why nor care. This was it. This was her moment. Squandered. Lost forever. But, then…

"Come here, bitch. Come here."

She ran in the kitchen and pulled out the drawer, then grabbed the biggest knife she could find. "Stop!" She turned and pointed it.

"Oh, you's about a dumb bitch, ain't you?" He smiled as he pointed the gun. "Never brang a knife to a gun fight, bitch!"

"Aahhh!" She covered herself and turned.

*Clink.*

"Oh, shit!" she panted.

"Yeah, ain't no fun when the rabbit got the gun, huh, bitch?" His smile fell to a grimaced frown. "With yo stupid-ass."

"Jaquanna, what is your problem?"

Benny turned just a slant. "She just stup—"

*Gunsh!* Jaquanna stabbed him in the heart.

*Poooow!* The shot rang out through the house. And beneath the stunned silence, there were sirens and this:

> *Jingle bell, jingle bell, jingle bell rock*
> *Christmas time is here.*

# Chapter 11

*Aint no sunshine when she's gone*
**- Bill Withers**

It was a storm unlike any other.

"Quanna? Quanna?" Little Ricky called. "Quannaaa?"

It was a cry.

Jaquanna was being walked from the house with a blanket thrown over her shoulders. She had tears in her eyes and a stunned look on her face. The entire world, as she had once known it, had changed. Today was a different day. Tonight was a different time. Who she was had gone away. Buried deeply. Somewhere. In there. Away.

*Ain't no sunshine when she's gone*
*It's not warm when she's away.*

There was a crack of thunder and a flash of lightening. The rains came down in gusty sweeps. Kirk Jr. was standing there, soaking in the pouring rain but feeling nothing but the echoing pain inside. No amount of warmth could ease his chill.

*Aint no sunshine when she's gone*
*And she's always gone too long*
*Any time she goes away*

How fitting, as he stood in the rain. No sunshine. The music played from inside the open door to his silver Camaro, and every word of it stuck to his heart. He'd never felt so torn before, so powerful yet so empty; so powerless when it mattered. What could he have done? How could he have helped? Had he given her the gun sooner would it have mattered? Should he have asked her for what it was needed?

The block was filled with flashing lights. Police. Paramedics and Coroner. It was Christmas Eve. It was Christmas.

The rain upon his face was a comfort. It soothed. It hid. It came.

"You okay, Quanna?"

"Yeah," she cried deeply as they led her away. "I'm okay, Big Boy."

Little Ricky cried, as he stood in his mother's arms.

*Wonder this time where she's gone*
*Wonder if she's gone to stay*
Lay-Lay was broken, as she stood there speechless. She
didn't say a word. Her man was dead and her child was taken,
and no how, no way could she understand why.
*Ain't no sunshine when she's gone*
*And this house just ain't no home*
*Anytime she goes away.*

"Hey," Kirk Jr. called to her. "I got you," he told her.
Jaquanna sniffled and nodded.
"You gon' be good, baby girl." He walked along as close
as he could while honoring the distance upon which the officers
insisted. "Whatever you need I got you."
"Thanks."
"Attorney. Money. Doctor. Whatever, baby, I got you."
She sniffled loud and cried harder. "Thank you." They
helped her into the back seat of the waiting black and white unit.
She was soaking wet in just that short little distance. They closed
the door.

*And, I know, I know, I know, I know, I know,*
*I know, I know, I know, I know, I know, I know,*
*I know, I know, I know, I know, I know, I know,*
*I know, I know, I know, I know, I know, I know,*
*I know, I know, I know*

As the car pulled off, Kirk Jr. walked, then jogged, then
ran as fast as he could beside it. Watching her as she smiled
through her tears and proud knowing he had given her just that
wee bit of comfort. Until finally the car pulled away.

*Hey, I ought to leave the young thing alone,*
*But ain't no sunshine when she's gone,*
*Aint no sunshine when she's gone*
*Only darkness every day.*

He headed back with his head hung low, walking slowly. Full of thought. It was a storm unlike any other.

*Ain't no sunshine when she's gone,*
*And this house just ain't no home*
*Anytime she goes away,*
*Anytime she goes away,*
*Anytime she goes away,*
*Anytime she goes away,*
*Anytime she goes away,*

# Chapter 12

*Lord, protect me from my friends;*
*I can take care of my enemies.*
**-Voltaire, 1694-1778**

*Sunday, July 2nd*
*Four and One Half Years Later*

"Next!" A woman's voice called but went unanswered. "Next." The air terminal was crowded with the rush of holiday traffic. There was no time for delay. "Next."

Some people get a chance to take a different path, while some are simply stuck with the path that they're on. But, like airplanes headed in different directions or old beat up clunkers destined to never leave the hood, there's a choice. After all, even that clunker was once new and able to go where it wanted. Yet, somehow, it decided to stay until it slowly rotted away. Never having gone anywhere; never having seen anything, its driver was its brain. And so it stands to say, what you do with your life is based simply on what you chose. In the terminal of life, you are the brain; your path is your plane. So choose wisely while you still have a chance,

"Excuse me, sir," the anxious lady behind him said. "Excuse me. Hello." She waved in his peripheral intent on getting his attention. "Are you next?"

"Oh." Mark was startled to his senses. "Yeah, I got next. I'm sorry." Hurriedly he moved forth to the ticket desk to choose a path and claim a journey. He was early, for, as Big Daddy said, 'A conscious man never loses tack of time. And when it comes to an appointment he's never late.' Big Daddy never carried a watch and never rushed anywhere. 'If you leave early enough you'll be there.' It was as simple as that. Mark smiled as he checked his watch and thought of his big ole country grandpa. He wondered if it was even possible to love any man more. He doubted it.

~ ~ ~

Mississippi had been a blessing for him. Raised by a man and taught about life, he'd shined all through high school, made good grades and earned a full scholarship. He was now a part of the starting lineup playing for Georgetown University. Mark Mitchell. M and M, they called him, and it seemed the whole world knew his name. "Aren't you that guy…" Yeah, those moments happened all the time. And to think, he was the product of a drug-addicted mother. How much his life had changed. How fortunate he'd been. Mississippi had been his blessing. "It's really hard to grasp," said Nana Mama when he'd first arrived. "It used to be that folks jumped on trains and headed to the big city to get out the south with all of the old outhouses and cotton fields or whatnots. Yeah," she said in her cute little dreamy way, so you knew she'd gone off to that place. "We was some cotton picking fools," she chuckled as she did so often. "Don't seem like it was long ago. Not long ago at all." Her face grew grim. "1955 to be exact…"And then she told it.

"It was right over there in Money, Mississippi, 1955. It wasn't a time to come from Money, nor come for Money either, no sir. Money was what Money was and it whatn't no place to be. Especially not for no Black boy."

He loved it when she told her stories. It was as if she was re-living a time. The emotions took her face, painting it with every passion.

"There was a boy what come down from Chicago," she explained, "by the name of Emmett Till. This had to be along round ole maybe August sometime. Young boy, 14 I thank he was. He come from a different place, coming here from that city. He wasn't raised for no south." She shook her head like a mother hurting. "He whatn't learnt to deal with these white folk." As if, there was some subtle art. "It was a different time, baby, oh, such a different time." She told her story in her own lazy way, not rushed by the eagerness of youth.

"Emmett Till, he come down here, and was accused of whistling at some white woman. Just whistling at her that's all. 'Cause that was kinda the thang to do back then. Rude, but the thang to do. Man seent a woman he thought was cute he might let a little old funny sound come out his mouth." She chuckled as she remembered. "Yeah, they'd do that. I didn't much like it but they'd do it. Lord knows, they'd stayed on whistling at your grandma."

He didn't doubt it. She was still a pretty girl. Like Cicely Tyson: full of love and wisdom filled cheer.

"But, he come down here and he whistled at that woman, is the way the story goes. And what came outta that was one of the most gruesome lynchings this world has ever seen." The anger in her jaw. The pain in her eyes said more than the words could describe. "Aw, man, that was a different time." She shook her head. "They say they beat that boy like he was a wild animal. They ain't seent no human being in him. They cain't have or they cain't a done all that. I mean, they beat that boy, then they shot him in the head, then they ripped his eyes out for looking at that woman. Then they tied an old cotton gin fan around the boy's neck, with the use of some barbed wire. That's what they did. Then throwed the boy's body off in the dang on Tallahatchie River, weighted down with that old thang. That's what they did here in Mississippi," she told him. "And two white mans was charged but the white jury set 'em free. Yeah, they sho did." She took a breath, filling her lungs with the only relief that there'd ever be for Emmett Till. "Strange Fruit. That's what they called it when they hung black folk from a tree and left his rotting body to blow in the breeze. Strange Fruit. You saw it, you smelt it. You knew. But, at 14 years old, that boy ain't knowed and he was from a whole different world from this here."

As she ended, she stopped and looked him straight in the eyes. He wondered how much of that was a warning.

"Mississippi ain't like no big city, baby. Whatn't then and it ain't now."

Mark nodded. Yeah, now he understood. She taught with story, and he'd never forget.

"This here something altogether different," Nana Mama went on. "Oh, we done come along way, ain't no doubting that. But we still got a ways to get, 'cause we ain't there just yet. Especially not here in Mississippi."

Mark nodded.

"Yeah, but," and she smiled as she came back to the now, "it's good seeing all you babies coming on back home. And all the family reunions and carrying ons; it's beautiful. The oniliest thing I don't understand is why y'all hate each other so. You use to run outta here to keep from getting hurt. Now, y'all out there hurting yourself." She shook her head. "Like our people ain't got enough problems as it is. Drugs and guns." She scoffed with the pain. "Coulda went and gave that stuff to a bunch of monkeys and they prolly'da had better sense."

Colorful. That's how he described her. 'My colorful old sweet granny.' Yeah that was Nana Mama. Colorful for shitty damn sho.

~ ~ ~

As he boarded the plane, he took his seat and looked forward to getting to L.A. It was summertime, a time to relax a bit and just share a little time with Mama. After all, you only got one mama and one mama was all you'd ever get. Each moment was its own treasure. No matter with whom or where she'd been, she was Mama. Every flaw, every imperfection, every touch; every smile, every crazy silly awkward thought, every back-woods superstition; every meal, every measure, every hug: she was Mama. Every sacrifice for a better tomorrow, every five dol-lars spent that she really couldn't 'spare,' every dream lain at the altar of youth, just so you'd have something else. Wherever she went, whomever she was, as surely as you drew your every breath: she was Mama and you only get one Mama. M 'n' M, the great Mark Mitchell, was now headed home to his.

# Chapter 13

It was a sunny Sunday, just before the 4th of July. It had been four and a half years. Jaquanna was now 18, and she was on her shit, as she crept up the block beating in her brand new red and black rag top Camaro.

"Heeey, bitch?" Shamika waved.

"What that shit do?" She had the rag down, as she pulled to the curb. They were on 105th between Main and Wall, just behind the elementary school yard where they'd all grown up playing. Jaquanna pulled into her mother's driveway and parked.

At 15, Shamika was a little chubby now, after having her baby. Her days of Double-Dutching and hopscotching had long since been done. Another cutie with a booty slain, and relegated to baby mama status. As she sat around waiting on Welfare and complaining about who ain't gave her what, and how everybody want something from her. All the while, the little boys kept tryna get it and, in some twisted way, this made her feel extra cute and special simply because they wanted it. Jaquanna had seen it all before and, for herself, it was something she never wanted.

"Hey you." Jaquanna bent down to greet her friend with a warm welcoming hug. Rosa was in a wheelchair now. "Ain't seen you in a minute."

"Iknowhuh?" Three syllables one word. She'd been gunned down by one of Kirk Jr.'s boys, caught up in a crossfire. A senseless call made of blind emotion. And, though it had happened over a year ago, Rosa still didn't know the totality of what had happened or even that Kirk Jr. was behind it. But, Jaquanna knew. She was on the inside now. She was Kirk Jr.'s girl. She knew a lot of things. Just as she knew that the crippled girl once said to be destined for the WNBA, was turning into a young alcoholic who lived with a struggling mother and sexually abusive brother she both resented and adored.

"What you bitches got on my forty?" Jaquanna had her hand out.

Shamika hitched little Dwayne Jr. up on her hip. "Shiit." She rolled her eyes like she thought she was cute. Ashy little bay-bay all wide-eyed with dirty feet. And a round bubblehead face.

"Girl," Rosa said, "I'm so broke, they got my picture on a warning poster at the church."

Jaquanna was like "warning poster?"

"Yep."

"And what it say?"

"Miss this bitch with the collection plate." She smirked and rolled her eyes.

"Damn, you wrong."

"And then the sorry-ass Deacon got the nerve to pat my ass down when I come out."

Shamika chuckled. Jaquanna laughed.

"But them stupid muthafuckas don't never check my shoes." She pulled a five-dollar bill from under her heel. "I stay getting they ass."

Jaquanna laughed again. "Girl, you's a fool." She got behind Rosa's chair and pushed her off towards Main Street. "Come on," she said, "let's go to the liquor store up on 103rd, I'll buy y'all a drink."

"Shit, girl," Shamika said to her ghetto fabulous home-girl, "get me some Pampers. I need some Pampers for this baby."

"Some Pampers?"

Shamika hitched her load again and nodded. "Hm-hmmm."

"Big Wayne ain't taking care of that baby?"

"Naw, naw. He manned up. He manned up. Shit, I know how to pick them. I ain't one of these little dumb bitches out here, just having babies for niggas who can't take care of them and shit."

"Oh, yeah." Jaquanna gave her that look that said, she thought she was even dumber than the rest, for even thinking she had it figured out. "And what you look for? I mean, how you know, like?"

"I don't know." Shamika shrugged but spoke through a thought-filled whisper, as if searching her mind for some magi-cal, stored away, secret. "You just kinda like know, you know?"

"Hm-hmmph." *Bull shit-ass bitch.* Jaquanna smiled. *Always just popping off at the mouth like she done figured out what made Kool-Aid.*

"It's kinda like hard to explain," Shamika added. "But when you know, you just like really really know. Know what I'm saying? It's like woman's intuition or some shit." It's amazing how those who always thought they'd figured stuff out, can never really quite tell you how they figured it. They "Just Know." No matter how senseless it is, they "know." Like giving you the answer to a complex math problem but they can't explain how they came up with the answer, and they swear nobody ever told it to them, and, on top of that, they swear they know. It's a good thing those folks don't take that intuition and other mystical, magical, all-knowing, hocus pocus, bullshit and play the damn lottery; the rest of us would never win shit. "Yeah, but you know what I'm saying. Know what I'm saying?"

Yeah, a whole bunch of nothing with that young crowded-ass brain.

*Go Shamika! Go Shamika! You can do it! You got it! Palease.*

"So let me ask you this." Jaquanna bent the corner on Main. It was a real nice day. Gentle breeze. Warm sun. Things were quiet and peaceful. Like church took all the bad asses off the block for a moment or something. Naw. What it was, was them little badass muthafuckas had been up and out acting a damn fool all night Friday and Saturday nights. So thugs rested on Sunday while everybody else went to church. Praise Him. Rest was important too. Praise him. "If you so good at picking them and you picked yo ass some Wayne, why yo ass ain't got no diapers?"

"Aw, fa'get you, bitch." Shamika chuckled. "He 15, Ho."

"Oh, and that make a difference?" asked Jaquanna.

"It's his mama," Shamika explained. "She be on that bullshit. Tryna tell Wayne the baby ain't none of his and shit. Like I'm just some ole jump off ass rat out here screwing every damn body."

"Oh, so he don't help?"

"I mean, sometime."

Rosa smirked. "So why you pick his ass then, damn psy-chic?"

Shamika chuckled. "Aw, fuck you," she said. "Y'all get up off my g-strang with all that hating."

"Bitch," Rosa told her, "You need to go wash that damn g-strang."

The three girls laughed as they walked past V-Market and headed down to 104th.

"Whatever." Shamika made them talk-to-the-hand. "Haters."

At the light, there was a tall, slim, brother. Handsome. Clean cut. Well-toned body. He had on Georgetown gear. Tank-top and shorts. Ball tucked under his arm.

"Excuse me." Jaquanna stepped up from behind him to push the little pedestrian button. As if he'd just been standing there and had been too lame to have pressed it himself, or as if her now rapid five pushes were gonna somehow magically click the light green like a charm.

"Damn, girl, he fine." Shamika had a finger in her mouth and a dusty-butt baby on her hip, mumbling just loud enough for him to hear as she stripped him with her eyes. And welcomed him with her smile.

"Iknowhuh?"

"You bitches is nasty," Jaquanna said, as the smiling young man turned around. "Don't pay my nasty-ass friends no mind."

"Don't I know you?" he asked.

"I don't think so." She looked repulsed. "From where?"

"I got next," he said.

"Huh?"

"I got next, remember?"

"Next what?" Jaquanna was straight confused. "I mean…what?"

"107th Street School. You came and cut me in line."

"I cut you in line?" She demanded with offence. "How you figure?" She smiled.

"Remember I said I had next and—?"

"Aww, yeaaah." She tapped him on the shoulder. "Heeey whassup?" She was bubbling now, as she touched him again on some touchy-feely shit. "Damn, that was you?"

He nodded and licked his lips as he stared her up and down.

"And what you mean, I cut you?" she said. "I ain't cut you."

"Yeah you did. But I ain't tripping."

"Yeah, whatever."

Shamika switched over and tossed Wayne Jr. on to the other hip. "So is you gon' introduce us to baby or what?" she asked Jaquanna.

"Iknowhuh?" Rosa chimed in. "Fuckin slut."

"Damn, I don't even remember your name." She pointed at the tall handsome stud. "What is it again?"

"Mark."

"Mark?"

"Yeah, we never exchanged names before."

"Oh, huh?" She laughed for no reason. "That's crazy."

"Well, bitch?" Shamika cocked her head and threw an eye at her girl like 'I'm waiting'.

"Oh," said Jaquanna, "Mark. This my little super slutty ass homegirl Shamika."

"Hiiii," Shamika waved, looked him up and down like she was hungry and he was a T-bone steak, smothered in A-1 Sauce, then bit her lip, as if not biting it would cause her mouth to hang perpetually open. "Howyoudoing?" One word three syllables no breath. Almost on some Wendy Williams shit, but not quite.

"I'm good, ma. How you?"

"Fiiiine."

"That's what's up." Mark nodded.

"And this here, queen on her own damn throne," she pointed, "is the ever lovely and sometimes demanding ride or die, Miss Rosa."

"You know we can go fuck if you want to." She blew him a kiss as she extended her hand.

"Aw, hell naw!" Jaquanna said and they all laughed. "Bitch, you nasty."

"Shit, I'm just keeping it real."

"Okaaay?" Shamika offered. As if, her panties were an option too.

"Well, I don't know how Miss Jaquanna would feel about that," he said.

"Oooh," Rosa rolled an eye at Shamika. Shamika gave that uh-oh-um-I'll-say look. Then they both looked at Jaquanna.

"Thought you said we ain't exchange no names or nothing?"

"Bitch." Shamika put her girl on blast. "That ain't what the hell he talking about. And, if you don't want it, pass that shit on."

"Okaaay!" Rosa and Shamika exchanged a horny hi-five.

"From when you went to jail that day," he said simply. Jaquanna frowned.

"When they tased you," he explained. "I was in the crowd."

"Oh. Okay."

"Plus when you kilt your daddy."

"He whatn't my daddy." Her voice was stern and serious. The memory, not one desired.

"Um, my bad." The light turned and they stepped across. They were walking side-by-side. "But you kilt him though?"

She turned and looked at him now. "He died."

Mark nodded. Well enough would be left alone. For now. "Did you get some time for that?"

"A little bit."

He nodded.

Feeling a little rude, she added, "I just got out."

"Oh, how long ago?"

"About six months."

"So you did about four years?"

"Damn!" She was obviously flattered. "You know everything, huh?"

"I never forgot."

"Whaaat?" Her face lit up like a little child's who knew she had a fan. "Well I'll say."

"Well spoken."

She sucked her teeth and smacked his arm. "Forget you."

"What?" Mocking a fake injury, he danced away.

"Um, excuse me." Princess Shamika raised her hand. "But, bitch, you got a man." She pointed at Jaquanna whose mouth instantly fell open with wide-eyed surprise. "And I need one." She pointed to herself. "So, um," She turned to Mark. "What it do, Daddy?"

"I know the fuck this bitch just didn't." Jaquanna had stopped pushing Rosa and now stood with her hands on her hips, smiling wide but for sure surprised. "With them little hot-ass guts."

"I know huh?" Rosa laughed. "Leave them both, Papi," she told the blushing Mark. "Come with Rosa. Rosa make you feel like you never felt before, huhn?"

Mark shook his head and bounced his ball. "Man, y'all crazy."

"See what happen when a bitch is in heat." She pointed at her giggling girls. "Fucking sluts. Need to tie they draws up."

"Hell," Shamika reached under her short skirt. "He can just pull these muthafuckas aside and hit this."

"Yeah," said Jaquanna, "that's prolly how you made that damn baby."

"So." She rolled her eyes. "Shit. Daddy can get him one too."

"Damn, like that?" Mark smiled.

"Hell yeah, just like that, Daddy." She licked her top lip, straight across, real slow. "Um. And it'll be fun too. I bet ya."

"Shit," said Rosa, "I need a baby too."

Mark was a dribbling speechless fool.

Jaquanna hit them both with the shame-finger-cross. "And on Sunday morning too," she said, "you Ho's is sick."

They were at the store now and Jaquanna walked around to find one of the guys who normally hung out on the crates out back and played dominoes. She gave him the money and sent him inside to buy the drinks. Shamika and Rosa had already gone in. She stayed outside with Mark.

"So you got a man, huh?"

"Yeah, kinda."

"Well, can I get next?"

"Next?" She laughed with a frown. "What you mean next?" She bit the inside of her cheek, to keep from breaking her face with her smile.

"You know I always liked you, right?" He was quiet. Serious. In a softer more emotional place.

"Oh, you did?" She joined him.

"From the time I first met you."

"Damn. For real?"

"I followed everything about you. About your case. The police abuse. Whatever. Whatever I could find."

"Aww."

"I got something for you, Jaquanna, and I'm not all the way sure what it is. But I'm feeling you. Always have."

As Jaquanna stood there talking, she thought about Kirk Jr., and the man he had become. She remembered when he felt like this. Young love. Foolish love. A love without definition. She was grown. She knew better than to believe in that nonsense. "Yeah, well, you know—"

"Just put me in line." He sensed her rejection. "That's all I'm saying. Just let me know I got next."

"I mean, but—"

"Is that asking too much?"

"No. I mean…" She shook her head as she looked for the words.

"You're thinking too hard." He grabbed her hand. "My Nana says: when you think you can't feel." He explained, "You gotta shut off your mind, Jaquanna, reach inside of you. Close your eyes. Feel. And, the next time I see you—" He looked her in her wide brown eyes.

She nodded slowly.

"—Then you give me an answer."

She kept the nod and felt the words. "Kay," she said. "I will."

"Then I look forward to it."

"But," she began, "what if I never—"

He released her hand and touched a finger to her lips. "Then it was never meant to be."

She understood. She nodded.

"But," he said, "we can't afford the luxury of a negative thought: Napoleon Hill."

"Huh?"

"It's a quote."

"Oh."

"What the hell y'all back here all whispering about?" Cock-blocking ass Shamika bent the corner.

"Iknowhuh?" Rosa rolled up right behind her.

"Hey, man," the old drunk pointed to Mark as he handed Jaquanna the bag. "Ain't you Mark Mitchell?"

Mark smiled and nodded.

"Well, I'll be damned." The old man laughed with a hearty roar. Then did a little spin and a snap. "Ah-hhha! Mark-muthafuckin'-Mitchell." He extended his hand and Mark took it. "How you doing, man?"

"I'm good, Pops." Mark nodded. "What did you say your name was?"

"William," the old cat said, "William Burk, man."

"Good to meet you, man."

"Man, I be damned. Mark-muthafuckin'-Mitchell," he said, "M-ah-god-damn-M."

"Yep. M 'n' M," he said. "That's me."

"Good to meet ya, man." O.G. patted him on the back. "Good to goddamn meet ya." He shook his hand again. "I always did love me some Georgetown," he declared. "You going pro, boy. You just watch and see. See if what Ole William tells you ain't true. I ain't wrong about no shit like that. I'm telling you. Pro, boy. Pro. You hear me?"

"Yeah, that's what's up, Mr. Burk. I'll remember you said it."

"Damn right, I said it."

"I make it." He pointed at William. "You get a ticket to my first game, how's that?"

"Well, god damn it, best to get me something to wear, 'cause, I'ma be there, boy!"

"It's a date." He shook the old man's hand again.

"What was all that?" Jaquanna asked.

"Hold up." He turned. "Mr. Burk?"

"Hey?"

Mark tossed him his ball. "That's all you, O. G."

"Ah, man, thanks."

"Won my last game with that one."

"What?" William Burk looked at the ball. "That half-court, three pointer, right at the buzzer against UCONN?"

"Oh, you saw it, huh?"

"Man, I'ma treasure this damn ball." He looked down at it amazed, as if it were a gift from his own child.

"You do that, O. G."

"What, you s'pose to be somebody?" Jaquanna asked.

"Okaaay?" added Shamika. "Who the hell is you, man?"

"Iknowhuh!" said Rosa, "Big, sexy, ball playing stud." She tossed her head and stared at his crotch. "Rosa always likes to play with balls." She nodded as if to confirm.

"Slut," Jaquanna said. "You little Hoes need to go wash your damn draws out in gasoline."

"It's physical therapy, Ho."

Mark shook his head and smiled.

"So who is you?" Jaquanna demanded.

"I'm a ball player." He pointed at the jersey he wore. "Play for Georgetown."

"Oh." She nodded. "That's real cool," she said, "that's real cool."

"I think so."

Dreams are like that: They're filled with all of these wondrous joys and wholly unrealistic expectations. Until, one day, they're suddenly confronted with the harshness of reality. Some dreams are lost, some are given away, some are taken, and some are put on hold. But, dreams are not one dimensional, and they're highly unpredictable. And, sometimes, when we least expect it, and, yes, maybe even doubt it: Sometimes… Dreams…Do…come true.

On her way home, Jaquanna stopped to get a pregnancy test. Just maybe. Oh, maybe. She was about to be somebody's Baby Mama. Yeah, it was getting juicy and only bound to get juicier.

# Chapter 14

*...the time has come to move over and let*
*Those of younger age prepare for their ascendancy.*
                                        - **Robert Greene**

As they moved through the city, it looked like a presidential entourage. Two cars up front, three in back, with Kirk Jr. smack dab in the middle, and a loose chain of roving cars behind. There were close to two million dollars on dazzling display. And as the entourage passed, folks all stopped and stared, as they shielded their eyes against the sun's glare, to see who it was inside the new pale sapphire colored $330,000 Bentley Mulsanne.

The souped-up engine was a gentle purr, as he relaxed in the back, finding comfort within one of the soft, massaging seats, a cloud on wheels. A racing cloud, able to hit top speeds of 184 mph. It was luxury, it was eloquence, and it was strength. It looked it, it felt it, and it smelled it. And the Flying B emblem said nothing but the best and 'money ain't a thang'. And all that saw it knew.

Kirk Jr. and his crew were chipped out the muthafuckin' game. They'd made it. With him today were 'the inside Dime'. These were the men who knew, as much as there was to tell. The inside Dime. The trusted ten. The Modern pirates with whom he'd broke bread. Yeah, they'd made it.

Even Big Dick had to know when he was fucked. But, he saluted with a proud smile. His nephew was doing his thing. A new generation, a new turn, anyone with some sense understood. We each have a chance and we each get a turn. Some make it and some don't, but we all waited and hoped, shining brighter than the rest hollering I got next. Today was a torch passing turn.

As they slithered across the city in the mild traffic of the noon day, Kirk Jr. felt like a proud father — if that truly made any sense — for, though Preacher was 26 years old now and Kirk Jr. was only 20, Kirk Jr. had practically not made, no not made — what's the word? Practically discovered. That's it. Discovered. Kirk Jr. had basically discovered the man who now frequently spoke to the nation. And, today, Preach Patterson, as he had taken to being called, was being honored in the dome at the Crenshaw Christian Center, a social gathering, the likes of which, the esteemed, and honorable Pastor Dr. Fredrick K. C. Price had never been known to permit.

The dome was huge and as they pulled in to the crowded lot, the entourage was ushered to the tiered double-deck parking structure for the spaces, which had been reserved for them. Though the church was always crowded throughout the various Sunday services, with today's practiced gathering of speakers, it was packed near capacity — as was to be expected.

As they walked in and took a seat, Kirk Jr. noted the likes of Al Sharpton, and Jesse Jackson sitting up on stage. Some said that Louis Farrakhan and even President Obama might make an appearance. Preach sat calmly and humbly waiting. He'd told Kirk Jr. he didn't see what all of the fuss was about and that he was no way as learned or knowledgeable as any of the men who were set to honor him. But, as Kirk Jr. pointed out: It wasn't the bursting well of his knowledge that mattered; it was his connection to and ability to understand and reach the streets that counted. It was a different day. A different time. And it was time for a different voice, one that the youth could relate to, accept as their own, and rally behind. And, like a game of tag, or a sprinter in the relay as he receives the Olympic torch, Preach Patterson, from this day, was it.

~ ~ ~

"In the words of Dr. Martin Luther King Jr.," Rev Jenkins said, "A genuine leader is not a searcher for consensus but a molder of consensus." And he paused. "It's been a long time, since we've had one of our own who has been willing to stand up, in the face of oppression; someone willing to stand, for more than just himself, without fear or regard for the consequence to self, over and above, how the lack of standing, might affect the people." He spoke in that long, slow southern way that preachers so often do. In fact, by closing your eyes one might even hear the delivery and intonations reminiscent of a long revered and remembered Dr. Martin Luther King Jr. Reverend Jenkins had known King and being from Alabama himself, he'd walked for freedom's sake and he'd even kept the shoes. "The people first, over and above all else, it's the greatest sacrifice a man could make. And here today, today we've come to honor a man who has found it in his heart to do just that." With a slow wave, he pointed. "Preach Patterson."

As they nodded at the introduction, Jaquanna strutted in and slid next to her dude, looking every bit the raw dime that she was. Chocolate, smooth, sweet and delicious, with just a little danger if you chewed off too much or tried to consume it too fast. "Sorry I was late, Baby."

Kirk Jr. nodded as she sat. "Just started." His eyes danced all over her, eating her, devouring her, savoring her. Remembering all that she was.

She'd missed the entourage, because she'd gotten caught up getting her shit whipped. She now had her shit in a long, flat, China-doll style, weave, and shot-through with red highlighting streaks. The weave fell to her armpits, while the bangs were blunt-cut right over and across her brows. She was Prada down in her sexy black suit. And stepping hard in her Manolo Blahnik crocodile heels. Red claws on her hands and toes. Diamonds on her wrists, neck, and ears. She hadn't told him about the pregnancy test. But, now was not the time for that.

"You see, everybody's got a story," Reverend Jenkins was saying. "It's not about just hearing the story and, then, just letting it be. We have to look at these things, see how they affect the greater good, and then, in that, we must decide. We must decide, whether to get involved, and, if so, to what measure. But, a decision must be made." Reverend Jenkins gestured with emphasis and searched the measuring eyes of the nodding congregation. "So you see, it's about hearing the story and, then doing something about the story we hear."

"Welllll," a man in the front row said.

"And everybody ain't made to do that."

"I know that's right," a shout came from nowhere.

"But we done found us a leader, who is." He gestured again with a wave of his hand. "You see, the days of Martin done gone; the days of Malcolm done gone; the days of the Black Panther Party and Revolution, all them days done gone too. But, Lord have mercy, our troubles ain't gone yet. Not yet they ain't."

"What you talking 'bout, old man?" someone shouted. "You tell 'em what you talking 'bout."

Reverend Jenkins smiled and continued. "I'm talking 'bout the ways of our leadership has been divided long enough."

"Welllll."

"Our philosophies and beliefs done changed."

"Welll."

"Our struggles done changed."

"Hush!"

"It's a new day out here now," he said. "It's a new struggle, a new pain, a new need for direction, and a need for somebody to lead in a whole new way."

"Welllll."

"Amen."

"The church has always been our place, because the church was the one place we had."

"Yes Sir."

"On Sundays we could all get together and talk, and, from there, we launched our hope for change."

"Sho did."

"But we ain't got to hide no more."

"Well I don't know about hiding."

"We can come out and say what we feel now. Because today is a brand new day," he declared, "and we need to go about things in a whole new way. 'Cause we done had our turn. Al and Jesse," he turned and pointed," they done had they turns too. We just the throw-a-ways from the King days. Which the youth can no longer seem to relate to." He didn't say it with regret. "But, I tell you it's a brand new day," he said. "We done our part, now, it's theirs. It's their turn now. We've given them what we could. We've shown them what we've learned. But it's their turrrrn!" he shouted. "It's their turn now."

"Welllll."

"At some point we gotta stop, and pull off the training wheels and let 'em riiiide!"

"Yeah."

"Yeah."

"Hm-hmmm."

"Cause it's their turn now. The strength of a future is gauged by its youth and if we don't give it to 'em now, while we can stand by and teach them, then when will they have the chance to learn?"

Heads nodded. Heads shook.

"An ex-player becomes a coach, because he knows the game. A mother teaches her daughter to cook. And if we take off the wheels we wanna be there, so we can hold 'em up in case they look like they might be ready to fall."

"Oh, yeah."

"Wellll."

"Hmmm."

"It's their turn now," he said, "It's their turn now. Just like the Olympics, it's time to pass the torch. It's a dark road. But with the torch there is light and with the light we just might see some things and make a difference in the stories of the lives up ahead."

"Amen."

"Hmmm?"

"Wellll."

"In the days of darkness, while we stared up at the mountain, and could only wonder what lied at the top, he saw. He saw the other side."

"Wellll."

"Sho did."

"He told us about a dream and a vision that he had. But, I tell you, the man was a prophet."

"Hmmmm."

"A prophet to our people and a visionary of the times, a psychic—as surely as if there ever was one—who saw, so clear-ly, what the future held."

"Yes."

"And it's a new day."

"Wellll."

"We done did a lot, but we got a ways to go."

"Hmmmm."

"In the words of his greatness; in the words of a King. I say unto you, and I say it loud: FREE AT LAST!"

And they all joined in. "FREE AT LAST!"

"Yes. Yes. Yes."

"Thank God Almighty, we are Free at Last!"

"Hallelujah!"

Reverend Jenkins then picked up an old rugged pair of well-worn shoes, whose strings were tied together. "I'm all through walking now." He held the old shoes up in the air. And the huge dome fell into a hushed silence. His voice was a mournful whisper, tinged with tears. "I've walked for many, many miles. But I'm all done walking now. I'm all done walking and I'm all done talking. This is the last leg in the relay. 'Cause I done stood at the mountain top and I stared."

"Yes. Yes."

"I can see it now."

"Hmmm."

"And it's a beautiful thang too." He smiled.

"Wellll."

"Never thought we'd get this far," he said, "Never thought we'd see the top, or peer down at the other side." He paused. "But, we here now. We climbed that mountain rock by rock and stone by stone."

"Yes!"

"Scraped our knees, ripped our nails, and stubbed our aching toes! But good God we made it!" He said, "We're not there yet. But, the valley is before us. And the fight don't seem so hard." He smiled. "This new generation is ready y'all. I don't thank they hate us that much."

"I know that's right."

"Jim Crow done gone. And they even gave a Black man a chance at the throne!"

"Hey now!"

"Naw, it ain't over, but, it sho feels better now."

"Yes. Yes. Yes."

"The future seems brighter now."

"Yes."

"And, so, with that," he turned to face Preach, and extended his old shoes. "Let the next leg of the journey begin."

Amidst huge applause, Reverend Jenkins took his seat and dabbed at his sorrowful eyes. One could only wonder what all he'd seen on the leg of his journey in the fight.

Preacher stood with the shoes held high, like a heavy weight champ just handed a belt. "Kinda hard to follow on the heels of that one." He nodded over his shoulder at Reverend Jenkins. "But I'm honored for the chance to try." He looked around with a stern expression and waited till they fell into silence. "One more time for Reverend Jenkins, and all the other great leaders who stand here with us today." He set the shoes on the podium. They'd be his inspiration and a trophy he would honor.

"Come on now, come on with it." An old man encouraged from the front pew.

"I stand on the platform of truth and I stand to speak for what I mean." Preacher spoke with speed and aggression. He had a strong face and an angry scowl, which one might have called anger. His presentation could be intimidating to those who didn't quite understand the source of his emotion and the focus of his intent. "I stand here and I weigh my opportunities, 'cause I realize that it's not every day that I can get the Black man to stop and pay attention to my words. You see, and I got things I wanna say." He looked around at the tense expressions as they waited to hear him out. "I guess I was always meant to stand here. Who woulda thunk it?"

"Well come on then "

"They call me Preach Patterson, but I am not a religious man." He shook his head as if to confirm it. "I speak to the streets, for the streets and from the streets. Just let me say that now. But, now, having said that," he rushed on, "let me also say that I appreciate being so openly welcomed into your house of worship. And, for that, I say thank God." He took a small breath. "Now, maybe I should take just a short moment to explain. Just so that it's not deemed disrespectful, 'cause I wouldn't wanna disrespect anybody's home any more than I'd want anybody to disrespect mine."

Heads nodded.

"You see, I walk with God," he said. "I walk right there with him, and I carries his truth where you dare not go. And then I come back and I tell you what they said. I walk into the Devil's den and I face him as sure as I stand. I don't walk with fear. I walk with truth and I walk unafraid."

"Yes. Yes."

"I'm not talking 'bout some Sunday morning stretch or some bowtie wearing brother beating on the door. That's not what I'm saying. Now, don't get me wrong, we all have our way; we all have our time. But I cain't put a title on mine." He shook his head. "The truth won't let me. Cause, you see, I takes the truth from wherever I find it and I look for ways to apply it. And not just on no Sunday either. I speak to the men on the block and I look 'em in they face; I look 'em in they eyes, and I don't judge 'em. They know I don't judge 'em. Judge not less you be judged. If they didn't welcome me, they'd tear my head off. They know it and I do too."

"Hmmm."

"Naw, I don't judge 'em. And I don't tryta preach to 'em either. I try to listen, teach, and share. I share their burdens 'cause their burdens are mine. And I listen, because their troubles are mine too. Yeah, so…" He looked around at the patient crowd. "I'm not gon' hate. I'm not gon' hate on the likes of Freeway Rick. I'm not gon' hate on Supreme. I'm not gon' hate on Big Meech or Harry-O, Bo Bennett, Felix Mitchell, or the likes of Lil Dee. I'm not gon' hate!" He struck the podium with the side of his fist. *Boom!* They gaped they listened they stared. "I'm not gon' hate on the drug lords and the thug gods who have or who do run these streets. They've earned their place in history, and no matter what we feel, history can't erase that."

"You right, you right."

"Yeeeeah."

"The 80's created a different culture. Drugs flooded our street. Ain't no sense in standing here talking about how or why, not right now. Not right now it ain't. Sure, we can get to that. And we need to get to it. But not right now. Right now it's important that we understand that we cain't hate. We cain't look at one of our own and see an enemy simply because of circumstance. I'm not gon' stand here and hate. I'm not gon' stand here and point fingers or act like I don't understand. I'm not! And, at the same time," He lowered his voice. "I'm asking you not to either. 'Cause we ain't got no time for that. I'm tired of being better than some group, or tryna point out some group that's worse than me. I'm done. I'm through. It's over. Y'all not gon' make a hater outta me. It ain't gon' get done. And, instead of us sitting around hating, we might just wanna think about something."

"Talk to us."

"You know, it could well be argued that, without the drug game, there'd be no rap or hip hop culture. Or, that it most certainly would not be all that it has become. And while some could argue whether it's good or whether it's bad, that's not my position, not now. Not today," He said. "I'm only saying to you today that the past is what the past is, and ain't no sense in us pointing no fingers."

"Hmmmm."

"But, how could we know what would be, in the absence of what was?" He continued, "And while we can look at all of the billions and billions of dollars, and all of the success, and promising futures which the Hip Hop world has brought us. It does not mean we turn a blind eye to all that it has cost us."

"Yes."

"Damn near everybody's dead or in prison."

"Ain't that the truth."

"Or on they way or been there."

"Hmmm."

"We're dealing with a bunch of young men and women, within our communities that are searching for themselves. Carving their own identities; defining who they are. Looking for a way out. And how can we say we don't understand?"

"Hmmm."

"I find that things happen and we don't always understand why. Why does not always have an answer," he said, "Sometimes these things go on to become some of the greatest mysteries of our lives. But, this ain't one of those mysteries, and these ain't one of those times."

"Talk to us."

"You see, the first part of reaching anybody is first finding out who they are. Because once you understand them, you don't fear them no more. These are our brothers and sisters. Our sons and daughters. Our mothers and fathers."

"Huhn!"

"What we scared of them for?"

"Uhn!"

"It's time for us to build a bridge of communication and, instead of talking to them, sit down, and talk with them."

"Well alright."

"I don't see why not."

"Cause then they may listen when we talk about 'Hood credibility' or the lack of it."

"Hmh?"

"How most of the people they look up to ain't living the lives they portraying."

"Hmmm."

"Somehow along the way we got things all mixed up and confused." Preacher seemed upset. "Back in the days when guys was on the mic talking about 187 on a m.f.ing cop or screw the police. It wasn't because they was out there doing it. When the song 'If I Ruled the World' came out, people understood it was a vision, a concept, a fantasy. I mean, just because Queen Latifah and Jada Pinkett-Smith played bank robbers in 'Set it off' you don't expect to see them actually out there doing it. You don't expect to look up and see Jay-Z arrested for running some drug smuggling operation or even having been in the same room as no drugs. If he did you'd call him a fool."

"Yeah."

"If Ice Cube was robbing or selling dope we'd all say he was crazy. It's entertainment. Every rapper hollering about millions ain't got them. Most of the dudes in the studio talking about guns ain't shot them. And if he really was a killer, he wouldn't be in there recording it. When Pac got shot, he made a song about it. When 50 Cent got shot, he made a song about it. But we got our folks out here tryna live the life they listen to and tryna be somebody who don't exist. All in the name of some hood credibility. It's entertainment. The characters aren't real, like the characters in a book or a movie. Of course, some part of those characters come from some true part of the creators' own lives, but ain't no way it can all be real. That's foolish. A writer may talk about prison or murder or drug dealing on the top-notch scales, but that don't mean they lived it. It's an alter ego; a fantasy; a creation, a character. Learn from them. Learn from them all. But understand the real cats that get the breaks in the game are not sitting in the pen talking about it. The real cats that make it are locked in a room somewhere writing, rapping, and acting. They not out there hitting the corner with Jimmy-Bob and Joe-Blow ready to kill up something."

"Hmmm."

"And these are the sorts of things we need to get them to see and share. Cause ain't nothing wrong with Hip-Hop, per se, I mean, they been making war movies, and gangster movies, and cowboy movies and terminator type shows forever. But that don't convince little Johnny and them to go out there and rob, shoot, stomp and kill each other. Now, it can be argued either way. But we need to have the talk. Especially when hood credibility and a street reputation has now become some defacto requirement demanded of the new artists who are trying to get in the game. It's crazy y'all, it's absolutely senseless. We're expecting too much evil of ourselves. And that's the stuff that's got to stop."

"Yep. Yep."

"I can see that."

"But, as I take up this torch, I'll swing the sword wherever I see fit."

"As you should. As you should."

"I'll go where the truth takes me."

"Yeah."

"And I won't be afraid."

"Um."

"And I won't be a 'yes man' either. For a yes man is no more than a weak brained individual looking to be liked. A coward who's afraid to stand on the truth. Or he simply has no valuable information or opinion to add or offer. A yes man is a man's worst enemy—"

"Why is that?"

"Cause he'll sit back and let you do yourself nothing but harm, and then laugh at you as you go."

"Humph. Ain't that something?"

"He so afraid of hurting your feelings, or just don't care to the point that he won't even tell you you got a bugga in your nose."

A few scattered chuckles.

"Let you walk around thinking you looking all cute. All the while he whispering about you while the world laughing at you."

"Humph."

"If the outfit don't match, tell me," he rushed on, "If the shoes don't fit, tell me. Don't have me standing in line at American Idol if you don't think I can sing."

Laughter.

"That's wrong. That's wrong, people." Preacher smiled. "All those people standing in line all those hours, and then got the nerve to pitch a fit and cry 'cause they sound like a bag of cats hanging out in the storm. That's wrong."

Laughter.

"But what's even worse than that, is somebody; somebody they believed in, and thought they could trust, done told them they thought they could sing."

"Yeah."

"Somebody let them out of the house with a bugga in they nose."

Laughter.

"Cause they wanted to be a yes man," he said. "I ain't no yes man, and I'ma let you know if you cain't sing."

"Okay then. Okay."

"But I'm not easy to digest either. And I don't intend to be. I refuse to come pleading and begging. When I stand, I stand with demands and my anger may cause fear. 'Cause although most people don't wanna be the guy to make waves, I'm not afraid to make waves."

"Hmmm."

"But at the end of the day, I come with a tender heart and a love for people that helps me to want to inspire the best in every person that I meet."

"Yes."

"I come with an evil eye towards injustice, and a need to speak out against it wherever I find it. I come with open arms and a knowing embrace. I come with God's truths spilling forth unhampered. And I'll leave just like I came." Preach held up the old worn shoes and looked out over the Dome as he held them overhead like a heavyweight fighter; like an Olympian with the torch.

They all stood and politely applauded. He wasn't sure of the effect he'd had. But the best speech wasn't always the point. Sometimes it was just about knowing that the conversation had been had. Planting the seeds. For now, he was proud to be so acknowledged. And he nodded his head at Kirk Jr. who was standing with the rest, beaming as he applauded. The king maker witnessing his own take to the throne. Drug money.

Drug money. It was woven into the very fabric of America. From the jobs, it created for prisons and law enforcement, the billions that churned through the justice system. The Wall Street backers, the politician feeders. The discovered and developed rappers, the rappers then turned actors, the homes bought, the cars bought, the bling bought, and all of the colognes, perfumes, clothes, headphones, shoes, even some pro athletes and now a speaker for the people. All, every last bit, products of what the pursuit of drug money becomes. The winners. The losers. And the ones in wait. Drug money.

# Chapter 15

"Come here, little nigga." Later that night, as he walked into the 'new house' on 105th and Wall Street, Kirk Jr. wrapped his arms around Big Boy, bringing him into a headlock then kissing him on his forehead. "This my little nigga right here," he told Leon as he pointed at the young advancing recruit. "This nigga gon' do big thangs, watch."

"That's what's up." Leon nodded. He'd been checking Big Boy out himself and he was digging the youngster too.

"How your grip looking, my nigga?" Kirk Jr. Had been using Big Boy as a look out at several locations, but had recently elevated the youngster to a much more rewarding position making pick-ups and drops. So he was curious about how the man was coming along.

"I'm doing alright, big Dawg. I'm just getting it, you know?"

"Bout ready to buy a car?"

"Naw." He shook his head with a smile. "I ain't all the way there, yet."

"How much you pick up?"

"Where that bag at, Poo?" Big Boy turned to the older woman who'd been basically driving him around to make his stops

"Right here." Twenty-four years old, she was a big high yellow cutie, like on some Melanie Amaro type shit. She hit the cigarette and passed the leather shaving kit bag.

Big Boy unzipped the bag and set it on the table. 'The new house' was bought, paid for, and fully furnished now, but still was more of a clubhouse or local depot for the crew. Very little actually took place here. It was mostly a hang out. "It's seventeen-fifty," he announced.

Kirk Jr. dumped the bag on the table. It was all counted and separated and banded together in $5,000 chunks. He took the three chunks and slid the change. "Here, young nigga, put that with your shit."

Damn, all this?"

"Nigga, that's nothing," K. J. told him. "You family, boy, we eat."

"That's right. That's what's up." He looked at the man with love and admiration. Kirk Jr. had been there for him and his mom after Benny was killed, and even though the attorney wasn't able to get the charges dropped. Kirk Jr. had stayed true to his word and stayed 100% down for Jaquanna throughout her whole time in the halls and while she served her time up at Ventura School Youth Authority in Camarillo, California. He'd even gone up to visit her twice. Kept her books flooded. Made sure she didn't need a thing and then blessed her with the rag top red Camaro as soon as she was released.

"How old is you now, Big Boy?"

"I'm fourteen."

"Fourteen?"

He nodded.

"You had you some pussy yet?"

"What?" Big Boy's embarrassment showed in his smile.

"Naw, nigga, you ain't had none." Kirk Jr. and Leon laughed.

Poo-Poo Pat rolled her eyes. "Y'all stupid," she said.

"Poo-Poo?" Kirk Jr. pointed at her. "Go on and take the homie back there and break him off."

"Man, I ain't messing with that kid."

"Kid?" Big Boy grabbed himself. "Ain't nothing but man here, girl."

"Please, boy. If you don't you go home and jack that little thang off."

Leon and Kirk Jr.'s laughter only acted to rub that shit in.

"You just mad 'cause don't nobody want your fat ass."

"Fat?" She stood up now, white boy shorts, wife beater and sandals. "Boy I ain't hardly no damn fat." She spread her legs and dropped her hands on her hips and had every nigga up in there feigning. "Yeah, and I bet you that."

"So what." Big Boy turned away as he waved her off, already his little pecker was peaking.

"Go on hit the Homie off with a little of that good." Kirk Jr. and Leon had already experienced it.

"Uh-uh, he too young for me."

"Young? Girl, I'm fourteen."

"And? You say that like you can vote or some shit."
They laughed.

"Oh, okay, you got jokes," said Big Boy.

"What you gon' do with me, huh?" Poo-Poo walked up and pinched his cheek. "What you gon' do with me? What, fall in love?"

He sucked his teeth.

"What, you gon' be my baby daddy?" She already had two kids. He sho whatn't feeling that shit. "You are kinda cute," she whispered huskily in his ear.

"Well, let's make it happen, shit."

Poo-Poo cocked her hip and dropped her hand. "And what you got for me?"

"Damn like that!" Leon laughed.

"Don't be turning the homie into no damn trick," Said Kirk Jr.

"Aw, hell naw." Big Boy laughed.

"Boy, I'll take you back there and take your little virginity and have you feeling like the stars is angels around this muthafucka, but, shit, I gots needs too. What the hell?"

"What you want?" Big Boy asked.

"Aww!" Leon breathed into his fist.

"Aw hell, naw."

"I ain't no ho," she hugged him to let him feel her. "What you gon' gimme?"

"Naw, fuck that," Kirk Jr. jumped in to separate them. "I ain't finna let you work the homie. Put yo' money in your pocket, Big Boy, I'm telling you she vicious."

"Aw, fa'get you," Poo-Poo Pat nudged Kirk Jr. "Want me to get my guts all smashed and I cain't get nothing." She walked away with a nice wide strut. "Shit, I got kids."

"Don't trip, I got you," Kirk Jr. told her. "Just take his young ass down."

She took her finger and beckoned. "Come on, little boy," she said as he followed. "First I'ma teach you how to use your tongue."

She looked over her shoulder as she closed the door.

Kirk Jr. and Leon shook their heads. They already knew the drill.

When he got to the House, Jaquanna was all dolled up. Hair still loose and banging brightly, and a sexy little red satin two-piece set with black lace trimming. She was curled up on the couch with her feet tucked under her. The lights were dimmed. She was smoking a cigarette and having a drink. The TV was on but she didn't seem to be really watching it. Their condo in Los Felix was a modern style two-bedroom with sunken dining room area and a balcony. They were about 30 to 45 minutes from the hood. Out of the way but close enough to get there. Only Leon, Coo-Coo, Big Dick and the immediate family knew where they stayed. And even as they headed over to visit, for whatever reason they were encouraged to watch their rear views and to be alert. The jackers, kidnappers and cops were always lurking, and to be caught sleeping was to be caught slipping.

"Hey, babe."

He could tell she was feeling a little romantic. "Damn!" He fanned the air. "Why you smoking and shit?"

"Oh, my bad." Jaquanna rushed to put the cigarette out. "I'ma need to quit this shit anyway."

"Shit, you need to." He closed the door.

"Oh, here we go."

"Shit, here we go my ass. Smoking that stupid-ass shit. Don't make no sense."

"I know," she took a sip, "Mister Surgeon General." He was always preaching about the harm and addictiveness of cigarettes. It was a nasty habit.

"And you don't need to be in here drinking and shit either," he chided. "Conscious mind equals—"

"Conscious movements," she completed. "Yeah, I know Mr. Discipline Danny."

"Oh, that's how you getting it?" He smiled.

"Just calm the fuck down." She stood and came over. "I got this. I know what I'm doing." She kissed him.

"Move." He pushed her away. "Ashtray Face."

"Oh, like that?"

"You taste like a damn gin factory."

"So?" She kissed him again. "You like it."

As she turned and walked away, he could see the bottom of her rich chocolate ass cheeks hanging low and firm. "Now, don't you?" she demanded. In that awesome way, that youth just knew its tantalizing power.

"Yeah. Whatever."

"Yeah, I know whatever." She stuck her tongue out playfully.

Kirk Jr. went in the bedroom to put some money away and change into his casual house slippers. Coming back, he was smoking a huge cigar.

"Damn." Jaquanna fanned. "And you talking about me."

"Shut up."

"You shut up, shoot!" She turned up her nose. "Nasty ass thangs."

He smiled and blew a cloud.

"And go in there and wash your little nasty ass hands." She pointed as she headed for the kitchen. "I'ma feed you first."

"Ummm," he nodded.

"Then I'ma take you in there and bathe yo ass."

"Oh, I like that."

"Then I'ma tuck you in."

"Whoa. Wait a minute. Hold up," he said. "Ain't you forgetting something?"

"Um." Frowning a bit, she looked up into the great nowhere. "No, I don't think so."

"Oh." He nodded. "It's like that then, huh?"

She spread her legs and bent straight over. Chocolate cheeks every damn where. She pulled a pan from the back of the oven. "What?" She smiled.

"Oh, okay, I got your number."

"What is it?" She hugged him close and looked up into his handsome face then grabbed his growing bulge. "Huh?" She squeezed and jiggled his jewels. "What is it?"

"It's 68." He pushed her down to her knees where she giggled and unzipped him. Gimme mine and I'ma get you later."

"Hm. Hmmm."

Slowly and with a loving tongue, she complied with his urgent desire. It was a skill she was learning and she loved to practice. Jaquanna gave herself with passion, moaning loudly.

Dipping sharply. She'd spent many many hours listening to the girls in the juvenile prison tell stories about how to do it and she'd also read several porn type novels that talked about it. She couldn't understand why white girls got so much credit though, like they'd just invented the shit or something. From the top, she had been determined to be as good at it as any. Besides, she was serving her a Boss nigga and she knew he had his pick of many. She had to both earn and maintain her seat on the thrown beside him. And she ain't had no problem with that.

With a growing urgency, Jaquanna sucked him and worked him over, coaxing and stroking with even louder moans and whines as he smoked his cigar and grunted. She felt like one of the porn stars in the films she liked to watch. And when he gave it to her, she took it. All.

"Yeah." She licked her lips seductively. "Now, get that shit re-loaded for round two damn it." She wiped him with a paper towel.

"Damn, like that?" He smiled as he blew a cloud and zipped.

"Shit, I need mine too," she told him. "Now eat." She pointed to the food then headed off. "I'ma go make your bath water for you, Boo-Boo."

They had been living together for roughly four months now and, in some ways, Kirk liked living with Jaquanna. He liked knowing there was someone there at home waiting. Sometimes. But it also cramped his style a bit. He wasn't use to sharing his space and it sometimes made it hard to keep private things private when you had an extra set of eyes right up under you.

Big Dick didn't like the idea of Jr. allowing Jaquanna to come and stay with him. He told Kirk Jr. it was a 'fool's move.' A fool's move based on pussy he'd said, and pussy was like a drug; it'd make a man do what he knew he ain't had no business doing.

Kirk Jr. had been all excited about the idea at first, but now he wondered if he'd done the right thing. After all, most men were set up by the women they slept with. Fact. And it was also another fact that, no matter how sweet they were in the beginning, most relationships weren't meant to last forever. And, on some levels, it just created extra drama and chaos. The home is a man's haven, a place where he is supposed to be able to come in, put his feet up, and relax. A place to think, sort through his thoughts and make plans. It's supposed to be a quiet place without worry, concern, or distraction. Because, although being a Street Boss is a job, it is a job unlike any other, a job where even just one slip up can cost you both your freedom and/or your life. There were no oopsies here. A Street Boss is like a top management position in a company or corporation: people answered to him. He was expected to have answers and provide leadership; he guided and controlled men's lives; men's futures. Kirk Jr. wasn't just an average Willie-in-the-wheel. He moved money and he changed lives and, sometimes, it was a bit uncomfortable having someone share his space and look over his shoulder. Even now, he had to think about the more than $200,000 he'd left in the bag in the closet. He knew he should've put it in the safe. Hopefully she wouldn't go in the cl—

"What's this?" Jaquanna held the bag as if it were a dirty diaper. Other hand on her hip.

"Put that back."

"Shouldn't this be in the safe?"

"Yeah." He cleared the dishes. "I'll get it."

"Uh-uh. You go get yo self in the tub," she said. "Give me the combo, I got it."

"Humph. Not gon' happen."

"Oh, what? Like that?"

"No how. No way."

"Oh, you don't trust me?"

The relationship was different when she was in jail. She had needs and he provided for them. She wrote or called when she could, they laughed and talked about how good it was going to be 'that first time', shared a few giggles and memories of how they'd both been forced to grow up so quick. And that basically was pretty much it. But now things had become more real. The 'first time' was done, the needy jail shit was in the past, and now, they were thrust sharply into the world of the real.

He took the bag and tucked the cash then met up with her in the bathroom.

Kirk Jr. had grown into a tall, lean, well-sculpted man with a natural strength and sexy sheen. He'd hit the gym two or three times a week with Big Dick, just to stay on his toes and catch up with things — light weight, high-reps, and plenty of cardio on the bike or treadmill — and it was all paying off in some super sexy ways. The girls loved to talk about the little muscles in his legs, and whenever he wore a wife beater or peeled up out his shit, there was always some hot tail hoochie on point to play games.

"You thank you the shit," Jaquanna told him. "You ain't all that."

"Damn. Where that come from?"

"I just know you. You thank you the shit. Sit down." She pointed to the frothy bubble bath. "Before you accidently fall and bust your damn head."

"Oh, accidently, huh?" He was standing in the tub, naked and trying to adjust to its heated warmth.

"That's what I said." She pinched his taunt little ass cheek.

"Stop, girl." Flinching, he covered his butt. "Always playing."

"Quit crying."

"Why you make the water so hot." He still hadn't sat.

"Why you always crying and complaining?" she retorted. "With your spoiled ass."

"I ain't spoiled."

"Humph. Yeah, okay."

"Damn this shit hot."

"Here, boy." Jaquanna ran some cold water into the mix until he'd finally sat his ass down. "Big ass baby."

"Yeah, whatever." He picked up a soap cloud and threw it at her.

"Stop, boy." She tossed suds in his face. "You gon' mess up my hair."

"So."

"So my ass shit."

"Get it redone." He poked her in the chin and gave her a white sudsy beard.

"Man, fuck all that! Stop playing damn it." She wiped it off and took a handful and smothered his ass, then pushed him under the water. "Muthafucka." She stood away and strutted proudly.

"Oh, okay." He shook the water off. "I got you."

"Stop, K.J, I'm serious now, stop." She put her hands on her hips to reinforce it in case there was any doubt.

"Hm-hmmm."

"Alright, I'ma leave my ass up outta here."

"Yeah, go in there and get me my cigar; that way I can smoke it while you do my back."

"Yeah, I need a drink any damn way."

"Alkie."

"Just remember…" she bent over, slapped that chocolate thang, and shook it till it wiggled. "You like it."

"Umphn!" he grunted as he watched. "Naw, baby I love that there."

"Oh, that's all you love?" He'd never said it; though she was sure, he loved her.

"Girl, go get my cigar." He grabbed a new handful of the bubbly cloud.

"Don't! Stop." Jaquanna skipped away, and then strutted with what her mama gave her. All of what her mama gave her. And boy was it a lovely lot. Her mama should surely be proud.

When she returned Jaquanna washed his back and helped to scrub his whole body clean. And soon they were in bed as she served him with a reminder.

"Ummn," she purred as she spread herself wider and stroked the back of his head. His tongue moved slow and strong. "Oh, I like that. That feels so good."

Kirk Jr. swirled, stabbed, and lapped with his eager tongue. Did the entire alphabet A thru Z, and then did the whole thing in reverse. Just as Poo-Poo had taught him. Poo-Poo Pat had been one of his first. They'd grown up together. In fact, he'd been the one who gave her her name, 'Poo-Poo Patty who lives by the alley'. Yeah, they went a long way back.

"Damn, I love when you do that." Jaquanna pulled both of her knees back to her shoulders and let herself be had. "Ooh, lick that thang, Kirk, baby, lick it. Oh, it feels so good."

He remembered when, what seemed like just yesterday, Miss Chocolate thang Jaquanna was a little girl and he'd stalk her fine ass from a distance. He'd waited years to hold her and have her, but now she was his own.

"Give me some, baby," Jaquanna whispered. "Come on give me some."

As he stood, Kirk Jr. looked down at her. The cute little toes, the shapely calves, the curve of her thighs, the turn of her hips, the tight tummy and bulging breasts with the tight tiny nipples over dark creamy tips. Everything about her said, 'I am woman, woman I am'.

If only such moments could be placed in a bottle, corked and revisited at times. A mind's sweet treasures. A time etched forever. A sweetness without taste. Defined.

"Ooh, yeah!" She opened her legs as he climbed between them. "Come on, give me that."

He pushed into her, shoved her open. Bullied a path to her depths. She was his. His treasure to open. His joy to behold. As her breaths grew to sharpened gasps he rode her deeper, with each intake remembering, now, why she was here. Yes. He knew.

Having her here was more than alright. Having her here was meaningful, it was bliss, it was special, and it was perfectly timeless. Having her here was as it should be; as well as it ever was. Having her here made his house a home, a place to come home to; rush home to. A place to be; a place to be made whole, a place to become as one. In this place was richness; it was purpose; it was joy. Yeah, he remembered now, as he gripped the headboard and hovered over her, riding high in the saddle, staring down into the eager warmth of her desirous eyes, he knew. He remembered and he knew. The light sheen of sweat on his young hard body, the feel of her pink parts massaging his tool, while her nails gripped his hips and her ankles folded over his calves; all said one thing. The one thing that he knew: He remembered. The smell of her, the taste of her, the feel of her, the sound of her — HERE! All added to what it equaled. The math was simple. The meaning undeniable, the passion long and thick as it drove him to his edge and crashed into her with its purpose: it's very designed intent. She was woman. He was man. No doubt. And, here, now, was everything that love defined. All that love should be. Here, having her. Here.

"Ooh!" Something from deep inside of her uttered. "Oh!"

"You like it, baby?"

Too emotional to speak, she nodded.

Holding the headboard gave him an added drive to his leverage. "Huhn!" He slashed into her juicy softness pushing into her with a pound. "Gimme this. Huhn." He punished her joy again.

"Oh!" Jaquanna rolled her hips and took all that he had to give. Unafraid. In pain but wanting more. Hurt because there was never enough and hurting because she could take no more. Filled with joy and filled with fire. Afraid to let go. Afraid to hold on. Wanting, needing, giving, taking. Accepting *all* of the man, she loved.

'"Urghn!"

"Ooh!"

The music of lust filled the room. The scent of joy filled the air. Where was there a thrill to match this? Who felt but could not feel? Gave all that they could get? Held what they feared to hold? What power? What energy? What now? Of course, she was supposed to be here, where else in this world could she be but here?

"Oh, God!" she prayed aloud, "Oh, God!"

And He came. Making them whole. He came.

"We need to talk," she said when they'd finished. She'd gotten a warm towel and wiped him off and then put her lingerie back on. He was sitting up in the bed smoking a cigar. She lit a cigarette.

"Why, what's up?"

She took the little pee-pee stick and held it where he could see it, waving it like a damn magic wand. Her smile was nervous and unsure. "I'm pregnant."

"You what?" Kirk Jr. frowned.

She gave him that what-the-fuck look.

"By who?"

"Boy, aw, uh-uh. I know the hell you just didn't."

"It's mine?"

"Who else it gon' be?" She rolled her eyes and placed her fists on her hips. "I know you not fucking serious?"

"Shit, I don't be with you all day."

"I ain't the one fucking."

"What the hell you talking 'bout, girl?"

"You heard me," she insisted, "I ain't fucking stupid."

"Girl, you don't know what the fuck you talking 'bout."

"Oh, naw?"

"Hell, naw."

"Okay." She strutted over to the closet and reached into a pocket of one of his trench coats. "What the fuck is this then?" She whipped out a long-ass strip of rubbers.

"Girl." Kirk Jr. jumped up and snatched the strip. "Don't be going through my fucking shit."

"Well what you doing with them?"

"Man, I ain't gotta answer that shit."

"Yeah, that's what I thought."

"Look." He pointed with his finger just micrometers from her forehead. "Don't get stupid."

"You don't get stupid, shit."

Kirk Jr. turned to put the condoms back in the pocket.

"Got me fucked up," she added.

"I'ma tell you off top." He looked down on her. "You really need to go on with all that shit."

"Or what?"

He shook his head and stepped away.

"Shit." She added.

Kirk Jr. turned to face the angry woman again. "Push with the bullshit, okay?"

"You push with the bullshit. Getting all turnt up and shit. Fuck that, man. I ain't in the wrong. You is."

"Let it go, Jah."

"No, you let it go, Kirk."

"Yeah, okay."

"Okay then. Shit."

"Look." He bit his lip and pointed again. "I'm cool on that bullshit."

"You cool? Shit. I'm cool too, shit."

"Man…" Kirk shook his head and put on his boxers. Then hit his cigar.

"I mean who does that?" Jaquanna shook her head. "I'm sitting up here pregnant and shit, thinking shit is all lovey-dovey sweet and shit, and here you go turning into Count Fuck-himself or some damn body. Aw, uh-uh."

"Stop, Jaquanna."

"Stop? Stop what, Kirk?"

"Stop."

"Stop what?" She stepped up on him and peered up into his young strong face. "Huh?" She was hoping to calm him. "Being pregnant? Carrying our baby? Huh?"

"I ain't ready for no kid."

"You what?"

"You heard me."

"Oh, but you sitting up here bare-backing a bitch like it's all good, huh? Just dumping your little nut all up in a bitch, like what? You ain't think my shit work? You ain't think I'd get pregnant? Or what, you just didn't care?"

"Stop."

"Stop my ass, Kirk! I'm good enough for you to fuck bareback and shit, but I ain't good enough for me to have your baby. That's bullshit!" She knocked the ashtray to the floor. "Yo stupid ass. Cain't even tell a muthafucking bitch you love her." She reached up and slapped his cigar to the floor, just as he was about to take a hit.

"Girl." He shook his head as he picked it up. "You better go the fuck on."

"Or?"

"Stall it out, man. On the real Quah, stall on all that."

"Man, fuck you! You selfish, spoiled bastard."

"You ain't ask me if I wanted no kid."

"And you ain't ask me if you could put on no damn rubber either."

Kirk Jr. chuckled a bit and shook his head.

"Oh, I'm glad your stupid-ass thank this shit is funny," she told him, "'cause I ain't laughing worth a fuck."

"Look, I ain't ready to be chasing around no little dusty nose muthafucka all like that."

"A who?"

He laughed again. "You heard me."

"A little dusty nose muthafucka," she repeated as she shook her head in a fog. "Man, I don't fucking believe this shit."

"Hey, man, look. You know what I'm saying. Don't try ta make me seem like I'm the bad guy 'cause I'm not."

"Man, I ain't asked for none of this, Kirk. You know, you all on your muthafuckin' high horse like I'm asking for some favor or some shit. Like you know, like I just jumped up in here and said 'Hey, honey, God gave me a baby, I wish you'd be the daddy'. Shit. And that ain't even hardly the fucking case, goddamn it. God made the fucking decision to allow this life to be created at that instance. God figured it was this child's time to breathe and that it should come to us. Not me." She held her chest. "I ain't do shit, God did it. I ain't tricked or played you or lied to you, none of that. So miss me with all this victim-with-a-dick dumb-ass shit."

"Oh, victim-with-a-dick, huh?" He smiled. "V.W.D. that's what it is?"

"Man," she waved him off. "You know what, forget you, man."

"What you mad at me for?"

"'Cause you sitting up here test driving my muthafucking guts, like I'm just some ole bust-head ass bitch and—"

"That ain't the truth."

"It is the fucking truth."

"Man, you on some bullshit." He waved her off and took a puff.

"You know what," she decided, "since I'm on some fucking bullshit, I'm just gon' get my shit and go."

"Man…'" He shook his head as he watched her pull on some jeans to make good on her promise.

"Yeah." She went on in that way that women so often love to do. "That way you ain't gotta put up with my bullshit."

"Oh, now, you gon' get all diva on a nigga, huh?"

"You muthafuckin' right." She took a huge hug full from her side of the closet and tossed it on the rumpled bed, which just moments ago nestled her love. The spot was still wet. The love had grown cold. "Move my little shit out the way; that way you got more room for your little condoms."

He shook his head and laughed then decided to take a sip from her glass.

"That way you can bring all your little hood rats up in here and ain't gotta worry 'bout me catching you or me finding out or no shit. I mean, not that I give a fuck no more. Shit. You can go fuck whoever the fuck you wanna, far as—"

"Oh, so you gone?"

"What you thank?"

"So you breaking up with a nigga?"

"Naw, I'm just making room for your little condom crowd."

"Man, that's crazy, man."

She spun then and got in his face. Finger hovering. "Naw, you crazy. Shit."

"Get out my face, Jah."

"You get out my face." She frowned.

"You trippin nahmean?"

"You trippin ole bitch-ass nigga."

"Watch your mouth."

"You know what, fuck you!" Jaquanna slapped him

*POW!*

*Blam!* The thick glass he'd had in his hand smacked hard against her left cheek and dropped her to the floor.

"Muthafucka!" She sprung back up and swung an open claw.

"'Stop, Jah," he pointed and bit his lip.

"Man you fucking hit me, man." She held her cheek. Tears fell. A trickle of blood dripped from her nose. "Aw, uh-uh." Just the site of the blood took her back to a fucked up past.

"It was an accident, man."

"Accident, my ass. How the fuck was that an accident when you just smacked my ass with a fucking glass?"

"It was reflex."

"Man, reflex my ass." Her wrist wiped her nose.

"I told you to let it go. You don't put your hands on no man."

"You ain't no man. You fucking little dick bitch. You prolly a damn faggot." She was emptying her drawers and throwing more clothes and whatnots into the pile. "Ole under-cover fuck-boy on some stupid-ass down low shit."

He shook his head.

"Prolly why your gay ass got them condoms, huh? What, you like dick, you little bitch? That's why you don't want no kids?"

"Yeah. You know what. Yeah, just get your shit and go."

"I'm leaving muthafucka. Shit."

"Well, bye."

"Bye back, bitch."

"Watch your mouth, Jaquanna."

"Suck a dick, Kirk."

"Yeah, I'ma suck yo dick, keep it up."

"You prolly wish I had a dick, huh?" She was back in his face. "That way you'd have something to play with."

"Yeah, you got lyrics."

"Oh, I got lyrics, huh?" She touched the growing knot on her cheek. "Yeah, well, right now my muthafucking record scratched."

He chuckled and shook his head. "Man you stupid."

"Oh, you think it's cute, huh? With your stupid ass."

"Ain't you s'pose to be leaving?"

"Yeah, and I'm finna do me too."

He wanted to tell her to leave the car and all of the other shit she was so busily packing, while she popped off at the soup cooler. But he knew that that would've only been an emotional kid-like gimme-my-ball-back type response that was totally un-called for. It would've been like trying to hurt her simply be-cause she was hurting him with her words. Maybe Big Dick was right after all. He didn't need chaos in his home.

Jaquanna had went and gotten some plastic bags and she was angrily shoving stuff inside. "All this stupid-ass shit just because you got me pregnant. Humph. What the hell?" She shook her head. "Who does that? Man I am just too through. For real, man. On every thang. I'm done, man."

"Man, stall that shit."

"Man, suck my ass, Kirk. Little gay boy."

"Man, what's with this gay shit, man?"

"You ain't no man." She tied her third bag, tossed it, and approached to meet his challenge. "Cause if you was you wouldn't put your hands on no woman and—"

"I told you that was an accident."

"Accident, my ass, you bitch." She smacked him but he blocked most of the strength from the blow and dipped away.

"Girl, you better go on some god damn where." He pointed as she approached.

"Fuck you." Jaquanna looked around as if to find something to throw.

"Don't throw nothing at me, Jah." He danced from the room. "I'm serious, Quan, don't try me."

"What the fuck you just call me?"

He knew she hated it and that it only reminded her of Benny now. It had been a slip of the tongue. It seemed their Heaven had turned to Hell.

"My bad," he said. "I whatn't even tryna go there."

"Yeah, right, whatever. Bitch-ass muthafuckin' boy." Jaquanna cried openly and hard. She'd lived with that memory for four long miserable years. Suffering each day for simply having defended herself. Victim's rights. Or victim what the fuck ever. But what about her? What about her right to defend herself? What about her stolen virginity? What about her stolen youth? Or the trauma of it all that she'd have to live with, every day for the rest of her life? No treatment. No understanding. No nothing. Just a damn sentence and a torturous memory every night for four damn years. Her only knowledge of sex had been at her victimizer's hands. So, for four long years, every time she even thought about sex and what it might feel like to be with a man, all she had to hold on to or to satisfy her curiosity was the memory of the man she'd hated most. What about her? There'd been no mercy for her. Just a black and white page with simple non-emotional and unknowing judgments dictating her punishment. Damn the circumstances. No one was allowed to seek vigilante justice. Bottom line, she should have waited on the cops and let the police handle it. Period. The fact that she'd taken matters into her own young hands that night made her the perpetrator as opposed to the victim. And now, Kirk Jr. had shot that dart at her, just enough of a reminder.

"Naw, but on the real, that's my bad right there, Jah."

"Naw, uh-uh." She headed back to the room, grabbed a bag, and dragged it.

Out of the past? Into the future? Who knew where she would go. Life can be so temporary. Even when it seemed so permanent. Just the click of a finger, the flash of a flame, and suddenly a house was burning.

Ashes to ashes.

Dust to dust.

But then, there's a certain resilience within young love, isn't there?

# Chapter 16

***Monday, July 3rd***

"You need to leave that boy," Lay-Lay told Jaquanna the next morning as they sat at the table drinking coffee. It was the same house and the same kitchen. Jaquanna hated being here.

"But I love him, Mama."

"Uh-huh. I know," she said, "Just like I thought I loved Benny."

"Naw, Mama, this ain't the same."

"Well, it still got your eye all swole up just the same."

"Naw, but it really was kinda really my fault though, Mama."

"Making excuses for him, huh?" She sipped her coffee to hide her cocky grin, as if she'd seen and heard it all before.

"Naw, it ain't that."

"But?"

"But he a good man, Mama, and you know that."

"But even good man's got problems," Lay-Lay said, "and, hell, he cain't be all too damn good if he whupping on you and carrying on."

Jaquanna and her mother had gotten closer during their time apart. It had taken Jaquanna awhile to realize that her mother was just as much a victim as she herself had been. At first, she truly resented and even thought she hated her mother. Number one: for bringing that beast into their home, and number two: for not standing up for her kids and defending them against him. She'd felt her mother was weak and spineless. Later, she understood better as she realized just how often women found themselves in economical, emotional, and/or physical bondage: simply staying because they were afraid to leave, even when they weren't truly happy with what they had. Afraid to be without; afraid to be alone; or afraid of what the man might do to her if she tried to leave.

Letters, visits, phone calls all led to Jaquanna getting to know the person within Lay-Lay's being. This helped her to dis-cover just how beautiful a person her mother truly was, and all of the time and communication simply brought them closer.

"Yeah, I hear you." Jaquanna relented.

"I mean, I like the boy," Lay-Lay admitted. "I like all he done did for you. I like how he came by and checked on me while you was gone and everything. He's been real good about all of that, but once they start putting they hands on you, Jah, it only gets worse. Trust me. I know. I done been through it. Not once, not twice, but three times." She held up her fingers so Jaquanna could count them.

Jaquanna knew the stories of old boyfriends and their mistreatment of her mother. She surely didn't want to follow in that pattern. 'That shit's for the pigeons' she'd taken to saying.

"So, but why though?" she asked her mother. "I mean, like why do you think you kept being with those kinda dudes like, you know what I'm saying?"

"Well, I'm a little woman," Lay-Lay said as if that meant something. "And I've always liked great big old strong men." She explained, "You know the big, wild, angry brute that would tear my goodies up but also stand against anything but God himself to protect me."

Jaquanna nodded as she understood and recognized the description as well as the desire.

"And if they had the will and the ability to help pay the bills then that made it all the better."

Jaquanna sipped her coffee and lit a cigarette. 'A fool learns from experience and a wise man learns from the experiences of others' she'd once read somewhere. As she recalled it, Jaquanna made a conscious decision to sit back for a minute and just practice being wise. 'Might learn something,' she figured.

"But see," Lay-Lay went on, "what I ain't get was that that same big ole temperamental brute with no understanding and a short fuse, though it was the bomb to have on my side, it was a live damn bomb when it turned against my ass. See, it's cute when you feeling like 'hey, look what I got.' Like here's this big old bodyguard or some shit and I got all this control over him. I guess it's like one of those countries who be having the nuclear bomb and all that kinda stuff. It's the shit when you the one in control and you got your finger on the button. But when you drop that shit or that shit get to leaking, boy, I tell you. Boy, lookie here."

"Now, instead of it tryna protect, you it's tryna kill you."

"Exactly." Lay-Lay sipped. "Hm-huh, that part and why you thank they be like that though?"

"Spoiled."

"Spoiled?"

"Hm-humm."

"You thank so?"

"What else could it be?"

"But, I mean, how it like—"

"Look," Lay-Lay took a hit of her freshly lit Newport. It was her third one in the chain. "When a little boy grows up always having his way or use to having his way; then, when he gets older, he gets to where he be 'specting the whole dang world to cater to him and he ain't good for nothing or no body. He just one big old overgrown kid, constantly looking 'round for the next somebody he can lean on to take care of him or cater to him. And with his women he looking for a damn mama, one he can control with all of his whining and sniveling, the same as he did his mama. And the first time you don't come running, he pitch a fit 'cause the universe ain't right with the stars and you done forgot how amazing and special he is. Like you s'pose to feel lucky he shares his breath in your presence."

"Okay." Jaquanna was lost in the sauce tryna follow her mother. It seemed like Lay-Lay was just venting on some old shit that must've at once had her vexed, but Jaquanna didn't see how any parts of that fit in with her situation. "But I don't see how like—I mean, I get it. I do hear what you saying, but—"

"Okay." Lay-Lay took a breath, a sip, and a nice long puff. She was trying to sort things in her mind and looking for a different approach. She enjoyed these kinds of motherly chats with Jaquanna. It made her feel needed and important. It made her screwed up decisions of the past somehow seem meaningful. Like all of that hell and the bitter pains of those travels, were somehow meant just so that this conversation; this day with her daughter, could be had. It made her feel old now, realizing she was the source of advice. After all, she was still only 33 and pretty much still trying to figure things out for herself. But now, here she was; the time tested voice of experienced wisdom to a grown child of her own. And it seemed it'd happened overnight. But Jaquanna was all grown up.

"Okay," she repeated in thought. "Let me say it like this, then." Lay-Lay began, "you know how you get a baby and you put him in like a crib?"

Jaquanna nodded.

"Okay, so then you know how he might get in there and get to throwing a fit?"

"What, 'cause he want his mama?"

"Yeah, well, that too. But naw, he just gets to wanting what he wants or wanting whatever. It could be a bottle, a toy, someone to pick him up and make him the center of their universe: whatever," she said. "A baby like that is gon' make sure you know he is in the room! He will not be ignored, because, to him being ignored means being neglected and if you ain't get to him or get whatever he wants done fast enough, you bet your last money on God's green grass he gon' make sure you hear about it in as loud and in as dramatic a way as possible."

Jaquanna nodded and smiled knowingly, those were always the cutest little babies. On some, 'aw him want his mama' shit. 'Ain't that sweet?'

"But where the problem come in at," Lay-Lay continued, "is when he get use to throwing his bottle across the room to get his way or make a point and everyone comes running over to pinch his little cheeks or see what's wrong. Well, when he gets to being older his little brain is still working the same, but now, the only thing is, instead of him throwing his bottle and toys around the room, now he throwing your ass around the room."

"Uh-hmm, huh?"

"Either that or he'll just go to pouting, lip all turned out, whining and complaining or just disappear off somewhere, like he refuses to play with you 'because you're not a good friend', or some ole crazy madness. Just big ole babies." She took a hit. "Acting like us girls is s'pose to act. But they more spoiled than we is."

"Sho is."

"Like I say, when you first bring them kind around, boy they just like a little trophy. Big, strong, intimidating, the women be wanting some and the men be looking all up to him or scared of him. And you just sitting there with your little finger on the magic button. It's like you done created you a damn Frankenstein." She giggled at her pun. "But, Lord have mercy Jesus, when he roars and he's roaring at you, it's like you trapped with an ape in your own damn cage and ain't a damn thang you can do but try ta remember what it takes to make him happy. But you see, the more you ripping and running trying to remember how to make him happy so it'll calm his ass down, then the more it's just fitting into that same old pattern from when he was a kid."

"Hm-hmmm. Sho is, huh?"

"Yeah," she said, "we all just grown up babies, that's all we is. And when they say the squeaky wheel gets the grease, who you thank they talkin 'bout? I know I don't want no squeaky wheel all up in my damn ear." Another sip. "And that's what they be knowing, if he creates enough havoc or raises enough hell, then the people around him gon' give him what he want."

"Yeah, you ain't lying about that."

"And let me tell you, it's better when you live in his cage, 'cause you can just get up and go. But once you got an ape in your own damn cage, it's just all bad."

Jaquanna laughed.

"Cause ain't no way to get rid of him," Lay-Lay added. "He'll kick everybody's ass."

It was early Monday morning, eve of the Forth. The heat of the summer's sun was already beginning to burn its presence into the conscious. Jaquanna could hear little Ricky in the bedroom apparently just getting up. She checked her watch. 10:39 a.m. Figured. She shook her head.

"But the one thing you got to understand, Jah, is this," Lay-Lay explained, "Once they put they hands on you it's over."

Jaquanna wasn't feeling that statement. After all, she'd been in love with Kirk Jr. and waiting for their time together, for four years. She'd dreamed of these moments and felt like a true queen as she lived in them. It was like a modern day ghetto fabulous rags to riches Cinderella story. When Jaquanna came home, it was as if the world was hers. All she had to do was think that she might've wanted something and it was like Kirk Jr. read her thoughts and it was hers before the thought was even completed. So, yeah, okay, she was thinking now, so he wasn't ready for a baby yet. So, but that didn't make him a bad man, did it?

"Once they put they hands on you it's a whole nother thang else entirely, girl," Lay-Lay insisted. "It's just like learning to ride a bike: there may be some build up and mighta took a while before it went down that first time, but once you rode it once it's just easier and easier the next time. It's like driving a car or having sex or whatever; once that first time happens the fear ain't the same. The scary part of the consequences don't seem so much. And so when it comes to a man popping you upside the head, once he crack your ass in the eye that first time, next time he wanna make his point or punish you for not jumping when and how he want you to. Then he'll just be popping your ass again, till next thang you know, you'll stay in your big ole Dark Diva shades, like them MJB, Mary J. Blige things you got there now; just using them as shields to hide behind and cover all your black eyes and whatnots."

"But it whatn't even like that though, Mama."

"Yeah, okay." She puffed her cigarette and leaned back. "Experience gon' teach your ass what I cain't tell you."

"Naw, Mama, for real though."

"Yeah, well, what you want me to say?" Lay-Lay shook her head. "I cain't teach you what you already know. And Lord knows I hope you right and I'm wrong. Cause I likes that boy, but I loves my daughter."

"Thanks, Mama." Jaquanna reached over and touched her mother's hand. She could tell her mother was worried. But it wasn't like Kirk Jr. had Chris Brown'd her or no shit. So what if she had a black eye. Shit happens, right? Plus, she did cause it. It wasn't like he had chased her down and beat her. She just wanted to be fair. He at least deserved that.

"So when you going back home?" Lay-Lay asked her with a certain smugness.

"I don't know." She looked saddened by the thought.

"Well, you welcome to stay here as long as you need."

"Thanks, Mama."

"And what you gon' do about that baby?"

"I mean, what can I do?"

"You can do a whole lot."

"Yeah."

"But that's up to you."

"I know."

"But you still got time to think about it, Jah."

"Yeah."

"But," Lay-Lay stood, "if you is gon' keep that baby, you might wanna think about them cigarettes and drinking and stuff you be doing."

"I know, huh?"

"You want the baby to be healthy."

"Yeah, I thought about that too."

"What up, sis?" Little Ricky bounded into the room looking like an ashy blue-black refugee on crack. He'd grown tall, dark, and skinny. And already his eyes had that flat hardened dimness to them: the eyes of too much seen. His smile only reached his cheeks. In some ways, he was 14 going on 100. But Jaquanna could sense a certain extra bit of cockiness and swag that wasn't just there before.

"What's up, Big Boy?" She smiled and tapped his naked tummy.

"I don't know why; when you say that, it just don't sound the same."

"Oh, what you too hard core now?" she teased.

"I know, huh?" Ricky smiled broadly.

"Member you *my* little brother, boy."

"And you my big sis." He hugged her.

"Whenever," she said.

"Wherever," he replied.

"However," they said together.

"Aw. Yeah, that's cute," said Lay-Lay. "Now you go in there and put a damn shirt on, boy."

"Aw, man, it's hot," he cried. "It's too hot for all that. Plus, I'm finna go anyway."

"And where you finna go?" Jaquanna asked.

"Kirk wanna have us go down and pick up some jet skis and stuff for the function." He hadn't said anything about her eye. Though he knew she'd spent the night and why. That was their thing he told himself and he intended to stay out of it. After all, Kirk Jr. was almost like a big brother to him now. That was his big homie, his idol, his boss, and damn near his brother. He wasn't getting in that. Period. Yeah, it was still whenever, wherever, however, but that shit there was different.

"Umph," she rolled her eyes and took a sip.

"Plus, he finna have one of the homies start teaching me to drive."

"The homies?" asked Lay-Lay.

"Drive?" added Jaquanna.

"Aw, uh-uhn," Lay-Lay said. "I don't want you out there in that mess, Ricky. I ain't brought you into this world to be none of one of them." No matter how hypocritical it may have sounded coming from a woman who had no qualms accepting and benefitting from its fruits. It was the ghetto. Poverty. Survival. "I mean that."

"I ain't doing nothing, Mama," he mumbled as he sat to eat.

"And who teaching you to drive?"

"The Homie Coo-Coo."

"For what?"

"K.J. say he gon' help me get a car."

"Umph."

"Aw, Lord," Lay-Lay shook her head. "Boy, you ain't ready to be doing no driving." She looked over at him. He was a tall, slim handsome boy. She didn't know where he got all his height.

You teach them and then you set them free. But when do you cut the string? It was every mother's mystery. Hope and pray for the best. What more could you do?"

## Chapter 17

The obvious is only obvious once you see it. And, sometimes we can be blind to what's right in front of us. And even when we think we see it, sometimes we realize we don't. Sooner? Later? Never? Who knows? Does it matter? Will the universe be altered? Well, okay, maybe so. With the new babies formed or new energies shared or expressed in new environments and locations, okay, yeah, I guess the universe would be altered. Since everyone in some way will be shifted, changed or effected by the arrival or bonding of the newly formed energy: He's not with her so now she's over with him, and, now they have a baby when it could've been their baby, but now he has a baby with a new her and now she's stuck with him. Okay, makes sense. But still, how can we know the future? And who thinks of energy shifts while in the midst of searching for love? I mean, come on. Ridiculous. Or is it? Should it be?

If love is so deep, then how deep should the questions be before we go bonding our energies with just anyone somewhere and then just blindly falling so deeply into the undefinable? Love, oh, Love, makes us do foolish things. Or how about, it takes a fool to learn? Oh, so deep, when we pay attention. But who's got time for that?

Yes, sometimes it just feels so right and you can tell. I mean, you just know, right? But then too, no matter what it is we think we might feel, sometimes we get it all wrong. Like the words to a love song written in reverse; the meaning upside down: EVOL. LOVE. Hmmm.

As he approached the school, the midday sun was riding high. He had hoped she'd be here and to his happy amazement, she was.

Jaquanna was at the free throw line. She took a shot. Missed it. No one else was on the court so she lazily retrieved the ball and tried again. Another shot. Another miss. She was wearing a loose set of gym shorts and a tank top. Tennis and big round dark glasses. MJB's.

"I got next," he called.

"Say what?" She turned and looked. Her stern face melted to a smile. "Uh."

"Who next?"

"Ain't nobody here but you."

"Um." Mark peeled off his top and laid it over the bench. He wore gym shorts and tennis. "I like the sound of that."

"I bet you do." She shot. She scored.

"Lucky."

"Who? Me or you?"

"How 'bout both?"

"Yeah, I guess both **is** okay."

"My ball or your ball?" He held his up.

"I don't play with just anybody's balls.

He smiled. "Didn't think I was just anybody."

"Oh yeah?" She stepped out of bounds. "Who'd you thank you was?"

Her words burned into him like a high noon sun behind a magnifying glass. "Ouch."

"I thought you liked pain." Her sneer was false.

"Why you say that?"

"I told you I got a man."

"He the one did that?" Mark pointed to the not so hidden mountain behind her Diva stunners.

"I had an accident."

"Check ball."

Jaquanna thrust the ball with meaningful force, bouncing it into his big, strong waiting hands. "Nice hands," she told him.

They're patient."

"Umm." Jaquanna dribbled in with a confident stroke.

Mark spread his arms but allowed her.

She was bent low and backing her way in towards the goal.

Mark pushed up on her. Bending over her from behind, as he reached in and tried to swipe what he wanted.

She turned away; she disappeared. There one minute then gone. Charging, leaping. She'd gotten away. Back board, lay-up, *and boom!*

"That's two," she told him. First, the back of her hand then the front of her hand. "Two."

Mark had the ball and he smiled as he walked slowly forward. She was a wonder to watch and a thrill to touch. He liked her smile. Her daring deviance. The challenge in the toss of her chin. But the little girl was still right there, just right below the surface. And she is what drew him. "Close," He said.

"Not even."

"Check that shit."

Again, she checked it.

Jaquanna bent low and used her butt to try to push him backwards. But this time Mark stood firm. His strong legs anchoring him as he leaned over her and reached for what he wanted.

She was forced to stand still. To take it. She stopped dribbling. Looked for a shot, but he was too big, too strong. She could feel his weight as he thrust up against her. Feel his rock hard firmness as it challenged her.

"Go head foul me." She pushed her ass back into his stomach. "Come on, do it," she told him. "Bring it on."

Mark loved the way she looked bent over in front of him. He could wait forever right in that spot. But then, Mark wasn't a loser. Mark played the game. "Gimme that shit!"

"Ahhh!" she yelped as he took the ball and dribbled away. "You bastard." She smiled. "Why you do that?"

"I believe in taking what I want."

"Umph." She rolled her eyes. "Scared of you."

"Don't be."

"Why?"

"Cause I'll only take what you give me."

"I didn't give you my ball."

"That's 'cause you was being stingy."

"Well, you still ain't s'pose to take it." She popped a hand on her hip.

"You gave it to me."

"What?"

"You know you wanted me to have it." He took a shot and made it. He'd caught her slipping, standing there with her hand on her hip, too busy trying to look cute.

"Why you do that?" She approached.

"Check ball." He threw it at her.

"Oh, okay, I see you like to play rough." Jaquanna went over and took off her glasses. "Come on, boy. You ain't said nothing but a word."

"Oh, yeah?" He held his hands out waiting. His smirk was smug.

"Yep." She bounced it back. Firm, hard, solid.

"What word was that?"

"Might as well've been pain."

"Oh, yeah, and why is that?"

"Cause I'm 'bout to hurt your little feelings."

"Is that right?" He waited, moved the ball back and forth, and swung his hips with misdirection. Sure, he wanted to give it to her, but he also wanted her to fight for what he had, for what she needed. And what he knew she wanted. "I could give it to you, but what you gon' do with it?"

"I takes what I wants. Bring it."

He came in low and pushed in to her, shoving into her with an easy force. "You want this?" he demanded. "Huh? Think you can take it?"

"Yeah, give it here." She rushed into him. Gave what she had. "Bring it," she told him. "Gimme that shit."

Mark worked his hips. Used his legs. Arched his back. Dipped in deep. Spun hard then slammed it. *Blam!*

"Ohh!" she gasped as the board vibrated.

"And there's more where that comes from too." He smiled as he stepped out with a cocky stride.

"Damn, that's how you gon' do it?" She smiled.

"I'm just tryna stay in the game."

"Stay in the game?" She threw him the ball.

"Yep, and take whatever you'll let me have." He caught it.

"I ain't letting you have it if you take it."

"Sometimes people don't know what's best for 'em till you show 'em."

"What that's s'pose to mean?"

"I can only take what you want me to have."

"Well, I don't know about that."

"Well, quit holding back and I'll show you."

"We are talking about basketball, right?"

"Of course," he said with a teasing smile. "You're trying to keep me from getting to the little hoop and I'm doing all I can to get to it."

"Hm-hmmph!"

"With my ball."

"Yeah." She nodded.

"So I can get it in there and slam it, till it throbs and snaps back with a yawning bang."

"Ooh!"

"Like that?"

"Love it," she said. "Now try it."

A nice wind blew and swept through the playground. The glistening sheen of sweat that coated his hard strong body turned a gentle chill and caused goose bumps. His nipples hardened.

He checked the ball.

She caught it. "Ummph!"

"How you want it?" he pressed in to her.

"Bring me you're a-game. Don't step to this shit playing."

"Umph. That could be asking for a lot."

"And who said I cain't handle it?"

"You say that like you was raised up on Top Ramen and gun powder or some shit."

Jaquanna smiled. "Maybe I was."

They heard the loud beat of the driving bass then looked up to see the silver grey Jaguar XJ. Leon slowed as he passed outside the fence of the elementary school. Nodding his head, he waved to Jaquanna with one of them I-see-you looks.

"Oh, Lord," she said as the car pulled away.

"Who was that?" he asked. "The competition?"

She had her hands on her hips as she looked up at him. She shook her head and smiled. "Boy."

"That's not him?"

"Naw, that's his homie."

Mark nodded knowingly. Call it profiling if you want to, but a young black man in the ghetto driving around in an $80,000 car could only mean one thing: unless he was a rapper, ball player or dope dealer, he had just stole that damn thing.

The screaming jets of the passing plane were loud, as the 747 came in low on approach, readying itself to land at nearby LAX International Airport about ten miles to the west and right off the Pacific Ocean. 107$^{th}$ Street School is on the East side of Main Street, which means it is on the East side of Los Angeles. On the other side of Main Street is where the West side begins. The yellow line in the middle of the street is the actual demarcation line: the divider. The further west you go, the cleaner the streets and the nicer the homes become until finally you reach the airport and then the ocean and take off to disappear from the hellish paradise altogether.

Deciding to leave the games behind for now, Mark and Jaquanna decided to jump in her car and go grab a bite to eat. They settled on Tam's on 101$^{st}$ and Figueroa where they ordered a big plate of chili cheese fries and split it. They parked the car at the diner and sat with the top down to enjoy the last rays of the dying sun.

"So I see you didn't buck 'em."

She furrowed her brow in confusion.

"Your teeth."

She laughed at that. "Oh, yeah, huh?"

"Yeah, pretty smile," he said. "I always did like your smile."

"You still bite your nails?"

He showed her. "Occasionally."

"That's bad." She shook her head disappointed. "See, I listen. You don't."

"Oh, so you stopped because of what I said that day?"

"Yep. Sho did. Not right off, but yeah, eventually."

"See. And here I didn't even think you remembered me."

"I don't know, just, when you said that that day, it just kinda like stuck with me. And I guess I didn't wanna have buck teeth knowing I coulda prevented it."

"Yeah."

"Cause ain't no way I coulda afforded no braces, and really wouldn'tna even wanted none."

"I don't know; braces are kinda cute sometimes."

"You think so?"

"Well, yeah, they kinda fall into the plaid skirt, school teacher glasses, or librarian bun sorta category."

"Just hot for no damn reason, huh?" She laughed.

"Yeah, turn ons," he admitted, "and braces can have that effect."

"Or the opposite."

"Okay. Fair."

"Where'd you say you was from again?" She chewed slowly with her mouth closed. It was just something he always noticed. Her legs were open. Legs shiny, smooth, and tight. Her breasts were ripe. He liked that she hadn't put back on her glasses. It showed that she wasn't afraid to be seen for who she was. It told him that she was comfortable around him.

"Well, I'm from here. But, basically, I was raised in Mississippi."

"'With your grandparents."

He nodded. Happy to see that she remembered yet another thing about him and their long ago encounter.

"Wow."

He didn't ask what that meant. He knew it meant nothing, a space filler. "I see you like reading."

He nodded to the book in her windshield.

"Yeah, I've always loved reading. Ever since I was a little girl I use to read and just escape."

"I think that's super sexy."

"Do you?" She smiled brightly. "Why?"

"It just says that you like learning new things and that you're okay in the world of your individual thoughts and opinions. Plus, the more you read, you just learn more about things, and that also means there's more of you to give. I mean, our minds are who we are, and they define us, so if we broaden our minds, we can only broaden who we are. That make sense?"

"Yeah, I think I know what you mean."

"So do you prefer fiction or non-fiction?"

"Well, I guess both really. I mean, when I was in jail, I read just a lotta lotta like religious and like self-help and just how to type books. I don't know, I really just wanted to learn and understand things. I was in a real dark place and I just, I don't know, I needed to find meaning and purpose, like, you know? You understand what I'm saying?"

"'Man's search for meaning is the ultimate motivation in his life.' Viktor Frankl."

"Viktor Frankl? What he write?"

"Honestly, I don't know. Just one of those quotes I picked up from somewhere."

"Damn." She laughed at this. "And here I was thinking you was all deep and shit."

More laughter.

"No, I just always had a thing for proverb-like quotes and just deep reflective words and poems and stuff. Plus, my grandparents are vast sources of pure knowledge. That down home, cut-you-to-the-quick type stuff and I just love it."

"Cool. Cool."

"So what is this?" He touched her book.

"It's one by an author named Godfather called *'Everything She Should Know: what Daddy never told you and Mama never knew.'* It's a self-help kinda advisory book, just about how a woman should handle things from how to dress, how to handle money, catch the man you want, raise kids, deal with all kinds of games and sexual situations. Like how to avoid rape, molestation, dealing with players, cheaters. Just a bunch of stuff."

"Um. Any good?"

"It's the bomb! It says every woman should have it by her 13$^{th}$ birthday or at least before she turns 50. I mean, there's no substitute for a girl being raised by a loving father, but other than that, she needs this." She pointed at the book. "Matter of fact, she might still need it. It says it's like the 48 laws of power for women."

"Sounds cool."

"Get it."

"But for who?"

"Any female you care about."

"My mama?"

"She'll love it."

"Okay, so besides promoting books…"

"Okay. I know, my bad."

"So who Sugar Shaned your eye?"

"Who did what?"

"Sugar Shane Mosley. The boxer."

"Oh, naw, uh-uh." She touched it. "It ain't even all like that. It was just an accident."

A police car raced by with its sirens blaring.

"I saw you at the church yesterday."

"Oh, you did?"

"That was him?" Mark asked. "The guy you were with?"

Her voice fell. She looked down for some fries. "Yeah."

"Surprised they didn't mention you."

"For what?"

"Well, it was kinda your situation that got Preacher started."

"Oh, yeah, huh?" She asked. "You know him?"

"Yeah. Been knowing Preach and a couple of those other guys for years."

"What guys."

"The ones you and your boy were sitting with."

"Oh."

"But don't worry." Mark smiled. "I won't tell on you."

"I ain't worried about... Tell what?" She smiled. "What you gon' tell?"

"I'ma tell how you fell in love with me and tried to sweep me off my feet."

"'Yeah, whatever."

"Tell how you lured me into your car and offered me some candy." He pointed to the Now and Later pack she'd given him earlier. "And told me I better behave."

"Yeah, I said you better behave 'cause I ain't want your ass to try nothing."

"I'ma tell how you shared a plate with me—"

"It was too much!"

"And how you stole my heart with just your laugh," he said seriously. "Punctured my soul with your touch." He touched her eye and cupped her face as she melted in his hands. "And made me believe in magic, first love, and fairy tales simply," He leaned in, "with your," moved closer, "kiss."

It was a soft, hesitant, emotional kiss. Shocking. Breath-taking. Heart pounding, forbidden. Sweet.

"Why do you like me?" she asked once the kiss had broken.

"I don't know, Jaquanna. For me it's like asking why do birds fly or why does the sun rise only to fall and rise again. I mean, it's nothing that you did or didn't do, nothing that you said and no one moment that defines it. If you believe in love at first sight, I guess that's what it is."

"Love ? Seriously?" She looked him in the eyes. "Is that even possible?"

"I don't know what's possible, Quanna, I just know that when I look at you my heart floats. When I hear your voice or see your smile I feel like I'm witnessing perfection: like you were created with just the perfect bit of beauty with an added sense of flaw. Strong yet vulnerable; sweet but deadly; young but knowing; you're timeless to me. Like a Now and Later," he pointed at the package of sweet candy. "You're the kinda girl I could've loved in 1950 as well as 2020. You're her; you're that chick. Your beauty isn't a beauty of the day, like a fad or a fashion; it's a timeless beauty because your beauty is in the way that you carry yourself, the way that you do without trying and speak without saying. You're the kinda girl my granddaddy married and the kinda girl I can only hope to one day have. I mean, okay, here's this." He paused as if searching his mind for the right words. "You're the kinda girl when you walk into a room everybody looks and don't know why, but they see her. You're her."

"Damn, you sure know all the right things to say."

"You inspire me."

"Do I?" She blushed. "Humph."

The clapping pound of the black and white copter raced overhead. They heard more sirens approaching.

"What the hell?" They looked as two more units shot by.

It was the background of their lives. Another felony in progress. Another cage awaits. It was like a military operation the way they zoomed in and captured their prey. It was the norm here. It barely garnered any attention. It was like living in a war zone. Sooner or later, you just got used to constant helicopters and sirens. And you simply went about as if they weren't even there. To imagine, there were actually places where this wasn't the truth. Kinda odd when you think about it, because there were only very few places where such chaos was the norm. But when you grew here, then all you knew was here and here became your norm. In the war zone, under constant siege. Like a kid out playing kickball in Iraq.

"L.A. at its finest." Mark shook his head.

While a movie or video could highlight the drama and sell it to entertain the masses, it could never capture the pain and anguish of the many who felt trapped here without option or escape. In the war zone, there was constant battle; collateral damage; wounded souls; innocent victims and victims made of innocence.

"Something must've happened," she said.

"What happened to you?"

"What you mean?"

"The unthinkable," he said, "what happens when the unthinkable happens?"

"I don't know what you mean."

"Maybe I shouldn't?" He could tell she was uncomfortable. Maybe he'd gone too far. "Don't wanna talk about it?"

"I mean what's to talk about?" She hitched her shoulders. "I mean…"

"Why'd you kill him?"

"I hated that man. He used to just do like every fucking thing to us. He tortured us. He was nasty. He was sloppy. He was disrespectful. He was just like a monster that use to just sit up and burp and fart loud as he could, and then eat like a broken jaw cow or something. Urgh! I hated him."

Mark chuckled at the thought. Typical. Arrogant. Selfish. Male.

"And then he used to just beat on my mama like he owned her or something. Like she was born to serve him and keep him happy, and if he whatn't happy, then it was okay to just beat her like a fucking dog."

"And that night?"

There was a long pause. He wasn't sure she'd continue. There was a gentle breeze. The temperature shifted.

"He went too far."

Mark nodded. He could read the rest.

"He made our lives miserable. His mama shoulda killed him years ago." Her eyes grew distant. She was in another place, another time. "That kinda man don't deserve to breathe."

"Regret it?"

"Nope."

"So you were at peace doing the four years?"

"I shouldn'tna done no time. I did the world a favor." And she looked him right in his eyes.

He nodded. "Can I kiss you again?" But he knew the moment was lost.

"I don't know. I don't think I should do that."

"'It is not for outward show that the soul is to play its part, but for ourselves within, where no eyes can pierce but our own': Michel de Montaigne. Just another one I stole from somewhere. I don't even recall."

"And what it mean?"

"I don't know really. Just," he looked at her, "follow your heart."

She nodded thoughtfully.

"Where ever it leads you. Because the quiet voice is the loudest voice, or at least it should be. But sometimes it's drowned out till its words become silenced."

# Chapter 18

As he walked into the place, he stopped and stared. His entire aura spoke of confidence and money. As he stood in the doorway looking around, allowing his presence to dominate. His emotionless face demanded notice. Kirk Jr. had now entered the building.

They had arrived in a three car caravan; all three cars were low key. The people at the Cadillac dealership were clearly nervous and unsure about the meaning for the presence of the entourage. There were nine men and two women altogether.

There were two Escalades on the showroom floor, one blue, and one black. Kirk Jr. pointed. "I need both of those fully loaded," he told the now wide-eyed white man.

"Oh, well…" He had a red face and a huge palm. He was a big, beefy, burly man with soft hands and a gentle touch. Kirk Jr. thought he'd probably have been more the image of a line-backer, but, surprisingly, he wore a suit well, and it was a nice expensive suit. "I'm John." The strong simple name fit him and so did the strong handshake. "I can help you with that." He handed Kirk Jr. his card.

The crew was over at the trucks. Doors open, climbing in and out like they already owned the damn things. All of the people at the dealership had come out of their offices to take in the scene. Even the manager came out to see what all the fuss was about.

"Excuse me." The manager came over. He removed the glasses he'd had balanced on the tip of his slightly sun burned red nose. "May I help you?"

"Yeah, I just told John I want both of those…" He pointed to the two shining hunks, which dominated the showroom floor. "…fully loaded." Beside him, Poo-Poo chewed her gum like a true ghetto Diva. Popped it, chewed with an open mouth, and smiled. She was Gucci'd down from head to toe, stiletto heels and a big Gucci purse.

"Ah, yeah. Well."

"And I'll be taking those with me today."

"Well, I guess you most certainly will," said the manager, though not seeming to totally believe. "Just get with John here and he'll take you through the paperwork and we'll go from there. Ah, may I ask you what type of work you do, Mr. Ah? I didn't catch your name."

"Blackman." He shook the manager's hand. "I'm an investment broker."

"Investment broker? Oh, well, those are some nice vehicles and pretty expensive but nice."

"I'm sure I'll enjoy them, but, look; I don't have a lot of time, so I'ma leave Patricia here to handle this."

John and the manager nodded.

"And, ah…" The manager looked back and forth at them even more unsure. "Just how will you be making this purchase today?"

"Oh," Poo-Poo popped a bubble and said in her sweetest voice, "we'll be doing that in cash."

"Cash?" The blood drained from the manager's face. "Do you have any idea…"

She took off her shades and shook her head, stared him straight in the eyes and said, "It don't matter." She strutted and they followed as she slung the Gucci bag up over her shoulder and beckoned.

As Kirk Jr. turned and walked away, he waved for his crew to follow him. Next, they went and bought two jet skis and a small speedboat. He then went and got his whole crew fitted and bought Big Boy and two other new recruits the platinum and diamond chain and the pinky ring all of the full recruits wore.

"You doing your shit, my nigga." Coo-Coo hugged the man. "How much all that shit cost you?"

Kirk Jr. shrugged.

"Damn, like that?"

"I was always taught, if I had to ask, then I couldn't afford it, and if I had to count it, then I ain't made it."

"Yeah, well, you done made it, my nigga."

"We all have, my boy." K.J. hugged him again. "We built this together."

"Backs to the wall…" said Coo-Coo as he threw up the W with a proud smile.

"…we shall not fall…" Kirk replied.

"… balls in the street…"

"…cause we bang Wall Street, baby."

"You better know it."

"Live with them and die with them, my balls is all I got," Kirk Jr. declared.

"And it's all a real nigga need."

"True dat."

"Yeah," Coo-Coo added, "cause you know we up in this shit with two boots and a broom: stomping hard and sweeping shit."

"Ain't that what it is?"

"Real business, my boy."

# Chapter 19

*The people are always impressed by the superficial*
*appearance of things.*
*The [Prince] should, at fitting times of the year,*
*keep the people occupied and distracted*
*with festivities and spectacles.*
**-Niccolo Machiavelli 1469-1527**

*Tuesday, July 4th*

"Blood on the ground. Blood on the ground. Looking like a fool with your blood on the ground; gat turned sideways; blunt in your mouth," Preacher yelled out over the crowd. He was thinking of the message the older brother, who sang 'Pants on the ground' on American Idol, intended. The words caught on but the dress-style stuck. He wondered what he could say to this crowd here today that might stick. Something that they might actually carry in their hearts and feel encouraged to share with others. "Blood on the ground. Blood on the ground. Looking like a fool with your blood on the ground; Gat turned sideways; blunt in your mouth…"

They were up at the lake and having fun. The barbeque pits were burning and the crowd was growing. It was a party on wheels, and boss players in the game from all over L.A. had been invited. This was Kirk Jr.'s show, but Big Dick and his boys were on point too. It was a regular who's who of the Los Angeles underworld and everybody with a mama was tryna be seen, as they all brought out their finest rides, their finest women, and their brightest mid-summer bling and relaxed while setting out to shine in the burning sun. There were speedboats and jet skis galore and a rainbow of honeys strutting their thang. Bow legged, pigeon toed, light, and dark, short, tall, chunky, thick, or skinny. Even had them young, old and in between. Kirk Jr. was the talk of the gathering, with his new trucks and toys. And, as a boss should, he was enjoying his moment. It was about then that

Coo-Coo pulled up and all eyes turned with a different kind of focus.

"Fuck's up with this nigga?" Leon's eyes were spitting deadly darts at Coo-Coo. Beside him, he could sense Kirk Jr.'s growing heat. As Kirk took in the scene, he had to consciously catch himself and slow his breathing. He glanced over at Big Dick and saw that he was watching him too. Kirk Jr. had been put on blast and he knew it.

"What's this nigga fucking dense or something?" Leon was amazed as he watched Coo-Coo pull up in the brand new H3 Hummer. It was fire engine red with creamy-soft peanut butter interior and bright chrome-dipped every damn thing. Stuck up on some 30 inch Ashanti Stilts, with red alligator mags with chrome lips and run-flat tires. And if that wasn't enough, the icy package was topped off with a matching red, peanut butter and chrome speedboat and twin Ashanti's on the rack, and Jaquanna was sitting right next to him.

The old school cut 'If I Ruled the World' by NAS was blaring loudly over the monstrous system, as a load of fly females slithered from the back. The nigga was kicking in teeth and stomping the mud with both boots. As he approached, he had a blunt, a drink, and a smile. Imagine that.

~ ~

"Blood on the ground. Blood on the ground. Looking like a fool with your blood on the ground; gat turned sideways, blunt in your mouth." Preacher spoke louder to try to maintain the focus. "There's a difference. I said…there is a difference between criticism and constructive criticism. See, criticism, that's that stuff we call hatred. Just knocking somebody just to be knocking them. Sitting there refusing to give them their props, even though you know in your heart that they've earned it. That's just criticism. That's hatred. That's bull. Everybody wanna be a damn critic. Well, you got to earn the right to be a critic, either by what you done or what you qualified to do.

'The Album sucks.' 'The book was no good.' See, that's the job of a critic. But he's paid to give a non-biased opinion. That's what a critic does, but he has to be qualified before he can do it. 'The album sucks'; or 'the book was no good, I give it three stars.' See, all that means something if you're reading a newspaper or magazine where they review the types of materials you like. Especially, once you've come to know the critic and agreed with his opinions in the past. Because, see, this way it keeps you from going out to waste your money on the poor material. You see, the critic as it were serves a helpful purpose for the consumer. But on a general basis, if I share a song with you and you tell me it's no good, but when I ask you why or what led you to that conclusion and you can't tell me, well, then you ain't doing me no good. You just a hater, you got a foul taste about what I've shared and you cain't even tell me why. You ain't qualified to be no critic and your opinion ain't worth a damn. Cause if it don't better me then all it does is leave me right where I was before I approached you. I got a bugga in my nose and you cain't even tell me where it's at. That's worse than an ole country music critic tryna tell me which rap album is good and which one ain't."

Scattered laughter erupted. Most of them had been at the church and they remembered what he'd said about a bugga in the nose and how a 'yes man' left you vulnerable and exposed.

"But see," Preach went on, "constructive criticism is a whole nother something." He smiled and nodded. "Constructive criticism is a beautiful thing. Constructive criticism is about construction. It's about construction and building." He paused as he nodded to Mark in the crowd. "It's about building through helpful suggestion. And let me show you what I mean. I'm a show you what I mean. Remember that guy talking about 'the album sucks'? Remember him? Remember I said he's a hater? Well see, here's the difference. When giving constructive criticism it's about not only what you did wrong per se, but also how to get it right."

"That's what's what," someone said.

"So with constructive criticism, I must also offer you an informed opinion. Offer you a solution, if possible, even. I can't just say to you 'the album sucks' or 'I don't know, dawg, I just ain't feeling it'. Naw, ain't nothing constructive about that. See, with constructive criticism I must also offer advice on how to improve, or at least where I believe the improvement should be, if I may not know exactly how." He raised a finger. "For instance, I could say to you, 'Yeah, my boy, the first verse, and second verse caught me, but then the third verse was a little weak.' Or I could say, 'the beat really just didn't grip me, you may wanna try a different tempo. Or I may even say, 'I can't really tell what it was but it never grabbed my attention. The beats were cool but they don't fit the lyrics; maybe you could try something a bit more up tempo'. See," he raised his finger again, "that's constructive because I added my two cents not just towards critiquing it but also towards possible improvements to it. We're building together."

Preach looked around at the crowd of faces.

"Blood on the ground. Blood on the ground. Looking like a fool with your blood on the ground..." He looked around. "You hear that? Did you hear it? There's a message in there y'all and I ain't talking no criticism either. 'Cause see, I'm from where you from. I breathe where you breathe. I see what you see and I know what you know: we tired y'all. All of us. Each and every one of us is tired. We tired of living a lie for a hood that don't honor us and don't love us. Giving our all to a turf that just turns its backs on us and forgets about us once we've given our all and we end up dead or in prison. We tired. We tired. But somehow, we have not acted on our exhaustion. Why not? Why not? Why the hell have we not said enough is enough? I'm tired? Sure, we get our money, and we have our cliques within our cliques for that purpose. And sure, the hood helps us to define who we know, who we're linked with, who has our back— supposedly—, and where we grew up—usually. But tell me this: why are we still recruiting kids? Why are we still passing out our nicknames and why are we helping to further a deadly situation, which is killing our own? Why?

'"Or maybe we're not tired. Maybe I got it all wrong. I mean, really, who am I? Who am I to say we're tired? Maybe I need to watch my mouth. Maybe I need to tuck my tail and sit back and not say anything. But I ain't no yes man and I walk not in fear. I speak what my spirit holds true and damn it I'm tired! All across this damn country our young sons are dying and being locked up on the new plantation in droves and no one's saying anything. We throw our hands up and we recruit the next of somebody's son. Sell him guns and drugs then promote the ghetto dream in movies, books, and videos. Make him think that's gon' be his truth, when we all know the real truth is that most of them is gon' end up in a prison cell or leaking with their blood on the ground and their mama sitting there rocking back and forth on some pew crying while. Hopefully, if she's lucky, a few of his so-called homies may come over and pat her hand and say they're sorry. I'm tired y'all! I'm tired of watching our youth self-destruct, following in the footsteps of the rest of our people who have fallen victim to the trap of the great elusive ghetto dream. So when does it stop? How does it stop? When are we done recruiting? All across the land, in every ghetto, we see the same trap set for self-destruction; they give us guns and drugs then watch us kill and slang, till we end up dead or in a cage. I'm tired."

The women were nodding with real enthusiasm but the men were naturally more reserved. One had to be careful about appearing too weak or seeming to go against that to which he was supposed to have vowed for life, regardless if the hood or homies betrayed you, abandoned you, or let you down. You, in turn, were never to appear to have betrayed, abandoned, or let down the hood. Preacher understood the politics of the entire situation, but he also knew that he was in the presence of some real wise top notch street bosses who could make a difference within their hoods if they so decided. The first measure was to simply put it out there; plant the seeds for change. And, hopefully, a few would nurture the concept and water it. Stemming the flow of new recruits would lay new hope for future generations of young Black kids. It could, in fact, render gang banging and street hustling to old folks' tales similar to the old tales of racial segregation. It had to start somewhere.

"Today is the 4th of July and we're here." He pointed at the grass. "We here to celebrate. But when are we gon' liberate ourselves?" He paused. "If we not gon' celebrate setting ourselves free from death and destruction, what the hell are we celebrating? Huh? Man, I tell you, we got a bugga in our nose y'all and we got blood on the ground."

Blood on the ground. Blood on the ground. We looking like fools with our blood on the ground.

~ ~ ~

Mark watched her as she climbed from the shiny SUV. And, in his mind, he wondered just what it was that was so special about her. It wasn't just her beauty. He saw beautiful women every day. So, no, it wasn't that. Hell, there were even more beautiful women at the park, let alone the ones he met at school, or those juicy young things he ran into down in Mississippi. No, it wasn't just her beauty or her body. It wasn't even like she challenged him all that much mentally. But still.

Jaquanna was wearing a red two-piece leather short pants outfit and some stylish red slip-on sandals with the back out. Big red stunna shades with gold accents. She had gold tipped red toes and claws. Her hair was freshly whipped. And her sashay had the stalkers staring.

Mark saw Kirk Jr. fix on her with a stony stare. Jaquanna had not gone over to him but, instead, had stopped over to holla at her girls.

Coo-Coo had gone and stood right beside Kirk Jr., but after a brief pound in acknowledgement, the men didn't look to have said much to each other.

As Preacher wrapped it up, Mark typed and sent Jaquanna  text. It read:

No matter the distance
Of time nor space, I
Find myself feeling u,
Wantg u, needg u. My heart
Still holds u both
Now AND later
IGN

Mark looked at her face from his distant post and smiled as he watched her reach for her phone. She looked over at him and smiled. He felt like the kid who had sent the 'I like you' note in class. Those notes had gone high tech. He saw her typing a reply and he held his phone in his hand, eagerly awaiting her reply. He was happy just knowing that in this moment, at that very instant. She. Jaquanna. Her. That girl was thinking of and about only him! He felt both honored and confused. I mean, he looked again. Just what was it about this girl?

She'd finished typing. Sent it. Looked up and smiled.

He waited. With his phone in his hand. He waited. He looked up at her again. She glanced and shrugged. He waited. He was anxious but patient as he waited. He shook his phone now, beginning to wonder if the damn message had maybe gotten caught up on the satellite. Like the satellite had hooks on it or some shit. He hit a button, hoping to jar the message loose from the texting gods. He wondered about his service. He looked up at her. She shrugged. And he not so patiently waited. But it would come. He just had to wait, that's all. He wondered what she'd said.

~ ~ ~

"Nigga, I'm finna go big, nigga," Big Boy said. "Watch."

"Nigga, I'm finna get my chicken-scratch-ula on," exclaimed Chicken-shit. "I'ma have Boo-Coo crazy racks and some mo' shit."

The boys were both shining like fresh cut diamonds. They were the two newest members of the Wall Street Boys and they'd each received their chains and rings from Kirk Jr. just that morning. Within the crowd of the 50 or so youngsters at the function, they were the budding young fireworks; the Hood stars, the would-be-when's: they had next and everyone around them knew it. The young and the old alike.

These budding young tycoons understood very early on that age meant nothing in the streets. Sure age and/or wisdom had its place, but nothing, absolutely nothing, outranked success. Success was the ultimate status. Money was power. Money bought and paid for rank and status. With money and status you could put your O.G. to work for you, or if you didn't like or respect him you could pay to have his ass stomped and run out of the Hood.

Money was God in the streets. With money, you didn't have to chase some girl. The girls chased you. With money, you could fuck not just some girl but sometimes you could fuck a dime-piece, her sister, her cousin, her aunt, and sometimes even her mama. Money was like that. It had its own rules, its own boundaries, its own language, and its own key to the goddamn world. And these two budding young bosses knew it. As did every ole ass kissing muthafucka around them. Boss: Bring on the Sun Shine! Getting it!

"Yeah, a nigga gotta get it how he lives and that's real," Big Boy insisted, "on everything. I ain't missing it, nigga, I'm getting it."

"That's what's real, my nigga." Chicken-shit held out his fist. "Pound that shit, nigga."

Big Boy was sipping and blazing purple clouds and so was Chicken-shit. He gave his boy a pound. "On Wall Street, boy, watch."

"Ooh, look. Look." Chicken-shit pointed. "There go your girl."

"Who?" Big Boy turned and saw Poo-Poo pushing past with some other girls. He'd told his boy about how he'd smashed that. "Ah, nigga, you wrong, nigga."

"Was it good though? Shit. 'Cause that shit be looking straight right." Chicken-shit sipped and stared as her apple bottom jeans had that ass locked up like an old Chevy. "I'll beat that old bitch guts out her back."

They laughed. And a couple of the nearby youngsters who heard them joined in too.

"Yeah." Big Boy licked his lips. "All I'ma say is this, nigga."

"What's that?"

"That shit is like the crust of a sweet peach cobbler…"

"Ooh."

"Yeah, and when I opened that shit up, all I was wondering, was would she go better with a scoop of ice cream."

"Man double dip that shit!" Chicken-shit was also only fourteen and the twenty-four year old vixen had his shit running on overdrive. He liked the old girls. The young ones were too much with the bullshit and games.

"All I can say is this, my nigga. She made a boy love pussy for life."

"Man. I know that's right." One of the other young Homies gave him Dap. "Ain't nothing like some good pussy."

"That's real!" Someone else declared.

"Break a bitch back!" added another.

They all knew that most of them were lying and hadn't had any yet. But what young boy would admit that when he was with the guys?

"I'd be having her ass bent over a pillow and just be digging that shit."

"Man, I'd have her get on top; that way she can teach me some shit."

"I just want her to suck these young nuts."

"Damn, I bet that pussy good."

"Nigga, I just wanna hung-gun that old bitch and have her bent over begging."

And so, for the moment at least, Poo-Poo Pat was the mental pin-up at the party. But young boys are pretty easily swayed and as the wind blows so would their desires.

"Damn," someone from the stalker gallery said, "look at this bitch! Now that's hot!"

The new object of the moment was a younger girl. About fifteen or so and on some Boss Bitch Kim type shit. She was short, real short for her age, maybe five feet even, and this gave them confidence. At least she was their height. But she had her uber Diva Wendy Williams thing popping too, and that intimidated most of them. You could tell just by how she was dressed in all the extras with the big purse, iPhone, jewels, pampered toes, and nails etc. You could tell that she or someone she knew had some money. Probably her dude or one of her family members, but the only way to know was to get at her ass.

"How you think I should pop at her?" Chicken-shit asked Big Boy.

"You finna get at that?"

"Hell yeah." He checked himself over nervously. "What you think I should say?"

"Shit, nigga, I don't know."

"Let me see your knot."

"What. Fool! Where yours at?"

"I left my shit at home," Chicken-shit said. "Let me see yours. I'm just gon' flash it. I'll give it back."

"Man. Here." Big Boy handed him a wad of bills. "That's four racks and I want all my shit back too."

"Nigga, you gon' get this little ole shit." He rolled the bills into a huge wad with the big face hundreds to the outside, and then wrapped a rubber band around it. "Watch this, nigga, I'm finna knock baby's little fine ass."

"Handle that shit then, Young Boss."

'"What you think I oughta say though?"

"Shit, I don't know."

"Come on, give me something."

"Alright." Big Boy thought. "Here, tell her you like her nails."

"Her nails? Come on, my nigga. That's kinda slow. I don't need no yellow-bus type game."

"Alright. Tell her you like her smile or she just make you think naughty thoughts inside your Christian mind."

A few of the guys laughed.

"Come on, my Dude, fa real." Chicken-shit tapped his chest. "That's how you gon' send your kid?"

"Alright, her hair." They looked over and admired her long luscious tresses. "Women be liking when a nigga like notice they little hair and shit. Cause they spend hours tryna whip that shit."

"Alright. Fuck it." Chicken-shit popped his collar and slipped up on the young cutie. She was posted in the middle of talking to another girl. Big Boy and another guy trailed over.

"Ah, say, ah, you got a minute?" Chicken-shit smiled his best smile as he nodded at her.

"Me?" She held her shoulder and raised a brow.

"Yeah, I'm tryna holla."

"Bout what?" She frowned.

"Well, I was kinda like checking you out, and, like, I don't know. I just wanted to like, you know, say I like your hair and shit."

"Thanks." She grabbed it. Shot a phony smile. "It's fake." She rolled her eyes and took a breath. Like lame-o.

"Okay, your nails," he rushed on. "Them muthafuckas cool too."

She held them up. "Fake." And rolled her eyes.

"Well, you got a pretty smile."

"Invisible braces, see?" She opened her mouth to show him.

"Okay, fuck all that. You got a nice ass, a bomb nest and that Gucci bag is tight."

"Fake, fake, and knock off."

"Aw, well, bitch, you need to knock it off with all that ole fake-ass shit then."

She laughed and the whole little pack erupted.

"Looking like a fake ass Lil Kim wanna be. Bitch, if you don't knock it off. And give Jennifer Hudson her booty back 'cause she need that shit."

"Aw, you wrong." She was laughing. "That's my girl."

"Yeah, my bad, Jenny got it good with me too. She just need to eat and quit starving her damn self. "

"Okay," the little cutie said. "You got me. So what's your name?"

"Baby, I'm Chicken-shit."

"Wait." Both girls laughed. "You're who?"

"I'm Chicken-shit, precious. Know it and record it." He popped the collar on his white wife beater, skinny muscles on full display. "The Young Boss."

"Pa-lease, boy." She cocked her chin and gripped a hip. "What kinda name is Chicken-shit?"

"It's young Hoodlan."

"Wait, it's young what-ian?"

"Young Hood language, Mama."

"Oh, well, I must be from a different kinda hood, 'cause I ain't never heard no shit like that."

"See." He smiled proudly.

"See what?" She rolled her eyes and bent a brow, confused.

"You already learning something from a young boss."

"Negro, please."

"Here." He reached in his pocket and pulled out the huge rubber-band-wrapped knot. The girls exchanged knowing smirks. "Here," he repeated as he pulled his phone out from beneath the wad.

"Oh, you just had to floss all that, huh?"

"Naw, baby, I was tryna get you this." He extended his phone to her.

"What the hell I need this for?"

"Go on type in your math, so I can see what you add up to later."

"Boy. Here." She typed in a zero and handed it back.

"What the—Oh, so you's a zero?"

"Aw fa'get you!"

"Well, that's what you say your math added up to."

"Here, gimme yours." She held her thumbs ready on her phone.

"You gon' call?" He read her off the number.

"I don't know, maybe. 'Pend on how bored I get."

"Damn, like that?"

"Why they call you Chicken-shit?"

"My mama really kinda like gave me that name."

"Yo mama?"

"Yep. I was out with the Homies and she came and chased my ass home with a belt, and I was running and hiding around bushes and cars and all kinda of shit. So she gon' yell out 'Nigga, you better brang yo' little chicken-shit ass here' and, well, you know how Homies do, they ain't never let me live that shit down. Every day they'd be on a nigga's head talkin 'bout 'brang yo little chicken-shit ass here' till, finally, it kinda like just stuck."

"That's crazy."

"Yeah, but," He shrugged, "it's different."

"Yeah, it is that."

"So what's your name, you ain't told me."

She chuckled a bit. "Kim."

"Aw, hell naw, you bullshitting?" He laughed at the irony.

"Nope. That's what my mama named me."

"Oh, so you gon' be my little Kim?"

"Boy." She blushed and smiled like the dime piece she was.

"I'll even get you a real Gucci."

"Shit, I know that's right." She rolled her eyes. "With all that money you better."

"When you call me, we'll talk about it."
And, what you know, her ass gon' press SEND?
Chicken-shit's phone rang. He answered it.
"Hello," she said.
"Man, you crazy."
"Let's talk about that purse though."
They all laughed.
"You know what I'm gon' get you that."
"Aw, look at the big boss," Big Boy laughed into his fist. "Handle that shit."

~ ~ ~

Mark was happy, as the long awaited text finally arrived. It read: IGN?
Reply: I got next
Jaquanna: Oh. LOL
He watched her as she talked with her friends. They were in the same park and at the same function, but they may as well have been worlds apart. He noticed that, for some reason, he didn't like her with all of the flossy bling bling garb. He much more preferred his simple Jaquanna. The girl he'd met all those zillions of years ago. Not that he was knocking, just noticing.
"What up, M 'n' M?" Preach extended a hand, which went to a grip and a pull: ghetto hug, thug embrace style. "How's my kid?"
"I'm good, man, I'm good."
"That's what's right."
"Nice piece you spoke on," Mark told him. "Kinda risky though, 'specially with the crowd."
"Yeah, well, that's just the thing see, 'cause it's all about social responsibility, and if I cain't speak on the ugly side of our truths, who will?"
"Yeah, true that."
"That's part of the reason the cancer—if you will— keeps seeping into our soil and spreading to more and more of your young. How can we be afraid to speak our truth? Who's gonna warn our kids?" Preach was thinking as he spoke. "Look at it this way, Mark. If we're at a point when the parents are afraid to, or feel they can't speak to, or reach the kids, and the older guys, the so-called O.G.s are afraid or feel they can't reach

them, and the only people who feel they can step to our young and get them to listen is some angry face with a gun and a badge. Then what are we saying? What are we accepting? What are we setting our kids up for? So, what if I wanna 'save' my kids then I need to go in and call some angry somebody with a badge and a gun to come in and teach and retrain or ship my kid off? Are we that helpless? Has it truly come to that?"

"Yeah, that does sound sad."

"We just can't be afraid of the life and the problem that we ourselves created. If I can't speak on it, then who can? Do I have to get an angry face, a badge, and a gun and then come back and say it? Do I have to watch my back because I'm sick of seeing our brothers, sisters, mothers, fathers, uncles and aunts trapped in prison or laid in the dirt with their blood on the ground?"

Mark nodded. A few others were gathering around. Preach was right in his element.

"I refuse to be afraid of Frankenstein. We made this damn monster. And I'm not gon' just run and hide from it. I will not fear the task my spirit gives and my spirit has placed it on my heart to say something, to plant a seed. See, we got this street thing all confused, the logic don't add up. How are we gon' sit here and bitch and cry about somebody calling 'dem folks' on us when it's only 'dem folks' we willing to listen to?"

The women really understood that one.

"Who else we s'pose to call when Lil Rakim goes on one? What, do we just let him do his shit and tear up some shit? What? Can't call his daddy. He ain't around or probably in jail or dead. Step-Dude at the house has no say-so or authority, his mama still wanna hug his little bad ass and tell him how cute he is and plead with his ass." He took a high-pitched voice. "Stop, Rakim, you stop that, that's not right. You better than that. Come on, please, baby, Mommy loves you." He waved that off and went back to his own voice. "Please! That shit there don't make no sense."

There was a scatter of laughter. The crowd grew.

"Rakim don't need nobody to hold his hand. Rakim need to sit his ass down and learn. But mostly Rakim and them are in a different world. Our world is sometimes like a jungle. Remember that old school cut: 'It's like a jungle, sometimes it makes me wonder how I keep from going under'. Yeah, well, check all that out. Have you ever seen when those big game hunters go zipping into Africa whooping and cheering as their jeep or Range Rover goes charging into the forest. Whoop-eee! Guns at the ready, nets in hand, copter swirling, they chase them a beast to the ends of the world just so they'll have a fond old story to tell about 'that time'."

"That's fucked up."

"But how can we be mad when we are too afraid to even speak to ourselves. I mean, just look at it. If Rakim decides to roar like a lion and everybody has to stand back for fear that, his holy mightiness may rip our head off, then what's the message? I mean, let's be real, people are scared out here. People are dying out here. Who can we call to try and get a handle on Rakim before the big game hunters get called in? Who?"

There were about 30 heads or so all gathered around. People wanted to listen and they wanted to learn. The situation just felt so helpless some times; to the point where most people who lived in and around it all were scared to death of saying anything about it or even trying to speak to the forces out there behind it. But that was Preacher's point exactly.

"I can't be afraid of my own damn people. I can't be afraid of the people that I love. I can't be afraid of the monster we created. I can't be afraid to speak my mind and offer my advice on how to do something about it. I can't," he insisted. "I can't be afraid and I won't. I will not! I refuse to. You know why? I'll tell you why. I won't be afraid; because if I should, in fact, die by the hands of my own; if I should take my last breath while trying to breathe my truth; if our own lions should turn on me and chase me away. At least I'll know that, in my heart, I gave all I had to give as a man. At least I'll know that I stood through my fears for the people I believed in. And, hopefully, they'll remember me too and maybe in that, find a change. Am I scared? No, I'm not scared. Am I nervous? Of course I am. Do I realize that the very people I am trying to stand up for and reach could very well, in fact, be the ones to kill me? Yes, I do. I do and that's just sad. It's a sure fact but it breaks my heart more than it worries me. But at the same time, we cannot cry, if we will not stand. We can't cry about Rakim getting shot or killed or Doo-Dog getting a million years in prison; a million years in the zoo, if we will not stand up and speak our piece."

"I know that's right."

"And when City Hall puts all of these commissions and special committees together and has all of these super-strategizers come in to form 'think tanks' about how to deal with gangs, drugs or local street cultures. We need to go down there, stand up in there, and let our voices be heard! Here they'll put together all of these master hunters and pay them millions of dollars a year to map out ideas about how to go into the jungle and calm the land. It never works, but, at least, by having some 'special study' or 'special report' with some blue ribbon commission, it justifies them taking our tax dollars out of our paychecks to hire these master hunters to come down from their suburban retreats, to come sit in some room and look over a map and come up with some half-cocked plan."

"Humph."

"And we'll pay them an average of $150,000 to $200,000 a year to do this for us, since we are just so incapable of doing for our own selves!"

"That's crazy."

"What's crazy is that we go for it! It's crazy that we sit there and pay these suit coat wearing suburban geniuses to come down and think for us, and then we sit up and cry about the conclusions they come up with. Hell, they don't care. They don't live in the Hood. Ain't no wild ass lions hanging out on their corners or stalking their children in the street. The bottom line is they don't know the answer and they really couldn't care less, because if they truly did come up with an answer, it would be putting themselves out of a sweet $150,000 to $200.000 a year job. And who wants to lose that?"

"Yeah, that's real."

"I mean, come on now, let's be real with this shit. Who wants to just shoot themselves in the foot?"

"Yeah, that's true."

"I bet if a mad man was running loose in the suburbs, they'd be all over it. Quick. Just like when gangs first started going out of town in the 80's. You figure gangs started spreading, what around '85 or '86? Shit, by November '88 they re-enacted the federal conspiracy laws—something that was originally designed to attack the Mafia and was sidelined by Congress in the 1920's as being too broad and invasive. But when gangs started spreading and the crack started popping up in the rural areas and suburbs, that was it. They were all over it. Feds moved in all over the country to try and control it. It was to become known worldwide as 'the War on Drugs'. America had, for the first time ever, declared a war against her own people. Oh, it was okay when we stayed in our own jungle and acted a fool in our own cage. Well then, it was just another happy day at the park and another nice juicy paycheck. But, low and behold, the walls of the zoo had failed to contain. All of the rampant influx of money had created the ability for the animals to travel. None of the pseudo-geniuses had thought about that, no one had anticipated the animals actually wanting to leave. That was a new one; something they hadn't even seen with the heroin trade. Instantly, troops were activated. Kill, contain, or capture! And the whole damn nation started building cages as fast as they could to try and stem the spread. Hell, it actually became known that an L.A. boy, Cali boy or some out of town local trying to gang bang was more likely to get strung up on federal charges, where they had their own three-strike thing going on based on any combination of drugs or violent related offenses. And they had these crazy outrageous mandatory minimum sentences, where almost anybody could get caught up. Hell, your own mama could be put in jail for conspiracy, if it could be proved that she knew, or reasonably should have known, that you owned a Benz and had no job, or that you handled large sums of cash and didn't pay taxes. Oh, and don't have a house or car in her name. It was a wrap; we all know the stories now."

Several heads nodded.

"Kill, capture, or contain. An invisible wall around the ghetto. Big game hunters, a war declared. And here I stand to speak and I have to be afraid? I have to be nervous? I have to watch my back? Hell, I ain't the enemy! How that make sense?"

There was a scatter of laughter and several nods.

"Naw, I ain't gon' fear what I hope to save. It is what it is," he said. "Now, on the issue about all those commissions and whatnots down at City Hall about what to do, when and how. I'll end with this; sometimes to get to it you've got to go through it. We are the professors of these streets. And just like going to a doctor: if you needed brain surgery, you wouldn't go to a heart surgeon, so why are we going to some college educated sociologist about what's going on in our hoods? Hell, he probably ain't never even drove through our damn hoods, so how he gon' tell us how to fix them? And tell us what the problems are? Now, that's crazy! With his cute little report with all of the percentages and colorful graphics. That's crazy! We ain't nothing but a job to him, some numbers in a graph. We need to demand that those commissions be broken up and disbanded and that a true commission of the people, for the people and by the people be formed where our own people; our true professionals, are paid to think for us. And then, maybe we'll get some answers."

Mark loved hearing Preach speak. He always took away something new to think about. Looking around he saw that Jaquanna had come over and was at the back of the loose crowd. She was turning away from him now. He watched. He thought. He stared. And then he glanced over at Kirk Jr.

"Hey, what that shit do, big Double M's?" Big Boy and Chicken-shit had come over to greet the budding young star and NBA hopeful.

"What's good big 'ems?"

"Shit. Shit. This my kid right here." He pointed. "Chicken-shit, the young boss."

"Hey."

"Hey, Chicken-shit. Cool name."

He smiled. "Well, you nahmean, your boy just tryna climb and be recognized you know?"

Mark knew what the rings on the young men's fingers stood for. "That's what's up."

~ ~ ~

"Aw, there she is." Jaquanna danced gayfully forward and hugged the woman she could not stand, and really couldn't give a shit about.

"No, there *she* is." They collided and even did the whole little air-kiss bit.

TanJeeka had been after Kirk Jr. for a cool little minute. Even before Jaquanna had come home, she'd heard about how the woman was always trying to squeeze up in his face. Though TanJeeka was two years older, and had been ahead of her at school, the two women had known each other for years and had never been able to truly stand each other. There was just always some backbiting riff between them.

"How you been, girl?" TanJeeka had the whole little pouty face I-need-to-know diva thing going on. "You been okay?" she sang.

"Yeah, girl, shit. Just doing it, you know?"

"And how is love and marriage? He didn't give you that eye, did he?" the tactless bitch couldn't wait to add. Ole poodle purse packing bitch always behind the times or mixed the fuck up in them. The kind of bitch that would rock some hot pink Spandex, some damn platform heels, and some other kinda crazy polka-dot or checker-board whoopty-doo-da, but, to her credit, she was just cute and stylish enough with the shit that she'd not only pull it off, sometimes she'd even start a damn trend, ole Wendy Williams wig wearing bitch.

"Aw, you mean this little ole thang!" Jaquanna raised her glasses.

"Oh!"

"No, just an accident."

"Well, it looks just very very very bad."

"Looks worse than it is; it's nothing."

"Well, I'll just have to go over and spank his little tail." TanJeeka pointed.

"Well you do that," Jaquanna told her. "And you tell him I said what's up."

"Oh, you guys didn't wake up together this morning?" Her face looked intrigued. You think Wendy Williams loved gossip. "Is everything okay?"

"Yeah, girl, we good. You know that's my Wigga-ma-Jigga."

"Umm. Well, I'll say. Well, I'll be sure to speak to your Wigga-ma-Jigga for you then."

"You do that, girl."

Fake hugs and kisses.

"I will." And then she wiggled her little van-glorious ass off and headed straight for Kirk Jr.

Jaquanna was steaming inside as she stared after the little temptress. She just knew TanJeeka would find some way to twist some shit. The girl had more spins than a Dr. Dre album and her little guts were probably just as famous. Wendy Williams would probably just shake her head. Jaquanna damn sure did.

Just then, a new text message came from Mark. Jaquanna looked up from her phone to see where he was. He was at the water's edge smiling. Her heart suddenly felt lighter. She smiled for no reason. Or for every reason actually. But then, well, I guess that all depends on perspective.

The text message read:

Don't worry Be happy

There was a big round yellow happy face and the words from an old Beatles song played:

Yesterday, all my troubles seemed so far away
Now it seems as though they're here to stay'
Oh, I believe in yesterday.

Jaquanna typed:

Aw, thank u
I needed that

She wondered if he'd sensed that the exchange between her and Jeeka had left her stressed.

| Mark: | Can he be burnt? |
|---|---|
| Jaquanna: | Wat? |
| Mark: | Burnt. Can he be burnt? |
| Jaquanna: | Wat u mean? |
| Mark: | Can I have you? |
| Jaquanna: | Who said I could be had? |
| Mark: | Who said u couldn't? |
| Jaquanna: | Maybe I did |
| Mark: | Well I'm glad u let him knw! Itz about time! |
| Jaquanna: | ROTFL |
| Mark: | I eva tell u I like ur smile? |

And, of course, this made her smile. She looked over and he laughed.

Jaquanna:     Thanx. Thanx 4 u.

Mark:         In Life therz winnerz,
              Loserz n waiterz; I'd
              Rather wait than Lose.

But sometimes waiting is losing, isn't it?

We wait so long; we lose a part of ourselves. Or we wait as others walk by. Choosing while we refuse to be chosen. Sitting there waiting. While losing hope and faith. All the while committed to the uncommitted. And, if we do love, we can only love with half a heart because we don't own a whole heart to give. Stolen. Our most precious jewel sits on a shelf somewhere. But no, that may not be true, because, sometimes love does come back: it wakes up and sees itself, and like the fine rays of a brilliant sun, there's no denying its light. And in those times, the old tales of love's troubles are merely stories for our kids: 'Oh I remember when I first met your mama'. Sounds so much better than 'She was the one who got away'. Or, worse yet, 'Bitches ain't shit'.

# Chapter 20

"Nigga, fuck that bitch. Nigga!" Kirk Jr. was on one. "Matter of fact fuck you and that bitch!"

"Aw, come on, dawg, it whatn't even like that." Coo-Coo shook his head with a melancholy expression. He was hoping to calm the man down.

"Nigga, I don't care how it was, nigga, you outta line. And that bitch outta pocket too."

"But come on. How you figure some shit like that, my nigga?"

They had pulled off to the side. It was just the 'inside dime' bunch, but with all of Kirk Jr.'s animated antics and posturing, others throughout the park were beginning to turn a curious focus in their direction. Coo-Coo knew that the more of a show and crowd this drew then the more potentially out of hand it could become.

"What the fuck you mean how I figure some shit like that?" Kirk Jr. was in the middle of the loose circle they had formed beneath a large shade tree. Coo-Coo had his back to the tree. "Nigga, how you figure?"

"Kirk, it whatn't even like that, my dude. It—"

"I ain't yo muthafuckin' dude."

"Aw, like that?"

"If I was your dude," K. J. told him, "nigga, you wouldn'tna pulled that bitch-ass shit."

"Damn, that's how you getting it? That's how you get at your kid?"

"Man! Ssswoo! Man!" He was pacing back and forth with his hands on his hips and shaking his head as he bit his lip. Just this side of ugly.

"Kirk, man, calm down, homie. A nigga ain't meant you no dis."

Leon stepped out and looked crossways at Coo-Coo. Leon was taller, wider, the better fighter. Coo-Coo was a proven killer.

"Plus, you know you ain't s'pose to shit where you shine at, my nigga," Leon told Coo-Coo. "That, plus you pushing with a nigga's bitch? Come on, dawg."

"Aw, man, y'all seriously on some shit, man." Coo-Coo looked around and noticed that a couple of heads actually nodded as if they agreed with the duo's logic. Others said nothing. They would take the position of self-preservation and simply not add an opinion or step in in any way. Their position was silence.

No matter what, Coo-Coo knew he was on his own. He also knew that Kirk Jr. would automatically be given full support. When you sat on the top, you could do no wrong. Who was there to question you?

Money. Power. Respect. Money brings power; power brings the money. And who don't respect the power of a dollar? Almighty.

Coo-Coo had always been a lone wolf within the folds. Sure, he had ambitions and, of course, he was proud of his rise and shine. But he'd never meant to cross Kirk Jr. Never. Kirk Jr. was the one who'd helped to make him. Why would he try and cross him? He just wasn't getting the reasoning.

"Naw, nigga, yo' ass on some shit." Kirk Jr. was right up on the shorter man and breathing down on him. "If I wanted you to bring the bitch I woulda asked you to bring the bitch. That bitch got a car. Shit."

"Well, my bad, dawg. On the real, homie, I just peeped her about to push off, and I figured we was headed to the same spot, so I said fuck it and asked her if she wanted to push—"

"And then you bounce up just flossing all on a nigga and shit. And my bitch jumping up out yo' cage, like y'all just finished swinging from a tree somewhere. Naw, my nigga." Kirk Jr. shook his head. "That shit whatn't even cool."

"Come on, now, Kirk." He smiled. "Everybody already know you's a boss. Nigga, my pockets ain't nowhere near as deep as yo shit—"

"That ain't the point though," Leon said. "Why you had to bust out today?"

"Specially when you knew I was coming hard and about to get my gleam on—"

"Kirk, my nigga, look at that truck, man, look at my shit. I been had that shit in the shop. I ain't just went out and—"

"Well, why you ain't said nothing?" asked K.J. "You coulda put me up on it and let me know off top."

"It was a surprise! You know niggas be tryna get they gleam on for the summer—"

"But, come on, nigga."

"I figured you'd be proud to see one of your inside niggas shining. I ain't try to come with no shenanigans, dawg, I came up in here thinking you was gon' be proud as hell."

"You getting too big headed, nigga." He turned away. "Don't try ta turn this shit around."

"Man, how you gon'—"

"Cause I said so." He was back in his face.

"Man, go on with all that shit."

"Or what, nigga?" He had his finger in his face now. "Huh? What?"

Leon grabbed Kirk Jr.'s arm. "Come on, man. Niggas is really starting to like look and shit. You even got Big Dick and them at the domino table looking up over here."

"Man, fuck this nigga." Kirk Jr. shrugged Leon off.

"Man, go on with all that, Kirk." Coo-Coo gripped the glass in his hand with a tighter grip. His blunt was down to a nub. He tossed it. "I told you—"

"Told me what, huh?" Kirk Jr. bit his lip. "Told me what, nigga?"

"Let it go." Leon tried again. "We don't need—"

*Bam!* K.J. clocked Coo-Coo upside the head with a hard right hook.

The glass fell. Coo-Coo stumbled.

"Whoa. Whoa. Whoa." Leon jumped between them.

Someone else was helping Coo-Coo to regain his balance.

"What the fuck, nigga?" Coo-Coo gripped his left temple. His pride was wounded more than his flesh.

"You got me fucked up," Kirk Jr. told him.

"Oh, that's how you getting it? That's how you feel?"

"What, fool?" He tried to push around Leon. "You want it, nigga?"

Leon was doing his best to keep the men separated. Mostly everyone in the park was tuned in now. Big Dick got up and headed over.

Coo-Coo was hot but he knew he had to be careful. He had no win under the circumstances. He had no crew. His boys were all Kirk Jr.'s boys. He felt vulnerable. He felt defenseless. He'd have put his life on the line for, or in place of Kirk Jr. He was hurt to learn that Kirk Jr. could turn on him so easily. He felt totally betrayed.

"Leave that shit alone," Leon said to K.J. "This ain't how we do it, my boy."

"Man, fuck this nigga with this oh Hoe-ass shit. He wanna play we can play," said Kirk. "*However* the nigga wanna do it."

"That a threat?" Coo-Coo was steaming. "That's how you coming?"

"Take it how you wanna."

Coo-Coo shook his head. "This ain't even cool, man. This ain't even it, dawg." He fought a tear from his eye. This was supposed to be a day of happiness and celebration. Instead, it had become a day of shame. It hurt Coo-Coo even more because he felt that Kirk Jr. was like a brother. How do you harm a man you love and admire? But then, how could Kirk Jr. harm him? And how was he to save face now? Bottom line was, with Kirk Jr. turning on him, the fact was Wall Street had turned on him. Kirk Jr. was Wall Street. Wall Street was Kirk Jr. Never again, Coo-Coo decided. Never again would he trust or feel so completely safe within the folds of Wall. But Wall was all he knew.

"However you want it, nigga, you can get it." Kirk Jr. was still jockeying around Leon. Big Dick was approaching.

"What's up over here?" he asked.

Coo-Coo knew that no matter what, Big Dick would take K.J.'s side. There was no way he'd be fair or impartial.

"Man, I'm gone." Coo-Coo backed away. "I'm cool on all this shit."

Big Dick stopped him. "Hold up," he said. "You welcome to stay, Coo. I don't know what y'all got popping but you welcome to stay. We family."

"I'm cool." He shook his head sadly then he threw up the W. "Backs to the wall, my nigga."

~ ~ ~

"Damn, what the hell was that all about?" Shamika was pushing Rosa over to where Jaquanna and a couple of other girls were standing.

"Hold up." Jaquanna stepped with a strong stride as she made way to cut Coo-Coo off. "Coo!" She cupped her mouth and yelled. "Coo?"

Coo-Coo stopped and turned to her as she approached. "What's good, Jah?"

"What was that?"

"Bull shit." He waved it off.

"It ain't had nothing to do with me, did it?"

"Aw, naw."

"Sure?"

"Just different ways of seeing some shit, that's all."

"Y'all good?"

"Yeah," he said. "We cool."

"You look a little down, Coo."

"Aw, yeah, you know. That shit kinda caught me like way left, nahmean? I mean, I don't know..."

"You leaving? You ain't leaving is you?"

"I thought about it, but naw I'm here. We came to have fun and that's what I'ma do. I'ma drop this boat and see what that shit do."

"Yeah, that's what's good."

"You might wanna holla at your dude though, nahmean?" He tapped his chest. "All love, Jah, me and you good. You already know that."

"Yeah." She pushed his shoulder.

He smiled. "But let me go drop this ship though."

As Jaquanna headed back towards Shamika and the girls, she noticed that Kirk Jr. was serving her with a stern stare and an ugly scowl, as if she were the bottom of his boot. TanJee-ka pushed up and hugged him. He gave a one-cheeked smile then looked back at Jaquanna. He knew she couldn't stand her.

Jaquanna rolled her eyes and waved him off.

"Where them hits at, girl?" Shamika was sipping on something strong. And whatever it was, it had both her and Rosa with the giggles, swaying like it whatn't no body's business.

"Put that shit in the air, right?"

"You bitches is a mess." Jaquanna smiled.

"Oh, and I seen your little stud over there too." Shamika tossed her head in the general direction of Mark.

"Girl, that ain't my stud. Don't start me on no bullshit."

"Blaze it," Rosa insisted. "Let's smoke some good and then talk."

Jaquanna handed Rosa a chocolate honey-blunt she already had rolled up.

"Ooh." Shamika sniffed it. "This that boo-yah-bank-bank right here." She did a little happy dance. "This that shit have a bitch head bouncing off a ceiling."

"Naw, bitch," Jaquanna told her. "That's that nigga who dug your ass out last night, had your head banging against that damn headboard. Your drunk ass prolly just thought it was the ceiling."

"Damn, that what it was?" She rubbed her head as if it may have been true. "Well, shit, okay. I'm good with that too." She shrugged and looked for a light.

"Fucking Skanka," Rosa told her.

"That's alright," Shamika pinched Rosa's cheek. "Next time I'ma come get you and we gon' do a threesome."

"Ugh." Jaquanna frowned. "You bitches nasty."

Shamika had a mouth full of smoke and had to speak in that little hold-your-breath-squeaky-voice kinda way. "Now, you know Butch-ella had your ass bent over the bunk in there!"

They all laughed.

"So just stop tryna act all un-licked around this bitch," she added.

"Aw, fuck you bitch," Jaquanna told her

"See, yeah." Shamika nodded. "Now that's what I'm talking 'bout. That part right there."

"You just want my pussy."

"Well who gives a fuck?" Rosa reached. "I just want the blunt. Passa."

"What the hell?" Shamika looked with a frown and they all followed her line of vision.

"This bitch." Jaquanna saw that TanJeeka had wiggled her ass on the back of the Jet Ski that Kirk Jr. was driving and she was happily waving her hand in the air and screaming like she was at Magic Mountain on a damn high-intensity roller coaster or some shit. "Man." Jaquanna turned back to her group. "I'ma need me a drink and y'all need to pass that blunt. Cause I might go over and kick this bitch's ass."

~ ~ ~

"So what you prefer," Chicken-shit asked Big Boy, "a girl with hips? Thighs? Or ass?"

"Shit all three."

The guys laughed and nodded. They were passing blunts and drinks while checking out the ladies. Oh, what a wonderful hobby. Just watching as they stepped with grace or stumbled and giggled. The female form at its absolute best. Young, tight and shiny like a beautiful black diamond.

"Okay, yeah, of course all three," Chicken-shit continued, "but if she only had ass like say Tisha Campbell, where there was really no hips, but when she turned sideways you'd see it like blam."

Several guys nodded and smiled.

"But then there's some chicks who just got cool hips and as they walk toward you it look like a bomb whole like figure eight thang. But then from the side she really ain't sitting on nothing," Chicken-shit added. "But then some girls be having like some cool ass legs and nice thighs but they really ain't got like no real hips or ass or whatever."

"Well," Big Boy said, "for me I likes mine with them hips like pow!" He did the figure eight. "Cause with hips a broad just look right in like a cool dress or even in some jeans. Plus they say if she got hips she can make babies…"

"Man," Chicken-shit challenged. "Who the hell say that?"

"Shit, I don't know. They. Them. Everybody."

"Yeah, right. You made that up."

"I'm just telling you what I heard," said Big Boy. "Plus, with too much ass, all it gon' do is bounce a nigga up off some shit."

They nodded and smiled, puffed and passed.

"Hips though," Big Boy continued. "You can give me an itty-bitty bitch with hips or a big old bad bitch with hips. Hips make that shit just do what it's s'pose to do."

"That's real."

"Okay and what about titties?" Chicken-shit asked.

"Fun but not a major."

"Shit," another young cat said, "Naw, fuck all that, I need me some tig ole bitties. Damn the bullshit." He high-fived and exchanged nods with a few others.

"To each his own on that one then." Big Boy smiled. "But I can suck a flat one or a big old juicy one and still have me a ball."

More nods and jeers.

"Okay, how about lips?"

"Juicy," Big Boy said.

"Yabba-dabbas," declared another.

"Aw, naw, y'all crazy. Just some little cool soft shit."

"Man, I need a bitch with pillows on her face, a bump on her back and a gap in the saddle."

"A gap?" Chicken-shit asked. "What about you, Big Boy, you like 'em with a gap?"

"Gap. Cameltoe. Panty lines. All that!"

"Man!"

They laughed and cheered.

"I want a bitch that look like she love some dick," Big Boy said.

"And ain't afraid to come get it," someone else added as they exchanged a pound.

"Cool ass, hips, and thighs, with them chinky-eyes, plumped up lips and tits'll keep the boy on rise."

"Aw, here this nigga go with his America's next top rapper ass."

They chuckled and chilled. Bonding in the way of youth. Spending time just feeling each other out. Exchanging thoughts, scents and stories…like young cubs in the wild. Watchful and learning while constantly growing. You better trust they didn't miss much and they were ready for whatever.

And then there was the mating call, universal, passionate, deep.

Watching her was like watching a porno. Soft porn. Real juicy oh, so soft porn. "Good God!" She was 5'10", honey-gold-graham-cracker colored, about 180 lbs, small tits, nice wide hips, juicy thighs, and perfectly heart-shaped ass. She had her hair hanging down in a cascade of golden curls, and she was Baby Phat black and gold down, with super tiny, tight, black boy shorts and a black and gold tube top. She looked over the tops of her Diva shades at Big Boy.

"Girl, you done broke the damn law," he said.

"And what you gon' do, call the police?"

"Shit. I should."

"You snitch." She smiled. "How old is you?"

"I'm as old as you need me to be, baby," he swagged forward with a contemptuous grin. "And as young as you want me to be, mama."

"Mama, huh?" She smirked and smiled. Her girls rolled their eyes like she was wasting her time. She looked to be about 16. "Your mama know you up here?"

The girls chuckled.

"Oh, she got jokes." He laughed. "Tell you what…" He reached in his pocket and pulled out one of the business cards he'd had printed up the day before. "Call Daddy when you need a spanking."

"A spanking? Like that?" She smiled even harder. The shear sheen of sweat had her skin just glowing.

*Damn she fine.* He had butterfly flutters in his tummy. He could just imagine her ass-hole naked and posing. The girl was the business and she knew it.

"Big Boy, huh?" she read. "And what's this mean?" She pointed. "Investment Broker. What's all that?"

"Aw, yeah, I work on Wall Street," he told her.

"Oh, Wall Street, huh?" She smirked. "Yeah, uh-huh," she said. "And I went to Dumb Ass U."

"Damn, did you graduate?"

"Aw," she laughed, "Forget you."

"Hey, I'm just tryna congratulate, that's all."

"Alright." She pointed and nodded. "I'ma call you." She turned to step.

"What's your name though, like?"

"Just call me Mama."

"Well, shit, you gon' call me Daddy?"

She laughed. "I might," she said with a teasing lick of her juicy ass lips. "If you lucky."

"Yeah, well, hopefully I don't change my number before then."

"If you do, you lose."

"You make it sound like I already won."

"Humph." She dropped the card. "Ooops," and slowly bent at the waist to pick it up.

"Damn!" all of his boys jeered as they witnessed a vibrancy of beauty, which only God could've created.

She twitched her neck with a cocky turn. "My bad." She smiled. "But I'd say you won when I called you."

"Well, we two winning muthafuckas then."

"Humph." She rolled her eyes and peered over the rims.

"We should take our ass to Vegas."

"And do what? Get married?"

"I'm already married."

"Oh, yeah?" She frowned as if perplexed.

"I'm married to the game, baby." He showed her his brand new pinky ring."

"Humph. Yeah. Well, ain't that something."

~ ~ ~

Kirk Jr. had seen her coming and he'd turned his back on her approach. Sipping a bit, he tried to relax but now this. It was only bound to happen.

He was just about to get in the boat, as she walked up.

Jaquanna had both hands on her hips. Kirk Jr. was alone. "Take me in the boat," she said.

"Bitch, get the fuck up out my face."

"Oh, I see you just got your clown suit on, huh? And who the hell you calling a fucking bitch?"

"Get on, Jah. I ain't in the mood."

"I don't care."

"Go!" He pointed with a darting jab. "Get."

"Get? Man, who the fuck you thank you talking to? Don't let that liquor go to your head."

"I don't wanna—"

"Man, I don't care what the fuck you don't wanna do. I know you don't wanna keep calling me out my fucking name though, or talking to me like I'm some damn dog. Get! What the fuck kinda shit is that? Nigga, you getting too big in your head. Don't get your bubble burst."

"You through?" The glass split his smile. The Grey Goose burned with a loving warmth. "Ahhh!"

"Oh, you drinking now, huh?"

He turned away and looked in the air whistling Dixie.

"Uhg! What is that? Who does that?" She frowned as if disgusted. "I mean, come on, man, for real?"

"'What do you want, Jah?"

"Whatever happened to all that, 'I need a real queen I can build and grow up with, Jah; somebody I love more than the streets, Jah!' Or, here, how 'bout this one: 'I'm crazy about the ground you walk on, Jah!' Huh?" She demanded. "Tell me, what happened to all the-fuck that, huh? Huh, Kirk? Yeah, answer me that, damn it."

Kirk Jr. was rolling his eyes, smiling and sipping. Now he shook his head.

"Oh, you cain't say nothing now, huh?" Jaquanna went on. "Now, you act like you don't know the god damn human language." Now she looked really disgusted. "That's what I fucking thought," she added, as if she'd just realized she had a point to end all others. "Shit."

"What do you want, Jah?"

"What you mean what I want?"

"You making a scene." Kirk Jr. looked around then twirled his finger. "People is starting to stare at us, man."

"I don't fucking care, Kirk." She took off her shades to put her black eye on display. "You think I really fucking care? Huh?"

He shook his head. "Man, you tripping."

"Oh, was I tripping when you bust me in the eye too?"

"Aw, come on, man, it whatn't even like that."

"Oh, it whatn't?" Her voice was rising. "Well, how the fuck was it, Kirk? Huh? How the fuck was it, you big boss? I socked myself in the eye? Huh?"

"You getting loud and you making a scene."

"Scene pa-teen damn it, I don't give a fuck."

"Put your glasses back on."

"Make me."

Kirk Jr. stared her straight in the eyes. He had rocks in his jaw and ice in his eyes.

"What the fuck is that?" She stretched her neck and wormed in closer. "What, that's s'pose to scare me?"

"I forgot, you the big bad killer."

"Oh, you just had to bring that up, huh?"

"Man, get out my face," he told her.

"You get the fuck out my face!" she replied. "You on some bullshit, Kirk."

"I'm on some bullshit?" Scoffing he pointed at himself. "Me? Me? Is you fucking serious?"

"Hell, yeah, I'm fucking serious!" Jaquanna insisted. "You on some stupid shit."

"Man, this cain't be real." He shook his head.

"Why? Huh? Why it cain't?"

"How the fuck you gon' say I'm on some bullshit?"

"Cause you is, shit," she said, "that's how." Her voice fell just a tad but her face was tensed to a ten. "Getting all stupid."

"Bitch, you getting stupid."

"I done tole you about calling me a muthafucking bitch. O, Ho-ass nigga."

"Ho?"

"Yeah, you a Ho. I seen you over here with that bitch all out there riding around smiling and shit. You prolly fucking that slut."

"Yeah, I prolly am." He nodded with a facetious grin.

"That's why yo ass needed them fucking condoms, out here just sticking your little-ass dick in every fucking thing."

"Yeah, well, maybe you shoulda bought you some too."

"For who? For who, you?"

"I don't know; whoever the fuck got your ass pregnant."

"Whoever got me pregnant? You not serious, right?" she said. "I know you not fucking serious, Kirk?"

He served her with a stop-sign hand. "Man, just get out my face."

"Man what is wrong with you? Huh? Why is you acting all like this?"

"Like what?"

"You just done all of a sudden turned all ugly and shit. I don't even know you."

"Oh, naw?"

"Man, you changed."

"You the one just up and left a nigga."

"Left a nigga? Left a nigga? Is you fucking serious? Huh? Seriously? That's how you gon' play this, Kirk? Seriously, Kirk? Huh? Seriously?"

Now the nigga was staring around like he was looking for butterflies, and whistling some damn 'Don't worry be happy'.

"Orrgh! Oh, I pray to God!" she said. "I pray to fucking God, Kirk. You is so stupid. I mean you got to be fucking kidding me."

"What, man? What?"

"What is wrong with you? That's what," she said. "I mean, I just don't get it. I mean, what? You scared 'cause I got pregnant? What?"

He was taking a sip from his cup.

"I mean what? What is it, Kirk, huh? I mean you got somebody else or like?" She shrugged. "I mean, seriously, what?"

"To be honest, I don't even know, man."

"Don't even know? Don't even know what, Kirk? Don't know if you got somebody else? What?"

"I'm on some other shit right now and I just, you know."

"No, I don't fucking know. You ain't saying nothing. Why the fuck won't you just say what's on your mind? This shit is stupid, man. You all mad or whatever and I don't even know why. Tell the truth. I think you just wanna get rid of me. Huh? Is that what it is, Kirk? Huh? That it? Huh? Look at me, man. Is that it? You wanna get rid of me? Huh?"

"Man why is you making a scene, Jah?"

"Just answer the fucking question."

"Man, you turnt up on dumb shit."

"Me?" She was pissed. "Nigga, naw, you turnt up on dumb shit."

"Man, just get the abortion alright?"

"Man, I'ma be happy to kill this muthafucking stupid-ass baby."

"Well, fine."

"Well, fine, shit. Stupid bastard."

"Watch your mouth?"

"Oh, the bitch gotta watch her mouth?" she asked. "Man, you got Jah-to-the-Quah fucked up."

"Oh, Jah-to-the-Quah, huh?" He snickered.

"You heard me. I ain't stutter. Big Boss."

"That's right."

"Aw, uh-uh. Not fucking even. You done just got way too stupid."

"Let's just remember something, stupid-ass bitch. You hit me; I ain't hit you. You left me; I ain't leave you. And you pushed up in my function flossing on me with one of my own muthafuckin' niggas in front of God and a witness. So don't just stand here like you wanna claim victim's rights or some shit. And quit making a fucking scene."

"You wanna see a scene?" Jaquanna took off her shoes. "I'll show you a fucking scene." She was looking around as if wanting something to throw. "Yeah, I'll show—"

"Quit tripping, girl. I ain't playing, Jah."

"Nigga, you know what, fuck you." She was in his face with her finger hovering and her lips tucked.

"Don't hit me," he said. "I ain't playing. Don't hit me, Jah."

"Or what?" she said. "Or what, huh?"

"Get out my face."

"What you gon' do, beat my ass? Huh? You gon' stomp the baby up out me?"

"Go." He pointed. "Get."

She scoffed and laughed. "You comedy, nigga. Go. Get." She repeated with a chuckle. "Nigga, you better buy a dog. You fucking flea."

"Oh, well, then, you must be a tick, little stupid ass bitch."

"Don't call me no more bitches, Kirk." She was deathly serious now. "That's all I'ma say."

"Or what?" He was breathing right down on her. The stench of alcohol wafted with a strong burn. "What you gon' do, stupid?"

Oh, how we can all remember a time of staying up on the phone, all night long, too afraid to fall asleep, as if the love of our lives simply would not exist in the morning. Saying nothing; just hearing them breathe: 'what you doing?'; 'nothing'; 'me neither'. There's no happier feeling in the world. Everything is funny; everything is right. 'Listen to this song'. And then we'd even try to sing it. Oh, those were the days. Yeah, well, this wasn't one of those times.

"Man, get the fuck out my face." She nudged his chest.

He raised an open palm and reared it back. "Man, girl." He held himself but shook his head with tucked lips. "I'm telling you."

"Yo." Leon approached. "What's good over here, man?"

"You better get her." K.J. pointed as he backed away.

"Man, fuck him."

Leon was between them. "Y'all need to kill this shit, man. This ain't even the business."

"That's his stupid-ass." Jaquanna looked like she'd just sucked on a sour lemon.

Kirk Jr. calmly sipped his drink and shook his head.

"What's the problem, man?" Leon was looking at Kirk Jr. "What's good? We s'pose to be having fun."

"And that's all I fucking said," Jaquanna offered. "Was could he please just take me out on the damn boat so I could have some fun."

Kirk Jr. cut his eyes to the woman. Smiled and shook his head. The re-tell was always better than the truth. Her approach hadn't had half that much sugar.

"Well, fuck it, want me take her on the boat?" He told Kirk Jr. "I'll take her out if you want me to."

"Man, shit, tell her to have Coo-Coo take her ass. He got a damn 'boat'."

"Naw," Leon told him. "You don't want that to happen. That wouldn't be no good look at all."

"Okay?" Jaquanna offered. "That shit would look just outright damn stupid. My man got a boat but I gotta ride in somebody else's and all these people watching."

"They was watching when you crawled up out his damn Hummer too!"

"Well, if you wouldn'tna left me."

"Bitch, I already bought you a car."

"Okay." She shook her head. "I ain't gon' be too many more bitches, you little-dick-ass-boy."

"I bet your mama'll like it."

"Prolly will. You got enough condoms; get at her. But she ain't got no dick, you faggot."

"Bitch, I done told you 'bout playing me with that gay shit." He pointed and turned to head towards her.

"And I done told you, I ain't wearing no strap-on for your ass. You want a man; you get you a man, Bitch."

He headed towards her. "You know what…"

"Whoa." Leon stopped him. "Chill, my boy."

"Don't tell his stupid-ass nothing."

"Tell you what," said Leon. "I'ma take her out on the boat for a minute. You go on kick back."

"I'm finna use the boat," Kirk Jr. said. "Me and TanJeeka 'bout to hit that thang."

"Well—"

"Y'all can use one of the jet skis; take her ass out on that. I'm 'bout to use the boat."

"Fuck it." Jaquanna picked up her shoes. "Come on, Leon, let lover boy do his thang."

# Chapter 21

"Oh. Daddy!"

Big Boy had the big ole gold and black stallion bent over in the back of the Escalade. As he hammered that shit, sweat was dripping and the whole damn truck was rocking.

"Oh, yeah!" She was loud and she was wet. And she was slinging that shit like Venus with a racket. Baby had brought the business and served it with some fire. "Yes, Daddy! Yes!"

Big Boy bit his lip, threw his head back, and rubbed on those wide, tight, yellow hips. He couldn't imagine feeling more perfect. Her boy shorts were around one ankle. She was bent over and dropping it low. A perfect heart-shaped yellow moon.

"Ooh, yes, Daddy. Do it, Daddy, yes! Oh, do it, Daddy! Break mama off that good."

He was sweating like a big dawg. Ramming hard and fucking fast. Man that shit felt boss. He wanted to put a baby up in that shit and lock it in for life. Her juices were smacking. She was moaning and, all of a sudden, Big Boy's knees were shaking and his eyes were tripping the fuck out as the tip of his dick felt like it was about to explode! He was holding it, not wanting to cum, not wanting it to end. "Uurgh!" Needing it to last. "Ohh! Ssuu-oy!" Never wanting to forget.

"Do it, Daddy! Yes!" She rode back hard and slow then did some little wiggle type shit. "Yes, Daddy, yes!"

"Ssu-ooh!" Big Boy melted and flooded into her with everything he had.

~ ~ ~

As they headed over to the jet skis Leon helped Jaquanna slip into her life jacket.

"I don't know what all that was about," he said. "But don't let that shit faze you, ma. You feel me?"

"Yeah, I feel you." She was more depressed than mad. After all, she'd never been with another man. She couldn't believe the way he was acting.

"You a dime, nahmean?" Hunching his shoulders, he looked down into her eyes.

She nodded sadly.

"You always have been top shit, Jah, nahmean?" He placed his hands on her shoulders. "We like you," he said. "We all do. We always have. Just somehow, well…"

"What?" she asked, "Somehow what?"

"Naw, I might be outta line. Just know that a muthafucka feel you, nahmean?"

"Outta line for what though?" She turned to him and looked up into his strong young handsome face. "Say it."

"I don't know; it's just always been something about you, Jah. You got like that 'it' thang popping, you know? Nahmean?"

She smiled. "Oh, do I?"

"Yeah." He smiled back. "That's real shit, though. You top notch, girl."

"Well, thank you."

"My boy, Kirk, that's a lucky dude."

"Yeah, well…" She pointed to TanJeeka and Kirk Jr. zipping by in his boat. "His ass might not be lucky too much longer."

"Naw, you don't mean that."

"Shit." She turned her nose up. "This nigga a fucking embarrassment."

"Don't do nothing you'll regret."

"Humph!" She pulled her hair back and tied it up. "What the fuck I'ma regret for?"

"Don't be just letting no nigga slide up under you, you know?"

"What you mean?"

"I saw you and M 'n' M at the school."

She smiled. "So?"

"Hm. Hmm."

"What that mean?" She popped him on the arm. "Forget you."

"I mean I ain't saying nothing. I know how to keep my mouth closed. The question is, do you?"

"Do I what?"

"Know how to play yo shit close to your vest."

"Why?" She twisted an eye. "Why you ask that?"

"I'm just saying. Nahmean?"

"Hm-hmmm."

"Sometimes secrets is valuable."

"What?"

"Sometimes secrets is priceless."

"Huh?"

"I'm just saying," He smiled. "I like secrets." He looked dead at her. "When they matter."

"And when they matter?"

He hiked his shoulders. "When they do, nahmean?"

"Hm-hmmm." Though she didn't. "Yeah, ole KGB, secret CIA ass shit."

He laughed. "Why you say that?"

"Shit." She laughed.

"Naw, I just gotta mind my mouth, feel me?"

"Why, what's wrong with your mouth?"

"It could get me in trouble."

"Not if I can keep a secret."

"Aw, wow." He climbed on board. "Check all that out."

She slithered in behind him. "So, somehow what? What'd you mean when you said somehow? What was you about to say?"

"Somehow Kirk got lucky and came up on you before I did."

She smiled brightly and squeezed his sides. "Oh yeah?"

As the Jet Ski spun and swirled out on the lake, the vibrations warmed her with naughty sensations. She was happy for a time. And so she held on to Leon and laughed.

And then she looked up and saw the impossible: Tan-Jeeka had her head in Kirk's lap, bringing the heat under the holiday sun.

~ ~ ~

Burgers, ribs, chicken and hot dogs along with a few choice steaks. All of the beer, soda and liquor you could drink and together, the crowd of about 80 heads were having a party.

There were the domino games. The girls throwing Frisbees. Low riders all shined and heated, castles on wheels galore.

In the distance, Coo-Coo was out on the lake zipping back and forth with a couple of the girls he'd brought. There was no way he could've left and ruined their get down. Regardless of what. Coo-Coo was a boss and he was gon' boss the fuck up. Drink in hand, blunt blowing in the wind. Hookers dancing all nasty like whoa. He'd never let a man put his hands on him and get away with it though. Never! And he was having just a little bit of a hard time digesting that.

As Kirk Jr. raced by with his dick shoved all down Tan-Jeeka's throat, Coo-Coo instantly wondered about Jaquanna. He was angry. *How could he just do Jaquanna like that?* he wondered.

Coo-Coo noticed Jaquanna swooping up and around smiling behind Leon on the Jet Ski. And as Kirk Jr.'s boat raced towards the Jet Ski and Jaquanna turned, Coo-Coo witnessed the exact moment she saw it.

"That's foul," he said to himself. "Straight-up fucking foul."

He wondered what would happen if he made a move on Jaquanna. Sure, he liked her, but he also had a bit of spiteful bitterness in his heart.

He'd *never* let a man hit him and get away with it before. *Never!* No matter what. He didn't like being shit on. Not some, not a little bit, not never!

Coo-Coo nodded his head, sipped and puffed. His mind was full of thoughts.

~ ~ ~

"Where Big Wayne?" Poo-Poo Pat asked Shamika. "Why he ain't here?"

"Girl, his ass went to jail last night."

"For real? For what?"

"Same ole shit. You know how they do." Shamika shook her head. "In and out. In and out. Life on the installment program."

"Iknowhuh?" Rosa shook her head. "It's crazy, man."

"And, watch, his ass gon' be calling." Shamika smirked and shook her head.

"For what?" Poo-Poo said. "Shit, whatn't he with that other bitch?"

"Yep. But you know how they do." She took on a high-pitched feminine voice. "Let me speak to my son. How my son doing? Don't be having my seed around no man."

"Aw, uh-huh." Poo-Poo laughed at the memory. "All of a damn sudden."

"Yeah, all of a sudden he wanna be a damn daddy."

"Why didn't he come around when he was out here?" Preach had been standing there listening.

"He all confused, talking about he ain't sure it's his."

"That's crazy," Poo-Poo said.

"That's his mama put that shit in his head."

"So why not just get a DNA test?" Mark asked.

"I mean, I would," she explained. "But, shit, I ain't got to. I know who baby it is. Plus, it look fucking just like him."

Mark snickered. "But a test could make it for sure. So why guess?"

"I mean, but I ain't got no money for that no way so..."

"All these people." Preach looked around. "All this money spent on fun, food, drugs and recreation. You mean they wouldn't pitch in to help two of their own find out about the paternity of a baby?"

"I don't wanna ask nobody for nothing. Naw, uh-uh. I'm cool. I am so cool." Shamika shook her head and waved her hand. "It'll just be Mama's baby and Daddy's maybe, shit. It's all good."

"Maybe for you, but not for that child," offered Mark.

Preach picked up on that thought and added, "If the father has doubts, for whatever reasons whether senseless or not, and these doubts cause him to pull away from the child, then it is only the child who suffers. Saying 'Mama's baby Daddy's maybe' is like saying nan-nan-na-nan-nan. But the mother doesn't win and the father doesn't lose, because it was never about those two. The only winner or loser here is the child. Every child should have the right to know its parents. If a parent's no good, that's not for one or the other parent to decide, it's for the child to decide. And there's no way to call a man a deadbeat dad, if the mother is the one standing in the way of the connection. It doesn't matter if he's in prison or even if he strung out on drugs. I wouldn't care if he's gay or a member of the Taliban. That child has a right to know. Period. And it's a mother's job and a mother's duty to help her child to know its father. And if it means taking a DNA test in order to help the bond between the father and child, so that the father might become more involved and help the child to become a better, more well-rounded individual, then why not? God decided he was good enough to be the father. You made your decision when you decided to pull your pants off. God did the rest and it's on us to get out of the way. Help the child. He may be no good to you but a hell of a father, or the child may even bring out the man in him. If not, at least your child will never be made to look back, years later, and blame you for standing in the way."

"Yeah, you right." Shamika felt preached to and looked like she wanted to go kick rocks with her head hung low.

"My bad," said Preach. "I didn't mean to kill the mood. But serious issues do deserve serious moments."

"And, you know what; as soon as he get out this time I'm a straight do that shit, 'cause I do want my child to have the best chance to make it out here. And little boys is gon' need they daddies." With that, she hugged him in her cute little way. "Thanks." To Mark she said, "See if it was your baby, I'd know whose it is."

"Fucking hot ass!" Rosa reached out and smacked her on her wide young butt.

"Ow! Bitch!" She cupped her butt. "Don't get me wet," she warned. "I usually say, if you soak it you gotta poke it, but in your case, heifer, if it drip I need some lip."

"Ugh!" Poo-Poo said, "Y'all nasty."

"So why Poo-Poo?" Mark asked. "Why they call you that?"

Poo-Poo laughed.

"Aw, man." The girls knew.

"Long story," she said.

"One day, in elementary school…" Preacher looked to check her reaction as he told it. "Let's just say, she didn't make it home in time."

"Aw, you wrong!" She was smiling. "Y'all wrong for that." She blushed. "Just gon' put my shit all in the streets. Oops! I mean—"

They all died laughing.

"Naw, bitch, you said that shit," Shamika said. "You had your shit all in the streets. Shit was all across Wall and shit."

~ ~ ~

"Yes, Daddy, yes!" Chicken-shit was laughing. "That's what the bitch was saying, man. 'Yes, oh, yes, Daddy. Oh, do it Daddy'."

The guys all fell out laughing.

"And then this nigga," he pointed at Big Boy, "When he come up out the back of that muthafucka he looked like he had been chasing chickens for a muthafuckin' hour in the sun."

"I'ma chase your muthafuckin' ass, nigga, keep it up," Big Boy smiled.

"If he do," Chicken-shit told them, "Y'all better change his muthafucking name to Top Ramen 'cause I'ma knock his muthafuckin' noodle."

"Aw, damn, that's crazy."

Big Boy damn near choked on his smoke then recovered and told him, "I'd be careful if I was you."

"And why is that?"

"Cause, nigga, when I was born the doctor sent me home in a body bag and I sleep in that muthafucka erry night."

"So what is you, Count Dracula, nigga?"

"Naw, but I'ma be Count Smackula you keep fuckin with me."

"Naw," said Chicken-shit. "But on the real though, y'all wanna hear some cold shit?"

"What's up?"

"For my first birthday I ain't really get shit."

"Aw, nah?"

"Hell, naw," Chicken-shit lamented. "All I got was a Glock and some muthafuckin' tube-socks."

"Aw, damn, like that?"

"Hell, yeah. And I only got them muthafuckas 'cause it was cold."

"Nigga, I'm thanking 'bout getting me a hearse, nigga, and cut that bitch, front-back, side-to-side, and then put a casket and a body bag in the muthafuckin' back and I'ma keep me one of them mortician fools on the payroll. That way I'm ready for whatever whenever, nigga," Big Boy declared. "I'll knock me a nigga and drop his ass off, then come back and scoop his ass up when he ain't nothing but ashes in the muthafuckin' glass."

~ ~ ~

Mark:   I don't need money
I don't need fame.
All I need is a Honey
To wear my name.

And in the background was an old tune by young Michael Jackson.

Just look over your shoulder, Honey
And I'll be there.
I'll be there.
Just call my name
And I'll be there.

As Jaquanna stood and scanned the park, she saw that Mark was indeed right over her left shoulder. He smiled and her heart was lifted.

~ ~ ~

Enemies. We make them without even thinking. Friends, they also come without thought. The problem is, sometimes we don't know our enemies or...or...or... You see, we confuse some and call them friends. Who decides and how do you know?

# Chapter 22

On the way back, the Escalades were pulled over as they got off of the freeway on Century Boulevard. Kirk Jr. and a few of the other guys were taken to jail after a gun was found in a stash inside the vehicle in which he was riding. The bail was set at $5,000 and as soon as Jaquanna got to her mother's house, Lay-Lay ran out and told her.

"Let's find out where he at," Coo-Coo told her.

They dropped the other girls off there and Jaquanna started making calls to find out what she could, as Coo-Coo swung his truck around and headed towards 108th and Main Street, location of the southwest division of the LAPD.

Big Dick told Jaquanna that he'd gotten the news also, but it was almost 10:30 p.m. and he saw no need to make a big fuss about it. Kirk Jr. was being held at the 108th Precinct and Big Dick said they'd get him bailed out first thing in the morning, after they'd all had a full night's rest. The guys were probably tired and just going to go right in their cells and fall asleep anyway," he reasoned.

"Naw, Big Dick, I cain't leave him," she said. "I cain't."

"It's good, ma. Get some rest."

"No. Just give me the money. I'll do it."

"Well, it's like eight of them altogether."

"Yeah, well, I ain't concerned with all them. I'm not leaving him in there. Just give me the five thousand and let me go get him. Seriously."

"Alright, cool," he said. "That's your call."

Coo-Coo tapped Jaquanna and gave her the cutthroat signal. He was shaking his head.

"Wait a minute," she told Big Dick. "Hold Up." She pressed mute. "What's up?" she asked Coo-Coo.

"Tell him don't trip on the money. I got this."

"You sure?"

"Yeah, it's nothing. I got that shit in the back."

"You sure, sure?"

"Yeah, don't trip."

She clicked off mute. "We good," she told Big Dick.

"What's up?"

"We good." Jaquanna explained, "I'm with Coo-Coo and he got the money right here. So he gon' go ahead and pay it."

"Alright, bet. Just tell him to come scoop that shit from me in the morning then."

"Get it from you in the morning?" she repeated while looking at Coo-Coo so that he could hear her.

Coo-Coo shook his head. "I got this."

"He say he cool, Dick. He got this."

"Well, that's his call, bet."

"Alright."

Jaquanna wasn't exactly sure what to do. There was a Blouman's Bail Bonds on 108th and Spring, right next to the station. But the place looked like they had closed up for the holiday. Jaquanna used her phone and Googled a few in the 90003 zip code to see what she could find that was near the station. What she came up with was one called Mom's Bail Bond on $82^{nd}$ and Broadway. The sister at the place who called herself Mom, explained to Jaquanna that she would be happy to come down to the station and help, though with Jaquanna paying the full amount she truly didn't need a bondsman. Still, Jaquanna thought it was best. And together, Jaquanna and Coo-Coo sat in the H3 Hummer and waited.

"You good?" Coo-Coo could see she was a bit upset.

"Yeah, I'm straight."

"Tired?"

"A little."

"You wanna hop in the back and get a nap? You can."

"Naw, I'm good." She lit a Newport and sat back trying to relax.

A helicopter raced into position and hovered at a distance. Several black and white units shot out of the fenced in lot of the station. They were parked just outside the station, on the other side of the wall, on Spring Street.

"I know he pissed you off today," Coo-Coo said.

"Yeah."

"Specially with old girl out there on the lake."

"Man, fuck that bitch."

"Yeah, but it was him too though."

"It was. I ain't gon' even say it whatn't, 'cause I know it was. I know he was tryna piss me off."

"Yeah, and that whatn't cool."

"Naw, it really whatn't."

"You a trophy, Jah."

"Thanks."

"Don't let that nigga scrape you."

"What you mean?"

"Drag you down. Make you look like just some ole ratchet loose leg hood chick," Coo-Coo said. "You ain't gotta reduce yourself to being the poster child for no hood spousal abuse shit either."

A soft chuckle. "Damn, I know, huh?"

"I know it seem lonely out here and shit, Jah, but your boy Coo is a real nigga." He squeezed her thigh lightly and left his hand there. "Just holla at your boy if you need something. Holla at me for whatever, Jah."

"Thanks." She smiled and nodded. "That's cool shit."

"We all need somebody. When we ain't got nobody. And sometimes needing somebody can be when you don't want nobody else to know."

"I know, huh?" She hadn't caught every word, but she understood the gist of what he meant.

Jaquanna's phone rang. She checked it. There was a message. It was from Leon. *What the hell?* she thought.

It read:

Leon: Hey, U.
Reply: Hey
Leon: U up?
Jaquanna: Yeah.
Leon: U felt nice on da lake 2 day.

This made her laugh and she didn't understand why.

Jaquanna: Thanx???
Leon: LOL

She didn't reply any further. It was odd and it was uncomfortable. It was as if the Damsel in Distress had brought all the boys out to play. It was really getting ridiculous.

"So why you here?" she asked Coo-Coo, "After how he acted towards you today. Why?"

"Shit, I should be asking you the same thing!"

"Well, mine is simple," she said. "No matter what, that nigga in there stood by me. He stood by me for four damn years and I ain't need for nothing. You hear me? Nothing. So I couldn't give a shit if I live to be a hundred damn years old and I'm married with ten damn babies, if that nigga in a cage, I'm coming and I'll do anything in my power to be there to help him through and support him."

"See, and that's the shit that makes you a dime, Jah."

"Yeah, well I'm just a real bitch. Shit."

"I sho wish I had one like you."

"Why you ain't got no chick?"

"Ain't found one I can trust and really like just feel all like that, nahmean?"

She nodded.

"I just be sticking and moving, man."

"More money, more problems?"

"That part right there." He nodded. "For real, man, you ain't even knowing."

"Don't know who to trust and everybody wanna act like they trust worthy."

"You feel me?"

"They skeeting and scheming at the same time."

"At the same damn time." He agreed. "But I don't think I'd trade it though, Jah."

"Hell naw."

"I whether have money and deal with the shit that comes with it then be broke and have to deal with the shit that comes with that."

"Yeah, but at the same time, you niggas is up. Y'all need to start planning on getting up outta this shit. Get some legit shit 'cause, shit, you already know they got cages and graves for niggas that don't. And you can only get lucky for so long."

"No shit, huh? Waking up every day 365 days a year and committing at least one felony." He thought out loud. "That's crazy. Three hundred sixty-five days out of a year and all it takes—"

"Is just one time for shit to go wrong…" she added.

"And it's over," they said together.

"That part right muthafuckin' there," he said. "See that's the kinda shit I need to really like get serious on."

"Yep."

"See Dick and them they straight. They got businesses and houses and apartments and mobile homes and all kinda shit," Coo-Coo acknowledged. "We getting too old for the minor league shit. It's time to grow our game up around this mutha-fucka too. You feel me?"

"Yep."

"We done ate in these streets. Now it's about time for us to slide over and leave a little meat on the bone for the next hungry nigga in line."

"Yep." Jaquanna hit her cigarette. "That's what it is."

"Yeah, that's real shit, Jah. That's real shit."

"Know what I always wanted to do?"

"What's that?"

"Don't laugh."

"No," he said. "What though, for real, what is it?"

"A food spot," she said. "A soul food kitchen like."

Coo-Coo nodded. "Naw, that's cool," he said. "But can your ass cook?"

"Yeah, I can cook."

"Man, all girls say that. I done seen Thelma on the re-runs of Good Times."

"Aw, you stupid."

"I ain't never seen you cook shit."

"Naw, but I can burn though. My mama can too. Shit, just ask Big Boy; his ass'll tell you."

"Soul food, huh?"

"Yep."

"Well, why you ain't did it?"

"Come on now. I ain't got no money. Shit."

"All that money K.J. got. He won't hook that up? That's nothing. Plus he could use it to clean some of his shit."

"Sho can."

"How much you thank it'll cost?"

"Shit, cain't be no more than what? Like ten thousand?" she guessed, "to find a place, hook it up, get the food, and put the word out."

"And what would you call it?"

"Shit, Me and Mama's."

"Oh, like M and M's?"

"Oh, huh? I didn't even think about that. I wonder what they M's stand for?" she thought aloud. M and M's Soul Food was legendary in Los Angeles.

"But you'd have your mama cook with you too though?"

"Yep, sho would."

"That's some shit to really think about."

"I mean, people always gotta eat," she said. "And y'all know all the ballers, so all y'all gotta do is have them start coming through meeting y'all there, or just eating there or whatever. We could even give free meals to like certain rappers and stuff y'all know, and then post pictures and shit up all on Facebook. We'd have a gang of business. We could blow up and be straight legendary just like M and M's or Roscoe's Chicken and Waffles."

"Yeah, that's some good shit."

"Simple, too."

"Who knows, maybe I can help you."

"Naw." Her smile faded as she hit her cigarette. "I'm cool."

"Why? What's up?"

"Uh-uh. Free shit cost too much."

"Who said anything about free?"

She cut a quick eye then cracked a small smile.

"I mean, I'm just saying though," he said.

"What you saying?"

He shrugged. "So is you and Kirk gon' be together or what?"

"I don't know. Shit." Jaquanna inhaled deeply. "I really don't fuckin know." She blew out a cloud. "So why you do it?"

"What's that?"

"You know, like put the money up, or whatever?"

"Kirk gave me life."

She nodded.

"I'll die with what I ride with. Feel me?"

"Yeah." She released another cloud of cigarette smoke as she nodded.

"I wouldn't never leave Kirk for dead or cross Kirk. That's my dude, you know?"

"Yeah."

"Bad as I may want to some times." He looked her in the eye. "I just couldn't do it," he said. "My nigga gave me life. And he changed my life, you know? My whole family straight because of that nigga."

"Yeah, wow."

"Yeah, so we can pitch a tent 'cause I'm here with you, mama. All night if I gots to."

"Okay?" She socked his fist with a pound.

~ ~ ~

It did take all night, and Coo-Coo and Jaquanna did wait. It was about 4:30 a.m. when a sleepy eyed Kirk Jr. stepped out of the 108th Police Station.

Brief embraces, hugs and thanks and they all piled into the Hummer and headed to the house on Wall Street.

But Jaquanna was done, and when they got there, she headed home.

# Chapter 23

*Two years later*
*Monday, December 21st*

It was time for the sad song singing; the sorrowful good-bye; a time for remembrance of all there ever was or might have been. Another life planted; blood to feed the soil, so that one black rose might emerge from the urban jungle concrete. You eat what you kill; fertilize what you feed.

"This don't make no damn sense. But here we are y'all. Here we are. Just four days before Christmas and here we are, sitting in the church ready to go plant one of ours in the dirt. Here in the hell we are," Preach said. "Well, I can talk until I'm dead in the dirt, but I can't make no body listen."

The church was huge. The pews were packed. Young thugs and hustlas from all over the city came to honor one of their own. There was a storm outside, but nothing was colder than the ice, which poured through the veins of the men. Black was the color of the day. Even the body was dressed in black.

"You think you got it all figured out. I know you think you got it figured out. But you ain't got nothing figured out." Preach was angry. He'd taken this one personal. "You cain't have it figured out. Cause if you had it figured out we wouldn't be here."

Lay-Lay and Jaquanna sat in front. Marnetta had the baby. Kirk Jr. had paid for everything and everything was right. He'd rode with the family and sat next to Jaquanna, in his super soft black chinchilla trench. His diamonds blinged brightly. His eyes were icy pools. Big Boy looked like he was asleep.

"We gots to understand that this ain't what it's about. This ain't nowhere near what it's about," he said. "Everybody talking about escape, but then how do we figure to make it out when we ain't even factored in what it takes to make a change, and we still doing the same ol' thang?"

Preach shook his head sorrowfully as he took a breath and looked down at his young friend laid up in a shiny box and ready to be returned to nothingness, long before his time. What mother creates a baby to die? For what was it worth man gave his life? So young. For no animal in nature was this considered the norm; a child wasn't to be planted by its own mom. But in the Hood, it was accepted with a look and a shrug. No more Black Pride, no more Black Love. We had to watch our back even when we lived where we were born.

"I'm tired of the same old thing. I'm tired. Ain't y'all tired yet? Ain't you tired of fearing your own? Of burying your own? Y'all not tired?" His face wore his confusion. "Not tired of young men dying or sitting up in cages till they too old to breathe? Ya not tired? How many more of our own we gon' feed to this," he said. "And the youngsters out here, I mean, I just don't understand y'all. I mean…"he touched his forehead. His face looked frustrated almost to the point of tears. "Help me understand something. Help me understand. Cause I don't get it. I mean, I just don't. So I'ma ask you to maybe just think it through yourself because maybe you can get me an answer. But here's what I don't get. In the 70's and 80's gangs were new. So I can kinda understand how some of the kids got caught up and confused by the whole thing; especially since all of the drugs and money started flowing and it looked like a wonderful escape. And you kinda linked up with somebody just to get out there and chase the money. One came with the other sorta. And, I guess, that's still true. With the drug crews or whatever. But now here we are. All these years later. Here we are. We here now and we still doing the same old thing!"

Preach took a moment to look around. He wondered if anyone was listening.

"I mean, to me, it's like a crack smoker. In the early 80's, if you got tricked into it then it was like a bad thang, but you were tricked. Kinda sad actually, but, hey you didn't know the stuff was so addictive, so, I mean, I can kinda see it a bit. But now? To do it now? I mean, come on!" He shook his head like he was listening to a fool. "Come on! It just wouldn't make no sense. Because to do it now, you gotta know where it leads: no home, no job, no future…you gon' lose everything including your kids, and you'll be 40 years old tryna start all over again. You know! It ain't no mystery no more. You know! And you'd be a damn fool to go running down that path on a quick escape to nowhere."

Several heads nodded and smiled to that one.

"And so how is it different with gangs, drugs and the street life?" He paused to let the question linger and draw out thought. "Huh?" He demanded with wide-eyed insistence. "I said how is it different with gangs, drugs and the street life? How is it different when, just like the crack smoker, this madness has been around long enough now and we know. We know it leads our young Black boys and girls to life times in cages or that." Preach was pointing at the casket as all eyes fixed on Big Boy's empty body. The soul too long gone.

"Cages or graves, y'all. We know. We know it now. So who else's kid do we go and recruit? Huh? Who else's Big Boy do we get? Who's next?" He had a stern face and a darting eye. He believed in what he loved and he loved what he believed in. "They say the true definition of insanity is repeating the same action but expecting a different outcome. Why don't we get it? Are we just insane? You know how they catch a monkey? They carve a hole in a tree, stick a damn nut in there, and when the monkey reaches in to grab the dag-gone nut, his fist is too big for him to pull his hand out. But, since he won't let go of the nut, he cain't pull out his hand. We got a hand full of nuts, y'all, and this crap is getting insane. Every shiny thang just ain't meant to be had. But then it ain't like they walking around with signs saying, built and designed with thugs in mind. A Rolls Royce wasn't built for a thug; a Porsche was around before crack was ever cooked. See, the shiny thangs was built before the drug game came, so what does that tell us? It tells us that these shiny things were built for the successful working people. It tells us that if we work hard enough we can go out and buy a Mercedes; it tells us that with the right education and the right job and hard work, we can get nice things and keep them. And it tells us we ain't gotta hide them from the Feds or put them in other people's names!"

There were a few light chuckles. Mark had brought a lady friend. He was sitting on the opposite of the church from where Jaquanna and the family were sitting.

"Okay, drugs brought money to the ghetto. I get that. Great nations have been built on the backs of criminals. Hell, America was built on the backs of criminals who were exiled and shipped over here from England. America is a damn prison colony. So I understand crime being a foundation, but. But," he repeated, "We've got to graduate and move with the times. Maybe before we could just go and pluck that nut off that tree, but they done got slicker now. They done put a hole in the tree and the nut ain't so easy to get. We need a stick, a rope or something else or we need to leave that nut alone. We cain't keep recruiting our kids and sending them to the tree."

He pointed to Big Boy's casket. "Knowing that if they're not caught and caged then more than likely they coming back in a box for the grave. We cain't. We cain't 'cause that's insane. Please don't recruit my little brothers, cousins, and nephews. They squares. They don't need no nuts. They don't need them!"

Lay-Lay and Jaquanna had both been crying softly. Their pain was his pain, but he had to share his thoughts and teach about the reason that the young man lay dead. It was easy to stand up and cry and talk about how great a person Lil Rakim had been and how much his family and kids will miss him. But who took anything from that? Who learned from that? Like everyone in the room didn't remember the bad ass, that Lil Rakim really was. No. Preach would teach. Preach would share. Prince Rakim was for somebody else.

"Now, you know," Preach continued, "you ain't got to hear me now. But I just want you to remember I said it. And I need to know that I said it, and hopefully, just hopefully, saying it'll mean something. Just saying it will hopefully mean something. And so here's what I want to say. I wanna say quit acting like a slave."

Preach paused and looked around. There was confusion in a lot of faces, restlessness, and irritation in others. Marnetta was rocking as she held Ricky Jr. That first time at the park had turned into a baby, and Big Boy and the big gold stallion had been together ever since.

"You see, it was on a plantation that a black man learned to hate work and fear education. And we carry that with us today. See, a slick nigga on a plantation was the big stud breeder. All he did all day was lay up with the different women and try to get them pregnant. He was big. He was strong. He was intimidating. And he was probably hung like a dang horse."

A few nods and laughs.

"So, see, the slick nigga found ways to get other people to do his share of the work while he lay up in the back and chilled. To be made to get up and work every day was considered weak. It was considered square, and then, even after slavery, we kept that same thinking—especially since, we were overworked and under paid. We stayed with the same thinking. We called it working in the 'slave factory' or would even say 'I got a new slave' or 'I be slaving down at the shop', or how 'bout 'I ain't finna be working for no white man.' We gotta quit acting like a slave."

Lay-Lay nodded.

"That's all we doing," Preach said. "Acting like a bunch of dang slaves, handing down that same warped thinking. As if a day's hard work is poison. We acting like slaves! Times have changed; we don't have to feel like there's a glass ceiling or like we can't earn a decent wage. Sure, there's still problems with certain groups of people being paid higher wages or being promoted faster than other groups. But there's a fight there and that fight will be had. That fight continues. I'm not telling you that there is no pain. What I am telling you is it's time to stop crying! It's time to quit hiding in the cut like a lazy slick ass slave, and it's time to stop crying like a helpless baby. We ain't helpless no more. We don't get whipped for standing up for change. We don't get sprayed with hoses or dog bit for standing up for change. You know what we get for standing up for change? Huh? You know what the fight for change gets us now? I'll tell you what it gets us: It gets us a Barack Obama in the White House," he said. "That's what change gets us. When Harriet Tubman stood up for change, she had to risk her life to sneak down into the deep south and help guide slaves safely up north out of slavery. When Martin, Malcolm, and all those civil rights fighters took a stand, they stood for change. And all the while out there on the plantation, the song was being sung about the coming of the change. And what was Barack Obama's slogan and message to the people?" He paused for thought. "That's right. 'Change we can believe in'; 'Change now!' Because everybody understands it's time for change. And it's time for us to quit acting like slaves. And you know how we do that? The way we do that is we become champions for education." Preach paused. "We got our kids thinking that school is a bad place to go! And now I don't know what the heck happened there, 'cause see, on the plantation a black child was not permitted to learn to read or write and every child wanted to learn. They would sneak off and try to learn on they own. Because it was a known fact that it was easier to control a dumb nigger than a wise man. Education was emancipation. Education meant freedom. If you were caught trying to learn to read or write, it was said that you had lost your place; that you were trying to be uppity. And, the cold thing is we still do that. We hear a man talking like he got some sense we say he's a sellout. He's a square. He's a nerd. And so what does that tell our kids? What? To fear education?

"Man, we acting like slaves! We gotta quit acting like slaves. See, they've always understood, even on the plantation, that education was the most important part to breaking away. If we had learned to read and write, we could pass messages and organize; if we could read or write we could've written our own passes and traveled up north to get away from slavery and escape. If we could learn to read and write, we could have read a map or street sign and newspapers and books! Books! Books! You know, they say the best place to hide information from a fool is between the covers of a book, because that's the one place he'll never look. So why are we still running around making fun of the kids who are trying? Don't we even see that education is the most powerful bomb on the planet? Hell, education is what led to someone designing the nuclear bomb. Man, education is the bomb! Education is the magical key to the world and it's right there in the library. Right there in a book, and we so dumb we won't even look!"

Laughter.

"Man, they got us trained." He shook his head. "And then the big dumb ignorant bully wanna beat up on the little kid who's trying. They wanna make fun of him for doing his homework, because no one's taught them enough sense to do theirs. Now how backwards is that?"

Preach shook his head in disappointment.

"We gotta quit acting like slaves. There is no limit to how high we can go if, if... I said *if* we change our thinking. If we quit sticking our hand in the tree like a monkey! If we turn off the TV, learn to read books, encourage education, and teach our kids how lucky they are to have today and the equal opportunity to learn. We gotta show them that school is the most wonderful place in the world to go, because it's their chance to learn the world and obtain the tools they'll need to run the world! Hell, even a rapper needs to know how to read and write not only to do his songs, but what about the contracts or endorsement deals? And if he hopes to own his own business, he'll need to know the basics of how to do a payroll, bank accounts, everything. The world is ours if we can learn what to do with it. But us having the world and not knowing what to do with it is about as useful as handing a pit bull a diaper; it's gon' be crap everywhere because he don't know what to do with it."

A few smiles and nodding heads. He could only hope he'd touched a few.

"We gotta quit acting like slaves and quit tryna slick the system sitting on our assess collecting pennies to stay out of the work force, and acting like we got it all figured out. We acting like monkeys, man. And we raising the next generation of monkeys to try and figure out how to get the nut out of the same dang tree before the hunters show up. Sure, some make it. But most. Most. 99.99% end up in a cage or" he pointed, "right here in a box."

Lay-Lay nodded sadly. Just hoping Ricky's life would mean something to his friends or those who listened, but she definitely intended to encourage education more in her young grandson. She wanted Ricky Jr. to have a real chance at changing things for the family tree.

"Naw. Naw. This ain't cool. We gotta quit acting like slaves. Let go of the quick 'easy-to-grab' nut and pick up a book. That way we can learn how to make an axe and chop down the tree and get all the damn nuts!"

They laughed and nodded.

"I'ma tell you something else. While the bully eats more food and may have more phony friends to cater to him, letting him walk around with his bugga in his nose. At the end of the day, just like the rabbit in the race, the bully comes out of the starting gates and he's on top of the world in elementary and junior high. By high school, he's too high or too high and mighty for school, but in elementary and junior high he's on cloud nine. But later in life when you see him, he's usually dead. In prison. Or off somewhere angry and crying about what life ain't gave him. While—and check this out—while the nerd is like the tortoise: the slow awkward starter whom everyone makes fun of; but he goes on to win the race. He or she becomes the next somebody. He or she becomes the owner of the rap label instead of just the rapper. He or she becomes Bill Gates, Oprah Winfrey, or Barack Obama. That dude that didn't go to school. He ain't finna be nobody. Who he gon' be? If the streets don't pay him and the entertainment industry don't think he's entertaining, it's a wrap! It's a damn wrap he ain't gon' be nothing but a low man on somebody's totem pole while he walks around banging his chest and talking about what he done did or will do to somebody. He's angry because life ain't right and ain't nobody taught him how to live. Who's next? Who's next, y'all?" Preach shook his head as he backed away and the music began. "Who's next?"

~ ~ ~

As the music played, they all lined up and began to view the body. Jaquanna insisted on going first and Kirk Jr. was right there beside her.

Jaquanna miscarried the baby when she'd gotten pregnant those couple of years back. But it didn't matter. She and Kirk Jr. never got back together after that. It all just kinda faded away. They didn't even talk about it. And before long, he was flossing through the Hood with TanJeeka or any number of other girls on his jock. He was a real live factor. He was Mr. Right now. It was Kirk Jr's turn and he was the man. Not just a figure, but a major figure in the streets. And through it all, they'd been able to remain friends. In fact, Big Boy had become one of Kirk Jr.'s main young troopers and they were all getting it good. Now this.

Jaquanna was bent over the coffin crying in heaves as Kirk Jr. kept a hand on her just for support and balance. She pulled away now and looked down at the handsome young face of her only baby brother. They'd always been so close. And no matter what they faced, it was always a comfort to have him there. She would miss him. And so would his son. The boy had died too young.

"Whenever; wherever," she whispered as she fought the tears and laid Doo-Doo Bear in the casket beside him. "However," she cried, "I'll always be here." Jaquanna bent over and kissed her brother's forehead for the last and final time. "Good night, Big Boy." And in her mind, she heard him say, "Good night, Queen. I love you, Quanna." There was thunder outside and it rumbled through the room. She held his hand. "Don't be scared, Big Boy. Quanna got you, kay?"

The music played louder as she cried out and when she fell to her knees, Kirk Jr. was there to help her.

The line formed to say their good byes to a soul whose journey was now complete. Sixteen and already done.

"Oh, he was too young!" Lay-Lay cried. "Ohhh! He was too young!"

It's like a Jungle, sometimes
It makes me wonder
How I keep from going under...

# *Chapter 24*

### *Wednesday, December 23rd*

Jaquanna wasn't sure what the hell was behind it, but she was pulling out all stops to get it. She'd made a promise to her baby brother and she intended to keep it. Whenever, where ever, however.

Business had been going pretty good. *Me and Mama's* was an instant hit. Coo-Coo had not only given her the money. He'd done everything in his power to help spread the word and promote it. Just as she'd hoped, *Me and Mama's* was on par with the legends and street bosses from all over came to sit at its tables and chop game. This, of course, brought out the hot tail honeys and the up and coming wannabes all trying to be in the place to be seen and eat at *Me and Mama's* plates. Even Dr. Dre and Eminem had come through twice, Snoop Dog was a regular, and Ice Cube chunked up the W with Kirk Jr. and W.C. There were pictures of everybody posted up all over *Me and Mama's*. The bigger glass wall mounted display cases were towards the front and by the cashier's counter. But there were smaller display mounts on the walls beside each table also; that way the diners could eat and enjoy. Usually the pictures showed rappers and other famous personalities eating at the exact same table the picture was mounted over. That way the diner could see who had once shared their seat. It was fun to eat and browse. Look up and see E-40 or Erika Badu or even Master P and his crew. They all came and the spot was doing well; so good that they were even talking about trying to open additional cafes at one or two other locations.

"Hey you." She sashayed over and slithered into the booth.

"Aw, hey." Leon was bent over a plate of fried chicken, home fries and *Me and Mama's* special honey-spice barbeque sauce.

"Hey back."

"What's good with it, Ma? You good?"

She knew he was talking about the loss of her brother. It'd only been two days since they'd buried him. "Yeah," she said. "Yeah, I'll make it, you know?"

"That's what's up. That's what's up. Nahmean?"

"I saw you at the funeral," she said, "but you ain't speak."

"Yeah. Naw, it whatn't that."

"I mean…"

"Big Boy. That was my kid. I'ma miss him, you know?"

"Thanks."

Jaquanna let the silence linger hoping he'd step inside. Her brain was racing. Her spirit was ill at rest. Something told her to listen to the whisper.

A police car raced by with its sirens blaring. Water sloshed and splashed. The storm was a lingering one. Wet blankets hung over the city. Only two more days until Christmas. She didn't look so forward to Christmas any more. First Benny, and now this? She struggled just to stay whole, but inside she was already broken. Whenever, wherever, however.

"You know…" She began after it looked like he'd never speak. "I remember you once told me that you knew how to keep a secret."

Leon looked at Jaquanna as he slowly took a sip from his glass. "What's up?"

"I need somebody I can trust right now."

"Well, holla at your boy. What's on your mind?" He was chewing slower.

"I remember you told me you liked me once, Leon."

He frowned now. "What you mean?"

"That day on the lake."

He looked as if trying to recall.

"A couple years ago. Me on back holding you. You coming to my rescue when Kirk was all upset. 'Member?"

"Yeah." He smiled at the memory though he might not have actually called it a 'rescue'. "Yeah, that was good."

"What was?" she smiled shyly.

"You. You felt good as fuck."

"Aw, did I?"

"As a muthafucka."

"Hmm." Jaquanna looked around and saw that Chicken-shit had just come in. "Thanks." Just seeing her brother's road-puppy made her think of Big Boy. The two had been inseparable.

"Hey, Quanna," Chicken-shit greeted her. "How's my big sis? You in the Holiday spirit yet?"

"Naw, I'm cool." He didn't know. She didn't tell him.

"Well, cheer up, old lady, it—"

"Wait. Wait. Old lady?" She cut him off. "Boy, I ain't finna be nothing but 21. I ain't hardly no fucking old, excuse you."

"Aw." He slapped his forehead. "Shit." He shook his head. "I'm tripping."

"What?"

"Man I thought you was some kin to muthafuckin' Jesus Christ."

"Boy!" she popped his arm as he jumped back.

"Somebody told me they saw yo' muthafuckin' birth certificate and it said you was born in 1809 or some shit."

"Man, you stupid," she laughed.

"Then I'm all like, shit, her ass do look like she old enough to owe back taxes from the 1800's."

"Aw, forget you!"

Leon looked at his young comrade with a nod and a smile.

Chicken-shit then grew serious. "I miss my nigga too," he told her, "but I know he always said you had a bright smile."

"Oh, yeah?"

"Yeah and I knew he'd wanna see it." He pointed to the ceiling. "He said he was proud you never bucked it."

"He told you that?" She smiled at the memory.

"Yeah, he said you stopped him from bucking his."

"Aw, he never told me that," she said. "I ain't even think he remembered."

"My nigga loved his sis, man. You was his queen, Jah. He used to say he gon' marry a woman just like his sister."

"Damn." She chased a tear with the back of her hand. "Damn, I miss him so much."

"Backs to the wall." He chunked up a W. "My nigga gave his all, you heard me." He touched her shoulder and then he left. She knew Big Boy woulda been proud and grateful for that.

"Them some good niggas there," Leon murmured.

"But what happened, Leon?"

"What you mean?"

"How my brother dead, man?"

Leon shrugged and dropped his head to his plate. "Shit." He shook his head.

"Why ain't nobody telling me nothing?" The whisper was there again. It was growing in meaning but still unclear. "What happened, Leon?"

"What you mean what happened?"

"Okay, let's just skip the bullshit alright." Jaquanna leaned down over the table, getting in closer but also trying to make eye contact. "You know and I know, this shit don't add up, Leon."

"Man, come on now, how you figure that?"

"Okay, well, for one they find him out in the City of Industry, and he ain't got no business even going out there. Come on now, it's the middle of nowhere. Ain't nothing out there but big ass office buildings and industrial parks and stuff. Ain't no people or nothing even live out there. So what he out there for, huh? Tell me that. What he out there for, if he ain't doing some business for y'all or whatever? And for two, if he was doing business for y'all, then how come he was by his self and didn't have no back up or nothing? And, I know my brother stayed heated so... I mean come on now, how somebody gon' just walk up on him and shoot him in his chest. Just like that? He don't be slipping all like that."

Leon bit off a piece of chicken and shook his head.

A big man lumbered in and took a seat at the booth with Chicken-shit. Jaquanna caught Chicken-shit's eye and shook her head. She didn't like them doing business inside the Diner. But, on top of that, the big man looked suspicious.

A police unit cruised by outside. The rain was coming down a little slower.

"You cain't say nothing?" Jaquanna leaned back. "Huh?"

"I don't know what you want me to say, Jah."

"Tell me the truth, Leon. I know you know the truth."

"I mean…"

"Don't even lie, Leon. Please. Don't."

"But…"

"You told me once that sometimes secrets are valuable; priceless, you said." She looked him straight in the eye now. "I can keep a secret, Leon. And it'll be worth anything."

"Wow."

"Anything, Leon."

He was looking at her, nodding and licking his lips. "But, like…"

"Anything, Leon." She reached out and touched his hand. "I need to know what happened to my baby brother. The truth."

"Jah, man." He shook his head. "Niggas play for keeps in these streets, nahmean? This shit ain't no game, man."

"What that's s'pose to mean?"

"I mean, it mean what it mean, nahmean?"

"No I don't. You ain't saying nothing, Leon."

"We all make choices, nahmean?"

"So you saying Big Boy made a bad choice?"

"Aw, wow. Come on. I ain't even saying no shit like that."

"Look, Leon, I told you before, that day at the lake, you kinda like to beat around the bush and speak in metaphors and riddles and just be all evasive and all kinda shit. I get that, Boo, I do. But like I told you then, you be on some like super crazy KGB, CIA ass shit. Well, I ain't got no time for that right now, Leon. I need the truth. Period and point blank. And I need you to trust me to know how to deal with it."

He took a sip and stared at her.

"Okay," she continued, "let's do it like this. Tell me this: Was it somebody he knew?"

"Aw, wow." He shook his head in that I'm-not-biting-fashion.

"It was, wasn't it?" She nodded. "It whatn't no fucking robbery. 'Specially if y'all ain't had him meeting nobody, 'cause what would he have on him, the little jewelry, and the car? But then, the car ain't even got took so... What?"

"Look, I ain't said that, Jaquanna."

"But you ain't telling me I'm wrong either."

"I ain't said shit, either way."

"Hm hmm!" She pursed her lips in a thoughtful pucker.

"I ain't said nothing."

"Okay, look." Jaquanna pulled out a pen and paper. "Here's what I'm finna do. I'm not saying I'm all that or nothing, but I'm willing to trade what I have." She wrote down the name and location of a motel. "Now, when I leave here tonight, that's where I'll be going. I'm gonna go there, get naked, take a shower then relax naked in bed. And I'll be there. I'll stay all night. You bring me what I want. You can get what I have. Not saying you no trick or nothing. But I need you to have my back. I need you to take care of me. And in exchange, I'm willing to give all of myself, in any way you want me. And it'll all just be our secret. You keep your mouth shut. I keep my mouth shut, and we'll both just be two little happy campers."

"But, holdup, Jah. Hold up..."

"Look, Leon. I know you got bitches. I'm not saying my body should sway you. But I'm willing to use my body to reward you for doing the right thing by my brother. Y'all got pretty tight, right at the end, and I know all about that. I may know more than you think I know, but—"

"Man." He looked directly at her. The whisper was getting louder. "What you talking about, man?"

"Hm-hmmm." Jaquanna stood.

"Hold up." His face was a furious ball of confusion. "Come here."

"Tonight, Leon. Please, come for me tonight. Let's talk, kay?" As she stepped away, she looked over her shoulder. "I'll be waiting. And I'ma keep the light on for you too."

He shook his head and smiled. Jaquanna rolled her hips. She knew how to work her pieces.

And the thunder roared. And the lightening flashed. And it looked to be another long. Wet. Hard driving night. Filled with the constant pound of enduring rain. And the soft gasping echoes of pain. Torment. That's what it was, torment.

It was a storm almost like another from so many years ago. A Christmas storm of stolen goodies where one man paid a price. For having claimed the priceless.

*I wanna wish you a Merry Christmas*
*I wanna wish you a Merry Christmas*
*I wanna wish you a Merry Christmas*
*From the bottom of my heart...*

Kirk Jr. stepped in and stopped at the door. He looked around and smiled as soon as he saw her. He still had that magic. That confidence. That glow.

# Chapter 25

"Hey, you. It's been awhile." Jaquanna hugged Kirk Jr. once he'd removed his jacket. He had three of his boys with him. They went and posted up with Chicken-shit. These days, he hardly went anywhere alone, 'cause not only was it lonely at the top, it was hella dangerous. More money, more problems. Another nigga on the bench waiting his turn.

"What's good with you, girl?" He stopped at the booth where Leon was sitting. He didn't realize it had been her seat just moments ago. Still warm. Hot even.

"Shit, I'm good."

"You good?"

"Yeah, I'm straight."

Kirk Jr. took a seat and ordered some food.

"I kinda miss my old girl, Jah, man." He admired the roll of her hips as she retreated. "That was some good pussy there, boy."

"Yeah?" Leon peered over and caught the end of the stroll. "She had that wiener-beater, huh?"

"Man. And that skull game was a monster!" Kirk Jr. boasted. "She used to like to sit up and watch porn and just learn new shit and try it on a nigga. Have a nigga straight. Just. Ooh! Man! Yeah, buddy, Jah had that good-good."

"Why you leave her?"

"To be honest, my boy, I was just on some shit. I saw an excuse and I took it."

"Like that?"

"I mean, she the one pushed off, it whatn't me. But then, I just figured, what the hell, I'm good."

"I know that girl was in love with you, boy."

"Yeah. Yeah. That's how she put it too."

"Shit, I saw it."

"She a good girl, Man," Kirk Jr. Admitted. He was watching her as she moved about. "Been through a lot too." He was thinking of her pain just the other day, when he held her as she cried. He also had a flash of that old scene when she walked in the rain and he couldn't touch her. When he promised he'd be there for her. Always. As he remembered that scene, he shook his head. "A whole lot," he added.

"Yeah, I remember."

"She cain't stand Christmas."

"Humph. I can imagine," said Leon. "I ain't never really like tripped on that though."

"Yeah, she just don't like reliving that shit, you feel me?"

"And now the funeral…"

"Oooh. I know, huh? I ain't even thought about that." He shook his head with a half-smirked smile. "I know this shit prolly fucking her up."

"Yeah, she was just asking me about it."

"Asking you what?" He frowned. "What she like ask you?"

"Just like do I know who like served her brother or what not, and whatever, nahmean?"

"Damn, she on it like that?"

"She say it don't add up."

"Yeah." Kirk Jr. shook his head. "She'll be cool." He hadn't stopped by the diner in a while. He liked how they were fixing it up. He saw Coo-Coo peek his head out. They exchanged nods. Coo-Coo had actually become a damn chef. Well, maybe not a chef, but he could burn.

"'She also asked me like why we ain't doing nothing about it."

"Doing nothing about it? What she want us to do?"

"I don't know. I guess find out who did it. Get some get back."

"Man, that's crazy." K.J. waved it off. "Man, I ain't finna have our goons all out there like that over this."

Leon shrugged.

"'Naw, that ain't even it right there, my dude. Feel me?"

"Hey, you know me, K. I've always been right beside you and slightly behind you. Whatever you call I answer to."

Kirk Jr. threw up his W in salute. "For the street, my nigga."

Leon chunked up his. "For the street."

"Naw, we gon' let this one ride though," said Kirk Jr. "I mean, unless we just really like come up on something, feel me?"

Leon nodded. "However."

"We get us a Fa Sho Fa Sho, then we at that shit 9000. But, other than that, ain't no need in branging the whole house down on no mystery type shit."

"That's what's good."

"Other than that, my nigga," Kirk Jr. asked his lifelong comrade, "what's good with you?"

"Shit," said Leon. "Just thanking 'bout going to get warm up out this rain."

"Oh, you got you one for tonight?"

"Always."

"That's right. That's what's right."

"So you ain't been hearing nothing on Big Boy either huh?"

"Hell, naw."

As Jaquanna approached and brought Kirk Jr. his food, he looked her up and down and smiled. "See any good um, movies lately?"

"What?" She cocked her head and glared down her nose. "What you say, boy?"

"Aw, my bad." He dug into his food. "What you doing tonight?" He was smiling.

"Why?"

"I don't know. It's cold outside."

"And?"

Kirk. Jr. smiled at Leon and tossed his head at Jaquanna like get-a-load-of-this. "I don't like being cold."

"All that money. I know you can afford a jacket."

"Yeah. Ha ha, nigga," he told her. "Why don't you call me?"

"Why don't you give me your number?" She held out the pen and pad.

"You ain't got it?"

"I don't know; I doubt it. And, if I do, I ain't called it."

"Here." He handed it to her. "You gon' call it this time?"

She tucked it in her apron. "I might be busy tonight."

"Oh, yeah? With who?"

"Wouldn't you like to know."

"What's up with you and Coo-Coo?"

"Oh, we tend to our business."

Kirk Jr. frowned. "What's that s'pose to mean?"

"Nothing. Not a damn thang."

"Damn, what's up with all the attitude?"

"I ain't got no attitude, Kirk."

"Humph. I sho cain't tell."

"Ain't you like s'pose to be married or something?" Of course, she knew it wasn't true, but oh, well.

"Where the hell you hear that at?"

"Just wondering why all of a sudden you got time for me."

"Jah. How far we go back? Huh?"

"I mean, you my nigga, I ain't gon' lie—"

"You never stopped meaning what you meant to me, girl."

"Oh, yeah?" She smiled.

"What color is they?"

"Aw, boy!"

~ ~ ~

There was a loud whoosh as the door swung open. Mark walked in with his lady friend and right behind them was Shamika and Big Wayne.

"Damn." Shamika shivered as her voice carried. The instant star of the room. "It's cold out there. What's up, bitch?" She looked and everyone followed. Like my girl Tasha Smith from *Why Did I Get Married?* She didn't give a mad fuck.

"'Girl, don't be making no damn scene." Jaquanna hugged her home girl. "With yo ghetto diva-fied ass."

"Man, fuck them, shit." She waved off the room. "You know Sha keep it shitty."

"What's up Wayne?"

"Shit."

Jaquanna hugged Shamika's recently released baby daddy. Word was that the two had decided to get back together and try to make it work for the sake of the baby, though Jaquanna and everyone else mostly suspected that Big Wayne just needed a place to dump his dick for a minute. But, as those things go, they looked good together. "Glad you home, boy."

"Yeah, it's good to be home too."

"I know that's right."

"I just wish people would quit asking me am I gon' stay out this time. I swear that's some stupid shit."

"Well, you should keep your stupid-ass outta fucking jail then," Shamika told him. "Shit."

Big Wayne looked down at the mighty midget with the huge-ass personality and bomb ass pussy. He shook his head and smiled. "Shut up."

Jaquanna wasn't sure why it bothered her to see Mark pushing around with this other chick. She just knew that it did. First, he'd brought her to her brother's funeral and now to her diner. It was like he was flossing the girl on purpose. Like he was just parading her all over Jaquanna's turf. Or at least that's how the little nudge in her gut took it.

Jaquanna and Mark had been staying in touch, mostly over Facebook, and she'd even watched a few of his games on TV. M 'n' M was big shit in the minds of those who knew. Some said he might even be a number one draft pick when he came out of college next year. For some reason, he intimidated her; made her feel like she wasn't really good enough. It was like they were from two different worlds and she didn't think she'd fit into his. Jaquanna knew Mark loved her in some strange little funny way. It was crazy, really. But then, there was no denying it: she felt a very strong possessive sense for him too. Especially now when he had the nerve to bring some ole random nobody chick to her diner.

"Hey, Mr. Man," Jaquanna said as she walked over to Mark's table.

"Hey back, Cadillac." He stood up and hugged her.

"So what brings you to Me and Mama's and who's that you brought with you?" You knew she was gon' ask.

"Aw, naw, my bad." He smiled as he stepped back and did the whole and-now-introducing wave with his hands. "Jaquanna, I'd like you to meet my cousin Elizabeth. Lizzy, this is the girl I told you about."

"Hiii," the girls said as they smiled forced joy, one not really giving a damn about the other.

"What you tell her about me?" Jaquanna asked.

"Well, I used to tell her how you were gon' be my wife and take care of me the rest of my life."

She had her hands on her hips and a twisted smile on her face. She had to stand back to look up at him. "Hm-hmmm."

"But then I finally told her how she was gon' have to come back here and help me kidnap you 'cause I was tired of waiting."

"Oh, where you from?" Jaquanna asked Elizabeth. "You from somewhere." She'd noticed the tinge of an accent earlier, now that she thought about it.

"Yeah, I'm from the crooked letter state." Elizabeth was a cute, tall, skinny, jet-black thing with long shiny hair and smooth shiny skin. "Heeey."

"Oh, you from Mississippi?"

"The one and only."

"Hmm. That's right, girl."

~ ~ ~

The quest for love has many many roads; some with lingering trails. You might think you're over one, but soon you're there again. Like old markets and old rest places, there's a comfort within the familiar. But then, the memory is always better than the reality, isn't it? With time, it seems the pain does die, but there's an echo in its place. But who listens to the echo anymore? Love: sometimes it's hard to see what is right there in front of you. No matter how hard you looked. Or, sometimes it's obvious too.

The whoosh told of a car passing by. It was very chilly weather.

# Chapter 26

**Thursday, December 24<sup>th</sup>**
**Christmas Eve**

It was almost 1 a.m. the next morning. Jaquanna had just about given up hope and was starting to doze when she heard the soft knock at the door. It was just a gentle tap. *Tap. Tap. Tap.* Behind it was the wind. *Tap. Tap.*

Startled into consciousness Jaquanna sprung up naked from the bed. That whisper was in her tummy and she couldn't understand why. She pulled her little .25 caliber pistol from under her pillow and crept slowly to the window. Sneaking. Peeking. Careful. The gun was loaded with one in the chamber. Ready. She clicked the safety off.

There was another knock. Just as soft. *Doom-doom-doom.* Just three. Deeper. From the window, she couldn't see anyone; the angle was just off. Whoever it was was probably standing off to the opposite side. The whole thing just seemed suspicious. The water on the window contrasted with the warmth inside. It was misted over. She couldn't wipe it, not without being seen.

As soon as she'd gotten to the room, Jaquanna had sent a text message to Leon to let him know the room number. He never replied.

She'd showered and crawled in bed. She waited but had figured he'd call. She could hear the shuffling outside the room as she walked over to check the peephole. Useless. The whole thing had been fogged over. The shuffle seemed to leave.

"Who is it?" She called loud enough for the retreating person to hear.

"Yo, Jah." It was a man's voice. A whisper. Deep and low.

"Who is that?"

"It's me."

She still couldn't make it. "Me who?"

"Man, girl, open this damn door." She knew then, it was Leon.

"Aw, shit. Hold up." Jaquanna ran over and tucked the gun beneath her pillow then slid on the slinky robe she'd brought.

As she opened the door, he peeked in on her. "You alright?" he asked. "It's good?"

"Yeah." She stood back to let him in. "Come on."

As they settled in, she poured them both some Grey Goose then lit a blunt, chiefed that shit, then passed it.

"So what's good?" Leon was sitting at the foot of the bed turned towards her. She was stretched out laid back. She still had on the robe.

"I don't know, you tell me.

"You changed your mind?"

"Never."

At that, he nodded and smiled. "That's what's up," he said just to be saying something. "I like that."

"So?"

"So, what?"

"Who killed my brother?"

"Damn, you don't be bull shitting, huh?" he said. "You get straight to the point."

"My brother's dead."

"Yeah."

"I love my brother."

He nodded.

"Who killed him?"

Leon took a nice long gulp.

"And why?" Jaquanna was staring straight at the man. Her legs were stretched out, just behind him, and crossed at the ankles. "Tell me, Leon. Please."

"Look, man, this shit ain't happened, nahmean?"

"Don't even trip. You good. I got this."

"And what is you gon' do? Huh? Tell me that."

"What you mean?"

"What, you gon' go to the cops?"

"Please, boy! I look like a snitch?"

He shrugged. "I'm just saying though, nahmean?"

"Tell me, Leon."

"But what is you gon' do though, Jah? What is you gon' do?"

"Come on. You really wanna know all that?"

"Yeah, I do, actually."

"Maybe, it just depends."

"Depends?"

"Yeah. Who it is."

"This shit is some way like serious shit though, Jah."

"It got something to do with you?"

Leon turned to face her now. Just like at the Diner, she'd gotten his full attention. "What you mean?"

"Look, my little brother loved me," she said. "My little brother trusted me." She took a moment to hit the blunt. She knew she had his attention; she wanted him to sweat a bit; just a tad bit. To wonder. "My little brother always asked me for advice, on everything." She looked him straight in his eyes. "There's not much I couldn't know."

"About what though, like?"

She nodded and smiled. Mr. Leon. Play it safe like a snake. Play it patient then attack. She knew it would be a snowstorm in hell before he actually came out and admitted anything though, of course. He knew by now that she knew everything.

"I mean," he said, "nahmean?"

"You ain't said nothing, Leon."

"Shit." He smiled and stood. "You neither."

"Okay, here's the deal." Jaquanna swung over to sit at the side of the bed so she could face him. "I'm just gon' put it out there, okay?" She sat at the head of the bed and absentmindedly slid her hand under the pillow. No reason. Just instinctively doing what the whispering caution said. And, all of a sudden, she felt she should look outside.

"Okay, shoot." Odd choice of words.

Jaquanna pulled the gun in a smooth motion and slid it inside the pocket of her robe as she stood. She was sure he hadn't seen her. She kept her hand in her pocket, walked to the window and peeped outside. Blurry. She used the side of her hand to try and clear away a bit of the condensation.

"What's up?" He looked confused. Worried? Cautious?

"Who's that you brought with you?" She dropped the curtain and stepped away.

"What?" Leon raced over to where she'd been standing and pulled the curtain aside. "Who? What you talking about?"

"You ain't bring nobody?"

"Hell naw!" He was still looking. "Who the hell you talking about? I cain't see shit."

"Uh…" She smiled. "Just checking."

"Girl!" He spun around to face her, towering over and above her feminine form. "Don't be playing, shit."

"Naw, something just told me to check."

How far should she go with this? How much should she say? Jaquanna was still wrestling with these questions inside. Whenever. Wherever. However. What more was there to say? Why was simply implied. What did he do? It really didn't matter what he did. Or did it?

"Look," she said. "I know y'all was planning to get Kirk."

"What?" He looked worried. "Who told you that? Big Boy told you that?"

"What you think?" Her hand was still around the gun. His angry face had her uneasy.

"Man, that ain't no cool shit to be spreading around right there, man."

"Who's spreading it?"

"That shit can get a muthafucka killed, nahmean?"

"Not if you know how to keep a secret it cain't."

He looked at her. She was smiling. "What all he tell you?"

"Who? Big Boy?"

He nodded.

"Just how Kirk was getting too greedy and not really leaving nothing on the plate for everyone else to eat. And that you and him were thinking of making it happen big for y'all selves."

"He mention any other names?"

"Chicken-shit."

Leon nodded.

"So is that what this is?' Jaquanna asked him. "Is that why I lost my brother?"

"Look, Jah, this shit cain't leave, you feel me? Nahmean?"

"I'll be dead before I tell it."

"You'll be dead if you tell it, you understand?"

The tiny gun sweated in her palm. Her finger was on the trigger. She nodded and raised her hand with crossed fingers. "Hope to die."

Leon dropped down heavy on the bed and sat where he had been sitting before. "I'm trusting you, Jah."

"We all need somebody."

"Do we?"

She returned his stare and nodded.

"Look, here's what it was." Leon took a huge breath then swallowed a gulp of Grey Goose. Jaquanna refreshed their drinks as he began. "We was gon' hit one of the stash houses, right?"

"Yeah, he told me."

"But that shit just whatn't cool, like."

She nodded.

"I mean, we coulda did it or whatever, but then like it woulda been obvious that it was some way like inside type shit."

Of course, she understood, she already knew the story.

"So the thang was, to set up some shit and make it look like a Jack, you feel me? We had to make it look like it was somebody else who like did they thang and got us and not one of us," he explained. "But then, we had to make sure it was a big enough lick too, so everybody be straight."

Jaquanna nodded.

"This was gon' be they thang, you feel me? Big Boy and Chicken-shit would get they turn to sit up at the table, nahmean? Instead of just getting worked and fed crumbs," Leon said. "We was finna do this. Form our own shit. Boss up, you feel me?"

"And so what happened?"

"The truth, Jah." He looked up at her. "The truth is I don't even fucking know."

"You don't know?"

"Kirk ain't claiming it, Jah." He stood up and walked to the other side of the room. "He ain't fucking claiming it."

"But you know it was him?"

"I mean, who else could it be?"

"So, you thank he on to y'all." It was a statement, a proclamation, not a question. "You might be next."

"Shit is tense, right now, Jah. Niggas is peeping; niggas ain't speaking. Nigga just thinking, feel me?"

"That why you had Chicken with you tonight?"

"Oh, you peeped that, huh?"

"Yeah," said Jaquanna. "No wonder Kirk all of a sudden show up," she observed. "And then his three boys just went straight and sat with Chicken-shit too."

"Kirk was also watching Coo."

"Coo-Coo?"

"Yeah."

"For what?"

"Well, you know, Kirk ain't never got over that stunt y'all pulled at the lake and he's a vindictive ass dude, you already know."

"Yeah, but—"

"Plus, the way Coo-Coo got his own crew and just started doing his own shit. Plus he in business with you. You know, everybody believe y'all fucking."

"Aw, man. And even—"

"So, I guess Kirk feel if Big Boy was in then Coo-Coo might be in on it too. Who knows? I don't know what dude is thinking, but dude ain't stupid and he ain't slow."

"But he ain't admitting nothing."

"But he ain't tryna investigate it either, so…" He turned up his palms.

"So his ass already know."

"You feel me?"

"What happened? I thought y'all was dogs?"

"Money, man. Money do that shit. Have you pat-searching your own damn shadow," Leon explained. "I used to be his ace-Boone, man. At least I thought I was. The inside dime was a part of everything. But, shit, there's millions being moved around now and I guess those of us that's close just know too much or whatever. So…"

"He done replaced y'all."

"It's like slowly but surely, he move by himself. Without us. He got like a new group of young goons right up in his immediate circle and we got no influence with them. He recruited, paid, and trained them and they don't really fuck with us. Like the fucking secret service or some shit. They just straight isolated from us. They eat the feast and leave us the bones."

"But he ain't paying them right."

"They don't expect as much and they don't know all that pass through. Basically, they just like paid security or body guards or some shit."

"Like he a fucking rap star."

"Pretty much. Yeah."

The picture was starting to become just a little bit clearer, but still she didn't have what she needed. "So what happened to Big Boy?"

He shook his head. "I don't know, nahmean?"

"Why was he out there?"

"Industry?"

"Yeah."

"That's a good question."

"Come on now."

"No, serious, Jah."

"Well, what you thank then?"

"What I think?"

"Yeah."

"I think Kirk sent him on a bullshit mission; slid up on him and popped him."

"So why not you then?"

"Man, who knows, Jah? A nigga walking on egg shells and staying in the rear view."

"Yeah?"

"I been eating No Doze like Chiclets around this muthafucka."

Jaquanna smiled and sipped. Again, she looked out the window.

"What's up?"

"I don't know, I just—" She shook her head without completing. "I don't know."

"Maybe I should go."

"What if you could kill him, Leon?"

His eyes shot up. "You serious?"

"I mean what if?"

"I don't know, man. That's…" He shook his head and stared at the floor.

"Before he kills you, I mean."

"Say what?"

"Well, you know he will, right?" Jaquanna went over and sat beside him on the bed.

"Shit." He shook his head. "He gotta brang ass to get ass, you feel me?"

"I'm not talking 'bout your ego. And I ain't talking 'bout your pride. I'm talking 'bout what if? The real what if."

"Man." He shook his head and stood. His spirit was heavy with the thought.

"What if, Leon?"

"I mean…what?"

"Would you take over? Would you change things? What? Do you think it'll be a war? What? I mean," she said, "what?"

"All that shit just like really depends, like, Jah. Come on now."

"What if you could kill him and nobody would know?"

"What you mean?"

"I know ways to kill him."

Leon's eyes were wide open, and if he'd seen a ghost, you'd know.

"Ways without getting caught."

"Damn. You serious?"

She looked him in the eyes. "I look like I'm playing?"

"Damn." He paced the room and thought it through.

Jaquanna sipped her drink and lit a cigarette. She slid the gun back under the pillow.

"But, I mean like how?" he finally asked, "and who would do it? You?"

"What's in it for you?" she asked. "What's in it for me?"

"What would you want, Jah? Real talk. What would you want?"

"What was my brother s'pose to get?"

"I don't know, we—"

"Three hundred thousand," she blurted out. "Just me and you and nobody else knows. Our secret."

"Damn, you on some serious shit, huh?"

"My brother's dead, Leon. That's serious shit." She hit her cigarette. "Now, do I have your help and can you guarantee me you can get me the money once it's done? Are you sure you can get to it?"

"And how you gon' do it though?"

She blew out a cloud. "I'll let you know when I'm ready."

"When?

"Tomorrow."

"Tomorrow tomorrow or today tomorrow?"

"Christmas."

"Aw, damn."

"Yeah," she said. "Jingle Bells muthafucka."

"Damn." Leon smiled at her stony expression. "You's a cold one."

"Well, come warm me up." Jaquanna stood and let her robe slip to the floor. She spread her legs and posed with her fists on her hips. "I'm ready."

"Damn." He licked his lips as he stared her up and down. "Like that?"

"A promise is a promise. My word is my word," she told him. "I ain't come to play and I hope you ain't playing."

"Shit." He set down is drink and went for his buckle. "You ain't said nothing but a word."

As he sat on the side of the bed and sipped his drink, Jaquanna slid to her knees and spread his thighs. Leon was one of them manicured niggas who shaved his shit bald. She didn't mind. It made it look bigger and was a little less of a bother, not having to worry about getting hair in her throat.

Jaquanna licked Leon from his nuts to his tip, and then eagerly swallowed him whole. "You gon' be the boss once we do this."

"Yeah. That's some good shit."

"It's your turn."

"Humph."

"You know…" She chased a string of spit that flipped down to her chin. "I really fucking hate Christmas."

She took him again and sucked him hard. Dipping fast, taking him deep. She was somebody else entirely as she rolled her neck and hummed her lust, loving what she gave.

"Damn, mama, slow down."

"Shut up." She stood and had him lie back. Reversed herself and climbed on board in the reverse cowgirl position.

"Oh, wow!" he exclaimed at the sight of her ass.

She fed the head then slid down on it; stretching open to take him whole. As he punched her center and her juices flowed, coating his driving rod with her yearning passion. She was breathing hard almost instantly, and forcing herself to ride on despite the stabbing pains. He was much bigger than she had expected. "Ooh!" she gasped. "He never shoulda killed my brother."

## Chapter 27

*Friday, December 25th*
**Christmas Day**

She was down on one knee. The rains poured down. The darkness was filled with storm. She was soaking wet beneath her black raincoat. The winds were biting as the forecaster had warned. Her teeth chattered and she shook with shivers. She huffed into her hands to keep them warm. It was almost midnight Christmas day. She'd been on the bridge waiting since 8 p.m. Waiting for Leon's call.

The plan was simple. She'd shoot and she'd kill.

Taking a page from the playbook of the D.C. snipers, the key was to find the place. The right location at the right time and *POW!* Just like the assassination of John F. Kennedy, life as they knew it would be over. A shot. A single shot to echo and ripple throughout the ghetto. Game over. Game kaput. A simple done deal. Like the buzzer shot at the close of a game. Make it and you're the champ. Miss it and who knew.... It was the shot of the century.

The 110 freeway, also known as the Harbor Freeway, runs from downtown L.A. straight through the heart of the chaotic jungle, then comes to an end in the City of San Pedro, which is right on the harbor. The 110 is the main artery. Thug Central. Kirk Jr. had bought himself a home in Long Beach and this was the route he took home. He always entered right on Century Boulevard then headed south to the Long Beach freeway interchange.

There's a pedestrian footbridge, which goes over the Harbor Freeway at just about 111th Street. The footbridge has a concrete flooring but then encloses the area with a metal mesh-like canopy that looks out over the freeway. On both sides, the bridge opens into narrow, dark, and quiet side streets, which then span into residential expanses. The location was perfect, especially with the raging storm. No one would be out and about on the surface, and hardly anyone ever used the footbridge. She'd been there more than 3 ½ hours and only one girl had passed. She looked like a hurried drug addict and barely even looked up as she went, basically just checking close enough to see if Jaquanna was a threat.

Jaquanna wore a black hooded raincoat with a thick black beanie cap pulled down low. She dropped her head, hunched her shoulders, and moseyed along past the lady as she went. She had a mini-14 with a 30 round clip, which she carried inside a guitar case. Jaquanna was sure the woman could never identify her, and she even more seriously doubted that the woman ever would. A nondescript nobody. All systems were go. She was just waiting for Leon's call.

Leon's job was to keep point on Kirk Jr. and give her a heads up when K.J. was on his way. He usually moved with at least two other cars; one in front, the other in the rear, and though he sometimes rode in the passenger seat, he very seldom if ever actually drove. Knowing when he was coming, which car he was in, and where he was seated would be crucial. For if nothing else, Jaquanna knew that if she missed on this attempt there'd be hell to pay and the Blackman's along with Kirk Jr.'s boys, would be on an all-out rampage.

The cars raced by with a constant *whoosh* and *purr* as their tires sliced through the standing puddles. It was dark. She didn't know what kinda shot she'd have, but she hoped he'd have a car trailing closely enough behind him so that he'd be backlit by its headlights. If she didn't get a shot on the approach she'd also have a chance to swing to the opposite side of the narrow walk space and catch the car as it passed.

Jaquanna had never fired a gun before. Let alone a rifle. Leon had shown her how to use it and she'd even played with it, pulling the trigger, and going *POW! POW! POW!* But it was unloaded when she played with it, so she truly wasn't sure what to expect. But for Big Boy it really didn't matter. Whenever. Wherever. However.

Big Boy. Whoa, how she missed her brother. Every time she thought of him, it tugged her heart. Even now, she held on to the rail, leaned back, and looked up into the falling rain; smiling at the one man, she knew who looked down on her with love.

"I got you," she said. "Whenever. Wherever. However. I love you, Big Boy."

And, again, she smiled as she heard it. "I love you, Quanna." Man, she missed that little voice with all of its questions and silly games. It seemed like so long ago, too long ago in fact.

"You mad, Quanna?"

"You sleeping, Quanna?"

"Ugh, Quanna, you stank."

She laughed as she thought about that one and remembered his silly games. He loved it when she smelled his feet, or tickled him until he peed. And, boy, could he run from a mouse or a 'rat as he called it. Jaquanna remembered the time he'd jumped on top of the living room couch with Mama and they'd both hugged each other and screamed. She laughed out loud at that one, and the soft rain hid her tears. Yeah, she'd miss her brother no matter what. Having him around she never felt like she was alone. Sure, she'd get lonely sometimes, as everyone does at some point or another, but she was never alone. Always, no matter what, no matter where, no matter how difficult the situation. She knew she wasn't alone. Whenever. Wherever. However.

"You bitch!" she said aloud as she thought of Kirk Jr. "How could you? Why?"

It hurt her to think that the man she'd loved could have caused her so much pain. Kirk Jr. knew how much Big Boy meant to her. He knew how much it would hurt her. And then, to add insult to injury, he'd had the nerve to ride in the limo and sit with the family. The nerve to act as if he were some big comforter and supporter when, all the time, he's sitting up there in his big old mink chinchilla trench coat gloating in the pain that he'd caused. And to put icing on the damn cake, he had the fucking audacity to try to get back in her pants.

"You bitch!" she said again, her heart racing. Her jaw tight.

*"Watch for the entrance, front passenger!"* Leon's voice was edged with urgency. *"Watch for the entrance, front passenger,"* he repeated.

There was no time to try to respond to the chirp. She had to get the gun out. She had to get it set up. "What the fuck?"

She was nervous and moving as fast as she could. "Come on. Come on. Come on."

Leon was supposed to have given her warning; given her time to get set up and ready. "Watch for entrance," meant that they were already entering at Century Boulevard. Century was bordered by 99$^{th}$ on one side and 101$^{st}$ on the other. Thus, Century represented 100$^{th}$ Street. The overpass was on 111$^{th}$. They'd be racing towards her and building speed. She'd be lucky if she had two minutes.

"Come on."

As she looked out over the freeway, it was dark and raining harder. Her vision was blurred and it was hard to make out the cars. They'd be right up on her before she was ever even able to identify the car.

"Shit!"

Leon hadn't even told her which car Kirk Jr. was in or if he'd brought an escort.

"What the fuck!" She squinted into the distance. The gun was loaded and ready. All she had to do was find her mark.

There was a small tremor. Just a warning.

"Oh, Lord."

The crack bit and the lightning struck. And there…there in the distance she saw it.

They were cruising along in Kirk Jr.'s new Mercedes Benz GLV SUV on 28-inch rims. It was canary yellow and stood out like an elephant-on-a-mini-bike-trying-to-beat-the mid-day-traffic. She smiled and breathed easier. No wonder he'd forgotten to mention which car Kirk Jr. was in. It just seemed so obvious. This was one monkey who'd managed to figure out how to get the nut, and he wanted the world to know it.

The water caused the cars to move slowly. But it was late and the freeway was practically clear.

They were cruising in the far right lane.

"*Look for 'em. Look for 'em.*"

Jaquanna held the rifle steady to her eye. "I got 'em," she mumbled to no one. She'd noticed that there were no escorts with him and she felt pretty good about her shot.

"*Take 'em. Don't wait.*" She heard Leon's voice over the chirp. "*Take 'em.*"

Slowly, steadily. Firmly. She pulled the trigger. *POW!* The shot rang out and her heart jumped. Nothing. She didn't hit nothing.

"Shit!" She raced to try and get off another shot. "Damn!"

Thunder roared and lightening cracked. *Bloow!* "Damn!" She tried to hold her nerve. "Damn! Damn! Damn!" That lightning could be a problem. She really had to rush now. The backlight of the flash, while having helped to locate the car, was also putting her on blast. Someone might have seen her standing there; may have seen the rifle.

The Benz had gone beneath her now. This was it: The final buzzer. The bell.

Jaquanna raced, stumbled, and scraped her knee. She was anxious. Frantic. Soaking wet and growing scared. "Come on!" She tried to still her heart. "Damn it, where is it?" The Benz was gone; she didn't see it. Had they stopped beneath her? Oh, shit. Had they seen her?"

She didn't think she had even hit the car, but she couldn't be sure. And, had the backlight given her away?

*"Jah!"* She heard Leon yell. But she couldn't answer. *"Jah!"* He seemed excited. Urgent. *"Jah! Answer me!"*

She was on her knee and breathing hard. Crying in frustration as she shivered an uncontrollable cold. The rains poured as she fought to catch her breath and hold the gun steady. This was it. This was all she had. As it passed, she'd have one last opportunity to get the job done. But the SUV would make her job just that much more difficult. There's no way she'd be able to hit him from behind.

*"Jah, can you hear me?"* asked Leon. *"If you can hear me, say something."*

"No time, Leon," she whispered to herself. Her voice held a steady calm. She wasn't cold and she wasn't nervous. The whisper had become a shout. It was a warm welcoming hug. "Now," it said. "Do it now." And she cried as she heard his voice. Big Boy still had her back.

*Clow! Clow-clow-clow! Clow! Clow! Clow! Clow!*

Jaquanna gave it up at they ass until; finally, the Benz slumped and spun. The rear windows were busted and she thought she'd hit a tire.

*Clow! Clow!*

She hit the front windshield and the car stopped. How poetic.

The SUV was stalled and had spun around until it stopped, cutting sideways across the lanes so that the passenger side was facing the bridge. Kirk Jr. looked straight up at her, his eyes as wide as shit.

Lightning flashed. She knew he saw her. And she knew he saw the gun. Quickly he tried to climb over to the driver's side, but Jaquanna wasn't done.

"You bitch!" she whispered. "You don't take nothing from me."

*Clow! Clow-clow-clow-clow-clow!* And she pulled it until it clinked, empty, and totally dead.

"Good night, Big Boy." She was crying as she rushed to put the gun back into the guitar case. She then strolled calmly from the bridge. "Sleep tight," she said.

~ ~ ~

It was Christmas. Two men had taken and two men lay dead.

*I wanna wish you a Merry Christmas*
*I wanna wish you a Merry Christmas*
*I wanna wish you a Merry Christmas*
*From the bottom of my heart.*

She smiled as she heard the song blaring in the distance.

She hated what that song reminded her of, but she knew she'd never forget it.

*Feliz Navidad*
*Feliz Navidad*
*Feliz Navidad*
*Y Prospero Felizidad*

## Chapter 28

*And ole Sally May*
*She went away*
*And left ole Paul at home.*
*Oh, Sally May*
*Sally May*
*Sally where you done gone?*
*Done ran off. Done ran off.*
*Done ran off with old long tail John.*
*Oh, Sally May*
*Sally May*
*Sally, girl, you done wrong.*
*Sally May*
*Oh, Sally May*
*Lordy where you done gone?*

The plaintive cries of the down-home blues. Big Daddy'd had Mark make up the song a long time ago, and every once in a while it would still pop into his head. Boy, how he missed old Big Daddy, a true man if ever there was one. Always sharing. Always teaching. And when he laughed, boy could he laugh! He'd laugh so hard he'd hack and he'd cough. But you still knew his joy. The cigarettes couldn't take all that away.

*"These are some of the best days of your life,"* Big Daddy had told him when he was in high school. *"This is your time to develop the friends, connections, personality and job skills to carry you through the rest of your days; what you do while you're young will determine the remainder of your life. These are your root planting days. So plant them strongly and plant them wisely. We don't always get a chance to start over. And remember, your life, body, and mind are like a canvas. Be careful what you paint on it, 'cause every stroke counts and every line, swiggle or smudge can determine the outline of the image."* Big Daddy also said, *"Whatever you do, make as many friends as you can when you're young, because they will be your doors to opportunities later in life. You never know who might go on to be president or simply even come up on a housing or job offer*

*for you. The wiser the friends and the more positive the friends you make, the better off you'll be."*

Always something to share. That was Big Daddy. Mark wondered what Big Daddy would think about Preach. But that was easy, he was sure Big Daddy would love the wisened budding young leader. He'd have to take him back home one day.

*Sally May*
*Oh, Sally May*
*Girl, you know you done wrong.*
*Oh, Sally, oh Sally*
*Ran off with old long tail John.*

# Chapter 29

*January 1st*
*New Year's Day*

It was a new year and a new day. The sun glowed with a gentle warmth. The birds chirped and there was a breeze. So much had happened within the week. So much, what's the word? Newness. So much newness. So much replenishment.

It was what it was and it was over.

Jaquanna was standing in her mother's front yard, right there on 105th behind the school. Mark had come over and asked to talk to her and they were there together.

Kids played in the distance and you could hear the screams over at the school. They even had the Double-Dutch going.

"Go Tamika! Go Tamika! You can do it! You got it!"

She smiled as she heard it. I guess some things never change. We pass it on from one generation to the next until suddenly your turn is over. You step aside and life, like a game, continues.

Hide-and-go-get-it. Who hasn't played that one? House anyone? Who wants to be the doctor? Show and Tell, now that's a no-no! And watch your little nasty thinking too. Nobody told you to remember all that. Just Nasty! Nasty for no damn reason! Um-um-umph! Look and the Devil got your mind too, huh? That's a zip damn shame. Nasty!

"You know," Mark said as he looked into her eyes and held her hands, "I was just a kid when I first met you. And something inside just never grew up I guess. But we've both had our burdens; have had to face some tests."

Jaquanna nodded with a sad expression, her mind playing over her tragedies.

"You know, most people's stories end here, but my story doesn't end here. I refuse to let it end here, Jah, I can't." He looked into her eyes. "And yours doesn't have to end here either."

"I know." A tear welled. "But it does." The tear fell. She left it. "This is Home. It's all I know, Mark. I don't know nothing else."

"But what's next? I mean…"

"I don't know what's next."

He shook his head with pain and confusion. "It's the same old story over and over I mean. Damn!"

"I know."

"I'm gon' go," he said. "I'm gon' go out there and I'm gon' make something of myself."

She smiled as she nodded and fought a tear.

"And then I'm gonna come back. I'm gon' come back and see if that's how you still feel."

The tears began to fall from her face, making warm wet streaks as they went.

"But why?" she asked. "I don't understand why? Why do you want me? Why do you think I'm worth it? Why, Mark? Huh? Why?"

"I don't know, Jah." He cupped her head as he took his thumbs and wiped her tears. "But just maybe everything's not meant to be explained, you know?"

She slowly nodded though totally unsure.

"Just remember IGN, girl."

"Yeah." She smiled. "You been telling me that since I was a little girl."

"And I'll probably be saying it until you're dead."

"How you know yo ass ain't gon' die first?"

"I'm already dying, Jah."

"Wow." She broke his eye contact. "Damn."

At the end they said what they always said, though they were sure they no longer meant it. As, sometimes, dreams clashed with reality. And the experiences of childhood created a different adult.

"I got next," they said.

And they again walked away from the now.

Jaquanna stood and watched him until he reached the corner of Wall Street. And just then, Leon shot past her in his brand new Range Rover. He also stopped at the corner of Wall.

She smiled as she thought about the symbolism of that, because, as they reached Wall, Mark made the *right* turn and continued on his way, while Leon made the *left* turn and stopped at the corner and stayed. One made the 'right' decision and the other was 'left' behind. Talk about a crossroad. Now, how poetic was that?

"Quanna?" She turned at the sound of Coo-Coo's voice. He was standing behind her in the open doorway. "You cool?"

"Yeah," she said with a last glance. "I'm good. Come on." And with that, she went inside.

Jaquanna's uncle would be home next week and she was really looking forward to it. She knew he'd be sad about Ricky, but he'd also be crazy about Ricky Jr. Uncle Lou's Rib Shack was already on the horizon. He loved to barbeque and now that she had the money, she was going to make sure he never went back to anybody's prison. It was indeed a new day.

~ ~ ~

"Game, fool!" Mark was drawn by the boastful winner as he passed the basketball court. "That's a wrap!"

"So what, nigga, I got next."

"Uh-uh," said a cute little chubby girl with a ball under her arm. "I got next, I called it."

"Oh." The little boy smiled. "Well, can I play with you?"

"Boy, please."

Mark smiled and wondered if the two would stay in touch or if he'd ever get over her.

*Sally May*
*Sally May*
*Tell me where you done gone...*

# If You Took Your Last Breath Today

If you took your last breath today, what would they say?
If you took your last breath today,
what would they say about you?
Would they say you lived your life the way
That you really wanted to? Chose to?
Would you wish you'd made a change
Or maybe even took a chance;
Climbed a mountain or got out and danced;
Took your money out your rubber band;
Helped a kid or even held a hand;
Had a meal and maybe just a laugh?
How would you really look at your past,
If yesterday, was all you had?
And what you got is really all you'd get
And what you left is really what you took
Cause what you took is really all you had.
Cause what you took is really all you had.
If you took your last breath today, what would they say?
If you took your last breath today,
what would they say, say,    say?
Say about you. Say about you.
If you took your last breath today, what would they say?
If you took your last breath today, what would they say;
About the life that was once alive?
Did she live or just shuck and jive?
What was the use?
Why did she have her eyes,
If she refused to see Or live her life?
Thrown away within the great confine

Because she never unlocked her mind:
Never unlocked her mind…
If you took your last breath today, what would they say?
If you took your last breath today,
What would they say about you?
If you took your last breath today,
What would they say?
Say about you.
Say about you.
Hush.
For everyone who goes there's another who comes.
Though some of us simply die while waiting in line….
Yeah, life is too short, so you must…

# Choose

# Your

# Lines

# Wisely.

# ABOUT THE AUTHOR

With over 23 completed, manuscripts, and having just signed with indie-major DcBookdiva Publications and Ben Official Books, you can expect that many more of Godfather's titles will be coming to market soon.

Having taught urban lit. classes, since in prison, added his ink to various projects, written poems and social political articles for various newspapers, etc. Godfather is no stranger to the art and craft of the pen. Author of fiction, non-fiction, self-help, howto, erotica, poetry, news articles, autobiography, as well as a fre-quent interviewer, blogger, co-host for luv4thelockdown on BlogTalkRadio.com/UrbanLiteraryReview and former Crips spokesman, Godfather, is now ready to make some noise and he's well prepared to do it.

For more detail/info check out the detailed interview titled INCARCERATED SCARFACE on the all new hot spot for industry news www.StraightChaser.com and get to know this all around talent as he emerges from the shadows to claim his place amidst Urban Lit. Royalty.

DC Bookdiva Publications
#245 4401-A Connecticut Avenue, NW
Washington DC 20008
dcbookdiva.com

## Order Form

Name_____

Inmate ID_____

Address:_____

City/State_____

| Quantity | Titles | Price | Total |
|---|---|---|---|
| | Dynasty 3, Dutch | 15.00 | |
| | A Killer'z Ambition 2, Nathan Welch | 15.00 | |
| | Smokin Mirrors, Mike O | 15.00 | |
| | Secrets Never Die, Eyone Williams | 15.00 | |
| | Up the Way, Ben | 15.00 | |
| | A Beautiful Satan 2, RJ Champ | 15.00 | |
| | Tina, Darrell Debrew | 15.00 | |
| | Trina, Darrell Debrew | 15.00 | |
| | The Diary of Aaliyah Anderson, Randall Barnes | 15.00 | |
| | Uppity, Jannelle Moore | 15.00 | |
| | I Got Next, Godfather | 15.00 | |

**Sub-Total   $**_____

Shipping/Handling (Via US Media Mail) $3.95 1-2 Books, $7.95 1-3 Books, 4 or more titles-Free Shipping

**Shipping   $** _____
**Total Enclosed   $**_____

Certified or government issued checks and money orders, all mail in orders take 5-7 Business days to be delivered. Books can also be purchased on our website at dcbookdiva.com. Incarcerated readers receive 25% discount. Please pay $11.25 per book and apply the same shipping terms as stated above